[...]S NOVELS

ALL OF ME

"[The characters'] physical attraction heats up the pages, but their personal development forms the heart and soul of the novel, a delicately revealing in-depth character study. Wilde's clever combination of humor, sorrow and love brings a deeply appealing sense of realism."

—*Publishers Weekly*

"A warm serene character study. Jillian is a fully developed person, but the relationship drama is owned by Tuck as Lori Wilde goes deep inside his soul. Fans who appreciate a sometimes amusing but always pathos second chance at life (and love) will enjoy this profound contemporary."

—*Midwest Book Review*

"Light and charming, this is a pure romance, which is a nice change... a satisfying read with excellent characterizations and real-life issues."

—*RT Book Reviews*

ADDICTED TO LOVE

"Entertaining and humorous...There's a seriousness to it also, as the heroine learns to recognize real love and caring. Wilde again includes secondary romances that are intriguing, entertaining, and hot."

—*RT Book Reviews*

"Wilde brings romance fans a feel-good, laugh-out-loud read...one of the best romantic comedies I've read in a long time." —NightsandWeekends.com

"Charming...lighthearted fun...strong secondary romances enhance an engaging Valentine tale."

—*Midwest Book Review*

ONCE SMITTEN, TWICE SHY

"Lori Wilde at her best...The magic and romance that Ms. Wilde began in her first book in the series, *There Goes the Bride*, continues in this novel...I really loved this story. The writing is wonderful and the plot grabbed my attention from the first page. I fell in love with the characters and couldn't wait to see how they worked everything out."

—ContemporaryRomanceWriters.com

"A definite crowd pleaser...Lori Wilde can write very engaging and quirky romances and *Once Smitten, Twice Shy* is one of them... [A] good read with some suspense to boot." —FreshFiction.com

"A wild ride on an emotional roller coaster."

—FallenAngelReviews.com

"Amusing . . . an entertaining contemporary romance."

—*Midwest Book Review*

THERE GOES THE BRIDE

"A wild ride." —*Booklist*

"I adored this book! I even kept it in my purse in the hopes that I would have a few minutes in which to squeeze a paragraph or two . . . I can't wait to read the next in this wonderful new series . . . Superb!"

—TheRomanceReadersConnection.com

"*There Goes the Bride* is a [Lori] Wilde madcap contemporary romance."

—*Midwest Book Review*

"FOUR HEARTS! Ms. Wilde conquers a whole new part of the romance genre . . . lots of funny elements and a great cast of characters."

—LovesRomanceandMore.com

"A dynamite novel that readers will treasure for years to come." —*RT Book Reviews*

Also by Lori Wilde

License to Thrill
Charmed and Dangerous
Mission: Irresistible
You Only Love Twice
There Goes the Bride
Once Smitten, Twice Shy
Addicted to Love
All of Me

Kiss The BRIDE

LORI WILDE

FOREVER

NEW YORK BOSTON

This book is a work of fiction. Names, characters, places, and incidents are the product of the author's imagination or are used fictitiously. Any resemblance to actual events, locales, or persons, living or dead, is coincidental.

Forever
Hachette Book Group
237 Park Avenue
New York, NY 10017
www.HachetteBookGroup.com

Forever is an imprint of Grand Central Publishing.

The Forever name and logo is a trademark of Hachette Book Group, Inc.

Printed in the United States of America

First edition: June 2012

10 9 8 7 6 5 4 3 2
OPM

Contents

There Goes The Bride

To my wonderful editor, Michele Bidelspach, who gently pushes me to reach my highest potential. Thank you so much for caring!

Acknowledgment

Many thanks to super agent Jenny Bent. Her support and encouragement were invaluable in the writing of this book.

Prologue

The summer issue of *Society Bride* declared the marriage of Houston's hottest bachelor, Dr. Evan Van Zandt, to his childhood sweetheart, oil heiress Delaney Cartwright, a classic friends-to-lovers fairy tale.

Texas Monthly, in its trendy yet folksy way, decreed their union the high-society equivalent of beef barbecue and mustard potato salad. Delaney and Evan simply belonged together.

A sentimental write-up in the *Houston Chronicle* dubbed their romance a heartwarming Lone Star love story.

Delaney's mother, Honey Montgomery Cartwright, pronounced them the perfect couple. Lavish praise indeed from a Philadelphia blue blood with impossibly high standards.

Her father grumbled, "This thing's costing us more than her liberal arts degree from Rice," as he wrote out a very large check to cover the nuptials.

And her long-deceased sister Skylar, who occasionally popped up in Delaney's dreams to offer unsolicited advice, whispered with unbridled glee that the ceremony was a glorious train wreck just waiting to happen and she insisted on front-row seating.

Skylar, being dead, could of course sit anywhere she chose. Everyone else had to cram into the River Oaks Methodist Church.

The cherrywood pews overflowed with five hundred invited guests, plus a dozen members of the press and a sprinkling of enterprising wedding crashers. The laboring air-conditioning system was no match for the double punch of a too-thick crowd and sweltering one-hundred-degree heat.

"Who gets married in Houston during August?" Delaney heard a woman murmur.

"I'm getting a heat rash in these panty hose," another woman replied.

Feeling chastised, Delaney ducked her head. She stood just outside the open door of the chapel waiting for the wedding march to commence, her arm looped through her father's.

"I heard it was originally supposed to be a Christmas ceremony, but the bride postponed it twice," the first woman said. "Do you suppose we could have a runaway situation?"

"Hmm, now that would make an interesting spread in tomorrow's society pages."

At that comment, her father tightened his grip. *No turning back now,* his clench said.

Delaney's hopes sank. Her mind spun. *A coyote would gnaw her paw off.*

The bridesmaids reached their places. Her best friend, Tish, wedding videographer extraordinaire, was filming madly. Every gaze in the place was glued to Delaney.

Everything was perfect. It was a true celebrity-style

wedding, just as her mother had planned. The purple orchids, accented with white roses, were on lavish display—in bouquets and boutonnieres, in vases and corsages. Her size-four, ten-thousand-dollar Vera Wang wedding dress fit like a fantasy. The flower girl was cute. The two-year-old ring bearer even cuter. And both children were on exemplary behavior. Delaney's antique wedding veil fetchingly framed her face, even though her scalp had been tingling weirdly ever since she put it on.

This was it.

Her big day.

The seven-piece orchestra struck the first notes of the wedding march. Dum, dum, de-dum.

Delaney took a deep breath and glanced down the long aisle festooned with white rose petals to where Evan stood at the altar. He looked stunningly handsome in his long-tailed tux, love shining in his trusting blue eyes.

Her father started forward.

But Delaney's beaded white Jimmy Choo stilettos stayed rooted to the spot. No, no, this was all wrong. It was a big mistake. She had to call it off before she embarrassed everyone. Where was her cell phone?

"Delaney Lynn Cartwright," her father growled under his breath. "Don't make me drag you."

A hard throb of distress surged through her temples. *What have you done? What have you done? What have you done?*

She forced herself to move forward. Her gaze searched for the exits. There were two on either side of the altar, and of course, the one directly behind her.

But Daddy wasn't letting go.

Closer, closer, almost there.

Evan made eye contact, smiled sweetly.

Guilt whirled like a demon tornado in the pit of her stomach. She dragged in a ragged breath.

Her husband-to-be held out his palm. Her father put her hand in Evan's.

Delaney's gaze shifted from one corner exit to the other. Too late. It was too late to call this off. What time was it anyway?

"Dearly beloved," the portly minister began, but that's as far as he got.

A clattering erupted from behind the exit door on the left.

And then there he loomed. Dressed head to toe in black. Wearing a ski mask. Standing out like crude oil in a cotton field.

Thrilled, chilled, shamefaced, and greatly relieved, Delaney held her breath.

The intruder charged the altar.

The congregation inhaled a simultaneous gasp.

The minister blinked, looked confused.

"Back away from the bride," the dark stranger growled and waved a pistol at Evan.

Excitement burst like tiny exploding bubbles inside her head. *Prop gun*, Delaney thought. *Nice touch.*

Evan stared at the masked intruder, but did not move. Apparently he had not yet realized what was transpiring.

"Move it." The interloper pointed his weapon directly at Evan's head. "Hands up."

Finally, her groom got the message. He dropped Delaney's hand, raised his arms over his head, and took a step back.

"Don't anyone try anything cute," the man commanded at the same moment he wrapped the crook of his elbow around Delaney's neck and pressed the revolver to her temple. The cold nose of it felt deadly against her skin.

Fear catapulted into her throat, diluting the excitement. Delaney dropped her bouquet. It *was* a prop gun, wasn't it?

The crowd shot to its collective feet as the stranger dragged her toward the exit from whence he'd appeared.

"Follow us and the bride gets it," he shouted dramatically just before the exit door slammed closed behind them.

"You're choking me," Delaney gasped. "You can let go now."

He ignored her and just kept dragging her by the neck toward the white delivery van parked at the back of the rectory.

A bolt of raw panic shot through her veins. What was going on here? She dug her freshly manicured fingernails into his thick arm and tried to pry herself free.

He stuck his gun in his waistband, pulled a pair of handcuffs from his back pocket, and one-handedly slapped them around her wrists.

"What is this?" she squeaked.

He did not speak. He wrenched open the back door of the van just as the congregation came spilling out of the rectory and into the street. He tossed her onto the floor, slammed the door, and ran around to the driver's side.

Delaney lay facedown, her knees and elbows stinging from carpet burn. She couldn't see a thing, but she heard anxious shouts and the sound of fists pounding the side of the vehicle.

The engine revved and the van shot forward, knocking her over onto her side.

"What's going on?" She struggled to sit. The veil fell across her face. She pushed it away with her cuffed hands and peered into the front of the van. "What's with all the rough stuff?"

He didn't answer.

She cleared her throat. Perhaps he hadn't heard her. "Nice execution," she said. "Loved the toy gun, but the handcuffs are a definite overkill."

He hit the street doing at least fifty and she tipped over again.

Her heart flipped up into her tightly constricted throat. She dragged in a ragged swallow of air. This guy was playing his role to the hilt.

When they made it to the freeway entrance ramp, he ripped off the ski mask, threw it in the seat beside him, and then turned to look back at Delaney.

Alarm rocketed through her. Saliva evaporated from her mouth. Something had gone very, very wrong.

Because the man who'd just taken her hostage was *not* the kidnapper she'd hired.

Chapter 1

Two Months Earlier

Glasses up, girls. A toast to the bride-to-be," bubbled Tish Gallagher. She smiled at Delaney, tucked a dark auburn corkscrew curl behind one ear studded with multiple piercings, and raised her drink. "May your marriage be filled with magic."

Delaney Cartwright and her three best friends were celebrating the final fitting of the bridesmaids' dresses by dining at Diaz, Houston's trendiest new restaurant hot spot. They'd already slurped down a couple of margarita-martinis apiece and noshed their way through blue corn tortilla chips dipped in piquant salsa and fire-grilled shrimp enchiladas laced with Manchego cheese and Spanish onions.

Everyone was feeling frivolous.

All except for Delaney.

Tequila made her edgy, but it was what her friends were drinking, so she'd joined in.

"Third time's the charm." Jillian Samuels winked and lifted her glass.

Her friend was referring to the fact Delaney had postponed the wedding twice. No matter how many times she explained to people that she'd delayed the ceremony because she was trying to get her fledgling house-staging business on solid ground, everyone assumed it was because she'd gotten cold feet.

But that wasn't the reason at all.

Well, okay, maybe there was a tiny element of an icy pinkie toe or two, but mostly Delaney didn't want to end up like her mother. With nothing to do but have kids and meddle in their lives.

"To the most perfect wedding ever." Die-hard romantic Rachael Harper sighed dreamily, her martini glass joining the others in the air. "You've got the perfect dress, the perfect church, and the most perfect man."

On paper, it was true. Rich, good-looking, affable. Dr. Evan Van Zandt was kind, generous, and thoughtful. Her family loved Evan, and he adored them.

The only thing not perfect in the whole scenario is me, Delaney thought and anxiously reached up to finger the bridge of her nose.

Rhinoplasty might have ironed out the hump, bestowing her with a flawless nose, but it hadn't straightened out her insecurities. She felt like a fake. No matter how many people raved about how gorgeous she was, Delaney didn't believe it.

The emotional repercussions of being a chubby, bucktoothed, nearsighted girl with a witchy nose resonated deep within. Never mind the weight-loss programs, intensive exercise sessions, braces, veneers, elocution lessons, LASIK, and liposuction. Inside, she still felt the same.

"To happily-ever-after," Tish said. "Come on, up with your glass, Del."

"To happily-ever-after," Delaney echoed and dutifully clinked glasses with her friends.

Remember, it's just like Mother taught you. Perceiving, behaving, becoming. Perceive yourself as happy and you'll behave as if you're happy and then you'll become happy.

Happy, happy, happy.

Tish lowered her drink and narrowed her eyes at Delaney. "What's wrong? Don't tell me you're getting cold feet again, because I'm counting on your wedding paying off my Macy's card."

She might be teasing in that devil-may-care way of hers, but it was impossible to slip anything past Tish. Her street-savvy friend had come up the hard way, but she'd never let poverty stop her. After years of struggling, she was finally gaining the reputation she deserved as one of the best wedding videographers in the business. Delaney was so proud of her.

"Nothing, nothing. I'm fine."

"You lie. Everything's not fine. Spill it."

"Honestly. Just pre-wedding jitters."

Tish didn't let up. "What's wrong? Is your mother driving you around the bend with her everything's-gotta-be-perfect-or-my-high-society-world-will-implode routine?"

Delaney cracked a half smile. People joked about Bridezilla, but no one ever mentioned that Mother-of-Bridezilla could make Bridezilla look like Bambi on Valium. "There is that."

"But it's not all. What else?" Tish pushed the empty salsa bowl aside, leaned forward, propped her elbows on the table, and rested her chin on her interlaced fingers. Jillian and Rachael were also studying her curiously.

She shrugged. "No relationship is perfect. I'm sure I'm making a mountain out of a molehill."

"You let us be the judge of that. Go on, we're listening." Tish waved a hand.

Talking about her romantic life made Delaney uncomfortable. Unlike her friends, she didn't enjoy freely swapping stories about her sexual adventures.

Um, could it be because you've never had any sexual adventures?

Besides, if she told them the truth, she couldn't keep pretending everything was fine. And yet, staying connected to those she loved was the most important thing in the world to her. If she couldn't share her fears with her friends, how could they remain close?

"Well?" Tish arched an eyebrow.

Delaney blew out her breath, trying to think of a delicate way to phrase it. "Things with Evan are..."

"Are what?" Jillian prompted when she took too long to continue.

Jillian was a dynamic young lawyer with exotic ebony hair, almond-shaped eyes, a body built for sin, and a Mensa IQ. She snared every man she'd ever set her sights on, but then dumped them just as easily as she collected them.

"Well, you know." Delaney shrugged.

"No, we don't. That's why we're asking."

"Okay, here goes. Not to complain or anything, but ever since Evan suggested we abstain from making love until our wedding night, I haven't been able to think about anything but sex. And now he's leaving for Guatemala next Monday with a volunteer surgical team to perform surgery on sick kids, and he'll be gone for six weeks."

"What?" Tish exclaimed. "You guys aren't having sex?"

"Evan thought it would make our wedding night special if we waited," Delaney explained.

"How long has this been going on?" Jillian asked.

Embarrassed to admit the truth, Delaney dropped her gaze. She wished she hadn't even brought it up. Evan was a saint. He was giving generously of himself to others, and here she was selfishly whining about their lack of a sex life.

She gulped and murmured, "Six months."

"Six months!" Tish exploded. "You're engaged, and you haven't had sex in six months?"

"I think it's romantic." Kindergarten teacher Rachael was a green-eyed blonde with delicate porcelain skin and a poetic heart. Her favorite color was springtime pink, and she favored flowing floral-print dresses. In the candlelight, through the haze of a couple of margarita-martinis, Rachael looked as if she'd stepped out of a Monet. "And very sweet."

"You think everything is romantic," Jillian pointed out.

"Oh," Delaney said quickly, "don't get me wrong. I was all for the idea."

"Why?" Jillian looked at her as if she'd said she was for a worldwide ban on chocolate.

Delaney shrugged. She wasn't all that into chocolate either. "Because honestly, our sex life wasn't so hot before and I thought maybe Evan was right, that time without physical intimacy would help us appreciate each other more. But now I'm thinking it was a dumb idea. What we really need are some techniques for spicing up our love life, not celibacy."

Her friends all started talking at once, each offering their version of how to rev up her romance with Evan before he left on his trip to Guatemala.

"Surprise him with floating candles in a hot bath," Rachael suggested. "Mood music. Massage oils."

"No, no, that's not the way to go," Jillian said. "Sexy

outfits are what you need. Stilettos, thongs, a leather bustier."

"Make love outside," Tish chimed in. "Or in the laundry room or in the backseat of your car. Pick someplace you've never made love before."

"Sex toys," Jillian threw in.

"Write him X-rated poetry." Rachael giggled. "Mail him a naughty poem every day while he's out of town. He'll be crazed for you by the time he gets back."

None of this sounded like the Holy Grail of sexual experiences that her friends seemed to suggest, but Delaney was willing to give their ideas a shot. Anything to prove to herself that this impending marriage wasn't a big mistake.

"Wait a minute." Tish snapped her fingers. "I've got the perfect scenario. Kidnap Evan from his office during his lunch hour tomorrow. Do something really daring, something that feels mysterious and taboo."

"Yeah, yeah," Jill joined in. "I can see it now. Delaney calls Evan and then tells him to meet her in the parking lot outside his office for a luncheon date. She dresses up in something super sexy, but throws a coat over her outfit and..."

"It's June," Rachael pointed out.

"Okay, a raincoat then."

"And," Tish said, "Delaney hides behind the door and when Evan comes outside she throws a tarp over his head, puts a dildo to his back—you know, like it's a gun—and tells him if he doesn't do everything she demands then she's going to blow him away."

"She forces him into her car," Jillian continued, "and takes him off to a secluded spot and has her way with him."

"Or," Rachael added, "she could take him to a really nice hotel where they have a big spa tub and flowers and candles and room service."

Tish fanned herself. "Whew, I'm getting hot and bothered just thinking about it."

Actually, Delaney thought, it wasn't a bad idea.

Longing to find something to accelerate her low-voltage sex life, she mulled over their suggestions. What if she did kidnap Evan from his office and take him to a secluded spot and seduce him? It might just be the catalyst they needed, and it would make for a great send-off so that he didn't forget her while he was in the wilds of Guatemala.

Be realistic. This is straitlaced Evan you're talking about.

Delaney shook her head. "Evan would never go for it. He's too dignified for stuff like that."

"Which is precisely why you take him hostage. Don't give him a choice. Bring handcuffs or duct tape or zip ties." Jillian pantomimed binding her hands.

"You never know," Tish said. "Evan could very well surprise you. He might be thinking you're the one who's too dignified, and you'll both find out you're horny as rabbits."

"Tish!" Rachael exclaimed.

Tish grinned impishly. "I'm just saying."

"You know," Jillian said, "there's a sex toy store in the shopping center across the street. Why don't we go check it out? Find a dildo Delaney could use as a pretend gun."

"Excellent idea." Tish flagged down their waiter and asked for the check.

A dark sinking feeling settled inside Delaney. Blabbing about her fears may have drawn her closer to her friends, but she couldn't help thinking that in the midst of their plans, she'd once again lost sight of herself and what it was that she really wanted.

And apparently she was now off to buy sex toys.

Five minutes later Delaney found herself being hustled across the busy thoroughfare. By the time they reached the shopping center, all four of them were breathless and laughing from dodging traffic. The sex toy place was located in the far corner of the strip mall, its neon sign flashing out a vibrant red—Ooh-La-La.

They trooped past a jewelry store with engagement rings prominently positioned in the showcase. Delaney glanced down at her own four-carat marquis-cut diamond set in an elegant platinum band. Funny, try as she might, she couldn't remember how she'd felt the day Evan had slipped it on her finger. She must have been happy. Why wouldn't she be happy? She just couldn't remember being happy.

There was a party supply warehouse, then a discount shoe barn and a lingerie shop. Inset in the small space between the lingerie shop and Ooh-La-La was a consignment store specializing in wedding attire.

Delaney shouldn't even have glanced in the window. Her mother was such a snob she'd have a hissy fit if Delaney dared to buy anything from a consignment store, but an enigmatic force she could not explain whispered, *Go on, take a peek.*

Cupping her hands around her eyes, she pressed her face against the glass for a better look inside the darkened store. And then, just like that, she found what she hadn't even known she was searching for.

The wedding veil to end all wedding veils.

It was encased in glass and mounted on the wall over the checkout counter. For reasons she could not comprehend, Delaney felt as if she were standing on the threshold of something monumental.

She could not say what compelled her. She already had a perfectly beautiful wedding veil from Bergdorf Goodman's that her mother had picked out for her on their last foray into Manhattan, but she felt compelled. There was simply no other word for it.

Her friends kept walking, but Delaney stayed anchored to the spot. Transfixed. Unable to take her eyes off the veil. It was a white, floor-length mantilla style, and so delicate it looked as if it had been created for a fairy princess.

I'm the answer you've been searching after, the veil seemed to whisper. *The magic that's missing.*

For the first time since she'd agreed to marry Evan, something involving the approaching nuptials truly excited her.

The veil was absolutely perfect.

Delaney's fingers itched to stroke the intricate lace, but the store looked closed. The lights were dimmed. She couldn't see anyone inside, yet her hand was already pushing against the door handle.

Drawn by the sight of the wedding veil waiting just a few feet away, she stepped over the threshold.

"Delaney? Where did you go?"

Distantly, she heard her friends calling to her, but she did not turn around. She just kept moving, pulled inexplicably toward the veil. She reached out a finger and stroked the glass case.

Up close it was even more compelling. The delicate lace pattern formed a myriad of butterflies sewn with thread so fine it was almost invisible.

"May I help you?"

Startled, Delaney jumped and tore her gaze from the veil to meet the eyes of a soft-voiced, black-haired woman in her early forties. The shopkeeper wore a gauzy, purple crinkle skirt and a lavender sleeveless knit blouse. She studied her quietly.

Delaney felt a subtle but distinct atmospheric change. The room grew slightly cooler, damper, and she experienced a strange but familiar sense of connection. "Have we met?"

"Claire Kelley," the woman said with the faint hint of an Irish brogue. Her handshake was firm, self-assured.

"Delaney Cartwright."

Claire raised an eyebrow. Delaney knew that look. The woman recognized the Cartwright name, but to her surprise, Claire did not ask her if she was one of those oil money Cartwrights the way most people did.

"Tell me about the veil," Delaney said.

"You have a very discerning eye. It's a floor-length mantilla style made of rose point lace, created with a very fine needle. Rose point is considered the most delicate and precious of all laces."

"May I see it?"

The woman hesitated and then said firmly, "I'm afraid it's not for sale, Ms. Cartwright."

Delaney's father, the consummate oilman, had taught her that everything was for sale for the right price. "If I may just examine the design up close, I'd like to have one just like it commissioned for my wedding."

"That's impossible. It's one of a kind."

She couldn't say why this was suddenly so important, but need settled like a lead weight in her stomach. She curled her fingernails into her palms. "Please, I must see it."

Outside on the street she could still hear her friends calling to her, but they sounded so very far away—on another planet, in another dimension, far outside her realm of concern.

Reluctantly, Claire took a key from her skirt pocket and ticked the lock open. She removed the veil from the case and arranged it with great care on the counter in front of them.

The majesty of it hit Delaney like a softly exploding eggshell. For one incredible instant she felt as if she were floating. She forgot to breathe. She could not breathe. Did not want or need to breathe. Terrified that if she dared inhale, the veil would evaporate.

A second passed, then two, then three.

At last, she was forced to draw in a deep, shuddering sigh of oxygen.

"Butterfly wings," she whispered.

The design was constructed of tiny roses grouped to form the butterflies. The veil was so white, so beautiful—almost phosphorescent. At any moment she expected it to fly right out the door.

Isn't it amazing, she thought, *to live in a world where there is such a work of artistic beauty.*

Delaney blinked, blinded by the dazzle and the image of herself wearing the veil as she walked down the aisle to meet her groom. The image swept in and out before her eyes as if she were in a slow, dreamy faint. She stared at the veil, seeing her future wedding, seeing the man she was about to marry.

But it wasn't Evan.

In his place stood a hard-jawed man with piercing dark eyes and a world-weary expression. He looked like a guardian, a soldier, a warrior. He exuded a strong, masculine quality. For the first time in her life, she had an overwhelming urge to kiss a man she knew absolutely nothing about. And she sensed, without doubt, he would taste like caffeine—strong, brisk, and intense.

A hard shiver ran through her.

She hitched in another breath. Her vision cleared and she was aware that while only an instant had passed, a vast expanse of time had swayed before her. A chasm into an unknowable dimension.

Claire was watching her, concern reflected in her pale blue eyes, yet there was also warmth and a steady quietness that reassured Delaney.

Whatever you see, it's okay.

The shopkeeper did not speak the words, but Delaney heard them as clearly as if she'd shouted.

Like a magnet to metal, the veil tugged at something deep within her. Her body pulsed with buoyancy and desire. She shut her eyes and found the alluring pattern burned into the back of her eyelids.

"This veil is very special." Claire's voice grew sentimental and her mouth softened. "It's over three hundred years old."

An illicit thrill shot through her at the possibility. Delaney's eyes flew open. "Impossible. It's snow white. A veil that old would yellow with age."

A slight, knowing smile lifted the corners of Claire's mouth. "It's rumored to be magic."

"Magic?"

"There's a legend."

Delaney adored history and ancient lore and had a secret longing to believe in magic, to have faith in something beyond the five senses. She leaned in closer, her eyes swallowing the veil.

"A legend?" she whispered.

"Here you are!" Tish barged through the door, Jillian and Rachael following in her wake.

The interruption, like a knuckle scraped against a cheese grater, irritated her, but she loved her friends, so Delaney tamped down her annoyance and forced a smile.

"What's up?" Tish asked, coming to stand at her elbow.

"Shh," Delaney said. "Claire was about to tell me the story of the veil."

"Oh." Tish blinked, seeing it for the first time. Delaney heard her sharp intake of breath. "Wow, that's some veil."

Jillian peered over Tish's shoulder. "It's brilliant."

"Strangely mesmerizing." Rachael tilted her head to study it in the muted lighting.

"Go on with the story," Delaney pleaded.

Claire paused.

"We want to hear it too," Tish said.

The shopkeeper eyed them all, and then she cleared her throat. "Once upon a time, in long-ago Ireland, there lived a beautiful young witch named Morag who possessed a great talent for tatting lace." Claire's lyrical voice held them spellbound. "People came from far and wide to buy the lovely wedding veils she created."

"I can see why," Delaney murmured, lightly fingering the veil.

"But there were other women in the community who were envious of Morag's beauty and talent. These women made up a lie and told the magistrate that Morag was casting spells on the men of the village."

"Jealous bitches," Jillian said.

Claire arrowed Jillian a chiding glance.

"The magistrate," she continued after Jillian got the hint and shut up, "was engaged to a woman that he admired, but did not love. He arrested Morag, but found himself falling madly in love with her. Convinced that she must have cast a spell upon him as well, he moved to have her tried for practicing witchcraft. If found guilty, she would be burned at the stake."

"Oh, no." Rachael brought her fingers to her lips.

"It's just a myth," Tish said, but Delaney could tell that her friend, who pretended to have tough skin to hide a tender heart, was as enraptured with the story as the rest of them.

"But in the end, the magistrate could not resist the power of true love. On the eve before Morag was to stand trial, he kidnapped her from the jail in the dead of night and spirited her away to America, giving up everything for her love. To prove that she had not cast a spell over him, Morag promised never to use magic again. As her final act of witchcraft, she made one last wedding veil, investing it with the power to grant the deepest wish of the wearer's soul. She wore the veil on her own wedding day, wishing for true and lasting love. Morag and the magistrate were blessed with many children and much happiness. They lived to be a ripe old age and died in each other's arms."

"Ah." Rachael sighed. "That's so sweet. I was afraid they were going to burn her at the stake."

Tish snorted and rolled her eyes.

"Humph," Jillian said. "I don't think it's fair that she had to give up the very thing that defined her just for the love of a man."

"The magistrate gave up his job for her," Delaney pointed out. "And he was exiled from his homeland."

"Morag was exiled too." Tish narrowed her eyes at the veil as if she didn't trust it.

"You must remember," Claire said, "this was three

hundred years ago. Things were much different then. And the magistrate wasn't just any man, but her soul mate. There's a very big difference. You can love all manner of people, in all manner of ways, but we each have only one soul mate who not only completes us, but challenges us to grow beyond our fears."

Was it true? Delaney wondered. Was there really such a thing as a soul mate?

Whether it's true or not, muttered a saucy voice in the back of her head that sounded a whole lot like her sister, Skylar, *one thing's for sure. Evan Van Zandt is definitely not your soul mate. You're too much alike. Peas in a pod. No challenge. No emotional growth going on in that relationship.*

Delaney nibbled her bottom lip, disturbed by the thought. Maybe Evan wasn't her soul mate, but he was kind and good and honest. As children they'd played in the sandbox together.

Evan was the one person who had told her she was pretty when she was chubby and bucktoothed and near-sighted and had a hump in her nose. Both of their families heartily approved of the marriage, and she did love him. Maybe not with a magic-wedding-veil-soul-mate-for-all-eternity kind of love, but she did love him. So what if there was no red-hot chemistry? In Delaney's estimation sex was way overrated anyway.

Too bad you don't have a magistrate to kidnap you and take you away with him.

It's my fault, Delaney thought, *not Evan's.* She hadn't tried hard enough to make their sex life something special and then she'd gone and agreed to the celibacy thing and now he was going off to Guatemala to heal crippled children.

She pushed the troubling thoughts away and leaned down to examine the veil more closely. Poetry in lace. It spoke to her in a singsong of the ages. It might not be rational or practical or even sane, but she could feel an enchanted force flowing through the air.

Goose bumps spread over her arms. What if there was some truth to the legend? What if she wore the veil on her wedding day and wished that her sexual feelings for Evan would grow stronger, richer, deeper, and truer? Would it happen?

A compulsion quite unlike anything she had ever felt before gripped her. The feeling was much greater than an itch or a whim. It gnawed at her. No matter how much it might cost, she had to have this veil. Weird as it sounded, Delaney just knew that if she had the veil she would get the happily-ever-after she so desperately desired.

But what about her mother? How could Delaney begin to explain this to Honey and convince her to let her wear this veil on her wedding day?

You can figure out how to deal with her later. Just get your hands on it.

There it was again. The undisciplined voice that sounded like Skylar. A voice boldly inciting her to do things she wouldn't ordinarily dare.

"I'll give you a thousand dollars for the veil," she blurted, surprised at her feelings of desperation.

Claire shook her head. "I'm sorry, but it's not for sale."

"Three thousand," Delaney said firmly, acting as if there was no way the woman could refuse. Three grand was probably twice what this little consignment store netted in a month.

"It's not a matter of money."

"Five thousand." Enough haggling. She was determined to possess the veil.

"You would spend that much for a wedding veil?" Claire's eyes widened.

"Her grandmother left her a two-million-dollar trust fund and she just turned twenty-five," Tish interjected. "She can spend as much as she wants."

"No." Claire shook her head.

"If it's not the money," Delaney asked, "what is it?"

The shopkeeper took a deep breath and looked as if she wished they would all just go away and leave her alone. "There are complications."

"Complications?" Delaney frowned. "What kind of complications are we talking about?"

"Um...well...throughout the years the veil has... er...backfired," Claire stammered.

"Backfired? What does that mean?"

"There've been a few incidents."

"Like what?"

"Whenever people hear about the legend, they feel compelled to wish upon the veil."

"What's wrong with that?"

Claire nervously moistened her lips. "Nothing in and of itself. The problem occurs when people wish for one thing and what their hearts really want is another thing completely. Because you see, when you wish on the veil, you get whatever your soul most deeply hungers for. It's just that some people aren't ready to face what's truly in their hearts and souls."

"Be careful what you wish for because you just might get it," Jillian said.

"Exactly." Claire nodded.

"But this wedding veil is absolutely perfect," Delaney

said, feeling wildly out of control, but unable to reel herself in. "I have to have it. Would seventy-five hundred dollars convince you?"

A long silence stretched across the room. All five of them were staring at the wedding veil.

"You really are desperately needin' a bit of magic in your life, aren't you," Claire Kelley murmured, her Irish brogue more noticeable now.

Delaney looked from the wedding veil to Claire and saw understanding in the shopkeeper's eyes. Eerily, it seemed as if the woman comprehended all of Delaney's doubts and fears concerning her impending marriage.

"Yes." *Far more than you can ever know.* Delaney raised her hands in supplication. "Please, sell me the veil."

"I cannot sell it to you."

An emotion she could not name, but that tasted a bit like grief, took hold of her. Why was possessing this particular wedding veil so important? There was no rational explanation for it, but an odd feeling clutched deep within her. The yearning was almost unbearable.

"Ten thousand." She felt like an acolyte begging a Zen master for enlightenment.

Claire sucked in her breath and looked around the shabby little shop. "You really want it that badly?"

Delaney nodded, too emotionally twisted up inside to speak.

"All right." Claire let out her breath in an audible whoosh. Her reluctance was palpable. "You may have it."

She felt as if someone had lifted a chunk of granite off her heart.

Delaney's breath came out on a squeak of pure joy. "Really?"

"Yes, but only under one condition," Claire cautioned.

"Yes, yes."

"You must swear that you will never, under any circumstances, wish upon the veil."

"I'll sign a waiver, a contract, whatever it takes. My friend Jillian is a lawyer; she can bear witness."

"Delaney." Jillian made a clucking noise. "Are you sure you want to do this? Ten thousand is a lot of money for a wedding veil."

Defiantly she met Jillian's eyes. "I want it, okay? Just back me up here."

Something in her face must have telegraphed her seriousness. Delaney rarely took a stand on anything, hardly ever expressed an opinion or even a strong desire, but because of this, whenever she did take a stand, people usually listened.

Jillian held up her palms and took a step back. "Hey, if it's what you want, I say go for it."

"Thank you." She turned back to Claire and reached inside her Prada handbag for her checkbook. "I promise never to wish on the veil. Now may I have it?"

Claire stuck out her hand to seal the deal. "Done."

And that was the moment Delaney realized that although she'd managed to find the special magic she'd been aching to believe in, she had just made a solemn vow never to use it.

Chapter 2

That night, Delaney dreamed of her sister.

Skylar had been dead for seventeen years, but she popped up in Delaney's dreams with surprising regularity. Although she couldn't say why her sister still played such a prominent role in her sleeping life.

Maybe it was because Skylar's passing had left her an only child. Afterward, her mother had tied the apron strings so tightly Delaney felt as if all the personality had been strangled out of her. Maybe dreaming of her outrageous sister was an avenue into her own subconscious. A way to express the feelings she'd learned to suppress.

Tonight, for some inexplicable reason, her sister wore roller skates, purple short-shorts, and a silver-sequined top hat. Other than the bizarre outfit, she looked exactly as she'd looked the last time Delaney had seen her—blond, beautiful, and sweet sixteen.

Skylar perched on the curvy footboard of Delaney's sleigh bed, enthusiastically chewing a persimmon.

"Who eats persimmons?" Delaney asked.

"I do."

"Of course you do."

"Persimmons are like me. Unique. If you were a fruit, Laney, you'd be an apple. Dependable, granted, but boring as hell."

"Watch what you're doing. You're dripping juice all over my new Ralph Lauren comforter."

Skylar rolled her eyes. "See? What'd I tell you? Boring. Go ahead and bitch all you want; you can't fool me. I know what you've been up to."

"I haven't been up to anything except protecting my expensive bedding from a persimmon-sucking ghost."

"Low blow, baby sis. But I am glad to see you're showing some spunk. Bravo," Skylar said. "However, insults aren't going to distract me from what you're hiding under the bed."

It was true. Delaney didn't want her sister poking fun at the wedding veil.

"Come on, pull it out. I know it's there. You might as well let me see it."

She sighed, knowing Skylar would pester her until she either showed her the veil or she woke up. "It's no big deal, just a wedding veil."

"Hmm, the plot thickens," Skylar mused. "What are you going to do about the veil that you've already got hanging in your closet? Remember that one? The veil Mother picked out for you."

"You're just trying to start trouble."

"But of course. Everybody knows stirring up trouble is what I do best." Skylar polished off the persimmon and chucked the remains in the trash can.

"I didn't know ghosts could eat," Delaney said, trying to deflect Skylar's attention.

"Technically, I'm not a ghost. Rather, I'm a figment of your dream imagination. You could send me packing if you really wanted to, but honestly your life would be pretty damn dull without me. So quit arguing and produce the veil." Skylar made "gimme" motions with her fingers.

Delaney flipped her head over the side of the bed and grappled underneath the bed skirt until she found the sack. She slipped it out, sat up, and cautiously handed her the sack. "Be careful with it."

Skylar peeked inside and whistled. "Holy shit, that's an awesome veil."

"I know." Her sister's approval meant a lot. Delaney felt eight years old again, full of wistful longing to be glamorous and grown-up. Hanging around Skylar's vanity, watching her apply makeup and change outfits as she got ready for a date.

"And I see that you found the veil at a consignment shop."

"Uh-huh."

"Mom's never going to let you wear it."

"I'm aware of that."

"You could fight her on this. Oops, oh, wait, I forgot. You're so into being the perfect daughter, you could never buck the flawless Honey Montgomery Cartwright."

"No need to get unpleasant." Delaney snatched the wedding veil away from Skylar and folded it back into the sack.

"Ah, perfect little princess. Lucky for me I died when I did. I would never have heard the end of how perfect you are, and how perfect I am not."

Skylar's comment shot her full of anger. Delaney remembered the raw horror and agonizing grief she'd experienced over her sister's death. Nostrils flaring, hands knotted into fists, she faced off with her. "No, it was not lucky! It was terrible the way you died."

"Okay, sorry. Chill."

"I won't chill. The way Mother and Daddy were afterward was awful. Losing you was the worst thing that ever happened to this family. I had to be perfect because you got your silly self killed, sneaking off to a KISS concert, drinking with your friends, and then getting smashed up in a car crash. If you hadn't been so damn rebellious, you'd still be alive and I wouldn't have ended up spending my whole life making amends for something you did. I had to have chaperoned dates until I was nineteen. Mother wouldn't even allow me to go to sleepaway camp, much less a rock concert. She refused to let me get my driver's license until I was twenty-one. And it was your entire fault."

"Ooh, where's all this emotion coming from?" Skylar applauded. "I approve. Usually, you're so pent-up."

"I don't want your approval."

"Why not?" Skylar crossed her legs and the wheels of her skates left dirty marks on the sheets.

Delaney cringed. "Watch the linens, will you?"

"What? Scared you'll become like me? Scared Mommy won't love you anymore if you do?"

That's exactly what she was scared of, but Delaney couldn't tell her sister that. "I am going to wear this veil on my wedding day. Wait and see."

"Sure you are," Skylar scoffed.

"I am!"

"Nah." Skylar pushed the top hat back off her forehead and assessed Delaney with a pensive stare. "You'll cave and our mother will get her way yet again."

"I won't."

"We'll see."

Delaney clutched the sack to her chest, knowing

her sister was right. If she responded true to form and accepted her mother's edicts for what constituted the perfect wedding, she would not be wearing the consignment shop veil.

"I have an idea on how to handle Mother." Skylar smirked. "If you've got the balls for it."

"There's no need to be crude." Delaney pressed her lips together. "What's your idea?"

"Why don't you sew a designer label on the veil, put it in an expensive box, and tell Mom someone very high up on the blue-blood food chain sent it to you. Like one of our Philadelphia relatives we've never met."

Delaney gasped. "But I can't do that. It's underhanded and sneaky."

"I knew you didn't have the balls for it. Night, Chicken Little." Skylar swung her legs off the bed, the wheels of her skates making a clacking noise as she stood. "See ya in your dreams."

"Wait, don't go."

Skylar paused. "Yeah?"

"Do you really think your plan would work?"

"Guaranteed." She winked.

Delaney worried her bottom lip. She wasn't a liar, but she wanted so badly to wear the veil at her wedding.

"I'll tell you something else," Skylar added.

"Oh?"

"I was hanging out tonight, eavesdropping on your dinner conversation with your friends, and I think they're right."

"About what?"

"Seducing Evan. Making him your sex hostage. Sounds totally hot. Go for it. Maybe it'll be the jump start you two need."

"Your glowing endorsement is all the more reason not to do it." Delaney glowered.

"You sound just like her, you know." Skylar wrinkled her nose and stuck out her tongue.

"Just like whom?"

"Who do you think?"

Skylar was right. She did sound just like their mother. Judgmental, inflexible, overly concerned with appearances. And that was the last thing Delaney wanted.

She dragged a hand through her hair. "This is horrible! How can I stop from becoming like her?"

"Do the most outrageous thing you can think to do. Kidnap Evan from his office, take him to the woods, and have your way with him. I triple dog dare you."

"Fine," Delaney said. "If that's what it takes to prove to you I'm not like Mother, I'll do it."

Skylar snorted. "Seeing is believing, pipsqueak."

Following that snarky comment, Delaney woke up.

Detective Dominic Vinetti watched Dr. Evan Van Zandt stride into the exam room, frowning at the chart in his hand and shaking his head. A bullet of dread ricocheted through the ventricles of Nick's heart at the serious expression on the other man's face.

"I've received the results of your follow-up tests," Van Zandt said, "and I'm sorry, Nick, but the outcome isn't as favorable as we had hoped."

Sweat broke across Nick's brow. He fisted his hands and swallowed hard. In this stupid paper gown he was nearly naked and felt too damn exposed. He scowled past his anxiety and mouthed toughly, "Whaddya mean?"

"It's been eight weeks since the injury and while your leg is improved, you're still healing at a much slower rate than I anticipated. I'm afraid I can't yet allow you to return to work."

Fear swamped him. Anxiety soup. Followed on its heels by a thick, rolling wave of despair. *Son of a bitch.* He could not spend one more hour watching bad television. Could not play one more video game or surf the net one more time or he'd lose his frickin' mind.

"I gotta go back to work, Doc. I'll take a desk job. Sit on my butt, no chasing suspects. I promise." He held up his palm as if he were taking an oath on the witness stand.

Van Zandt fidgeted with his tie, then flipped up the tail of his lab coat and took a seat on the rolling stool. He had the butter-soft face of a man who'd lived an easy life. "I can't in good conscience sign the release form."

Nick pressed his palms together, supplicating. "I'm going nuts, here. Please don't make me beg."

"Have you been doing your exercises?"

"Regular as a nun to mass."

Van Zandt threw back his head and brayed loudly at Nick's comment. "Well, at least you still have your sense of humor."

Irritation dug into Nick's gut. The guy laughed like a freaking barnyard donkey. "Yeah, lucky me. Ha, ha."

"Have you been taking your antibiotics?" Van Zandt asked.

"Morning, noon, and night."

"What about the pain pills?"

"Not so much."

"When was the last time you took one?"

"I never got the prescription filled when I left the hospital," he admitted.

"You're kidding."

Nick shook his head.

"There's no need to be macho. If you're hurting, take the Vicodin. Pain inhibits healing."

"Pills make me feel dulled."

"Take them anyway."

"I've seen a lot of people get addicted to those things."

"You're too strong-minded to get addicted."

"You have no idea how bored I am."

"Let's listen to your lungs." Van Zandt took a stethoscope out of his pocket. He placed the earpieces in his ears and pressed the bell of the stethoscope against Nick's back. The damn thing felt as if he'd just pulled it out of the freezer. "Deep breath."

Nick inhaled.

"Have you been eating a healthy diet?"

"I have a slice of pizza now and again, but otherwise I'm doing the whole rabbit food thing and staying away from beer like you said the last time I was here."

"Good, good." Van Zandt nodded.

"Why am I not healing? You really think it's just because I haven't been taking the pain pills?"

"Could be. How's your stress level?"

"I told you, I'm going stir-crazy with nothing to do."

"Anything else going on?" Van Zandt finished listening to his lungs and came around the examination table to lay the stethoscope against Nick's heart.

"You mean beside the fact my grandfather died two days after I got wounded on the job? And my income has been cut by a third while I'm on disability? And oh, yes, my ex-wife, who left me on our honeymoon last year, just sent me a wedding invitation. Guess what? She's three months pregnant, marrying a famous stand-up comedian, and moving to Martha's Vineyard."

Nick didn't like discussing his private business,

especially that bit about Amber, but he was playing the sympathy card, hoping Van Zandt would feel sorry enough for him that he'd sign that release form.

"Really?" Van Zandt looked surprised and dropped his stethoscope back into the pocket of his lab coat.

"Yeah, my life's a regular soap opera. You've heard it on TV, maybe read it in the tabloids. I'm the schmuck who got cuckolded by Gary Feldstein." It occurred to Nick that he felt as empty inside as those new plastic specimen cups lining the shelf over the sink.

He'd closed himself off emotionally and he was dead numb. Talking about it was like poking your arm with a needle after it had been submerged in ice-cold water for a long time—you'd already lost all the feeling, it was the perfect time for more pain, before the arm woke up and started throbbing like hell.

"Ouch," Van Zandt said.

"Tell me about it. See why I have to get back to work? My mind's a mess. I need the distraction."

"I see why you're not healing. Excess stress takes a tremendous toll on our bodies. I'm getting married myself in August, so I do understand the anxiety involved. Although I can't imagine what it must be like to get dumped on your honeymoon." Van Zandt tried to appear empathetic, but only succeeded in looking constipated.

"I would say congratulations, Doc, but I'm sorta soured on the whole subject of marriage."

"Understandably so."

"Word to the wise. Watch your back."

"I appreciate the warning, but I can assure you my fiancée isn't like that."

"Yeah," Nick muttered. "That's what I thought."

"My fiancée and I have known each other since we

were children. She's sweet-tempered, quiet, and modest. I've never met anyone so easy to get along with."

"Well, you know what they say about the quiet ones."

"I have no cause for concern."

The son of a bitch looked so damn smug. Like he had the world by the balls. As if he was so sure that something like that could never happen to him.

"Whatever you say." Nick shrugged. "Now that you understand where my tension is coming from, will you sign the form and put me back to work?"

Van Zandt's smile was kind, but firm. "Nice try, but no. Now let's have a look at that leg."

He pulled back the paper sheet to study Nick's injury, his fingers gently probing the knee. The wound was surprisingly tender, the scars still pink and fresh-looking. The kneecap was slightly puffy. Nick sucked in his breath at Van Zandt's poking.

"It shouldn't be this tender two months post-op." Van Zandt shook his head. "And you've still got a lot of swelling. You're going to have to baby it more. Take your pain pills. I know you're an intense guy, but for God's sake, man, try to find a way to relax."

Nick sighed. Dammit all. "How much longer?"

"I'm headed to Guatemala with a surgical team, and I'll be out of the country for six weeks," Van Zandt said. "We'll have Maryanne schedule you for an appointment the day after I get back."

"Six more weeks!"

"I know it seems like a long time, but it's what your body requires. If I allow you to go back to work too soon, you could have a relapse that would end your career as an undercover detective." Van Zandt scribbled something on a prescription pad, tore off the top sheet, and handed it to him. "This is the name of a good massage therapist. She'll teach you some relaxation techniques to get you through your recovery. In the meantime, try to find a low-key hobby to keep your mind busy."

Massage therapy? Relaxation techniques? Hobbies? What a load of crap. He needed his job back. It was the only thing that grounded him when the world was shifting beneath his feet.

"If you require anything more while I'm out of town, Dr. Bullock will be standing in for me."

Hmm, Nick thought. Maybe he could talk this Bullock character into signing his release form.

"And don't think Dr. Bullock will send you back to work," Van Zandt said. "I'm making a notation in your chart."

Ass wipe. "You know me too well."

"Go ahead and get dressed. You can leave through the doctors' entrance on the south side of the building. It's closer to the parking lot so you won't have so far to walk."

"Thanks," Nick forced himself to say.

Before he left the room, Van Zandt rested a hand on Nick's shoulder. "It's going to be all right if you do what I tell you. I promise. But if you don't..." He didn't finish his sentence. The warning was implicit.

Easy for him to say. He had a killer job and two good legs and a fiancée who loved him.

"Yeah." Nick nodded.

He'd come to his appointment with the expectation that he'd be returning to work on Monday. He was leaving with the realization he was stuck with himself for six more weeks, or risk losing his career forever.

Fuck it all. He felt like he'd just received a roundhouse kick to the head.

Again.

* * *

The sleek architecture of the Medical Arts Center in northwest Houston where Evan leased office space exuded a clean, faultless charm achieved only by brand-new buildings.

Feeling like an extra from *The Rocky Horror Picture Show* trying to sneak into the Oval Office for an audience with the president, Delaney paced the sidewalk outside the doctors' entrance.

The black, thigh-high, vamp boots Jillian had loaned her pinched her toes, and the pink raincoat covering her skimpy black bustier, garters, and fishnet stockings rustled noisily. A modest-sized dildo, which Tish had insisted she buy when they'd finally made it over to the sex toy store, rested in her raincoat pocket.

With both hands she carried a small, lightweight tarp pilfered from her father's barbecue grill. She had come fully prepared to carry out this sexy hostage-taking fantasy.

But doubt was making mincemeat of her already shaky self-confidence. Nervously, she nibbled her bottom lip, and then realized she was mangling her lipstick and forced herself to stop.

Remind me again why you're doing this?

To improve sex with Evan.

Is that really the reason?

Okay, if she was being truly honest with herself, she had to admit it was a last-ditch effort. Before she hitched her life to Evan's forever, she wanted to know if the possibility of sexual electricity even existed between them.

And if it doesn't?

Delaney shook her head. Tish and Jillian and Rachael

and even her dead sister, Skylar, felt certain that taking Evan hostage for an afternoon of unexpected sexual delight was exactly the thing their relationship needed.

But what if they were wrong? What if Evan hated this surprise seduction? What if he refused to play along? Or worse yet, what if he did play along, but the seduction did nothing to spice up their sex life?

She checked her watch. Twelve-oh-five.

Where was he?

She'd phoned Evan early that morning and invited him to lunch. He'd promised to meet her in the parking lot outside of his office at noon.

He's a doctor, his time isn't his own. Patience, patience. He'll be here.

Good advice, except the waiting was ramping up her nerves and making her palms sweaty. Quickly she peeked through the darkly tinted back door to see if she could spot Evan in the hallway.

Ooh, ooh, there he was, head down, ambling toward the exit.

Excitement spun through her. Pulse pounding, she jumped behind the door.

This is it.

She raised the tarp up in front of her, ready to toss it over his head when he came through the door.

Several seconds passed.

Where was he? What was taking so long?

Just as she was about to take another peek, the door swung open.

A thrill, unlike anything she'd ever felt, took swift possession of her. Delaney pitched the tarp down over his head, whipped the dildo from the pocket of her raincoat, and then pressed the tip of it against his spine.

"This is a gun," she growled in a movie moll voice. "Do as I say, or you're gonna get a bullet in your back."

In her imagination Evan's knees would quake. He would raise his hands over his head, beg her not to kill him, and then promise to do whatever she demanded. She was floored by the realization that having that kind of power turned her on.

But that was not what happened.

One minute she was teetering on her stiletto boots and the next minute she was lying flat on her back, pinned to the cool green lawn and peering up at the bristling stranger who was staring down at her. His hands were wrapped around her wrists and his knees were between her legs.

Everything had gone wrong. Her blood pumped crazily. Oh, God, oh, no, it couldn't be.

A bizarre sensation of déjà vu crushed her. This was crazy, insane, impossible.

Thunderstruck, she blinked, unable to believe what she was seeing. Instead of snaring her fiancé, she had bagged the man from that weird vision she'd had while she was in Claire Kelley's shop when she'd first touched the wedding veil. The hard-jawed warrior. The man she'd seen herself marrying.

You're imagining things. This can't be the same guy you saw.

But it was.

Same uncompromising chin, same dark mysterious eyes, same irresistible pull of attraction.

She gulped.

The barbecue grill tarp lay on the sidewalk beside them. Her raincoat hung open, revealing her scanty boudoir attire, and she was still holding that damnable dildo clutched in her fist.

Shame burned a red-hot blush up Delaney's neck, a rampaging forest fire of embarrassing heat consuming her entire face.

His gaze raked over her.

She watched him sizing up the situation with a look that told her he'd seen it all and done even more. Nothing surprised this guy.

Like her fiancé, he was dark-haired and had a similar build—slightly taller than average height, broad shoulders, narrow hips—but the resemblance stopped there. Evan's eyes were blue, but this guy's eyes were so brown they seemed black.

Like coffee. Or cocoa beans.

She sensed he was a man who felt everything intensely, and he didn't need much of a reason to fight. Or to make love. He was a man who dared. A man who took risks.

And he *was* the man from her vision.

Something in his face spoke to her. He would be fiercely loyal and protective, making his woman feel special and cared for. And, illogically, she wanted to be that woman.

His eyes kept drilling into hers as if on some level he recognized her too.

Silly? Fanciful? Or something metaphysical?

Delaney's chest tightened. It was as if every muscle in her body had converged around her heart and they were squeezing in rhythmic, synchronized contractions. Suddenly there didn't seem to be enough oxygen in the entire world to pacify her hungry lungs. She was breathless and struggling hard to regain some small shred of self-control.

Then again, he appeared to be doing some struggling of his own. Actually, he looked...*flattened.* As if she were a tornado and he was a trailer park.

His pupils constricted and he moistened his lips. His pelvis was pressed flush against her thigh and Delaney realized, to her total mortification, that he was halfway aroused.

"Is this the gun you were planning on shooting me with?" He wrenched the dildo from her hand and sent her a sardonic smirk. "'Cause it looks like it's already gone off half cocked."

Oh, God, kill me now. "I thought...I thought...you were someone else."

"Clearly."

He arched an eyebrow and took another look at her body, this one long and lingering. His eyes darkened from coffee-colored to inky black as he carefully cataloged the lacy details of her bustier.

Goose bumps dotted her skin at his appreciative stare. Her breasts prickled, her nipples tightened, and her throat closed off.

And Delaney was terrified he would notice how her body was betraying her desire.

She felt trapped, and the thought sent a shiver through her that she couldn't dismiss as being chilled. It was June in Houston. Hot, humid, sticky. Plus, she was startlingly aware that her thin plastic raincoat was molded tightly against her curves.

So was the good-looking stranger.

What had she gotten herself into? His lips hovered above hers, and she made the deadly mistake of staring at his mouth.

Anticipation raced her heart.

Perturbed by both his mocking and her stupidity for listening to her friends and dressing up like this, she splayed her palms against his chest and pushed. "Get off me, you big oaf."

Usually, she wouldn't have been so rude, but this was not a normal circumstance, and the roguish expression on his face was just begging for a bad-mannered comment.

"You're freakin' gorgeous," he murmured. "What gives? You shouldn't have to throw a tarp over a guy to get him to go out with you."

"Off!" She tried to sound tough and bitchy, but she wasn't good at tough and bitchy, and she came off sounding more scared than anything else.

"Yes, ma'am." He rolled to one side.

"And give me that back." She sat up and snatched the dildo from his hand.

He laughed then, a rich, melodious sound rolling over her like a spring breeze, and she almost liked him for it.

Almost.

Then a shocking thought occurred. What if Evan came out of the clinic and caught her like this? Sitting half naked on the ground like some deranged Victoria's Secret model. The notion was enough to propel her to her feet. Quickly she belted her raincoat closed and jammed the lurid sex toy back inside her pocket. She had to get out of here. Her mission of seduction had failed miserably.

Well, it wasn't a totally failed seduction; the oddly familiar stranger was looking at her as if he wanted to eat her for dessert. Unfortunately, she'd managed to arouse the wrong man.

Breathing heavily, Delaney snatched up the tarp and spun on her high-heeled boots, striding for the sanctuary of her car.

"Hey, lady," the guy called after her.

She wanted to keep walking, but years of good breeding wouldn't allow her to ignore him. Frustrated, she turned and snapped, "What is it?"

He stretched out a hand. "Could you help me up here? Seeing as how you're the reason I ended up on my butt in the grass."

For the first time she noticed the brace strapped to his right leg. He was impaired.

Guilt flooded her. She slapped three fingertips across her lips. "Oh, my, I'm so sorry."

"'S'all right."

"How did you do that, you know, with an injured leg?" she asked, hurrying back toward him.

"Do what?"

"Flip me onto my back."

"I'll never tell." His smile was pure wickedness.

Delaney felt something start to unwind inside her. Something she could not name, but it had been bound up tight for a very long time. Her breath escaped her lungs, rushing out over her lips. She stepped closer. She was looming over him, but it felt as if he were the one dominating her personal space and not the other way around.

How was that possible?

Clutching the tarp to her chest with one hand, she put out her other hand to help him up.

He took it.

His palm was hard and calloused, his grip strong. Her skin burned. Dumbfounded, she felt herself dissolving. Becoming something else, someone else. Her jaw dropped open. No words came out. What was there to say?

"Give me a tug." His fingers closed more tightly around her hand.

She yanked him to his feet and then he was standing right in front of her. Eye level.

He wasn't but a couple of inches taller than her own five-foot-nine height. Barely but distinctly, he leaned in toward her. Close enough for his black T-shirt emblazed with the Harley motorcycle logo to brush the sleeve of her raincoat. And for Delaney to feel the heat of his breath on her cheek.

A thermal wave of energy hit her and she battled the urge to push her body against his. The sensation was so compelling, Delaney realized that if she didn't move away right this instant, this very macho male was going to kiss her.

Defensively crossing her arms over the tarp and holding it close to her chest, she turned. Moving as quickly as she could in the damnable stilettos, she raced for her silver Acura.

Fingers trembling, she fumbled the keys from her pocket, jabbed them in the lock, wrenched the door open, and tumbled inside.

Consumed by remorse, she squeezed her eyes closed. Her breath came in heavy, irregular gasps.

What if Evan had seen them?

Where was Evan? Her eyes flew open, her gaze tracking to the digital clock in the dash. Twelve-twenty.

She tossed the tarp in the backseat, then took her cell phone from the console and flipped it open. She started to punch in Evan's number, but then saw she had one missed call. She entered the code to hear her messages.

It was her fiancé.

"I'm sorry to do this to you, Laney," Evan's recorded voice said. "But I've got an emergency at the hospital. Rain check?"

Rain check.

Delaney looked down at her pink raincoat and then stared up at the cloudless sky. It might be sunny and hot, but she couldn't shake the feeling there was one hell of a thunderstorm heading her way.

Chapter 3

Two days had passed and for some bizarre reason, Nick couldn't stop thinking about the sexy vixen who had ambushed him outside the orthopedic clinic.

Whenever he closed his eyes, he could see how she'd looked walking away from him, rolling and swaying, as if she were gliding on an ocean wave. Serene, calm, untouched by external circumstances. He wished he'd had hours to watch her, study her—okay, all right, *ogle* her.

Her light brown shoulder-length hair, streaked with enticing blond strands, had been styled in a straight sleek style that underscored her cool-as-a-cucumber aloofness. She wasn't voluptuous like the women he usually dated, like his ex-wife, Amber. Yet in spite of her athletic figure, she had sufficient curves. He'd gotten a pretty good look at what she'd been hiding underneath that raincoat.

Not bad. Not bad at all.

Something about her compelled him in a way no one woman had in a very long time, and it shook him. He thought he'd washed his hands of all that romantic junk.

She looked like a woman who had a lot to say, but never got to say it. Nick found himself wishing he could be the one to hear what was inside her head, learn the secrets she kept closed up behind those sphinxlike lips.

What was it about this particular woman that got to him? Was it her unflappable calmness that made him ache to rumple her? Maybe it was her wide, slightly crooked mouth that seemed out of sync with the rest of her? That mouth was the most interesting part of her beauty, precisely because it didn't fit.

Or perhaps it was her eyes—sharp, smart, and green as an oasis. Looking into the depths of her made him feel like a traveler lost in an enchanted forest. Of course, it could have just been the sizzling underwear peeping from behind the raincoat and her unexpected willingness for adventuresome sex play.

A shudder passed through Nick. Whatever the cause, the woman was F-I-N-E, fine.

He'd been damn tempted to ask for her phone number, but it was clear from the huge rock on her ring finger she was deeply involved with someone else. And to Nick's way of thinking, there was nothing more off-limits than a woman who was spoken for. Too bad. A little sexual healing would have been a very nice way to pass his recovery time until Dr. Van Zandt got back from Guatemala.

Yeah, right, like you would ever have a chance with her even if she wasn't engaged. She's filet mignon, and you're a hot dog.

Determined to burn her off his brain, Nick decided a workout was in order.

He ambled out to his pickup truck, favoring his achy knee, and drove over to Gold's Gym. Strenuous cardio was out of the question, but he could do upper-body strength training, and Doc Van Zandt had endorsed swimming.

After twenty minutes in the lap pool, Nick emerged winded, with water trickling down his bare chest and abdomen. He dried off with a thin white cotton towel, his heart punching hard against his rib cage, his lungs burning. Fatigue weighted him, but his thoughts were still locked on his mystery woman. He kept picturing her on his bed, in that girly pink raincoat, knowing full well that she was wearing next to nothing underneath.

What was the inexplicable pull? Where had it come from, this continual, aching need that had dogged him for two long, agonizing days?

He hit the weight machines. Working out his triceps, his biceps, his pecs. He pushed himself until his arms quivered, desperate to sublimate his sexual desires with exhaustion. But this time, instead of easing his mental torture, exercise seemed to have fueled it. He was doubly aware of his body, of his physical needs.

Face facts, Vinetti, you can't have her. The woman is already spoken for. Maybe that was why he couldn't stop thinking about her. Because she was strictly off-limits. Dammit. What the hell was so special about this one?

His cell phone rang.

Relieved to finally have something else to focus on, Nick snatched up the cell phone from his gym bag and punched the talk button. "'Lo?"

"Nicky, it's your nana."

Immediately the muscles at his shoulder blades tensed and his grip tightened around the phone. "Is everything all right?"

"Yes, yes. I just needed to talk to you about something."

"What's up?" Sweat ran down his forehead and he swiped it away with his gym towel.

"I'm ready to go through your grandfather's personal

effects. Could you drop by tomorrow afternoon, say three-thirtyish, and help me start packing things up?"

Nick hesitated.

It wasn't that he had anything else to do tomorrow. Nor was it that he minded in the least helping his grandmother. He'd move heaven and earth for her. What he hated was the thought of saying good-bye to his grandfather once and for all.

Nick had been just seven years old when his father, his two younger brothers, Richie and Johnny, and his sister, Gina, had moved in with Nana and Grampa in their three-story Victorian on Galveston Island. Over the course of the last year, everything in Nick's life had changed. His bride had left him on their honeymoon. His knee had gotten mangled, forcing him off the job he loved for weeks, and his grandfather had passed away. He simply wasn't prepared to handle any more changes.

"Are you sure now is the right time?" he said. "It's only been two months."

"It's time," she said. "It's got to be done."

"There's no reason we can't wait a while longer."

"Yes, there is, Nicky. I'm selling the house," she said, her firm tone telling him she'd brook no argument.

Nick couldn't have been more stunned if she'd reached through the phone and punched him squarely in the gut. "Nana, no, absolutely not. You can't sell the house."

"I can't talk about this now. There's someone at the front door. We'll finish this discussion when you come over tomorrow afternoon." And with that, she hung up on him.

The dial tone mocked his ear.

Nana had hung up on him!

Feeling as if he'd just gone fifteen pulverizing rounds

with a heavyweight boxing champ, Nick slipped his cell phone back into his gym bag.

All right then, if that's the way it was going to be, he'd look at the upside. At least he had something to do besides fantasize about the woman in the raincoat and fret over his knee—confront his grandmother and convince her she couldn't sell the only real home he'd ever known.

On Sunday evening, Delaney got her rain check.

Evan took her to La Maison Vert, the only five-star French restaurant in Houston. He wore a tux. She had on a little black cocktail dress. The decor was elegant, the service impeccable. And the pan-seared, pecan-encrusted mahimahi bathed in a rich buttery caper sauce was definitely worth the three additional hours on the treadmill the extra calories were going to cost her.

It should have been a magical evening.

Instead, Evan talked nonstop about his work, spoiling the romantic mood. Any other time, Delaney wouldn't have minded. Evan was passionate about his job and she was a good listener, but tonight she found herself wishing that he were half as passionate about her as he was about medicine.

She'd still planned on seducing him, but extreme embarrassment—following what had happened outside Evan's office—caused her to give up on the hostage-taking fantasy and go for something a little lower key. She had reserved a room at the Hyatt and worn a dress that showed lots of cleavage with sexy underwear underneath, and she'd ordered oysters on the half shell for an appetizer.

But Evan hadn't wanted any.

Glumly, she'd sucked down the delicacies alone while her husband-to-be extolled the virtues of a new hip replacement procedure. Delaney zoned out on the details. She didn't know how to tell him he was boring her to tears.

This is how the meals are going to go for the rest of your life. Skylar's voice rang in her head.

Now that was a depressing thought.

It's okay, she reassured herself. She had her work too, and she loved it. Evan probably got just as bored listening to her talk about All the World's a Stage as much as his shoptalk bored her. Except she never really talked about her job with him.

She'd gotten into the business of staging houses quite by accident. She had received her master's degree in liberal arts and was trying to decide what to do with it when Tish, who'd been struggling to make a big mortgage payment after her divorce, asked Delaney to help her fix up her house so she could sell it.

She had given her friend's place a complete makeover, and it sold the following week at ten thousand more than the asking price—and that was after the house had been on the market for over a year. Delaney had found her niche, and on the plus side, it was also a career her mother endorsed.

Excited by the headiness of that first success, she'd borrowed money from her father and started All the World's a Stage last summer. But while the business was breaking even, it was only because of her mother's friends. To date, besides Tish, only one other of her clients had not come from the pool of people who regularly kissed up to Honey Montgomery Cartwright.

But Delaney was eager to change all that. She was determined to succeed on her own, without her mother's help.

She ordered another glass of wine to loosen her up enough to proceed with her plans for seduction. Evan was leaving for Guatemala tomorrow morning. If she couldn't coax him into bed tonight, she wouldn't have another chance before their wedding.

She assessed him through the glow of a pricey zinfandel. He was classically handsome—flawless to a fault, perfectly symmetrical features, manicured fingernails, complexion like a baby's, every hair combed smoothly into place.

And Delaney couldn't help comparing him to the rugged guy she'd tarped outside Evan's office.

Now there was a man. *Ha-cha-cha.*

Immediately her mind conjured up a picture of him. Beard stubbling his firm jaw, calluses on his hands, tanned skin, unruly hair curling around his collar. He put her in mind of Gerard Butler, the rugged British actor who'd played the phantom of the opera in the recent film version of the famous musical. It was one of her favorite movies. He possessed the same hauntingly mesmerizing quality of extreme masculinity that Mr. Butler did.

Her heart thumped faster just thinking about him.

He was everything she had never wanted. Bold, brash, cocky. And yet, again and again, over the course of the last couple of days, her mind had been drawn to thoughts of him.

He's a fantasy; forget him. Your future is sitting right in front of you.

But those biceps. Those piercing dark brown eyes. She sighed.

She squinted at Evan in the candlelight and tried to get worked up, but an undertow of anxiety tugged at her thoughts. He was a very good-looking man. Why couldn't she get stoked over him the way she did over this stranger? What was wrong with her?

"And by then," Evan was saying, "we'll be ready to have kids, and then you can give up your business and stay home."

"What?" Delaney blinked, realizing she'd spaced out. "What did you say?"

Evan repeated what he'd said.

"I'm not giving up my business. I love my business. What made you think I would give up my business?"

"We don't need the money, and our children will require your undivided attention."

"What about your undivided attention? Don't kids need a dad as much as a mom? Why don't you give up your job?"

He laughed, the braying sound affecting her like fingernails on a chalkboard. When had the sound of his laugh first started to irritate her? She'd never really noticed before what an unattractive sound it was.

"Okay, point taken," he said. "You can keep the business as a sideline and we'll hire a part-time nanny."

"Oh, thanks so much for your permission."

"You're mad?" Evan looked bewildered. "Why are you mad?"

"Nothing. I'm not mad." She held up her palms. He didn't even realize he'd been patronizing her. "Never mind."

"No, no, let's talk this through."

His calm rationality was getting on her nerves. Which was weird. His steady sensibility was one of the things Delaney liked most about him.

Thankfully, her cell phone picked that moment to ring.

Evan gave her a gently chiding look. "You left your cell phone on? This is our last dinner together for six weeks."

"You leave your cell phone on whenever we go out,"

Delaney said, feeling a little defensive as she searched in her clutch purse for the slim flip phone.

"I'm a doctor; there could be emergencies," he said. "You stage houses for a living." There it was again, that slightly condescending tone in his voice.

She found the phone and checked the caller ID. It was from Trudie Klausman, the one client who had not come to her from her mother's sphere of social influence. "Excuse me, Evan, I need to take this."

Delaney put her napkin on the table, pushed back her chair, and hurried to an out-of-the-way alcove to take the call.

"Trudie," she greeted her caller. "How are you?"

"Fine, just fine."

"How's the new condo?"

"Wonderful, I love it. There's so much to do here, so many activities, and lots of handsome widowers to chase after in my golf cart."

"That's great to hear."

"Listen," Trudie said, "I've got a friend who's looking to sell her house."

"Really." A smile flitted across her lips. At last, a referral that had nothing to do with her mother.

"My friend lives on Galveston Island in an old Victorian. It's a beautiful place, but needs work. Her husband died a couple of months ago and she's really lonely."

"That's sad," Delaney said. "I'm so sorry to hear it."

"It's been rough on her. They were married fifty-two years, and Leo was the love of her life."

Delaney made a noise of sympathy. "Tragic."

"Well," Trudie said, "they did get fifty-two wonderful years together. Most of us aren't so lucky. Anyway, a condo came open here at Orchid Villa right across the courtyard from my place. But she can't afford the condo until she sells her house. The condo won't last long. You know how quickly the properties are going around here, so she needs to sell the house as soon as possible. Can you drop by tomorrow afternoon and give her your expert opinion?"

"Trudie," Delaney said, "I'd be happy to do what I can for your friend."

"Can you come around three? Got a pen so I can give you the address?"

"Three would be perfect. Hang on, I've got my BlackBerry right here." She dug the device from her purse and powered it on. "Go ahead."

"Her name is Lucia Vinetti." As Trudie gave her the address, Delaney felt her excitement growing. She hadn't had a project in a couple of weeks, and she was eager to work and get her mind off the wedding plans.

In the course of a two-minute conversation, Delaney had completely forgotten about seducing Evan. If she couldn't find the magic that was missing from her life through love, then she would do it through her work. Now, all she could think about was making sure Lucia Vinetti's house sold quickly and for the most amount of money possible.

And opening up a whole new aspect of her career.

Lucia Vinetti and her friend Trudie Klausman strolled through her garden in the gathering twilight, admiring the flowering bougainvilleas, inhaling the scent of red honeysuckle growing up the fence.

"I hope I'm doing the right thing. Messing with fate can be a risky proposition," Lucia Vinetti said as she pulled a small bottle of lavender lotion from the pocket of her apron and rubbed a dab of it into her hands.

She'd led such a wonderful life, she'd never really minded growing old. But these wrinkly brown spots on her hands, Mother Teresa, how she hated them. When Leo was alive, he would laugh about her vanity, kiss her hands, and tell her she was in luck, because brown was his favorite color. Remembering her husband, Lucia smiled while at the same time her heart welled with sadness. She was going to miss this place so much, the garden in particular where she and Leo had worked side by side, coaxing things to grow.

"I'm telling ya, Luce, Delaney is the one for your Nicky," her best friend Trudie said.

"But playing matchmaker? I'm not sure it's prudent to interfere in other people's love lives."

Even at seventy-five Trudie still dressed like the Las Vegas showgirl she used to be. Garish colors, styles made for women a third of her age, outrageous props. Tonight she had a lime green feather boa tossed around her neck. But Lucia never judged Trudie for her eccentric clothes. She might be outrageous, but she was the truest friend Lucia had ever had.

"The minute I met this girl, I knew she was the one for your grandson." Trudie sounded so certain. "But just to be sure, I did her astrological chart. The stars never lie. She and Nick are destined to be together."

"But you said she's engaged to marry another man." Lucia kept rubbing her hands long after the lotion had been absorbed. Nervous habit, but then playing around with fate was something to be nervous about. "That isn't a good sign. Nick's already been cut to the quick by one fickle female; the last thing I want is to see my grandson get hurt again."

"You were engaged to someone else when you met Leo," Trudie reminded her.

Lucia thought of Frank Tigerelli, the wealthy man her family had wanted her to marry. He'd ended up going to prison in some real estate scam. Thank God for her Leo. He'd saved her from making the gravest mistake of her life.

"If something goes wrong and Nicky gets hurt, I'll never forgive myself," Lucia said.

"We're just putting them together and letting nature take its course," Trudie assured her. "If they meet and the whammy doesn't strike, no harm, no foul."

Lucia nodded and took a deep breath. Her grandson needed something to jar him out of his doldrums.

"Will you tell me the story again about how you knew Leo was the one?" Trudie asked, absentmindedly twirling her boa. "I love that story. Look at me. I had to go through three husbands before I got it right, and then Artie up and dies on me. Men."

Lucia smiled. "Our first meeting was such a cliché, I don't get why it fascinates you so."

"You know why. Tell the story."

The truth was Lucia loved telling the story as much as Trudie loved hearing it. "I had just turned eighteen. A friend and I had been invited to a party thrown by a man in our office where we both worked as secretaries. The party turned out to be very dull. I looked at a clock on the wall and it was only nine-ten. I wanted so badly to leave, but my girlfriend who'd given me a ride didn't want to go. She'd found a fellow to flirt with."

"Not much of a party girl, were you?"

"No." Lucia smiled. "I seriously doubt that you and I would have been friends if we'd met back then."

"Probably not," Trudie agreed. "So then what happened next?"

"I was about to call my father to come get me, when Leo walked into the room. And then it hits me. A bolt from the blue. The whammy."

"What did the whammy feel like?"

"My heart started pounding and I wanted desperately to run away, but at the same time I couldn't take my eyes off him. Nor he me. He comes toward me and the crowd parts like the Red Sea. I'm barely breathing."

Trudie sighed happily.

"Leo introduces himself and we start talking and talking and talking. The room gets less crowded and quieter. We find a seat and keep talking. My friend shows up and wants to leave. Leo tells me he'll give me a ride home so I tell my friend to go on without me. Finally we're the only ones left at the party. Even the host went to bed. I looked at the clock and it says nine-fifteen. I'm starting to think I'm caught in some weird waking dream and then I realize the clock has stopped. It stopped the minute I saw Leo." Lucia's voice broke and tears sprang to her eyes.

"Aw, Luce, I'm sorry. I shouldn't have prodded you to tell that story," Trudie fretted. "I didn't mean to make you cry."

"It's all right." Lucia swiped at her eyes. "Even though it hurts, I like remembering Leo."

"See, don't you want that kind of love for Nick?"

"Of course I do."

"Then let go of your fears and put your trust in the magic that stopped that clock the minute you and Leo met. If Delaney Cartwright *is* Nick's soul mate, they'll know it."

"And if she isn't?"

Trudie shrugged. "She's still a whiz at staging houses."

Chapter 4

James Robert, what is this?"

Jim Bob Cartwright glanced up from the *Houston Chronicle* Sunday crossword puzzle he was working to help him fall asleep and saw his wife, Honey, standing in the doorway, holding something out in front of her as if it were going to give her a disease. Jim Bob pushed his reading glasses up on his forehead to see what she was talking about.

"Looks like a wedding veil."

"Exactly." Honey's lips were pressed together in a tight, disapproving line. If she hadn't just had a round of Botox, Jim Bob had no doubt she would have been frowning.

He slid his glasses back down on his nose. "What's a ten-letter word for flawless?"

"Perfection," she said. "I found it under Delaney's bed."

"What? Perfection?"

"No, the wedding veil. Perfection is a ten-letter word for flawless."

"So is Honey Leigh." He smiled at her.

"I doubt that's what the makers of your crossword puzzle had in mind," she said dryly. "Delaney bought this at a consignment shop. If she thinks I'm going to let her wear this shabby thing at her wedding, she's going to have to think again."

"I think it looks nice," he said.

"You would," Honey grumbled and set the veil down on the edge of the bed. "It's from a consignment shop."

"What's wrong with that?"

"It's tacky. It's been on other women's heads." Honey shuddered.

"What were you doing snooping in her room?"

"I wasn't snooping," she said defensively.

"No?"

"If you must know, I went to turn down her covers so she could slip right into bed when she gets home from her date with Evan. I expect they'll be out late since this is the last night they'll have together for six weeks. I saw the corner of the veil sticking out from underneath her bed and pulled it out for a look. What perplexes me is why she would want to wear a used veil. I've raised her better than that."

"You're too hard on her," he said, but thought, *Who are you, Martha Stewart?* "Cut her some slack."

"We've had this discussion a million times."

"And you always win."

"That's right, and don't make me say why."

Skylar.

Their eldest daughter's name hung in the air between them, painful as a third-degree burn. Jim Bob blinked and stared hard at the crossword puzzle.

He couldn't say for sure when his marriage had started to unravel; certainly Skylar's death had been a pivotal turning point. But if he were being honest, Jim Bob would admit the marriage had been fraying long before then, and he had no real idea why. He still loved Honey, deep down inside, but they hadn't been close in a very long time.

In fact, when he thought back on their life together, he wondered if they'd ever really been emotionally intimate. Honey was always on guard, worried about presenting a glossy image of the impeccable wife, hostess, mother, or what have you. It felt like she was a consummate actress who'd perfected a role in a long-running play, and she was determined to get rave reviews each and every night.

And she expected him to play the perfect leading man, although she never hesitated to let him know how he failed to live up to the role.

He supposed her insistence on living what she called the "proper way" came from being a blue blood with a pedigree she could trace back to European royalty. While his family, before his great-grandfather had struck oil back in the 1920s, had been nothing but dirt-poor farmers. For reasons he couldn't fathom, foolish things like not allowing Delaney to wear a used wedding veil mattered greatly to his wife.

With a clarity undiminished by the passing years, Jim Bob remembered the first time he laid eyes on Honey. He'd been attending a summer seminar at the University of Pennsylvania, and he'd seen her striding purposefully across campus as if she knew exactly who she was and where she was going and she wasn't about to let anything or anyone stand in her way.

That strong sense of purpose was what had initially attracted him to her. She possessed a special something that he lacked—a driving force that pushed her to continually better herself. He admired the quality, but honestly did not fully understand it. Honey was a doer, whereas

Jim Bob was just happy to be along for the ride. In that regard, Delaney had taken after him.

Growing up the youngest of the three Cartwright brothers, with a larger-than-life father, Jim Bob had gotten lost in the shuffle of his legendary family. He was laid-back and easygoing. Loved having a good time and believed that life took care of itself, that you really shouldn't have to work so hard at it. Unlike Honey, who discounted anything that came easily.

His family had loved Honey from the minute they'd met her. Both because her blue-blood status gave respectable cache to their oil field money and because they believed she was exactly what Jim Bob needed to give him some direction in life.

They were right on both counts.

Honey had taken to his family like, well, a duck to water. Her own mother had died shortly after they'd met and she had no other immediate family. She'd told Jim Bob she didn't get along with her distant relatives, since they'd forsaken her during her mother's long illness. Medical bills had drained most of the fortune her father had made in textiles. Even her family home had been mortgaged to the hilt. They'd never been back to Philadelphia, and none of Honey's relatives ever called or came to visit.

But her high-society cache and Honey's unerring sense of direction hadn't brought Jim Bob the happiness he'd thought their marriage was supposed to provide. His children had been the only things that had given him real joy.

And then Skylar had been killed.

Honey blamed him wholly, completely. Blamed his permissiveness and what she called his screwed-up priorities. Putting fun ahead of safety. And he couldn't fault her for it. He'd actually pleaded Skylar's case for less restriction, convincing Honey to untie the apron strings and let Skylar go to that damnable rock concert. Jim Bob never regretted any decision more.

When Honey had told him he would get absolutely no say in raising Delaney, he'd stepped out of the picture as far as discipline was concerned. Even when he didn't agree with something his wife was doing, like putting Delaney on a strict diet, or pressuring her into plastic surgery, or egging her on to marry Evan, he'd kept his mouth shut. Jim Bob's ideas on child rearing had gotten his oldest daughter killed. What in the hell did he know? He couldn't buck Honey on anything.

Jim Bob peered over the top of his newspaper. Honey was sitting on the edge of the bed, staring at the wedding veil as if it were a poisonous viper. She was so damn determined this wedding had to meet some impossibly high standard she'd set up in her own mind. It was costing him a fortune, but the money wasn't what bothered Jim Bob. He worried that Delaney was getting married simply to please her mother.

Not that he disliked his future son-in-law. Evan Van Zandt was a good guy and came from a very respectable family. Delaney could do far worse. It was just that, because of Honey's overprotectiveness, Delaney had never really experienced life. Evan was the only man she'd ever dated. She'd never lived on her own, nor was she well traveled. She hadn't even worked at anything other than this little business venture she'd started, except teaching undergrads when she was working on her master's degree.

If it weren't for Honey pressuring her friends into using All the World's a Stage when they sold their houses, he doubted Delaney could keep the business afloat without tapping into the trust fund his mother had set up for her.

Jim Bob couldn't help feeling that his daughter deserved so much more out of life.

But how could he advise Delaney on marriage when his own was in such rocky shape?

Where had things gotten so messed up?

He looked at Honey. A sweep of blond hair had fallen across her cheek, and his heart wadded in his chest. The past was gone, and he felt the future ebbing away like hourglass sand. God, he'd screwed things up so badly.

"I've let you down," he said to Honey.

"Excuse me?" She looked up, assessing him with cool green eyes that revealed nothing. The same inscrutable eyes Delaney had inherited.

"Over the years, I haven't been the kind of husband you deserved."

She stared at him for a long moment then said, in the oddest tone of voice, "I got exactly what I deserved."

"You didn't deserve an alcoholic."

"James Robert, you've been sober for fifteen years. It's all in the past. Forget about it."

"I'll never be able to forget it. Or what I did to you and Delaney," he said. "I haven't really made full amends."

"Yes, you have."

"If I'd truly made amends then why haven't you forgiven me? I'm so sorry I hurt you, Honey. So very sorry."

"You're forgiven. Now can we stop talking about this, please?"

"You should have divorced me."

"I'm going to keep this veil," she said, getting up and crossing the room to put the veil in her closet. "If Delaney wants it back, she's going to have to ask me for it."

It irritated him that she pretended to forgive him when he knew she hadn't. She punished him every day. Like she was doing now. By not allowing him to say what he needed to say. By dismissing his apology as inconsequential.

"I want things to be better between us," Jim Bob said. "Like they used to be when we were first married. Remember?"

"Let's go to sleep, James Robert. It's late."

"Stop changing the subject. I don't want to talk about wedding veils. I want to talk about us. How we're going to spend the rest of our lives once Delaney is married and off on her own and she's no longer the glue holding us together."

Honey looked at him with those calm green eyes that revealed nothing about what she was really feeling. "I don't know what you intend to do, but I'm planning on living my life exactly as I have been."

"Filling it up with what? Charity events and Pilates and spa dates with your friends?"

"Why, yes."

"Where do I fit into your plans?"

"What is it that you want from me?"

I want you to love me the way you used to! He wanted to grab her by the shoulders and shake some feeling into her. But you couldn't force people to feel something for you if they didn't.

His chest constricted. "What happened, Honey? What happened to the girl I married? The one who had big dreams and an even bigger heart? The one who used to laugh at my jokes and let her hair down once in a while? The one who told me we were a team and as long as we were together, nothing could break us?"

She reached across the bed and stroked his cheek with her index finger, the unexpected tenderness in her eyes cutting straight to his heart. "Delaney's grown now. We're in our mid-fifties. What's past is past. I can't be something I no longer am, and I can't bring Skylar back. Now please, can we just go to bed?"

He wanted to shout. He wanted to throw something against the wall. Anything to get her attention.

But he did not.

Jim Bob put the crossword puzzle aside, turned out the light, and slid down in bed. He reached for Honey and pulled her into his embrace. She did not resist, but she held her body so stiffly against him, he could take no comfort in her arms.

She was an ice queen. Beautiful, but untouchable. Impossible to know even after thirty-four years of marriage.

There was no getting through to her. He'd been trying for years. She had her idea of the way things were supposed to be, and Honey refused to budge. The terrible thing was, much as he still loved her, Jim Bob didn't know if he could live with that anymore.

Divorce was an ugly word, but he was almost ready to say it.

When Honey had finally fallen asleep, Jim Bob got up, went to the closet, took out the wedding veil, and put it back underneath his daughter's bed.

Someone in this family damn well deserved to hold on to their dreams.

On Monday, after seeing Evan off at the airport, Delaney guided her silver Acura south toward Galveston Island to meet Lucia Vinetti. Her mind wandered during the fifty-minute drive and for some inexplicable reason, she found herself thinking about the man she'd thrown the tarp over outside Evan's office. The man from her mysterious vision.

Why did she keep thinking about him?

She liked well-groomed, well-bred men. Not scruffy, tough guys who stared at her as if they could see every thought that passed through her head.

Even now, just recalling the way his dark eyes had stared at her caused Delaney's body to tingle.

She shivered. She didn't like feeling this way. It upset her equilibrium. And she had spent her life putting on a calm face. Passive nonresistance had taken her this far in life, and she was sticking with it.

Forget the guy. He's just an illusion. An image of masculine perfection you've conjured in your own mind. Focus on the job at hand. This is what you want. Your own base of clients and referrals, so you can prove to your mother that you don't need her interfering in your life.

Although it was just a small step, this new project represented the freedom she'd longed for, but had just been too afraid to reach out and grab. Winning this contract was a huge deal for her, and she wasn't going to let the memory of some studly guy she'd briefly brushed up against distract her from her goal.

She longed to make her business something special. Something that was hers alone, but until now she'd been floating along, just letting her mother make things happen for her. Taking the path of least resistance. It was her pattern.

Delaney crossed the bridge onto Galveston Island and traveled the main thoroughfare. At the next red light, she consulted her notes for the correct address. Lucia's place was several blocks north of the beach.

When she turned onto Seawall Boulevard, the sight of the Gulf of Mexico made her smile. Her mother hated Galveston, with its scandalous island history and touristy atmosphere, precisely the two things Delaney loved most about the town.

She found the adorable old Victorian residence without any problem. The lawn, while trimmed short, was not landscaped with any particular design in mind. A hedge here, a flower bed there, a clump of coconut-bearing palm trees thrown in.

The house was painted an outdated color of canary yellow and trimmed in powder blue. Wind chimes dangled from the porch and pink flamingos decorated the yard. Whimsical, kitschy, and cute, but definitely not for the more upscale clientele willing to pay top dollar for an island retreat. Delaney took out her notebook and jotted: *work on curb appeal.*

She parked in the driveway beside a white ten-year-old American-made sedan and hurried up the sidewalk. Before she even had a chance to knock, the door was thrown open, revealing Trudie Klausman dressed in a pink Bermuda shorts set and a bright red fedora and beside her stood a kind-faced woman in her early seventies. She wore a floral-print housedress covered with a well-worn, faded blue gingham apron.

The sight of the woman conjured images in Delaney's mind of chocolate chip cookies and pastries made from scratch with loving hands. Lucia looked like the grandmother Delaney had always longed for, but never had. Her mother's mother had died before Honey had even married her father. And her father's mother had been infirm with a debilitating illness, living the remainder of her years in a private care facility. Delaney had never known her grandmother when she'd been spry and healthy.

"It's so good to see you," Trudie said. "This is my friend Lucia. Lucia, meet Delaney Cartwright."

She held out her hand to Lucia, but the elderly woman ignored her outstretched palm and instead enveloped her in an embrace that smelled like vanilla extract and lavender soap. "Welcome to my home, Delaney. It's so nice to meet you. Trudie's told me so many wonderful things about you."

A glow of warmth at the woman's friendliness stole through her. After meeting Lucia, she wanted the job more than ever. "Thank you, Mrs. Vinetti. I'm honored that you're considering hiring All the World's a Stage."

"Please, call me Lucia."

"Lucia it is." Delaney smiled.

"Come inside," Lucia invited. "I can't wait to see what you think of the house."

In true Victorian fashion the rooms were small, but plentiful. While the house was exceptionally clean, and the woodwork phenomenal, it was a little worse for the wear. Fifty-two years of family living jam-packed the house with knickknacks and photographs and keepsakes.

It looked as if Lucia never threw anything away, and apparently a lot of people had given her many things over the years she felt obligated to display. Her homey style, while wonderful for living in, was too jumbled for enticing buyers. Nothing was cohesive. Not design or color schemes. Not furniture style or window treatments. If Lucia were to show the house in its present state, potential buyers would see it as overcrowded, old-fashioned, and out of step.

Delaney, however, loved it.

Lucia's house presented her first real decorating challenge. Her mother's friends and acquaintances were the kind of women who redecorated every few years. They were well aware of trends and fashions. Staging their homes for sale had usually consisted of little more than rearranging furniture for the best layout or bringing bits of nature indoors to create a breezy feel or simply giving the place a good cleaning.

"Trudie tells me you're engaged to be married," Lucia said.

"Yes, August fourth."

"That's wonderful." Lucia beamed. "How did you and your fiancé meet?"

"We've known each other since we were small children. Before that really. Our mothers met in Lamaze class."

"So you don't really have a story about how you two first laid eyes on each other?" Trudie asked.

"No," Delaney admitted. As far back as she could remember, Evan had been there. Like a security blanket.

"It's almost as if you're marrying your brother, huh?" Trudie asked.

"No, no." Delaney forced a laugh. Trudie's statement disturbed her because her relationship with Evan *was* more like brother and sister than passionate lovers. "It's nice. Marrying someone you know so well."

"I guess I could see it. Built-in trust and all that," Trudie said. "But I'd be afraid I'd miss the sparks of really falling madly in love."

"This window seat is adorable, Lucia," Delaney said, purposefully directing the conversation off herself as they entered one of the bedrooms on the first floor that had been converted into a library.

Bookcases lined the walls. Delaney took a peek at the titles. Georgette Heyer, Jane Austen, Mary Stewart, Daphne du Maurier. Many of the same books that lined her own shelves at home.

"My Leo made it for me," Lucia said with a sigh in her voice. "So I could curl up and read and still look outside to keep an eye on the children chasing butterflies in the backyard flower garden."

"The window seat is definitely the highlight of this room," Delaney said, relieved that she'd seemed to have sidetracked Trudie from talk of romance.

Lucia ushered her down the hallway, Trudie bringing up the rear. "And here's the kitchen. I raised six children of my own here and then my four grandchildren, after my daughter-in-law died and my son, Vincent, needed help with the little ones. They're all big ones now, but they come back to visit me often."

Delaney surveyed the room.

The wallpaper was faded. It would have to be replaced. The appliances were all circa the mid-eighties. The dining table was even older than the appliances and bore the scars of too many children banging on it with silverware and toys. The linoleum was peeling in the corner by the refrigerator, and there was a burn mark the size of a saucepan bottom on the Formica countertop.

"This is the heart of the house," Delaney breathed, surprised at the nostalgia welling up inside her. But that was silly. How could she be nostalgic for something she'd never had? She wished with all her might she could have grown up in such a home where kids were allowed to spill and sprawl and their growth spurts were marked in colored pencil on the wall beside the back door.

She immediately felt disloyal to her own family at such a thought. She'd had all the privileges the Cartwright money could buy. But that had included hired cooks and maids. She missed the boisterous camaraderie of cousins and siblings, of the numerous aunts and uncles and grandparents that this house clearly boasted. The Vinettis had what Delaney had always longed for. A close-knit, extended family.

"For sure," Trudie said. "This is where the family congregates when they visit. And it can get pretty rowdy in here, with all the laughing and teasing and eating. Lucia's an excellent cook, and she makes the best Stromboli you'll ever put in your mouth."

"So what do you think?" Lucia asked. "What needs to be done? Can you give me an estimate for what this might cost?"

"Just let me jot down a few notes."

"Sit," Lucia invited. "I'll make coffee and we'll have some tiramisu I baked this morning."

Delaney sat, took her calculator and her notepad from her purse, and crunched numbers while Lucia served up espresso and the ladyfinger cake.

Lucia settled in across from Delaney, anxiously pleating her apron with her fingers.

"I have some good news and some bad news." Delaney took a sip of her coffee. "Which would you like to hear first?"

"Oh, definitely I want the good news first," Lucia said.

"You have a beautiful home. I can feel the love in every room. Once we get it in shape, it's going to sell very easily."

"And the bad news?" Lucia gnawed her bottom lip.

Delaney longed to tell her that there was no bad news. That this warm, welcoming home was absolutely perfect as it was. But unfortunately, in a competitive real estate market, that simply wasn't the truth. "Trudie tells me you're on a limited budget."

Lucia nodded.

"In order to get the top asking price, I'm afraid you're going to have to invest about twenty-five thousand dollars in getting the house fixed up before we're ready to start staging it."

Delaney saw the hope fracture out of Lucia's face. "I don't have that kind of money."

"Could you borrow it until the house sells?"

"I was going to borrow the down payment for the Orchid Villa condo so I didn't lose my chance at getting the unit across the courtyard from Trudie. I don't have enough collateral for both loans," she said.

"Don't give up yet. Where there's a will, there's a way." Delaney reached across the table to touch the woman's hand. And then she had a brilliant idea that would give both of them what they wanted.

One of the programs on a cable home improvement channel, *American Home Design*, was running a contest to find the best home makeovers. The rules were simple. Send in "before" and "after" videos of your home improvement project. The winning entry would be selected for the most improved space. She had seen the advertisements on television, but she had never entered because she'd never made over a place with as much potential as Lucia's.

Now, with Lucia's home as her ace in the hole, even if she just made the finals, it would take her fledgling business to a whole new level and launch her career. Thinking about the potential got Delaney excited.

"Do you think your children and grandchildren and nieces and nephews would be able to pitch in to help you get the place ready?" she asked.

"Oh, yes, yes. Especially my grandson Nick. He's an undercover cop for the Houston Police Department, but he injured his leg on the job and he's been off work."

"But can Nick do the work with an injured leg?"

"What he can't do, his brothers can."

"Good, good. Here's my plan." Quickly, Delaney told them about her idea for entering Lucia's house in the *American Home Design* contest. "If your family can provide the labor in place of my usual crew, I'll be willing to waive my fee until after the house sells. All you would have to pay for are the supplies."

"Yes!" Lucia clapped her hands. "I love it. It's the perfect solution."

"Are you sure your family will be on board? Especially the grandson you mentioned? It sounds like most of the burden will rest on his shoulders."

"Why don't you ask him yourself?" Trudie interjected. "His truck just pulled up in the driveway."

"Come meet him," Lucia said.

Her mind lighting up with ideas, Delaney followed Lucia back into the living room. She couldn't wait to get started.

Footsteps sounded on the front porch. A man's voice rang out, "Nana, I'm here. Who does the swanky car in the driveway belong to?"

Delaney was standing with her hands clutched behind her back when she realized Lucia and Trudie had slipped out of the room and left her standing there all alone.

Where had they gone?

She turned her head to look, but before she had much time to ponder this question, the door opened and Lucia's grandson walked over the threshold.

He drew up short the second he spied her.

Their eyes met.

Delaney's heart stilled, and she felt a crazy, out-of-control sense of utter serenity.

Together, they gasped in one simultaneous breath.

"Oh, it's you."

Chapter 5

What'd I tell you?" Trudie whispered to Lucia. "I knew it. They're smitten."

"It seems like they already know each other," Lucia said. "Imagine that."

They were secreted in the small closet underneath the staircase. Lucia looked at the shelves around her, crowded with memories. It hit her. This was going to be a huge undertaking, clearing out a lifetime of living. The closet door was open, giving then a great and completely undetected view of Nick and Delaney.

Lucia had to agree, her friend was right. There was no denying the combination of surprise, delight, confusion, and distress on the young people's faces as they stared at each other.

"It's the whammy," Lucia whispered. "The way they are looking at each other is exactly the way I felt when I first saw Leo."

"Toldja." Trudie giggled gleefully.

"Delaney is so beautiful," Lucia breathed.

"And your Nicky is quite handsome in that rough,

tough way of his. They're going to give you the most gorgeous great-grandchildren."

"Let's not put the cart before the horse," Lucia said. "Remember, Delaney's engaged to someone else, and Nick's ego is still smarting over what Amber did to him."

"Yeah." Trudie sighed. "There is that. But what's a good romance without a little conflict?"

As Lucia and Trudie spied on the couple, Delaney glanced from Nick to her wristwatch. She tapped the face of it, shook her wrist, and then looked again before holding it up to her ear.

"Funny, my watch must have stopped," they heard Delaney say. "Which is a bit strange because I had the battery replaced just last week. Could you tell me what time you have?"

"Three thirty-five," Nick replied.

Lucia and Trudie stared at each other.

"You hear that?" Trudie nudged Lucia in the ribs with her elbow. "Her watch stopped! Just like the clock with you and Leo. It's a sign. There's no doubt about it. Those two are fated."

Hope rose in Lucia's heart. Could it be true? Was Trudie right?

But Trudie must have spoken too loudly because Nick raised his head and glared in their direction. "Nana? Are you and Trudie hiding under the staircase?"

"Uh-oh," Lucia whispered. "Busted."

Seeing the pink-raincoat woman standing in his grandmother's living room totally blew Nick away. He stared at her and she stared at him and he had no idea what to say or do next.

And then he heard whispering and giggling from

behind the staircase and realized his grandmother and her best friend must be up to something. They'd tried to play matchmaker for him before, but it was beyond his comprehension how they'd found out about Raincoat Woman and lured her here.

One thing was for sure, she seemed as surprised to see him as he was to see her.

Nick strode past her, heading for the small storage closet underneath the staircase where he used to hide as a kid to spy on the grown-ups when they entertained guests in the living room.

"Okay, you two, what's going on here?" Nick asked. His head was still reeling, but he was trying hard not to show it.

"Um, nothing." His grandmother had a guilty look about her.

"Who is that woman?" he whispered urgently, jerking a thumb over his shoulder.

"That's Delaney Cartwright," Nana said. "I just hired her to stage the house. Isn't she beautiful? Such a face."

"Do what?" Nick couldn't believe the strangeness of the coincidence. His grandmother hiring the woman he'd been fantasizing about for the last three days and trying his damnedest to forget.

Maybe it's not coincidence, a disturbing voice in the back of his head whispered. *Maybe it's kismet. Maybe it's the whammy.*

Except Nick no longer believed in all that true love, soul mate, Italian-strength romantic whammy stuff his grandmother had spoon-fed her grandchildren along with her macaroni, pizza, and tiramisu. Amber had knocked the faith right out of him.

"I've talked to a real estate agent, and she said if I

wanted the house to sell quickly then I should hire someone to stage it. So I interviewed Delaney. I like her and I hired her." Nana crossed her arms over her chest and gave him a look that just dared him to argue.

What? His grandmother had already talked to a real estate agent? Without waiting to discuss it with the family? This impulse of hers to sell the house was more serious than he'd guessed. "I don't get it. What's a house stager?"

"A house stager is a person who comes in and fixes up your place so that it will appeal to a wider range of buyers."

"Remember when Artie died and I couldn't sell my house?" Trudie added. "It sat on the market for over two years until I hired Delaney. She staged my house, and it sold three days later for three thousand dollars more than the original asking price."

That sounded impressive, but Nick didn't want Nana to sell the house. Everywhere he looked, the past beckoned. Whenever he glanced around the living room, he saw the windowpane that he, his brothers, and his cousins had once busted out playing baseball with a pair of rolled-up socks and a red plastic bat on a rainy day when they'd been cooped up indoors. Who knew that socks—properly whacked—could rocket through glass like that?

In his mind's eye, he could see the Christmas tree, drowning in presents for the huge Vinetti clan. Or the fireplace where they'd hung their stockings. He pictured the archway leading into the kitchen where Grampa Leo always strung mistletoe so he could catch Nana around the waist and kiss her in front of everyone.

Nick smiled, recalling the time his baby sister, Gina, had sneaked a kiss from her boyfriend when she'd thought no one was watching and their braces had gotten locked together. He had teased her unmercifully for weeks afterward.

He saw the kitchen, full of life and laughter, as his family gathered around, cooking and eating and swapping stories. The scents were in his nose—onion and garlic, oregano and basil. The tastes filled his mouth—marinara sauce, pesto, mozzarella.

The memories hung in his mind like a drop of rich honey, thick and sweet, caught in the cleft of time and held preserved in this house. He'd always imagined bringing his own children here someday—at holidays, during the summer, to visit their great-grandmother and give them a glimpse into his history.

Tight-lipped, Nick battled to keep his emotions in check. His chest tightened.

Delaney Cartwright stood with her arms crossed over her chest. Her clothes were a far cry from what she'd been wearing the first time he'd seen her. Her pale green suit was simple and tailored, but obviously expensive. She wore sensible one-inch heels. Tall, willowy, long straight hair that was either light brown or dark blond depending upon your definition. Her cheekbones were high and her eyes were green as the Gulf. Eyes a guy could dive into without a look back.

Charlize Theron had nothing on this woman.

Although sans the raincoat and risqué lingerie he'd seen her in before, she possessed the same regal aura as the actress. She had delicate bone structure and a way of holding herself that suggested blue-blood breeding.

What had happened to the hotsie-totsie who'd ambushed him outside of Doc Van Zandt's place? That was who had fired his engines. This sophisticated-looking woman flat unnerved him with her old money aura rising up from her like the scent of freshly minted hundred-dollar bills. Her serenity and his unwanted attraction to her set his teeth on edge.

He searched for a reason to dislike her.

She looked like the kind of woman who had been floating through life on her gorgeous looks and her stacks of money, never having to take a stand or fight for something she believed in. He knew the Cartwright name. It was familiar to everyone in Texas. No doubt about it. This one had been handed the world on a silver platter.

He inflated his resentment, hunting for anything that would let the air out of this powerful attraction. She was too polished. Too perfect. With a woman like her, a guy would always be on the hot seat, never able to live up to the expectations of Daddy's little princess.

"I don't understand why you have to sell the house," he said, turning back to his grandmother.

"Without your grandfather, the magic is gone. It's just a house now, no longer a home. It should be a home again, filled with laughter and love and lots of children," she said.

"You shouldn't be making such a major decision when you're still grieving, Nana. It's only been a little over two months."

"It's time to move on, Nicky. Wallowing in grief isn't going to bring your grandfather back. I'm lonely here on the island, and there's finally an opening at Orchid Villa in a condo right near Trudie's."

"Why didn't you tell me you were lonely? I can get the family together. Make sure someone comes over to spend time with you every day."

"All you kids have your own lives to lead and besides, someone comes to visit almost every weekend. But I need to socialize with people my own age. I need to start a new life."

"At seventy-three?"

"What would you have me do? Curl up in bed and wait to die? Leo would be pretty mad if I did that."

Nick knotted his hands into fists. He felt so damn helpless. Over the course of the last thirteen months so many bad things had happened, and he desperately needed for something to stay the same.

"I just hate to see you make a mistake."

"Nicky." She took his hand in hers and patted it. "It's okay to let go. Clinging serves no one."

"I'm trying."

"There's something else I have to tell you that you're probably not going to like."

He arched an eyebrow. "Oh?"

"I can't afford to hire Delaney's crew, so I promised you'd help her do the renovations that need to be done before the house can be put on the market."

"You did what?"

"Don't look at me that way. You told me yourself you're bored out of your skull. Well, now you have something to do."

Nick couldn't stop the disappointment, hurt, resentment, and regret from building up inside him.

Don't be a selfish jerk. Think about what Nana needs. Back her up. But did his grandmother actually know what was best for her? Or was she simply making decisions based on blind grief and loneliness? He might not be able to stop her from putting the house on the market, but maybe he could find a way to slow down the whole process. Keep it from selling too quickly and buy some time until he could talk sense into Nana.

Turning back around, Nick saw Delaney waiting patiently for him to break up the huddle under the staircase. She looked as if nothing could ruffle her steadfast aplomb.

It set his teeth on edge and stirred in him a mighty urge to do whatever it took to sabotage the project and chase this house stager far away from his grandmother's home.

He sauntered back toward her, eyes narrowed, lips cocked sardonically, arms crossed over his chest in an I'm-gonna-throw-you-out-of-here-on-your-ear stance. Delaney had overheard enough of his conversation with his grandmother to glean the gist of it. He was not happy about Lucia's decision to sell her house.

He trod closer.

Too close.

Crowding her space, making it hard for her to think straight. His shoulders were wider than she remembered, but her memory more than adequately recalled his muscular athletic body. How could she forget when he'd had it pressed against the length of her?

Delaney realized convincing Lucia to hire her was not the test she had to pass. Here was the challenge. Here was the threshold guardian. If she wanted this job, Nick was the one she was going to have to convince.

She thought of the opportunity she'd be missing out on. A shot at publicizing All the World's a Stage on television and making it a rousing success. A prospect to spread her wings and fly. A chance to prove that she wasn't just a spoiled Cartwright princess.

Years of kowtowing to her mother, of repressing her opinions, of being the good girl and doing the right thing boiled up inside her.

This time she refused to keep quiet, refused to back down. This time, she was going to get what she wanted.

Clearing her throat, Delaney gave him her most professional smile. "I didn't mean to eavesdrop, Mr. Vinetti, but when you were speaking to your grandmother I got the distinct impression you're not in favor of investing money to have the house staged."

"Your assumption is correct, Ms. Cartwright."

"If you give me the chance, I can prove to you the value of my services."

"Oh, you can?"

"Yes."

"How's that? By showing up on my doorstep in a pink raincoat?" His gaze took a deliberate road trip down her body.

He was bringing that up? She couldn't believe his audacity. She was mentally halfway to the door when she realized that was exactly his intention. To chase her off.

She ignored his comment, opened up her briefcase, and pulled out the glossy, tri-fold brochure for All the World's a Stage.

He looked it over, quickly flipping to the back page to find her fee structure. "Kinda pricey. I think maybe you're peddling your wares in the wrong neighborhood. Try The Woodlands. They can afford to be gullible up there."

"As I told your grandmother, I'm willing to defer the payment of my services until the house sells, and if it does not sell in a specified period of time, I don't get paid at all." She raised her chin.

A suspicious glint shaded his eyes. "Now why would you do that?"

"Your grandmother's house presents an exciting opportunity to expand my business." She told him about the *American Home Design* contest.

"Yes, I see what's in it for you, but what's in it for my grandmother?"

"Quick sell of her house for an asking price that will more than offset what I charge."

"Maybe we don't want a quick sell. Maybe we'd rather have the right buyer, one who could love this house as much as we do over someone with deep pockets."

"Your grandmother needs a quick sell in order to purchase the condo she's interested in."

He glared at her suspiciously.

"There's just one catch to my proposition."

"Of course there's a catch." He was looking at her mouth and it unnerved her. "There's always a catch. What is it?"

She regretted having to say this. Dragging the words from her mouth was almost painful. "In order to save your grandmother money, you're going to have to stand in for my crew."

Just what in God's name had she gotten herself into? She couldn't believe she'd be working so closely with the one man in the world she had hoped never to see again.

Delaney lay in bed, staring up at the ceiling. One pillow under her head, the other clutched to her chest. She must be out of her mind.

"I did it to stretch my wings. To prove I can take on new challenges. Who knows? This might lead to a whole new angle to my business, especially if I can win the *American Home Design* contest."

"That's not the reason."

The voice startled Delaney. She looked over and saw

Skylar perched on her vanity and realized she must have fallen asleep.

"What do you want?" She sighed.

"Dropped by to get the goods on the hottie you spent the afternoon with, and here I find you talking to yourself." Skylar tsk-tsked. "Keep that up, and people are going to start thinking you're crazy."

"I am crazy. I see dead people in my dreams."

"You don't see dead people. You only see me."

"You're dead."

"Yeah, but I'm not people. I'm a person. Singular. You see a dead person in your dreams."

"So that means I'm not crazy?"

"Please, you were raised by Honey Montgomery Cartwright. Of course you're crazy on some level."

"Touché."

"Wanna know why I think you took the Vinetti job?" Skylar grinned. "Hey, I like the sound of that. Vinetti job. Like you're in with the mob."

Delaney sighed again and pulled the covers to her chin. "I'd say no, but you'd just tell me anyway, so go ahead."

"You're hot for her hard-bodied grandson."

"That's not it. You are so far off base." Delaney laughed but it sounded hollow, forced.

"You want to prove yourself to him. He thinks you're a spoiled rich Cartwright, and you want to show him he's wrong."

Now that was probably the real truth. Delaney didn't have a comeback.

"Personally, I think taking the job was a great move. I mean, did you check out his butt? Makes a girl feel faint just looking at it." Skylar fanned herself.

"You're a ghost; haven't you gotten past physical lust?"

"Hey, indulge me. I never got to have sex when I was alive."

"Really? That's sad."

"Don't feel sorry for me, just let me live vicariously through you a little." Today Skylar was wearing a tie-dyed T-shirt and a blue-jean miniskirt and fisherman's wading boots.

"What's with the boots?"

"Borrowed 'em from Granddad. He said to say 'hi,' by the way."

"Tell him 'hi' back."

"Will do."

"What do you need wading boots for in whatever place it is where ghosts hang out?" she asked.

"You keep getting this all wrong, Laney. I'm not really a ghost. You're dreaming me up. Whatever I wear, you're the one who dressed me in it. For whatever weird reasons are churning around in that disturbed brain of yours."

"So I can change you out of wading boots?"

"Sure. Give it a try."

Delaney imagined Skylar in glass slippers, and darned if the wading boots didn't fade away and glass slippers take their place.

"Cinderella, cool." Skylar stuck her legs out in front of her to admire the shoes. "Now all I need is a Prince Charming."

"Okay, this is officially freaky."

"No, it's not. There's nothing more natural than dreaming. So anyway, back to the hottie. He's so much cuter than Evan."

"Evan's cute," Delaney said defensively.

"Please, Evan looks like he's been popped from a cookie-cutter mold. Handsome rich doctor from central casting, anyone? Come on, wouldn't you rather have a real man like that delicious Nick Vinetti?" Skylar licked her lips.

"You're not being fair to Evan."

"Yes, okay, he is a nice guy. But I remember the time when he was twelve and dropped a pocketful of change on the ground so he could get a good look up my skirt."

"Evan's not like that."

"Maybe not now, but he was back then. Believe me, I was there."

"How can I trust that tidbit of information if, as you claim, everything you say is something I'm making up in my head?"

"Good question." Skylar propped her chin in her palm. "Keep it in mind whenever you're talking to me."

"You're messing with my head."

"No, you're messing with your own head."

"Maybe you should just go away."

"Maybe you should just wake up."

"Maybe I will."

"Fine with me."

Delaney flopped over onto her side, refusing to look at Skylar anymore.

"You're not waking up."

"You don't know Evan the way I do. You don't know how he was there for me after you died. He comforted me. Helped me through it. He was my only real friend until I met Tish. He liked me when I was ugly, Sky. Before the surgery and the weight loss and the braces."

Skylar lay down on the bed next to her, stacked her hands under her cheek, and gazed into Delaney's eyes. "He's a compulsive helper, Delaney. He'll always be where someone needs help, and as soon as they're emotionally strong enough not to need him anymore, he'll find someone who does need him."

"Evan would never cheat on me."

"I'm not saying he would. I'm just predicting he'll always be standing you up in favor of his work. Unless you're in a crisis. Then he'll be there."

"He's a doctor, for Pete's sake. Surely you get that his patients must come first."

"My point exactly. You'll always play second fiddle."

"It would be pretty petty of me to be jealous of sick people," she said.

"You say that now, but what about when you have children? He can't ever make the Little League games or the dance recitals. Your Thanksgiving dinners and Christmas Eves are interrupted by hospital emergencies."

Delaney had never thought about the long-term repercussions of Evan's career. Honestly, she'd never even imagined what it would be like to have children with him. That was strange, wasn't it? She was marrying him, and she'd never pictured having his babies.

"Very strange indeed," Skylar whispered, reading her mind.

"I'm doing the right thing by marrying Evan," she said defensively.

"Even though you have zero sexual chemistry together?" Skylar asked.

"Sex is overrated."

"You only think that because you've never had great sex. Or great love."

"You never had sex at all, so buzz off with that advice." Delaney glowered.

"Don't you want to know what great sex is like? Why Tish and Jillian and Rachael talk about it with such passionate enthusiasm?"

"No. I like things just the way they are with Evan. Calm, sweet, tender."

"And orgasmless."

"I have orgasms." Delaney furrowed her brow. "At least I think I do."

"If you're not sure, then you probably don't."

"Once again, you would know this how?"

"It's going to be tough, working on Lucia's house with her gorgeous grandson Nick hanging around, keeping his suspicious eyes on you. And all the while Evan is far away in Guatemala."

Concern winnowed through her. This was what she'd been worrying about ever since taking the job. Knowing that she'd be around Nick Vinetti every day for the next several weeks.

"I have to back out of the job."

"No, you don't. I say explore it to the hilt. Find out if the chemistry you feel with this guy is real or just a passing fancy."

"What about Evan?"

"What about him? He's the one who took off for Guatemala just weeks before your wedding."

"That's lovely. My fiancé is away helping poor children to have a better life, and you want me to screw around on him with some cocky cop."

"I didn't say screw around on him."

"It's what you meant." Delaney glared at her.

"I'm going to go now. You're upset and need time to think. Besides, your alarm clock is about to go off." Skylar started fading away, getting smaller and smaller, dimmer and dimmer.

She lay there, watching Skylar go until her glass slippers were all that remained.

Her sister was right. She couldn't back out of the job. Lucia was counting on her. She was such a sweet woman, and she'd just lost her husband. It would be wrong to go back on her word now.

Delaney blew out a breath. One way or the other, she would just have to suck it up and learn to suppress her lusty feelings for the sexy Mr. Nick Vinetti.

Chapter 6

Honey Montgomery Cartwright ran a lint roller over her peach-colored Italian silk suit even though she'd just taken it from the dry cleaner's bag. She checked the sticky roller paper and spied a hint of fuzz. Hmm. She made a mental note to change dry cleaners. Clearly, they were not doing the job she'd paid them to do.

Squaring her shoulders, she double-checked her teeth in the bathroom mirror. She'd already flossed and brushed twice this morning, but she wanted to make sure she hadn't missed anything. She was having lunch with Delaney's future mother-in-law, Lenore Van Zandt, to discuss preparations for the wedding rehearsal dinner. Lenore, a noisy chatterbox, made Honey nervous, but she'd be damned if she would show it.

She scrutinized her reflection. Fifty-three, but none of her friends would ever guess it. Honey considered herself both smart and lucky. She religiously avoided the sun, worked out two hours a day, six days a week, spent a small annual fortune on antiaging potions and creams, and she had her dermatologist programmed on speed-dial.

When they were dating, James Robert had said that

with Honey's platinum blond hair, high cheekbones, flawless complexion, well-toned body, and rigorous self-discipline, she was like Princess Grace in boot camp. These days, he no longer commented on her looks, just grunted and asked her how much her spa treatments had set him back. As if he didn't clear twenty million a year. What was it about the ultrarich that made them such tightwads?

Resolutely pushing thoughts of her husband aside, Honey snugged the clasp of a three-carat diamond and emerald necklace around her neck, added matching earrings, and then bestowed her mirror image with her most brilliant, practiced smile.

There. Everything was perfect.

No one, especially not her husband of thirty-four years, would ever guess the real truth.

With a regal toss of her head, she walked like a runway model down the stairs of the sweeping Colonial-style mansion that had been in James Robert's family for three generations. Her four-inch heels clicked smartly against the granite tile. She might be over fifty, but she wasn't over the hill. Honey refused to trade in her Manolo Blahniks for Birkenstocks. She would rather break a hip first.

She grabbed a bottle of Evian on her way out the door. Honey carried bottled water wherever she went. She was convinced that was one of the reasons she had such a youthful complexion. Sauntering out to the garage, she paused a moment to smooth down her skirt before sliding across the Cadillac's plush leather seat. Once outside the security gate, she stopped to pick up the mail. Leaving the engine running with the air-conditioning blasting, she minced to the mailbox, collected the day's correspondence, and got back inside.

Quickly she leafed through the pile. Bills, a sales circular, a party invitation, a couple of catalogs, a fitness magazine.

And then she found it.

A plain white envelope with no return address or postmark. Her name was printed in block letters with a primitive hand.

It hadn't been mailed. Someone had placed it in their mailbox.

Honey sucked in her breath, flipped the letter over, and tentatively slipped a fingernail underneath the envelope flap. She opened it up and pulled out the sheet of notepaper.

I KNOW YOUR SECRET. IF YOU DON'T WANT YOUR HUSBAND TO FIND OUT THE TRUTH, COME TO THE ENTRANCE TO THE GALVESTON ISLAND AMUSEMENT PARK ON SEAWALL BOULEVARD. NOON TOMORROW. BRING TWENTY THOUSAND DOLLARS IN CASH.

That was it. No signature. Nothing else.

Feeling fragile as a dried-up autumn leaf, Honey stared at the note, not wanting to understand what she was reading. Someone had learned her terrible truth.

The past had caught up with her at last.

Air left her lungs. She gasped, felt the color drain from her face.

The deception had started out as nothing more than a little white lie, but it had become Honey's entire life. Day by day, for thirty-four years, she'd steeped in her secret until it eventually permeated every corner of her soul.

Hand over her mouth, Honey flung open the car door and, contrary to the ladylike delicacy she'd perfected over the years, vomited in the gravel.

When she was finished, she rinsed her mouth with the

Evian and in a great inhalation of breath calmly drove to her luncheon date with Lenore. The blackmail note she crumpled and stuffed in the glove compartment.

She didn't want to go, but if she didn't show up, Lenore would wonder why. And Honey had spent a lifetime doing her best to keep people from wondering about her. As she searched for a parking place, dark questions plagued.

Who had sent the letter? Why had this person only asked for twenty thousand? And after all these years, how had he or she managed to track her down?

She could guess the answer to the last question. The blackmailer must have seen her picture with Delaney in the recent *Society Bride* article on society weddings. Why, oh, why had she allowed herself to be photographed for a national magazine?

Her stomach roiled again and she closed her eyes, fighting back the nausea. So much time had passed, she'd foolishly thought she was safe.

Idiot. You can never, ever let down your guard. There's no room for mistakes. Not now, not ever.

Not with the secret she harbored.

But here was this letter, threatening to ruin the life she'd built. Threatening to destroy not only her marriage, but her daughter's chance at happiness. Honey simply could not allow that to happen.

She would meet with the blackmailer and she would pay.

What other choice did she have?

The following day, Delaney took Tish with her to video Lucia's house.

Luckily, Tish had been able to rearrange her schedule so she could film the "before" video of the house so Delaney and Lucia's family could get started on the renovations as quickly as possible. Time was of the essence, both for Lucia's financial situation and for entry in the *American Home Design* contest. They had four weeks to get the house renovated and decorated before the July 9 deadline.

When they arrived at Lucia's house, Delaney was surprised to find so many cars in the driveway. She parked along the curb behind Nick's red pickup truck, and her stomach did a loopy little swoon.

She spun her engagement ring on her finger. *Remember what you swore to yourself last night? Get over your attraction to the guy. You're taken.*

"This house totally rocks," Tish exclaimed. "I can see why you're so excited. It's got such great potential."

"I know," Delaney breathed.

Tish collected her equipment while Delaney gathered up the briefcase chock-full of plans, computer printouts, and sketches she'd prepared after she'd returned home the night before. Tish filmed everything as they went up the walkway. The tiled roof, the palm trees, the pink flamingos on the lawn.

Delaney rang the doorbell and a gorgeous black-haired woman in her late twenties, with coltishly long legs, answered the door. She looked a lot like Nick, possessing the same intelligent brown eyes and long, thick, dark lashes.

"Hi," she said, greeting them. "You must be Delaney. I'm Gina, Nick's baby sister; come on in. Most everyone is in the kitchen waiting for you to film the house before we start packing up Nana's things."

"Packing?" Delaney asked.

"Nana's moving over to Trudie's while the renovations are going on. She put a retainer down on the condo this morning, and Nick's taking her to apply for a bank loan tomorrow afternoon. With any luck, you guys will be finished renovating this house before she has to close on the condo."

Feeling concerned that Gina had unrealistic expectations about what she could achieve, Delaney touched the other woman's arm. "You do understand that the house might not sell immediately."

"Don't be modest. Nana and Trudie swear you're a miracle worker. Our family has complete faith in you."

Did that include Nick? she wondered. Yesterday, he hadn't struck her as being very trusting.

"That's more than you can say about your own mother," Tish whispered to Delaney as they followed Gina into the kitchen.

They found the place pleasantly chaotic with a dozen people all talking, teasing, and laughing at once.

"This is Delaney, everyone," Gina introduced her.

They all applauded.

Delaney blushed.

Gina introduced her to everyone. Cousins and siblings, aunts and uncles, plus Gina's own identical twin seven-year-old boys, Zack and Jack.

There were too many Vinettis for Delaney to keep straight. But she was happy to meet Nick's dad. Vincent Vinetti was a big bear of a man who owned his own shrimp boat and was still handsome in middle age. He clapped her on the shoulder. "We appreciate so much what you're doing for my mother."

Some of the relatives hugged her. Some shook her hand. They all told her how much they valued her help. Oddly, she felt more welcome in this roomful of strangers than she did in her own home.

That wasn't fair. By nature her family just weren't huggers and touchers. They didn't get together in big groups, although her father's brothers and their children lived in the Houston area. She should not compare the phlegmatic Cartwrights to the lively Vinettis. It was apples and persimmons.

Delaney introduced Tish, and she also received a rousing welcome.

"Jeez." Tish pulled Delaney aside. "You didn't tell me you'd formed your own fan club."

"What can I say? They're an affectionate group."

"Apparently. Can you keep the fan club entertained while I start filming the house unencumbered by onlookers?" Tish asked.

"I'll handle it."

With her camera rolling, Tish disappeared back the way they'd come in.

"Where's Nick?" Delaney found herself asking Gina, then cringed inwardly. Why had she asked about him?

"He went with my husband, Chuck, to rent a moving van."

Well, that was a relief. She had a little extra time to compose herself before she saw Nick again.

Delaney's eyes found Lucia's in the crowded room and she held up her briefcase. "I've got the renovation plans with me to show everyone."

"Tony, get up, please," Lucia instructed the lanky young man in his late teens sitting to her right. "Let Delaney sit here."

Tony popped up and Lucia patted the chair beside her. "Sit, sit."

"Would you like something to drink?" Gina asked Delaney as she settled in next to Lucia.

"A cannoli?" someone else offered.

Delaney smiled and nodded. Who wouldn't be happy around this bunch?

"Coffee, tea, soda, water?" Gina offered.

"Whatever you've got on hand will be fine."

"We've got it all on hand."

"Coffee would be nice, and one of those cannoli does sound delicious."

"They're to die for," Gina said. "Nana baked them fresh this morning."

Delaney tried to remember the last time her mother had baked anything from scratch and came up with that disloyal feeling again. To distract herself, she took the plans from her briefcase and spread them on the table.

Everyone crowded around for a look. It was a bit disconcerting to have a dozen pairs of eyes peering over her shoulder. But as she explained what needed to be done to the property in order to achieve top dollar, everyone seemed to approve of her plans. Consensus by committee, just the way she liked doing things. Heartened by the unanimous acceptance, she looked up to see tears shining in Lucia's eyes.

Anxiety had her fingering the papers. "Oh, my goodness, there's something you don't like. Please, if you don't agree with my proposal, tell me and I'll change it."

Lucia shook her head, pulled a handkerchief from her pocket, and dabbed at her eyes. "Your proposal is wonderful. That's not why I'm crying."

"The reality of leaving your home is finally hitting you."

"Yes." Lucia pressed her lips together in an attempt to stay the tears from spilling down her cheeks. "Leo and I had such wonderful memories here. I can't believe it's over."

"Are you sure selling the house is really what you want to do?" Delaney had to ask.

Lucia nodded. "I have to let go in order to move on. It's the right thing to do."

Delaney looked into the older woman's eyes and knew Lucia needed to talk about Leo. Her family surrounded her, yes, and she could talk to them, but they knew all her stories. Lucia needed a fresh audience.

"Tell me about your husband." Delaney placed her hand on top of the older woman's.

Soon Lucia was regaling her with stories of her life in this house with her husband, Leo. The children they'd raised, the hard times they'd endured, the fun they'd had, the love that had grown deeper and richer with each passing year.

"How did Leo propose to you?" Delaney asked.

A smile flitted across her face. "He didn't."

"You proposed to him?"

Lucia looked scandalized. "No, no. I was a demure girl. I would never have done something so bold."

"So how did you two ever get together?"

There was that knowing smile again. "He kidnapped me from the chapel on my wedding day."

"What?!" Now it was Delaney's turn to look scandalized. "You married your kidnapper?"

Lucia giggled. "It was very romantic. I was engaged to marry the man of my parents' choosing. They were very old-fashioned. Frank's family had money, and my father had a struggling business."

"Your parents were basically selling you to Frank?"

"It sounds so bad when you put it like that," Lucia said, "and I'm certain that's not the way they intended it. They just wanted to make sure I would be taken care of."

"Did you love Frank?" '

"I tried," Lucia said. "And then, a week before the wedding I met Leo at a party, and I just knew he was the one for me. But he was a penniless student who came from a poor family, and my parents would not hear of me marrying him. Leo knew what my papa was like. That he would never give him my hand in marriage. I felt so much family pressure to marry Frank. I'd known him since I was a child. We'd grown up in the same small village together, and I was not a young woman who voiced her own opinions. I'd been taught to be a dutiful daughter."

Dutiful.

That was exactly how she felt. Dutiful and damned. Delaney fingered her engagement ring and thought of Evan. He was off in Guatemala helping people, and she was here having serious doubts about their relationship.

"Leo knew there was only one way he could have me. So he kidnapped me from the chapel on my wedding day. We took jobs on a cruise ship to get to America, and the captain married us at sea."

One of Lucia's daughters started singing "That's Amore," and soon everyone joined in. Singing and crying and laughing.

Including Lucia.

"Come on, Delaney," Lucia invited. "Sing with us."

To her knowledge, no one in her family had ever broken into impromptu song, much less the whole bunch of them singing in unison. She liked it, even though it felt like she had a walk-on part in *Moonstruck*. She half expected Nicolas Cage to saunter through the doorway at any minute.

Instead, it was Nick Vinetti who came traipsing through the back door.

"People, people," he said. "'That's Amore'? You must be talking about the time Grampa kidnapped Nana. Knock it off. Eighty percent of you are off key. Face facts, you guys ain't the Von Trapps."

And then he spied Delaney. He stopped talking and stabbed her with his gaze.

Wham!

She felt it deep inside her. The forbidden pull. The taboo attraction. It made him all the more desirable.

"That certainly is a beautiful engagement ring that you're wearing," Gina said. "So tell us, Delaney, about the man you're going to marry."

"Yeah," Nick said, still holding her gaze. "Tell us. Everyone likes the story of a good romance." His tone was sardonic. The look in his eyes inscrutable.

"I...I...think we should go over the renovation plans. Map out the tasks in phases. The sooner we get to work, the sooner we sell the house and the sooner Lucia gets the money for her condo," Delaney said.

Lucia got up from her chair. "Here, Nick, take my seat. You're going to be the one doing most of the work. See what Delaney has come up with."

Before she could protest—and how could she?—Nick plunked down beside her.

She reached for the papers, eager to have something to occupy her hands and purposefully ignored the nutmegy scent of his cologne. Clearing her throat, she launched into a thorough explanation of what she felt needed to be done to achieve the highest selling price for the house and the estimated cost of materials if the Vinettis provided all the manpower.

Nick took the papers from her and studied the list for a long time. It wasn't going to be as easy to persuade him as the rest of the family. "Why should we strip off the wallpaper and paint all the walls white?"

"Wallpaper dates a place. It's a fact of the real estate business, plain white walls sell better."

"But plain white walls have no zip. Nothing to make it special," he said. "No magic."

"That's precisely the point. The more people who can imagine themselves living here, the quicker the house will sell. We could do an off-white if you prefer. Ecru. French Vanilla. Eggshell."

He leaned forward. "Let me guess. The walls in your house are all stark white."

She took offense at the way he said it. Like he was criticizing her for having no personality. She raised her head to scowl at him, but got distracted by his face. His hair was wind-tossed, his jaw strong and stubborn, his eyes dark and challenging. "As a matter of fact they are. Do you have a problem with that?"

"Noncommittal."

"Excuse me?"

"White is a color chosen by someone who is afraid to commit," he said.

"And you obtained this information from what psychology textbook?" What was it about this guy? She was never confrontational. In fact, she avoided confrontation like the flu. But around Nick the contrary side of herself popped out. He was an instigator.

"No textbook. Eight years as a cop."

"So what color are your walls?"

He shrugged. "Varies from room to room."

She found herself wondering what color his bedroom was painted, but didn't dare ask. "Look, whoever buys the house can paint it any color they want."

"If they're going to paint it after they buy it, why are we wasting time and money painting it?"

"You really don't get the concept of presentation, do you?"

"If you mean that I can look through a fancy exterior to the truth beyond, then no, I don't get the concept of presentation. It's all bullshit."

"Nick," Lucia chided. "No cursing in mixed company. I know you're a cop, but save that kind of language for the streets."

"Sorry, Nana." He looked chagrined. "By the way," he said to Delaney, "I accept your compliment. I take pride in my ability to ferret out bull..." He slid a sidelong glance at his grandmother. "You know what."

"I didn't mean it as a compliment."

"I'm aware of that."

Acutely cognizant that they were being scrutinized by a bevy of Vinettis, Delaney forced a smile. Presentation is everything. Or that was her mother's mantra. Nick had a whole different mantra that apparently involved an excess of cattle manure.

"Well, then," she said and looked at the people standing around them. "Shall we get started? Who's got a pickup truck? We need to make a run to Lowe's for the initial supplies while Tish finishes videoing the house."

"I'll take you," Nick drawled.

Dammit. Why him? Delaney slapped a hand across her mouth, worried that she might have spoken her thoughts aloud.

Nick was staring at her pointedly. As if he knew what she looked like naked.

He practically does.

Her cheeks heated.

Don't blush, don't blush.

He pulled his keys from his pocket. “Ready for a ride, Rosy?”

Rosy?

She put a hand to her cheek. Dear God, her face must be flaming red. She didn’t want to go with him, but she didn’t want to stay here and keep blushing in front of his family either.

Delaney stuffed the papers back in her briefcase. Stay cool. Presentation is everything. “Let’s go.”

“You’ll need a check,” Lucia said.

“I’ve got this one, Nana,” Nick said and hustled Delaney toward the back door.

“Dominic, you come back here and get a check. I’m not going to let you pay for the renovations on my house.”

“I grew up here. I’m responsible for some of the nicks and bruises this old house has suffered.”

“You didn’t take me to raise,” Lucia argued.

“No, you took me to raise. Let me pay my due,” he called to his grandmother over his shoulder as the screen door slammed behind them.

When they reached his red pickup truck, Nick opened the passenger-side door. “Climb in.”

Feeling as if she’d just made a pact with the devil, Delaney got inside.

Chapter 7

"Where should we start?" Delaney asked Nick when they walked through the door at Lowe's. "I always lose my sense of direction in these warehouse stores."

Commandingly, Nick snatched the piece of notepaper from her hand and ran his gaze down the list. "Paint department. We can shop for the rest of the items while they mix our paint."

His proprietary manner agitated her, even though she knew it was her own fault. She'd acted helpless and asked his opinion; he was just taking over as bossy men had a tendency to do. Well, to heck with that. Surprising herself, Delaney snatched the notepaper right back. "White comes already made up."

Amusement played across his full lips. "We should at least get beige. I'll go nuts painting all those walls stark white."

"The condition of your nuts is not my problem," she said tartly, shocking herself. Dear God, why had she said that? What was the matter with her? What were these absurd impulses he stirred inside her?

"Why, Rosy, are you flirting with me?" His eyes twinkled mischievously.

"No, and stop calling me Rosy. We're painting the rooms white because they're small. Traditional wisdom dictates pure white walls will make the space appear larger."

"Are you shutting off my opinion?"

She didn't answer, just gave him a look that said "I'm the professional here."

Nick didn't quite know what to make of her. She had this sweet, go-with-the-flow way about her, but if you pushed her in the wrong direction, she dug her heels in with surprising stubbornness.

Delaney breezed past him, heading toward the big overhead sign pointing out the paint department, and in the process her shoulder lightly brushed against his.

His head reeled from the unexpected contact. His body stiffened and his gut clenched in a thoroughly enjoyable way.

Damn, he thought. *Damn. She smells like morning glories, fresh and pink and perfect.*

He tried to keep up with her, but his bum leg slowed him down. God, he hated feeling weak.

She glanced back over her shoulder, saw he was limping, and slowed her pace to match his.

Nick hated even more that she had to slow down for him. "Go on," he said. "I'll get there."

But she didn't. She waited. Patiently, politely. And it pissed him off.

"I'm sorry," Delaney apologized when he caught up with her. "I forgot about your injured knee."

"Were you stalking transvestites in dark alleys behind seedy strip bars?"

"What?" Startled, her eyes widened and she stared at him as if he were ordering takeout in Japanese.

"Were you knifing he/shes in parking lots?"

"No... no...," she stammered.

He knew he'd confused her. That had been his intention. His defense mechanism. Keep your enemy off guard. "Then what do you have to be sorry for?"

"I'm sorry I wasn't more considerate of your..." She glanced at his leg. "Disability."

"My disability, as you put it, is not your problem. So don't apologize."

"I was just trying to express my concern. Go ahead, be a cold loner with a huge chip on your shoulder. See if I care." She turned away, but not before he saw the hurt expression on her face. "Obviously you don't want or need my concern, and that's fine with me."

"Obviously," he mumbled.

What the hell is wrong with you? She is just trying to be nice and you've hurt her feelings. Feel better now, asshole?

The truth of it was she knocked him off kilter. Nick found himself wanting her sympathy, and that was a dangerous thing to court. Better to deflect her than allow her to slip under his skin. He was already hellaciously attracted to her. He didn't have to like her as well.

They picked up ten gallons of pure white satin paint. They lined the cans up in the bottom of the shopping cart, along with drop cloths and paintbrushes and rollers and trays.

Delaney consulted her list. "What's the tool situation?"

Nick reacted without thinking, glancing down at his zipper to see if she'd noticed the state of semi-arousal he'd been in from the moment he climbed into the pickup truck beside her.

She followed his gaze, and that adorable pink glow

rose swiftly to her cheeks. She flustered so easily. Her embarrassment tempered his own and restored his self-confidence.

Nick cocked a grin, ramping up the sexual tension, trying his best to embarrass her. Maybe if he made her uncomfortable enough, she'd quit the job. "Healthy."

"Mr. Vinetti," she said, clearly shocked by his retort. "I was speaking about the tools we'll need to repair your grandmother's house. Since you apparently pride yourself on being a Neanderthal, I'm assuming that you have the requisite hardware."

Nick arched an eyebrow and started to make a joke about requisite hardware, but she rushed to finish her thought before he got a chance to gig her.

"Like hammers and screwdrivers and wrenches and such," she said.

"I can assure you, Rosy, I'm a card-carrying caveman. It's not an idle boast. I own a fully equipped tool chest, and I know how to use it."

"I'm so happy for you. Now shall we continue with our shopping?"

"We shall."

She scowled. "You're making fun of me."

He measured off an inch with his thumb and forefinger. "Just a little bit."

"Are you going to keep giving me a hard time during the entire course of this project?" She primly squared her shoulders.

"Depends on what you mean by a hard time." He lowered his eyelids and sent her his most charming smile. He was bad. He shouldn't be toying with her like this, but he just couldn't seem to help himself. He got a kick out of shaking her cool.

"Will you please stop with the sexual innuendos?"

Nick held up his palms. "Hey, I can't help it if you're reading things into what I say."

She narrowed her eyes. "Be honest. Do most women really find this troglodyte stuff charming?"

"You'd be surprised."

Delaney tossed her head and skirted around him, wheeling the shopping cart toward the plumbing department.

Didn't she realize how easy she was making it for him to tease her unmercifully? Clearly, she had not grown up with brothers. She had no clue how to defend herself against verbal sparring.

"Hey, Rosy, wait up."

"Feel free to gimp along at your own pace," she called out over her shoulder.

Nick burst out laughing. Feistiness. All right. He knew she had it in her, and he loved provoking it. Chasing her off was going to be a lot more challenging than he'd first thought, but also a lot more fun.

When her left hand shot up over her head with the middle finger extended, he laughed so hard he almost choked. Now that was a sight worth seeing.

Miss-Butter-Wouldn't-Melt-Between-Her-Thighs-High-Society flipping him the bird.

Delaney Lynn Cartwright, the daughter of a Montgomery blue blood, does not stoop to common vulgarity.

She heard her mother's chiding voice in her right ear, and the small sense of satisfaction she'd just derived from flipping off the arrogant Mr. Vinetti evaporated instantly.

Don't feel guilty. It's about time you showed some spunk, Skylar's voice countered in her left ear.

Terrific. Her highly developed superego, represented by her mother's voice, was pulling her in one direction. While her much-ignored id, in the form of Skylar-speak, was yanking her in the opposite.

Apologize to Mr. Vinetti for your rudeness, Honey's voice demanded. Delaney stopped, turned, and faced Nick.

He was standing at the end of the aisle, eyebrows cocked slyly, and a knowing smile playing across his lips.

To hell with that. Look at him. He's so damn sure of himself. He deserved the bird, Skylar's voice argued.

Delaney whirled back around and marched in the direction she'd been heading.

Just like when her sister had been alive, Delaney felt caught in the middle between two warring personalities much larger than her own. As a child, whenever Honey and Skylar went at it, Delaney hid in the closet or under the bed to avoid the fray. Her mother the perfectionist, and her sister the free spirit.

What am I? she wondered.

You're the people-pleaser, the Skylar voice and the mother voice echoed in stereo.

Feeling overwhelmed, Delaney clamped her hands over her ears to drown out the conflict.

When did she get to please herself? She was twenty-five years old, pampered and protected. How was she ever supposed to know what she really wanted if she kept letting other people tell her what to do?

Plumbing. Concentrate on plumping supplies and the repairs to Lucia's house.

She stared at the shelf in front of her, not seeing anything because her mind was in turmoil.

"Are you okay?" a deep voice curled through both her ears as a masculine hand touched her shoulder.

Startled from her reverie, Delaney leaped, hand splayed across her heart. "Eek."

"Sorry, I didn't mean to frighten you." Nick dropped his hand, but very slowly, and in the process grazed the length of her arm with his fingertips.

"No, no, I'm sorry." She wasn't prepared for the full consequence of being touched by him again. Her breath simply flew from her lungs, and she was left with her mouth hanging open at the razor-sharp jolt of awareness blasting through her body. Quickly she stepped closer to the shelf and farther away from him.

He was staring at her intently. As if he could make her disappear merely by focusing his mind on the task. He left her feeling tongue-tied, weak-kneed, and totally inadequate. "Don't apologize. You didn't do anything."

Her eyes met his. Prickles of primal excitement skidded up her spine. "I flipped you off."

"Yeah." He grinned. "You did."

"That was rude of me."

"Sometimes rude is justified."

Not according to my mother.

Their gazes were fused to each other, her pulse firing like a piston.

"Which size pipe do you think we'll need to replace the leaky one in your grandmother's upstairs bathroom?" Delaney pulled her gaze from his and ran her hand along the smooth hard length of metal plumbing pipe on the shelf in front of her.

"One and three quarters," he said.

"That doesn't seem thick enough."

"I measured it."

"Are you sure?"

"I know if I measured something or not."

"No, I mean are you sure you measured correctly."

"Go with this one, Rosy." Nick leaned around her to reach for the pipe and his chest brushed against her shoulder. The sleeve of his T-shirt rode up, revealing a wicked scar high up on his bicep.

Delaney felt something inside her start to unravel. She gasped. "What happened?"

"Huh?" He turned his head and saw her staring at his bicep. He was so close she could smell the clean linen scent of his soap. "Oh, that. Got shot."

Her whole body went cold. "You got shot?"

"Long time ago. Rookie mistake."

She swayed, imagining him hurting and in pain. She couldn't stand the thought of it and bit down hard on her bottom lip.

"You're looking pale, Rosy. You gonna faint on me?"

"Your job is very dangerous."

"Most of the time, no."

"But you got shot on the job, and your grandmother told me you hurt your knee on the job as well. That seems pretty perilous to me."

He laughed and gave her a droll stare. Apparently her distress over his risky employment amused him. "Don't worry. Two injuries in eight years is not that bad. It's not like I'm an Alaskan king crab fisherman or anything."

His eyes hooked hers. He was so alive, so raw, so electric. So the opposite of Evan.

If she were a braver woman, she would have met the challenge in his eyes. But she wasn't brave. His overt masculinity scared the heck out of her.

"Go with this piece of pipe," he repeated, straightening and placing the pipe in her hand.

She dropped it into the shopping cart. "This is enough

for now," she said, anxious to get outside where she could draw in a breath of fresh ocean air and clear her head. "We've got enough to get started. We can always come back for more supplies later."

Nick paid for the purchases and they left the store.

On the drive back to Lucia's place, tension permeated the cab of the pickup. Sexual tension. Taut and hot. Delaney stared out the window, focusing on the scenery. Condos and beach cottages and seagulls and tourists in brightly colored clothes.

But no matter how hard she tried to direct her attention outside, every cell in her was attuned to what was happening inside. Both inside the cab and inside her.

Her hands lay fisted against the tops of her thighs. Her throat felt tight, the set of her shoulders even tighter. Restlessly, she wriggled her toes inside her sandals. Even way across the seat, Delaney could feel the heat emanating off Nick's body. The truck smelled of him—musky, manly, magnificent.

The plastic hula girl, mounted on his dashboard, swayed her hips with the vehicle's movements. The faster he drove, the faster she danced the hula. Hula, hula, hula.

Her mother would have labeled the hula girl tacky and lowbrow. She supposed it did seem a bit chauvinistic, sort of like the silhouette of naked women on eighteen-wheeler mud flaps. But she liked the whimsy of it. Watching the plastic doll's undulating hips had a mesmerizing effect.

She reached out to touch it.

"No, no," Nick growled. "No touching Lalule."

She drew back her hand quickly as if he'd smacked her.

"Sorry," he apologized. "Didn't mean to snap. Reflex. The nieces and nephews are always trying to monkey around with her, and I'm so used to warning them off, I forgot it was you. Lalule means a lot to me."

"Why is that?"

"My mother gave her to me," he said gruffly. "Not long before she died."

"Oh."

He didn't say anything else.

Delaney didn't mean to be nosy, but she wanted so badly to understand him. Because she thought that if she could understand him, maybe she could figure out why she was so attracted to this man. And then she could sublimate that attraction in a healthier way. "What was your mother's name?"

"Dominique. I'm named after her."

"How did she die?"

"Brain tumor. When I was seven." He stared out over the hood of the truck, and Delaney knew his mind was rummaging around in the past.

"That must have been so difficult for you," she soothed.

"Yeah."

"You must have felt abandoned."

He drummed his fingers against the steering wheel, and she thought that was all she was going to get out of him. She didn't press. If he didn't want to talk about it, he didn't want to talk about it.

But then a few minutes later, he surprised her. "Mom's dying wish was to go to Hawaii. Dad maxed out the credit card and took us to Maui for three weeks on one last family vacation."

He paused again and glanced over at her. The raw pain on his face was almost unbearable. Nick was far more complicated than she'd guessed.

In that moment, she saw past his looks, beyond the

dark eyes that were often hooded to hide his thoughts. Beyond the high, masculine cheekbones, the thick black eyelashes, the nose that looked as if it had been broken a time or two. She peered beyond the promise of his beautiful mouth, which wasn't too full or too thin, but very well shaped with a distinctive cut to the borders and a curious firmness in the way he held it. As if if he were to relax his hold, it might give away too many secrets.

Delaney thought that was all he was going to say on the subject of his mother, but then he said, "I was a cowardly kid. I wanted so badly to learn to surf, but I was afraid of the water. I didn't even know how to swim."

It touched her that he would confess this vulnerability, that he trusted her not to judge him for his childhood fears. Most macho guys refused to admit any kind of weakness. But in Delaney's point of view, Nick's willingness to acknowledge his foibles only made him stronger.

"You?" she said, treading lightly in this swamp of emotion. "Detective Bullet-Riddled a 'fraidy cat? I don't believe it."

"Yep. I was. My little brothers could swim, but I was afraid of sharks, of drowning, of getting taken away from my mother."

"Do you think she knew that?"

"I know she did. She bought Lalule and told me she was my guardian angel. Whenever I got scared, Mom told me to just give Lalule a shake, and she would remind me to shake things up," he explained.

"Shake things up?"

"Mom said I could sit on the beach, play it safe, and feel sorry for myself, or I could be brave, learn how to shake things up, and make my life happen. With Lalule's help, in three weeks I'd learned not only how to swim, but also how to surf."

"Your mother knew she wouldn't be around to inspire you herself, and she gave you the doll as a reminder of her indomitable spirit," Delaney said softly.

"Yeah. I suppose she did. My mother was sweet on the outside, but tough on the inside. Sort of like you."

That sounded dangerously close to a compliment. Except Nick was dead wrong. Delaney wasn't tough inside at all. She was a total marshmallow through and through.

He took a deep breath. "Mom died just four days after we got back home."

Delaney's throat clotted with emotion. "Nick—I—"

"So you see why I don't like anyone messing with Lalule," he rushed in to say. She could tell he was struggling to sound casual.

She wanted to touch him, to comfort him for that long-ago pain, but she had no business, no right. Still, she couldn't just leave him with his shoulders tensed, his jaw clenched, his mind hung up in the past. She skimmed his forearm with her fingertips—briefly, lightly, just enough to let him know she cared.

"I understand the hurt. The confusion a young child goes through when they lose someone close to them. You blame yourself. You think that if you'd been a better kid, the person you loved wouldn't have died. That if you had done just one thing differently, you could have saved them."

He looked startled. "You too?"

"My older sister," she said. "When I was eight."

Nick made a noise, half empathy, half sorrow. His eyes glistened. "Life's a bitch sometimes," he said to be macho, but he reached across the seat and tenderly took her hand.

Every muscle cell in her heart ached. She looked over

at him. This shared intimacy forced a deeper understanding, a bonding between them.

"Losing Skylar changed me forever, you know." She swallowed. "While losing your mother made you braver, losing my sister made me more afraid."

"You seem brave to me."

"I'm not." She ducked her head. "Not at all. You have no idea how scared I am ninety percent of the time."

"What are you so scared of?"

"Of everything, but mostly of being scared." She laughed at herself. "Of not really living."

"If that's true, where did you find the courage to dress up in that bustier and raincoat and attempt to kidnap your fiancé?"

"I needed to feel something. Needed some magic in my life, I guess. But you saw how well that turned out."

"I thought it turned out very well. It made me damn jealous of your fiancé."

Delaney couldn't handle the swell of emotions flooding through her. She couldn't keep looking at him. Instead, she directed her attention out the window and told herself to breathe.

They were traveling down Seawall Boulevard. Sunlight streamed through a break in the soft covering of clouds, sparkling off the blue waters of the Gulf of Mexico. The water shimmered, rolling in toward the seawall.

For a split second, Delaney felt the way she'd felt the night she found the wedding veil. Caught up in a special sort of magic that could change everything. And then the feeling vanished, disappearing as quickly as it surfaced.

She saw a carnival-style amusement park situated at the end of the beach. The rides looked old and shaky, the garishly painted skins peeling and rusting in the salt air.

Delaney was at once both charmed and repelled by the rinky-dink amusement park.

When she was a kid, she'd always wanted to go to a carnival or an amusement park. Ride those scary rides. Eat sticky candy apples and funnel cakes dusted with powdered sugar. Breathe in the air rich with the smell of frying grease. Get taken in by the sideshow barkers. Play games of chance and win a giant teddy bear.

Her mother had hated carnivals and amusement parks with a passion verging on phobia. "Carnies are common street thugs," she'd tell Delaney. "You'll get germs from the rides. They'll cheat you and steal your money. Stay away from carnivals and fairs and small-time amusement parks."

So she had.

But her mother had made carnivals such a taboo, that whenever Delaney saw one, she experienced the lure of the forbidden deep in the center of her stomach. Calling to her. Urging her to defy her mother. To sin by climbing on the Ferris wheel and floating high above the crowd and then slowly coming down to earth. She had imagined it a thousand times.

She latched on to the amusement park with her gaze, using it to pry her awareness off Nick. Realizing that in spite of having grown up a very rich girl, she had missed out on a lot of the simple things. What she would have given for a Lalule of her own.

Then Delaney saw something totally unbelievable.

Her smartly dressed, perfectly coiffed mother.

No way.

But she could have sworn it was Honey Montgomery Cartwright standing on the seawall beside the entrance to the amusement park, talking to an elderly woman in a babushka and wading boots, wearing a black eye patch over her left eye.

The pickup truck sailed by.

Delaney blinked. No, it couldn't be. She must have imagined it. She couldn't conceive of a single reason that would compel her mother to visit a run-down amusement park on Galveston Island.

"Wait, wait," she exclaimed.

"What is it?"

"Back up, back up," she yelled at Nick, frantically making counterclockwise motions with her hand.

"Huh?"

"Put it in reverse, go back, go back."

"I can't back up in traffic."

"Make a U-ey. Hurry, hurry."

"Okay, okay, keep your shirt on." His grin turned wicked. "Unless, of course, you want to take it off."

Any other time she would never have said what she said next, but she was so stunned at seeing her snooty mother slumming at an amusement park that she was not her normal self.

"Shut up and drive, Vinetti," she snarled.

"Yes, ma'am." He obeyed and made a U-turn at the next traffic light.

She was amazed at his acquiescence. Hmm, maybe that was the way you handled a guy like Vinetti. If she'd growled "shut up" at Evan, it would have hurt his feelings so badly he would have pouted for an hour. Nick, on the other hand, seemed to respect her for it. Then again, Evan had never given her any reason to snarl "shut up" at him.

"Drive slower."

"Cars are on my ass, Rosy."

"Tough."

"When'd you get so bossy?"

When indeed? She wasn't acting like herself, but right

now that felt like a good thing. Delaney undid her seat belt and scooted over to Nick's side of the truck and craned her neck to peer out his window. She was sitting so close she could hear him breathing.

They crept along Seawall Boulevard, cars piling up behind them, drivers honking their horns in irritation.

"What are we looking for?" he asked.

"I thought I saw someone I know."

"And that's worth snarling traffic over?"

"In this case, yes."

"What? Do you think that you saw your fiancé with another woman?"

"No."

"Then what on earth could you have seen that would make you holler like a banshee with her hair caught in a chamois wringer?" Nick asked.

"That's none of your business."

"I hate to disagree with you on that, but your sighting is the reason these cars are kissing my bumper. You owe me an explanation."

"I saw my mother, okay? Happy now?"

"With a man other than your father?"

"What's with you and the cheating-loved-ones scenarios? Oh, oh." She tapped his shoulder. "Slow down even more, we're almost there."

They inched past the amusement park entrance.

Teeth clenched, Delaney scanned the area. She looked first left toward the Gulf, then right toward the collection of ragtag carnival rides.

Nothing.

No one.

Her mother had vanished.

Chapter 8

Shaking with fear and revulsion, Honey climbed into her sleek white Cadillac and sped out of Galveston as fast as she dared, desperate to reach home and take a long, hot, cleansing shower to wash away her sins. Her heart was in her throat, her stomach was a tight knot, and her hands smelled of the twenty thousand dollars she'd just counted out. She felt very dirty.

Blackmail was an ugly business.

Then again, so was the thing she had done.

All these years, she thought she'd gotten away with it. Thought she had fooled everyone. Thought no one would ever discover her terrible secret.

In retrospect, she'd been both foolish and arrogant.

Now she was trapped. Forced to pay to keep her shame quiet and never knowing how long the blackmailing would continue.

And she had to keep it quiet. For her daughter's sake. No one must ever discover the truth.

At least until after the wedding. When Delaney was married to Evan and safely out of harm's way.

* * *

Nick didn't know why he'd told Delaney about his mother. He rarely talked about Dominique anymore. He wasn't the kind of guy who liked stirring up the past, and he certainly didn't like examining his feelings and talking about them.

Unfortunately, once the memories of those old feelings had been aroused—feelings of loss and anger and sadness—he could not easily stuff them back down into his subconscious. Even after he'd gone home for the day, he kept replaying his afternoon with Delaney over and over in his head. To relieve the pressure, Nick was back at the gym, pushing himself, exercising his body in an attempt to free his mind.

It wasn't working.

Almost always, when things got too emotionally tough, exercise provided him with the release he needed. During the whole Amber/Gary Feldstein fiasco, he shed nine pounds, ended up running a five-minute mile, and bench-pressed two-sixty. Thanks to Gold's Gym, he'd been able to put the scandal out of his mind and get through the humiliation.

But this was the second time exercise had failed him where Delaney Cartwright was concerned.

He lost count during bicep curls because he kept thinking about Delaney's soft voice and the way her deeply green, intelligent, expressive eyes encouraged him to spill his secrets. He forgot how many laps he'd done in the pool and had to go around again to make sure he wasn't short-changing his routine because he'd vividly imagined kissing that slightly crooked little mouth of hers. He forgot to put the timer on the treadmill and ended up staying on fifteen minutes longer than he intended because he kept wondering how her silky hair would feel slipping through his fingers.

What was it about Delaney that loosened his lips? Why did he feel this need to explain himself to her?

He didn't like it. He didn't like it at all. She seemed to hold some kind of magic key to the trunk where he kept his vulnerabilities locked up tight. She knew just how and when to slip that key into the lock and turn it. Nick barely knew the woman, and he had already told her things he'd never told Amber. Not even after being engaged for eighteen months.

He'd never even told his ex-wife the story behind Lalule.

When she'd run off with Feldstein, Amber had cited Nick's inability to communicate as the reason she'd left. Ha! If she could see him now. With Delaney, he was communicating like Geraldo Rivera in the Middle East, spilling everything he knew. How laughably ironic.

Then it suddenly occurred to him why he would share his deeper feelings with Delaney and not with Amber. For one, Delaney was an empathetic listener, but he suspected that was secondary. He could talk to her because with Delaney, he had nothing to lose. She was engaged to someone else. He didn't see her as a threat to his self-image. With her, he wouldn't forfeit any macho points for revealing his tender side.

Once he realized that, he felt better.

Okay, he didn't have anything to worry about. If tears had misted his eyes a little when he'd talked about his mother, no harm, no foul.

Except whenever he thought about Delaney, something tightened in the dead center of his chest, and that disturbed him. A helluva lot. The woman was engaged to another man. He couldn't, *wouldn't*, have these feelings for her.

Clearly, he had to find a way to chase her off. Not only because he didn't want her succeeding at selling Nana's house, but for his own mental health as well. He had to be subtle about it. Nana loved her. Hell, the whole family was smitten with her. If he didn't handle this right, he'd come off looking like the bad guy.

Quitting the job had to be Delaney's idea. But how to accomplish that goal? What he needed was an underhanded plan.

A smile broke across his lips as the perfect plot popped into his head. He'd turn on the charm and pretend he was trying to win her away from her fiancé. That ought to do the trick. Pleased with his solution, Nick breezed through the rest of his workout.

Yep, Delaney Cartwright's days as his Nana's house stager were numbered.

"You've got to be mistaken. Our mom? At an amusement park? Talking to a one-eyed carny woman?" Skylar scoffed when Delaney dreamed of her again.

"Yes."

Tonight, Skylar was dressed in scarlet cowgirl boots and a fawn-colored suede jacket with fringe on the sleeves. "I can't imagine in what universe that scenario is even remotely possible."

"I'm telling you, it was her."

"Did you ask her about it?"

Delaney blew out a breath. "Yes... no."

"Did you or not?"

"I tried to, but I couldn't get the words out. I did mention that I had a job on Galveston Island."

"Well, that was straightforward and to the point." Skylar picked up a tube of lipstick off Delaney's vanity, plunked down in front of the mirror, and rolled some on. "Ick! Too pale. Ditch the pink and get some red."

"If you don't like my lipstick then don't use it."

"I don't have a choice. You're the only one who dreams about me."

"Mother and Daddy don't dream about you?"

"Not much. Not anymore." Skylar uncapped Delaney's mascara and leaned forward to brush it across her eyelashes.

"Then why do I keep dreaming of you?"

"Who do I look like, Sigmund Freud? How would I know? Anyway, back to Mother."

"I don't know why she was there, but I'm telling you it was our mother."

"If you're so certain, then you should have confronted her, not wishy-washed around. If it had been me, I would have just come right out and said, 'Hey, Mom, spied you on Galveston Island chatting up a one-eyed carny chick; what gives?' "

"Yeah, well, that's you."

Skylar propped her cowgirl-booted feet up on the vanity and cocked back in the chair until only the two back legs were left on the floor. "Remember how Mom used to carry on about the evils of carnivals and street fairs and amusement parks? What was her deal? If it wasn't for Uncle Lance and Aunt Maxie taking me with their kids, I would never have even gone to Sea World."

"I never did get to go to Sea World," Delaney said. "By the time I was old enough, you were dead and Mom wouldn't let me out of her sight."

"Wonder what her deal is with carnivals? A rock

concert phobia I get, but carnivals? Come on. Everyone loves carnivals."

"Not our mother."

"So what are you going to do about it?"

"About what?"

"Finding out what Mom was doing there."

"I'm not going to do anything about it."

"Why not? Scared of the one-eyed woman?"

Truthfully, yes. "What would be the point?"

"So you'd have something over on Mother. We spent our lives totally under her control, and now you have the opportunity to prove she was not only hanging out at an amusement park, but that she lied to you about it. And besides, aren't you just a wee bit curious as to why?"

"Why *would* she be there?"

"Maybe she was buying drugs. Mother always told us that behind the scenes, carnivals were a hotbed for drugs."

"Mother? Doing drugs? Please."

"Yeah, you're right. If she was doing drugs, she wouldn't be so uptight."

"I've been thinking about it all day," Delaney said. "It makes no sense."

"Maybe she went there to meet a lover."

"Hello, I saw her with a woman."

"Eeps! Mother's a lesbian? That's her big secret." Skylar leaned back too far and the chair hit the ground. She rolled on the floor, laughing hysterically. "Good thing I'm not real. Otherwise, that might have hurt."

"Until now, I never realized how silly you were."

"I'm forever trapped in your imagination the way I was when I died. Of course I'm silly. I'm sixteen."

"When I was a kid I thought you were so mature and sophisticated."

"We all have our shattered illusions. Like Mother at an amusement park. Life will never be the same."

"You're making fun of me."

Skylar shrugged. "Have you told Mother about the wedding veil yet?"

"No."

"Wanna get to wear it with impunity?"

Delaney eyed her sister. "What do you have in mind?"

"Go talk to the one-eyed woman. Get proof it was our mother you saw at the amusement park. Then tell her you want to wear the veil. If she refuses, you whip out your trump card and inform her that you'll tell Dad about her clandestine trip to Galveston if she doesn't put her stamp of approval on the veil."

"But that's blackmail."

"Uh-huh."

"I can't blackmail my own mother."

"No? Why not? She's been doing it to you for years."

"What are you talking about?"

"Using my death to keep you in line. Be perfect, live up to her expectations, or you'll end up dead. That's emotional blackmail. She's kept you from being the person you were truly meant to be. This, my sis, is the ideal time to declare your independence and break free. All it requires is a little daring on your part. You up for it?"

"I don't know."

"Yes, you do." Skylar winked, and then Delaney woke up.

Honey couldn't sleep.

She'd spent the night tossing and turning beside a snoring James Robert, thinking of what she'd been forced to do the previous day and fretting over something Delaney had said at dinner the night before, about having a house to stage out on Galveston Island. She'd announced it quite out of the blue and then stared at Honey as if she knew something.

Could Delaney have seen her at the amusement park?

She had to find out.

Just after dawn, she got up, dressed, and went to Delaney's room.

She knocked on the door, and before her daughter could tell her to come in, Honey was already pushing her way over the threshold. She found Delaney sitting at the vanity in her bathrobe, flatironing her hair. Delaney's hair, without the proper products and styling techniques, looked shockingly unruly.

"You're up early," Delaney said mildly.

"I thought maybe we could have a heart-to-heart." Honey made Delaney's bed and stiffly sat down on it.

"Is this about the wedding preparations?" Delaney eyed her from the mirror.

"No. Not really. We just haven't had much of a chance to talk lately, and I was feeling we were a bit disconnected. You've been busy with this new project, and I've been busy too." Honey came over to pat her shoulder. "Here. Let me have the flatiron. You missed a spot along your nape."

Dutifully, Delaney handed her the ceramic styling iron and Honey breathed a sigh of relief. The insurrection had been a small one.

"Sit up straight; you're slouching."

Delaney sat up, but kept her eyes lowered so Honey couldn't peer into the mirror and read her thoughts. But she could feel tension tightening the muscles along the back of her daughter's neck.

"Busy doing what?" Delaney asked.

Alarm spread through Honey. Was her daughter being cagey? "Why, planning your wedding of course."

"Right," Delaney said in that calm, unemotional tone of hers that at times Honey found slightly demeaning.

You're the one who stressed the importance of learning to manage her emotions. She's just doing what you taught her.

Ah, but she'd learned too well. Honey feared she never really knew what her daughter was thinking or feeling behind those enigmatic green eyes so much like her own.

The price of controlling her youngest daughter had been high, but it was a cost Honey had no choice but to pay. She refused to let Delaney end up like Skylar. Even after seventeen years, the memory of her oldest child painfully wrenched Honey's heart. Haunting guilt sent her gaze flicking over Delaney, looking for any problems to nip in the bud. She took in the serene sophistication of her daughter's large bedroom with its cool sage green walls, cherrywood sleigh bed, and haute couture–inspired accessories.

"Did you have a wedding-based errand at the amusement park on Galveston Island yesterday afternoon?"

Honey froze. *Don't reveal a thing. Keep your face emotionless.* "I don't know what you mean."

"Come on, Mother, I saw you."

The words, once spoken, were as powerful as a slap. Honey's cheeks stung. She gulped. How was she going to handle this?

Lie through your teeth. It's the only way to survive.

Grappling to control the terror mushrooming inside her, Honey laughed, trying to sound carefree, but she only ended up sounding nervous. "Don't be absurd. You know how much I hate Galveston and amusement parks."

"Yes, I do, which is exactly why it struck me as so odd to see you there."

"I wasn't there," Honey denied. "It wasn't me."

The flatiron hissed in the silence between them, steam rising up from Delaney's hair. The silence lay heavy. An accusation.

"Are you having an affair?" Delaney asked.

This time her laugh was honest. "Don't be silly, darling. I would never jeopardize my marriage for a fling. I love your father with all my heart. I've never loved anyone the way I love him."

"You couldn't prove it by me." Delaney's voice was flint.

"Excuse me?" This change in her daughter bothered Honey immensely. Skylar had bucked her, spectacularly and often, but Delaney? Never.

"You nag Daddy constantly. He can't ever seem to do anything to please you."

Honey was taken aback. "I do not."

But it was true. She did nitpick James Robert. It was for his own good. Without her he would just drift along, never taking a stand, never feeling strongly about anything.

"I know things between the two of you fell apart after Skylar died, but Mother, it's been seventeen years. Hasn't Daddy been punished enough?"

"I'm not punishing him."

Delaney's accusation was ludicrous. Wasn't it?

"No?"

"I'm helping him to improve."

"What if he doesn't want to improve? What if he likes being the way he is? You married him that way. How come he isn't good enough for you anymore? You criticize me all the time too. How come I'm not good enough either? What's this impossibly high standard you're trying to reach? Face it, Mother, we're never going to be good enough for you."

Shocked to her very core, Honey sucked in her breath. "Darling," she whispered, "I had no idea you felt this way. I only correct you because I love you so much. I want to see you excel. To have a rewarding life."

"Have you ever considered your definition of excellence might differ greatly from Daddy's and mine?"

"Please don't get me wrong. I'm not putting you down. You're a wonderful daughter, and you've accomplished so much. You've started your own business and it's thriving. You're about to marry one of the most eligible bachelors in Texas, who just happens to be a really nice person as well. People are going to be talking about this wedding for years to come."

Using the curling iron, Honey pointed to Delaney's framed "ugly duckling" picture she encouraged her to keep on her dresser as a reminder not to slip up and go off her diet. "See how far you've come. You were a size eighteen in that picture, and now look at you, a perfect size four. I'm so proud."

"Uh-huh," Delaney muttered. "That's what I thought. As long as I stay thin I have your approval, but let me dare to gain weight, and I risk losing your love. Gotta tell you, Mother, conditional love doesn't feel so swell."

Honey had to bite down on her tongue to keep from lecturing her about mumbling and saying "uh-huh" and "gotta." Truth be told, her feelings were hurt. How could her own daughter misunderstand her intentions so completely?

"There." She forced a smile. "All done."

"Thank you." Delaney unplugged the flatiron and headed into the adjoining bathroom.

Suddenly feeling exhausted, Honey sank down on the bed. She thought once she'd raised Delaney to adulthood, everything would be so much easier.

But it was not.

She had imagined they would be fast friends, going shopping, calling each other several times a day, sharing fashion tips and diet recipes, and laughing together.

But they did not.

Honey thought that preparing for this wedding would be the glue that would finally bond them, that once Delaney was engaged and on the road to becoming a married woman, she would finally understand the sacrifices Honey had made. That she wanted only the very best for her.

But it had not.

If anything, the impending wedding seemed to be pushing them farther and farther apart, with Delaney growing more apathetic with each decision made. She didn't seem to have any sort of opinion on the cake or the reception menu or the invitations. Her reaction to everything was a bland, "Whatever you like."

What was wrong with her daughter?

The staunch reserve she'd perfected over the years slipped, and tears she hadn't cried since losing Skylar sprang from her eyes and slid down her cheeks. In spite of trying her very best, she was a terrible mother who couldn't love her own daughter unconditionally. God was punishing her for her lies and deceptions.

What would happen if Delaney found out about the blackmailer? What if she learned the truth?

Fear thrashed inside her. She struggled not to give in to it. She kept her hands knotted tightly in her lap, her shoulders set straight, and with catlike concentration willed the tears to stop. She was not a weak person. She was strong, she was a survivor. She and Delaney would weather this storm and come out stronger at the other end.

The tears dried on her cheeks. Yes, yes. Everything would be okay. This was fixable.

She had to believe it. Had to believe she would not lose Delaney.

Otherwise, if she dared let herself think that her surviving daughter had withdrawn from her completely, Honey would totally fall apart.

Her mother was lying, but Delaney had no idea why.

She sat parked in her Acura beside the Galveston seawall, her father's black Bushnell binoculars resting in her lap. She stared at the amusement park sprawling out across the beach below. She couldn't believe she was doing this—checking up on her mother.

Curiosity nibbled at her.

At ten A.M. on a Thursday, only a few tourists haunted the rides and concession stands. Lucia wasn't expecting her until noon, when they were meeting with Lucia's real estate agent, Margaret Krist, to discuss Delaney's plans for the house.

She had two hours to locate the patch-eyed woman and quiz her about Honey. She'd brought cash in case the woman expected to be paid for the information. Delaney might be sheltered, but she wasn't dumb. She watched television. She was aware of how these things worked.

The main thing keeping her butt welded to the car seat was this inbred fear of carnivals and amusement parks that her mother had instilled in her.

Stay away from carnies. Those people are scoundrels

and crooks and pickpockets and thieves. They will rob you blind, and that's if you're lucky.

Delaney scooted over to the passenger seat, rolled down the window, propped her elbows on the sill, and raised the binoculars to her eyes. She surveyed the area for the one-eyed woman, but saw no sign of her.

This wasn't getting her anywhere. She was going to have to face her fear, walk into that amusement park, and ask someone about the woman. Too bad confrontation made her nervous. She took a deep breath.

If you can flip off Nick Vinetti, you can do this.

Smiling, her courage bolstered by the memory, she got out of the car, tucked her purse under her arm, and strolled down the seawall toward the cement staircase leading down to the beach. Almost immediately, she realized how inappropriately she was dressed for a stroll along the shore. White silk slacks, a silk navy-blue V-necked blouse, and high-heeled sandals. What had she been thinking?

Well, when she'd dressed that morning she'd been thinking about her meeting with Lucia's real estate agent, not a powwow with the carnival woman. It was only after talking to her mother and Honey acting so suspiciously that she had made up her mind to do this.

Carefully, Delaney picked her way down the staircase, holding tight to the railing. The minute she veered onto the walkway leading to the amusement park entrance, the wind blew sand into her open-toed shoes.

She ambled along through the grounds, trying to look casual as she studied the faces of the amusement park workers. Surprisingly, a pleasant feeling stole over her. The sound of the ocean was so peaceful, she almost forgot why she'd come.

After trailing up and down the walkway and not seeing

the one-eyed woman, she realized she was going to have to ask someone if they knew her. Taking a deep breath to bolster her courage, she sidled up to the bored-looking guy manning the Whack-a-Mole. No one else was around. He leaned across the counter and leered at her as she approached.

She forced a smile. "Hello, I was hoping you could tell me where I might find someone who works here. She's an older woman and wears an eye patch."

"What's it worth to you?" His look was lascivious and his gaze fixated on her mouth.

She pressed her lips together in a firm line. "I'll give you ten dollars."

He held out a palm.

Delaney dropped a ten-dollar bill into it.

"You're talking about Paulette Doggett." The man spat a stream of tobacco into the sand not far from her foot. "It's her day off."

"Do you have any idea where I might find Ms. Doggett?"

The leering man shrugged. "I 'magine she's out chasing the hounds."

"Excuse me?"

"Paulette came into a wad of cash yesterdee, and she likes betting on the greyhounds."

"Thank you." Grateful to be out of the man's company, Delaney hurried away. She had two choices, go to the greyhound track and try to find Paulette in the crowd, or return to the amusement park another day. Since she had a meeting planned for noon, she chose the later option.

"Well, well, well, will surprises never cease," said a familiar voice from behind her that made the hairs on her arms stand up. "If it isn't Miss Rosy."

Chapter 9

Delaney turned to find Nick Vinetti standing behind her, his grin wide and wicked. She felt a little woozy, like all the air had been leaked from her lungs.

"Hi," she said breathlessly.

"Hi."

"What are you doing here?"

"I asked first."

And that's when she noticed the boys standing on either side of him. "Gina's kids, right? Jack and Zack."

"We're twins," one of the boys said.

"I can see that." Delaney smiled at them.

"Identical," the other added.

"I can see that too."

"We're seven," they chimed in unison, charming Delaney with their gap-toothed grins, crew cuts, and skinned elbows. She could easily imagine Nick at their age, dark-eyed and full of mischief. Although she had no idea why that image would make her chest feel all tight and knotty.

"I'm keeping them occupied while Gina and Nana are packing up Grampa Leo's personal effects," Nick explained. His voice sounded as tight as her chest.

Her eyes met his. "That's got to be difficult for your grandmother."

Nick shrugged. "Yeah, that's why they didn't need these little sea monkeys around. With school out for the summer, Gina didn't have anyone to babysit, so I volunteered."

Delaney's heart twisted. Nick acted all macho and nonchalant, but one look at his face told her it was hard on him too, and he was happier watching the kids than being the one sorting out his grandfather's belongings. "That was nice of you."

"I don't mind. Sea monkeys can be a lot of fun."

"Hey," Zack, or maybe it was Jack, protested. It was really tough to tell them apart. "We're not sea monkeys."

"You sure squirm around like sea monkeys."

The twins made faces and jumped around, letting their arms flop loosely as if they had no bones in them. Delaney smiled. They were so cute, and Nick was adorable with them.

"How about you?" Nick asked her. "Why are you here, looking decidedly out of your element?"

She didn't miss the gaze that he slid down her body in a disconcertingly intimate fashion, and then his eyes lingered on her inappropriate footwear. The intensity of his stare should have made her uncomfortable. Instead it ignited the sparks that had been simmering between them from the day he'd flipped her onto her back in the grass outside Evan's building.

Delaney didn't want to tell him the truth, so she skipped over his question. "Did your grandmother tell you that she and I are having lunch with her real estate agent to discuss the renovations and a time schedule for listing the house on the market?"

"Yeah, she told me, but that still doesn't explain why

you're at the amusement park looking like you stepped from the pages of some fashion magazine."

"We wanna go on the Ferris wheel." Jack tugged on his uncle's hand. "You promised."

"Would you like to come with us?" Nick inclined his head toward the biggest ride in the carnival that jutted high into the cloudless blue summer sky. "Plenty of time before your lunch date. Unless you have something else going on."

She hesitated.

He'd leaned in close, his face just to the side of hers. "Come on," he coaxed. "Have a little fun."

Was it her imagination, or was he standing just a bit too close and pushing just a bit too hard?

"I...I..."

"I gotcha. You're too fancy for Ferris wheels."

"I'm not," she denied indignantly. He had a way of pushing her buttons.

A half smile hovered at the edges of his lips. His warm breath fell against her neck, heating her all the way through. Was he doing it on purpose? Was he *trying* to make her uncomfortable?

"Come on. What do you say? Please, don't leave me alone with the sea monkeys."

Delaney was about to refuse his invitation and then she thought, *Why not?* She was twenty-five years old, and she'd never been on a Ferris wheel because her mother had made her afraid of them. It was pathetic really.

He gave her such a winning smile she decided she must be reading more into his body language than he actually intended. He was a cop; crowding people was probably just second nature. Nothing personal. Right?

"Pretty please." His grin widened.

"Well, when you put it like that, sure," she said. "I would love to."

The sun shone brightly on her face, and rather than worry that she hadn't put on sunblock and was exposing herself to the risk of premature wrinkles, she simply threw back her head and laughed. Then, she stumbled over a thick extension cord running across the midway and fell against Nick's side.

"Whoa there, Rosy," he said and put a hand on her shoulder to steady her. "You okay?"

"Fine," she chirped, feeling finer than she'd felt in a very long time. She couldn't explain where this sudden exuberance was coming from, but it sure felt good.

Nick said nothing. He angled an odd look her way just before he bought their tickets. The twins climbed into one of the cars of the Ferris wheel ahead of them, leaving her alone in the second car with Nick. They were the only customers on the ride.

The operator lowered the restraining bar, locking them in together. He stepped over to the controls and started the ride.

The cars jerked forward.

Delaney squealed and grabbed on to Nick's elbow.

He chuckled and slid his arm around her shoulder. "Scared of Ferris wheels?"

"Never been on one."

"You're kidding me."

"My mother was a bit overprotective."

"I'll say. It's not like it's a roller coaster."

"I've never been on one of those either."

For the first time, she realized how high up they were and that they were just dangling in the air. She eyed the ground, feeling decidedly nervous. Were they supposed to be this high up? It didn't seem right.

"Have no fear, Nick is here," he teased. "I'll protect you."

Sitting so close to Nick with his arm draped around her shoulder, she felt too giddy and way too free.

"Do you have any idea how tempting you are?" he murmured and touched the simple gold hoop earring at her earlobe.

"Um." She raised her left hand between them, flashed him her engagement right. "Just a reminder, I'm engaged."

"So I see." He said it with such regret in his voice. She searched his face for the emotion behind his words. His smile turned tender, wistful.

What was with him? He was acting as if he wanted to date her.

Delaney huddled into herself. His arm felt too good resting over her shoulders. She felt safe and protected. But she shouldn't be feeling this way. It was wrong. In just over six weeks she was marrying Evan.

Around and around and around the Ferris wheel churned.

Her head spun dizzily. Her stomach clenched. She thought of all the horror stories her mother had told her over the years about carnivals and amusement parks. About people getting hurt or killed on the rides. About safety violations and bribed inspectors and drunken ride operators.

Around and around and around.

The ride seemed to be lasting forever. It wasn't supposed to be this long, was it?

Colors were more vivid. Sounds intensified. Time stretched. What should have been only seconds felt like an hour as the rusted old bucket of bolts creaked and groaned.

She heard the twins laughing in the car ahead of them. They were having fun. This was supposed to be fun. How come she wasn't having fun anymore?

They circled around to the bottom. This was it. The

ride operator had to let them out now. She shifted, getting ready to stand up.

Get out of here and far away from Nick Vinetti.

But the ride did not stop; it whizzed on by the operator and swiftly climbed back into the sky.

Delaney's mouth went dry. Her muscles contracted. She wrapped her fingers around Nick's forearm.

"Stop," she squeaked and laid a hand against his upper thigh.

"Stop?"

"You're a cop. Do something. Stop the ride."

"I can't. We're in midair."

She peeked over at him. He was trying hard not to laugh at her. She dug her fingers deeper into his flesh. Her breathing was fast and raspy. "Get me off this thing."

"You're serious," he said, his body tensing beside her. "You're really scared?"

She nodded.

Nick leaned over the edge of the ride just as they were cresting the top. "Hey," he shouted down at the operator. "We want off."

"Thank you," she whimpered. "Thank you very much."

His pulled her close against him. "It's okay. I'm here. I'm sorry for laughing at you. I didn't realize you were really scared."

Delaney went stock-still as his chest made contact with her breasts and a surge of unwelcome desire ripped through her. His body heat warmed her and the connection of his raw, masculine power overwhelmed her. Even more unsettling, his comforting scent of nutmeg and leather invaded her brain.

She wanted him.

Desperately.

Oh, this was a terrible state of affairs.

Nick tilted her chin up, forced her to look him in the eyes. “Are you okay?”

Emotions she couldn’t deny, but had held in rigid check ever since she’d met him, surged inside her. Stunned, she could barely nod.

“You’re safe,” he murmured. “I promise.”

The thing of it was, she did feel safe. He made her feel safe. Safer than she’d ever felt with anyone. And that was far scarier than the Ferris wheel ride. She was loopy and frightened and she wanted him to kiss her even more than she wanted off this contraption.

He dipped his head toward her and she was already opening her lips. Already eager and ready for him.

He’s going to kiss me, yes, yes, yes.

But he didn’t kiss her.

Just as his lips were about to softly brush against hers, the ride stopped.

And so did Nick.

Leaving her hanging, quite literally, her mouth open and wet and wanting him.

He pulled back, raised his head, removed his arm from her shoulders, and did not look at her.

Her mind spun with sensory overload. What was happening to her? The taste of frustrated anticipation lay bittersweet in her mouth. The lonely sound of the metal bar clanking echoed in her ears. The feel of the empty space between them as he got out of the car stretched long and lonely. The smell of ocean breeze and cotton candy came rushing in to fill the void left by his leaving.

But Nick did not stray far. He turned and reached back for her. Offering his hand to help her step out. His touch was a furnace, his body heat seeping into her skin.

She took his hand and he pulled her gently across the seat toward him.

Delaney felt the material of her pants tug tightly across her bottom. She heard a soft ripping sound, like the tearing of silk. She jerked her head around and saw that the seat of her pants had snagged on a small jagged hole in the aging metal. When she stood up, she felt the air against her bare skin and put a hand behind her to examine the damage.

The tear was much bigger than she'd feared. She gasped at the six-by-six-inch square of nearly severed material that had once been covering her left butt cheek, but was now flapping in the Gulf breeze. Unfortunately, she also happened to be wearing thong underwear.

"Hey, Uncle Nick, that was fun." Nick's twin nephews came walking toward them.

"Please, you've got to help me out here," Delaney whispered urgently to Nick. "Before the boys see me."

"What is it?" He ducked his head.

"Put your hand on my backside and you'll find out."

"An unorthodox request," he said, "but okay." He pressed his large palm flush against her bare flesh. "Uh-oh."

"Uh-oh is an understatement."

"Here, boys." Nick reached into his pocket with his free hand and pulled out several one-dollar bills. "Go get yourselves some cotton candy."

"Mom said we can't have any junk," Jack said. "She says it'll spoil our lunch."

The boys were peering at her curiously. Delaney gave them a shaky smile. "What kind of kids is your sister raising?" she whispered out of the corner of her mouth. "They can't be bribed with cotton candy?"

"Kids that will have all their teeth?"

"Look at them, they've already lost teeth."

"Baby teeth."

"This isn't funny," she said.

"Yes, it is." He grinned.

Her initial impulse was to get upset. Torn pants that had cost her a fortune. A blow to her dignity. Then she realized it *was* funny, and to get huffy was exactly like something her mother would do. It was just a pair of pants. No major catastrophe. As for her dignity, big deal. She was loopy from a cheap amusement park ride. Dignity didn't figure into it.

Delaney giggled. "Any suggestions, Detective? On how to make an exit without everyone"—she waved her hands at the twins—"seeing my . . . er . . . exit?"

"I've got you covered. I'll send the boys on ahead of us and I'll walk with my arm around you, holding up the flap of the loose material with my hand."

"I'm going to need a new pair of pants. I can't meet with the real estate agent and your grandmother looking like this."

"You and Gina are about the same size. I'm sure she's got something at Nana's that you can wear. Maybe not as snazzy as your outfit, but at least you won't be naked."

"Stop teasing," she pleaded. "I can't hold still while I'm laughing."

"Where's your car parked?"

"Along the seawall about a block up."

"Come on, boys, we're walking Delaney to her car. You guys lead the way to the seawall." Nick's arm circled snuggly around her waist and his big palm rested hot and heavy on her butt.

Animal instinct tussled with her sophisticated demeanor. Her pulse pumped. Her skin tingled. Self-control had been drummed into her from birth, but nature was nature. Polished manners and civilized etiquette didn't stand a chance against pure animal magnetism.

Delaney wanted to scurry back to her car as fast as her legs would carry her, but with Nick's leg in the knee brace, he couldn't move fast, and she was left plodding along at his pace.

"Ask him," Jack whispered to Zack.

"No, you ask him."

"You."

"No, you." The boys pushed each other.

"Ask me what?" Nick said.

Jack and Zack cast looks over their shoulders at Delaney and Nick. "Is she your new girlfriend? We hope she's your new girlfriend 'cause we heard Mama telling Nana that if you didn't get a new girlfriend soon, you were going to turn into a grumpy old man and she'd have to go find Amber and kick her skinny butt for breaking your heart."

"My heart's not broken," Nick growled.

"But you are grumpy," Zack pointed out.

"Who's Amber?" Delaney felt Nick's arm tighten around her waist.

"Nobody important."

"Amber was his old wife," Zack said.

"Mama says she ran away on their honeymoon," Jack added.

"With a famous guy from TV," Zack supplied.

Delaney looked at Nick. "What's this?"

Nick rolled his eyes. "I'll never live this down."

"What?"

"Gary Feldstein. My wife left me on our honeymoon for Gary Feldstein. Can we drop it?"

"I'm sorry."

"Hey," he said. "Don't apologize. You weren't the one doing the horizontal tango in our stateroom with Feldstein. You have nothing to be sorry about."

She could tell he was embarrassed. She remembered hearing something on one of the tabloid television shows about the fact that comedian Gary Feldstein's new bride-to-be had met him during her honeymoon with another man. To think that Nick was that man made her heart ache.

"Your sister sounds really protective of you," she said softly.

"So is she your new girlfriend?" Jack asked. "Or not?"

"Delaney's just a friend."

Just a friend.

Why those words would make her feel sad, Delaney had no idea. She couldn't be anything more to Nick than just a friend. She didn't want to be anything more than just a friend because she was engaged to another man. A sweet, kind, generous man who would be tremendously hurt if he could see her now, strolling down the seawall with Nick's arm around her waist, his hand splayed across her bottom.

She didn't know how to deal with this conflict of emotions. Wanting Nick to like her as more than a friend, but very glad that he did not. Guilt over the fact she was here with Nick, instead of with Evan, and not feeling very badly about it.

Honestly, she was a little miffed. Evan had gone off and left her for six weeks just before their wedding. But being miffed made her feel guilty again because Evan was doing such great work in Guatemala. What kind of person was she to be jealous of that?

A small, petty person, that's what she was.

She started to draw away from Nick, eager to remove herself from his proximity, but then she remembered he was the only thing standing between her and revealing her bare butt cheek to the tourists strolling the seawall.

Her stomach was in turmoil, her mind a mess. She wanted to sprint to her car and sit down ASAP, but of course she could not. She had to smile and walk slowly and pretend that she wasn't turned on by the feel of Nick's calloused hand. Meryl Streep couldn't have done an acting job this good. Luckily, years of trying to please her perfectionist mother came in pretty handy at times like these.

After what seemed an eternity, they finally reached her car.

"This you?" Nick stopped beside her silver Acura.

"Yes, yes."

"Boys," he said, "stay here on the seawall while I walk Delaney around to the driver's side." Thankfully, the twins were arguing about Hank Blalock's batting record and not paying them any attention.

"You asked me why I was here," she said. "Do you still want to know?"

"Sure, if you want to tell me."

"Remember when we were driving past and I told you I thought I saw my mother here?"

"Yes."

"She was talking to a patch-eyed woman and I came here to find her to ask her why my mother was talking to her. I found out her name was Paulette Doggett."

"Why don't you just ask your mother?"

"I did. She lied."

"Did you talk to Paulette Doggett?"

"No. It's her day off. But I was wondering, since you're a cop, if you could do a little investigating for me and find out exactly who this woman is before I approach her."

"I could do that," Nick said.

"Thank you. Thank you so much."

"Don't mention it. Apparently this is my day to be chivalrous."

Delaney unlocked her car door while Nick's hand stayed firmly in place. Heart thumping crazily, she turned her head to look at him. "I'm going to sit down now, you can let go."

"Ah," he said. "All good things must come to an end."

Blushing, she sank down into the seat.

"See you later, Rosy." Nick shut the car door and walked back to the boys, who were now seeing who could spit the farthest over the side of the seawall.

She sat there with the engine running, watching Nick corral the kids and feeling an emotion she couldn't describe. She hadn't found the one-eyed woman or her mother's secret reason for visiting the amusement park, but what she had found was a part of herself she never knew existed.

What she didn't know was if she liked what she had discovered about herself.

Or hated it.

Nick brooded through Happy Meals at McDonald's with his nephews. His maneuverings at the amusement park had backfired spectacularly.

When he'd seen Delaney standing in the midway, looking out of place and a little forlorn, he'd made up his mind to put his plan into action. He'd flirted with her and crowded her personal space. He'd coaxed her onto the Ferris wheel ride. The torn pants had been an added bonus. He'd felt her tension, knew he'd unsettled her.

But she'd unsettled him just as much.

Using sex appeal to chase her off definitely had its drawbacks. If this was going to work, he would have to keep his mind on his objective—talking Nana out of selling the family home, while at the same time keeping his mind off this powerful attraction to Delaney.

Nick plowed a hand through his hair. How had he gotten himself into this ugly kettle of sharks? He wanted a woman he could not have.

His sister, Gina, would call it fate.

Nana would call it the whammy.

But Nick didn't believe in all that bologna. Not anymore.

And yet, in a matter of days, Delaney Cartwright had burrowed deep under his skin and he couldn't figure out why. Why her? Why now? Why did he think she was so special? Once upon a time, he'd thought Amber was special too.

Maybe it's you. Maybe subconsciously you're looking to turn the tables and get even with fate by falling for someone who's already spoken for.

Nick grimaced. He hated to think that.

And yet, here he was, pining for a woman with a huge engagement ring on her finger.

Aw, crap. The truth of it was, he was too screwed up for this. Even if Delaney wasn't engaged—which she was—he had a lot of baggage he needed to unload before jumping into another relationship.

The knee, for one thing.

His grandfather's death, for another.

Delaney's watch did stop the minute that you met her.

Just like the clock on the wall at the party stopped when Nana and Grampa Leo met.

Yes, but that wasn't the first time he'd ever met her. If it really was the whammy, wouldn't her watch have stopped when she threw the tarp over his head?

He didn't have the patience for this whammy nonsense.

"Uncle Nick, the Ching Bada in my Happy Meal broke," Zack said, handing him the pieces of a cheap plastic toy.

Nick didn't even know what the hell a Ching Bada was, but from the looks of it, the thing was some kind of weird cartoon character on wheels.

Nick examined the shattered pieces. "Sorry, buddy, but I don't think I can fix this."

Zack's lip pouched out sorrowfully. "But I want it."

"I know, but sometimes we can't have what we want."

Strange thing, the forlorn expression on his nephew's face was exactly how he was feeling about Delaney. He wanted her, but he couldn't have her. The situation was broken beyond his ability to fix it.

One thing was for certain. Time wasn't on his side. He had to get rid of Delaney and get rid of her fast, before he did something totally stupid. Like fall in love with her.

In order to chase her away, he was going to have to turn up the heat and make sure he checked his heart at the door. He knew of only one way to accomplish his goal. Tackle getting rid of Delaney like she was an assignment. Use the three-pronged approach he'd developed. It had never failed to keep his professionalism in place undercover and his emotions tucked deeply away.

Chapter 10

For the rest of the week, Nick and his family worked to move Nana in with Trudie. They put the bulk of her things in storage, leaving only a bare minimum of furniture—at Delaney's advice—in the house for the staging. Once they had her possessions relocated, they spent the weekend cleaning the place from top to bottom.

By Monday morning, everyone else had gone home. Nana was ensconced at Trudie's, and Nick was alone at the house. He would be living there during the renovations. It felt hollow and sad with everything gone and the sound of his footsteps bouncing off the vacant walls.

Nana kept insisting this was a new chapter in her life, but to Nick, it felt like an epilogue. As he stared around the bare rooms, a moody thrust of emotions pushed against his throat. The book of his grandmother's life was coming to a close, and he couldn't do anything about it. He hated feeling powerless.

This house—and his grandparents' love—had been the sanctuary that had saved him after his mother died. For the house to go out of the family made him feel as if he were losing both his mom and his grandfather all over again.

Being here alone strengthened his determination to undermine the house renovation process, no matter what it took. With the family dispersed and Delaney on her way over for their first real day of tackling the repairs, Nick paced the kitchen, rehearsing what he'd planned. The initial phase of "Operation: House Stager Ouster, Tactic #1—Know Thy Enemy" was now in play.

Delaney appeared on the doorstep at eight A.M. dressed in a sleeveless floral V-neck tee, flip-flops, and clam-digger-style blue jeans. Her hair was pulled back in a care-free ponytail that swished about her shoulders whenever she moved. She had a sack of bagels and two cups of Starbucks coffee in her hands. The smile on her face wrapped him like an unexpected hug.

"Good morning." She beamed. "I brought breakfast. We need fuel to start the day."

Ah, clearly she was a morning person. Nick made a mental note. You never could tell what information would prove useful. "Come on in."

He held the screen door open and let her in through the mudroom, then led the way into the kitchen. He'd raised all the windows to let in the Gulf breeze—the house had never been equipped with air-conditioning—and while it was cool now, by noon the temperature promised to be in the high eighties.

"It's just me and you today?"

"Yep." *And you have no clue what you're in for.* "No one else can afford any more time off from their jobs. We're flying solo until the weekend." He held out his arms and said mischievously, "I'm your crew. Do with me what you will."

She set the bagels on the kitchen counter. "It looks so empty," she said. The word "empty" echoed in the room, underscoring her point. "It makes me feel a little sad."

Nick nodded. *Yeah, try having it be your grandmother's house and see how that feels.*

"I figured you for straight black." She held out a grande cup of coffee to him. "No fancy blend."

"You pegged me." He eyed her. "Let me guess. You're a low-fat hazelnut latte with artificial sweetener."

She canted her head. "I guess stereotypes are stereotypes for a reason."

Reaching out to take the coffee from her, their fingers touched briefly against the cup and he almost fumbled it. Nick was very aware of how close they were standing, but he wanted to move even closer. *Careful. Not too soon. That's Tactic #2. We're not there yet.*

"Bagel?"

"What kind?"

"Plain, cinnamon-raisin, and poppy seed. Not knowing what you like, I got all three."

"Plain."

She took a bagel from the sack. "Cream cheese?"

"Why not?"

She slathered the bagel with cream cheese and then held it out to him. Rather than taking it, Nick boldly leaned over and took a bite of it right out of her hand.

Okay, so he was blurring the edges between Tactic #1 and Tactic #2. It was an intimate gesture calculated to throw her off balance, but as his head went down and Nick got a whiff of her sweet, gentle-smelling cologne, he was the one thrown off.

"You've got cream cheese on your chin," she said as calmly as if men ate from her hand every day of the week.

Nick gulped. Where had his blushing Rosy gone?

She reached over with her thumb, then dabbed his chin with a Starbucks napkin. "There."

Then Delaney raised the bagel to her mouth and nibbled off a chunk right where he'd bitten into it.

She did it with such finesse he had to wonder if she possessed a few undercover tactics of her own. Blood pooled low in his abdomen. He stood there feeling awkward and unsure of himself, when just seconds before he'd been the one trying to unsettle her. How had she managed to turn the tables on him so swiftly? It was almost as if she knew what he was up to and was secretly paying him back.

She glanced down and he followed her gaze to see her staring at his knee. "Exactly how did you injure it?"

He shrugged. He didn't like talking about it. "I'd rather not say. It's sort of embarrassing."

"Hmm, sounds intriguing."

"Why, Rose, what in the hell are you thinking? Are you imagining me in a compromising position?" he teased. "Say, busting my knee falling from a chandelier during adventuresome sex?"

"No, I wasn't."

Ah, ah, she couldn't hide it. He saw a pink tinge creeping over her cheeks. He knew it. She wasn't as bold as she was pretending.

"Sorry, sweetheart. You can't lie. Your rosy red cheeks give you away."

"How did you hurt your knee?" she badgered, and he could tell she was determined not to let him get the best of her. He admired that. He made her nervous, but she wasn't going to let him steamroll her.

"A few months ago someone was assaulting transvestites in south Houston."

"Don't tell me you were having kinky sexcapades with a transvestite?" she teased.

He lifted his eyebrows and cocked his most seductive grin her way. "Now, Rosy, that's just wrong."

She acted immune—setting down the unfinished bagel, folding her arms over her chest, assessing him mildly. But she didn't fool him one bit. Nick saw the way her breath quickened, how the pulse at the hollow of her throat jumped.

"I've got it." She snapped her fingers. "You were assigned to dress as a woman, weren't you?"

"How did you know?"

"What else could make a tough guy like you blush?"

"I'm not blushing," he denied.

"Yes, you are."

"My face is turning red because whenever I think about what happened, I get pissed off all over again."

"Have a temper, do you?"

He snorted. "My captain gave me the assignment as punishment for not following orders on another case. He hates it when I don't follow orders and still end up making a good clean collar."

"Oh, you're one of those kinds of cops." She picked up her coffee and peered at him over the rim of the cup.

"What kind of cop?"

"The maverick-loose-cannon-Mel-Gibson-*Lethal-Weapon* kind of cop."

"More like Mel in *Lethal Weapon 3* and *4*. I'm not suicidal. I just don't like following orders when they're ill-conceived and could get me or my partner or an innocent bystander killed. And the dress the captain picked out for me to wear, good God, it looked like something from *Boogie Nights*. Cheap, polyester, and sequinned."

"So what happened?" She leaned in, obviously intrigued. Nick had to admit her interest flattered his ego.

"It's midnight. In a seedy part of Houston. Dive bars and strip joints and crack houses." He stopped and looked at her. "You have no idea what that part of town looks like, do you?"

"No," she confessed. "I'm from River Oaks."

"Somehow I'd guessed. You're one of *those* Cartwrights. Richer than God."

"Yes," Delaney admitted. "But let's not get sidetracked by the fact that I'm an oil heiress. About your story. You're in an unsavory section of the city late at night. Now what?" She took another sip of coffee.

"Don't you dare laugh."

She held up two fingers. "Scout's honor."

"You were a Girl Scout?"

"No."

"So your vow not to laugh has no oath to back it up."

The corners of her lips twitched and her eyes twinkled. "Nope. You're just going to have to trust me."

"Okay, here goes. I'm wearing gold lamé spandex, four-inch stilettos, and panty hose. By the way, how in the hell do you women walk around in those damn things? Panty hose are the most god-awful torture device ever invented. The Geneva Convention should have weighed in on those puppies."

"Next time try a bronzer on your legs instead."

"Trust me, there ain't gonna be a next time."

She laughed.

"It wasn't funny. And remember, you promised not to laugh."

"Sorry." She tried to school her features, but couldn't completely dampen her smile. "But I would have given anything to see you in that outfit."

"Trust me, it was ugly. My partner and I are strolling

down the street looking like Jack Lemmon and Tony Curtis from *Some Like It Hot* and this guy jumps out of the alley, grabs my partner, puts a knife to his throat, and starts dragging him back down the alley."

Delaney sucked in her breath, splayed hand across her heart, and looked sincerely concerned. "Oh, my goodness."

"It was a little hairier than oh-my-goodness," he said. "I went after the guy, but he threatened to stab my partner in the throat if I didn't step off."

"What did you do?"

"I threw my purse at the guy's head. My partner took that opportunity to bite the guy's wrist. The perp lost his grip on my partner, realized he was in trouble, dropped the knife, and took off down the alley. Stupid me, I just had to go after him. Word to the wise, don't sprint down a dark alley, in a seedy part of town, wearing four-inch stilettos."

Delaney hissed in her breath through clenched teeth. "Ouch. I can see where this is headed."

"Believe me, ouch doesn't begin to describe the words that came out of my mouth. The guy tried to scale a fence. I jumped to grab for him and came down hard on my right leg. My heel caught on some garbage and slipped out from under me. I had my hands locked around the perp's ankle when my knee gave way. I heard this horrible crackling sound like an elephant stomping on a big bag of pork rinds. To make matters worse, I pulled the punk down on top of me. What damage the fall hadn't done, the weight of a two-hundred-pound meth-head finished off. I tore all the ligaments and fractured my kneecap."

Delaney's face paled and she made a low noise of sympathy.

"So here I am in the emergency room, gold lamé skirt hiked up to my waist, panty hose twisted around my privates, howling like a werewolf at the moon."

She reached out a hand and touched his arm. "I'm sorry that happened to you."

"Hey, don't be sorry. It wasn't your fault." He didn't want to admit it, but he liked the way her hand felt against his skin. "Your turn."

"My turn for what?"

"Confession time. I tell you my most embarrassing moment, and you have to tell me yours." He'd been blabbing away, trying to gain her confidence so she'd confide in him, but so far he hadn't learned anything personal about her. If Operation: House Stage Ouster was going to work, he had to get her to talk about herself so he could figure out her Achilles' heel.

"You were present for my most embarrassing moment."

"Ah, yes, the tarp incident. That's the most humiliating thing that's ever happened to you?"

"I don't usually put myself in embarrassing situations."

"Tell me, what inspired you to dress in a raincoat and bustier to bag your fiancé and drag him off for an afternoon of hot sex?"

"Truthfully, I didn't really want to do it."

"No? Then why did you?"

"It was my friends' idea."

"I'm going to need a little more to go on. Fair's fair. I told you about the panty hose."

"It's embarrassing."

"More embarrassing than my story?"

"You're going to make me go through with this, aren't you?"

"Absolutely. We can't have the ledger go unbalanced."

"Okay, here goes." She inhaled. "I was telling my friends that my fiancé and I had entered a celibacy pack before our wedding. We haven't had sex in six months and I was feeling—"

"Horny."

She blushed. "Well, yes."

"What kind of red-blooded American male agrees to a celibacy pact?" Nick raked his eyes over Delaney. "Especially with a woman like you?"

"It was my fiancé's idea. Anyway, my friends came up with the scenario to kidnap him from his job for an afternoon of hot sex. To prove to myself I wasn't a stick in the mud, I decided to go through with it."

"Are you sure your fiancé isn't gay?" Nick cocked an eyebrow.

"He's not gay."

"Asexual then?"

"Maybe," she admitted. She wouldn't look at him.

"Do you love the guy?" Nick had to ask.

"I've known him since I was a child."

"That's not what I asked."

"I love him," she whispered. "But I'm afraid the love I feel for him is not the right kind of love. That's what I was trying to find out with the whole raincoat and bustier thing."

"If you don't love him that way, then for God's sake, do the poor schlub a favor and don't marry him," Nick said sharply.

"You don't understand. It's very complicated. My mother, she's a stickler for all that social registry stuff. Wants to make sure I marry the right kind of man."

"Meaning rich and well bred."

"Yes."

"What century are you living in?"

"You don't know what it's like. Coming from high society."

"Sounds like a pain in the ass to me."

She laughed. "It is."

"So you thought you were bagging your boyfriend and instead you bagged me. You must have felt like you were angling for whitefish and came up with a carp instead."

"I was so nervous about the whole thing that I threw the tarp over the first guy who came out the door. It never even entered my head that you weren't Evan."

He felt as if he'd been kicked squarely in the bread basket. His breath left his body in one long whoosh. "Evan? Your fiancé is Dr. Evan Van Zandt?"

Her eyes widened in surprise. "How did you know?"

Nick groaned. Of all the freakin' luck. His gut fisted and his pulse knocked for no good reason.

"What is it? What's wrong?"

"Trust me to get myself in this kind of situation," he muttered under his breath.

"What are you talking about?"

He tapped his knee. "Evan? Your fiancé. He's my doctor."

Nick's revelation rattled Delaney to her core. Evan was his surgeon?

"We better get to work," she said, ignoring the feelings churning inside her. She couldn't meet his eyes. She was still trying to deal with the implications of what he'd told her. Nick knew Evan. Evan had treated Nick. "Did you get to the plumbing repairs yet? Are we ready to move on to putting down the kitchen tile?"

"I finished the plumbing," he said. "Just waiting for you

to help me pull up the old linoleum; the new tile is stacked up on the porch, ready to go."

Delaney worried her bottom lip with her teeth. Being so close to him was unsettling. "Maybe we could skip to the painting today instead. You can do one room, I can do another."

"Wouldn't it be more effective if we worked together?" he asked, sizing her up with one long, cool stare. "And I thought you wanted the kitchen finished first, since it requires the most work."

She cleared her throat. "Um, I'm thinking it's better if we're not in the same room."

"What's the matter, Rosy? Scared you can't keep your hands off me?" he taunted her. "Scared Evan will find out we were in a room alone together? Shh, I won't tell if you won't tell."

"There's nothing to tell," she denied stridently.

"No?" He stepped closer, crowding her space, chasing all the air from her lungs.

"Absolutely not," she bristled.

"You're going to deny there's chemistry going on here." His gaze nailed her to the spot.

"I will not jeopardize my relationship with a man I've known for twenty-five years over a lusty affair."

"Whoa." He held up both palms. "You're moving a little fast for me. Who said anything about an affair? What makes you think I'm the kind of guy who would have an affair with an engaged woman? I'm outraged."

"You're teasing me?" She eyed him.

"I'm testing you."

She didn't know what to make of that. "I don't trust you."

He shrugged. "So quit."

"What?" Her eyes narrowed. "You want me to quit, don't you? That's what this is all about. That's why you've been coming on so strong."

He didn't say anything, his silence confirming her suspicions. He didn't want Lucia to sell the house so he was coming on to her, hoping to make her leave.

"I'm not quitting." She hardened her jaw.

"Fine by me."

"I've got work to do." Drawing herself up to her full height, she went over to the corner, picked up a putty knife, and started tackling the aged linoleum.

Nick came up behind her. "Why did you offer to wait to get paid until after the house sells? That doesn't sound like good business to me."

She didn't answer him for the longest moment. She was trying to decide if he even deserved an answer. "Because I needed this job as much as your grandmother needed it done."

"You?" He made a dismissive noise. "You're an oil heiress. You're engaged to a prominent doctor. You're stunningly beautiful. Why would you need a job?"

"It's complicated." Her face was burning red again as she felt the telltale flush creep up her neck. No matter how hard she tried to suppress it, he seemed to have a magical ability to make her blush.

"I've got two good ears."

She ignored him. She'd already talked too much, gave him too much ammunition to use against her. Darn her need to be liked. She wished she didn't care what he thought about her, but she did. Disgruntled with herself, she grabbed a chunk of linoleum and yanked it up from the subflooring.

"You blush every time I give you a compliment. Why is

that?" He came over to lean one shoulder against the wall in front of her.

"You're in my way."

"I know that."

She raised her head and glared at him point-blank. "I realize you're a cop and interrogating people just comes naturally to you, but I'd appreciate it if you dropped this whole line of questioning and helped me get this old flooring up."

He grabbed a piece of linoleum from the opposite end of the kitchen and pulled up a long hunk of it. He opened the back door, chucked the brittle strip out onto the back lawn, and then started again. In half an hour, they met in the middle of the room, the floor sticky and raw from the glue of the old linoleum.

They looked at each other, but neither of them spoke. Two people standing in the middle of a vacant room, uncertain what to make of each other.

"I was unattractive as a child," she said, not knowing why she was telling him this. "The proverbial ugly duckling."

Nick tilted his head and studied her. "Well, I'd say you've blossomed into a hellaciously beautiful swan."

"No, I haven't."

"You want me to haul you over in front of a mirror and prove to you otherwise?"

"What you're seeing isn't real, Nick. It's all packaging."

"What are you talking about? Don't you notice the heads swiveling and the tongues drooling when you walk down the street?"

"Nose job." She touched her nose with her fingertips. "Until I was fourteen I resembled the Wicked Witch from *The Wizard of Oz*."

"No way."

She put a hand to her waist. "Or you could say I looked like the Pillsbury Doughboy's blind date. And then there were the teeth." She raised her upper lip, revealing her teeth that she knew were perfectly straight and dazzlingly white. Five grand worth of veneers could do that for you. "I could have given Bugs Bunny a run for his money, except I stuttered like Porky Pig. Oh"—she snapped her fingers—"I almost forgot the Coke-bottle glasses."

"I'm sure you're exaggerating. Women have a tendency to denigrate their looks."

"It's true. Just ask my mother. She'll be the first to tell you I was a total train wreck." Under her breath she mumbled, "Lord knows she's told me often enough."

"I think I get it," he said.

"Get what?"

"Why you lowballed your bid on my grandmother's house."

"Really?"

"Lack of self-confidence," he said.

"Partially," Delaney conceded.

"And you lack self-confidence because your mother never believed in you until you had your nose done, lost weight, underwent LASIK surgery, got braces, and stopped stuttering."

Her eyes widened. "How did you know?"

"Why else would you be so hard on yourself?" His voice was kind, his eyes kinder still. "Come on, Delaney, it's way past time to stop beating yourself up for your sister's death. You didn't kill her. You weren't responsible. Let go of the blame."

Dammit, just when he was making it easy for her to resist him, he turned sweet. She couldn't bear the understanding expression on his face. It was too much. She could handle feelings of lust for him. Lust was just lust, but this feeling—this was dangerous stuff.

"I've just remembered something," she said, feeling bad about lying but knowing she had to get out of here before something really dangerous happened.

"Yeah?"

"I've got an appointment to give a bid on a house in west Houston at ten. With the traffic, I'll be lucky to make it. Sorry to bail on you like this, but we made a good start."

"You've been here less than an hour," he said.

"I know, I'm sorry." The way he was looking at her was making things worse. "I gotta go."

"See you tomorrow?"

"Uh-huh." She forced a smile, grabbed her purse, and ran from the house while she still had the strength of will to tear herself away.

Chapter 11

Okay, phase one of Operation: House Stage Ouster had been a rousing success. Nick had gotten Delaney to reveal her doubts and fears and insecurities. He knew where her vulnerabilities lay, knew just how to wound her. Problem was, he didn't want to wound her. In fact, he felt an overwhelming urge to protect her. From her mother, from her fiancé, from the entire world.

Shit. Shit, shit, shit.

Tender feelings were not part of the plan.

Last night, unable to sleep, he'd tiled the entire kitchen by himself in spite of the pain in his knee. This morning, he was tired and achy and ready to abandon his plans to chase her off. Face facts, he wanted her around. And that thought was scary as hell.

"Come on," he muttered. "You can't let your feelings for her derail your own needs. She's marrying someone else. It's not like you have a chance with her. Hell, you don't want a chance with her. You're through with all that romantic mumbo jumbo."

Oh, yeah?

"Yeah."

Then prove it, Vinetti. Tactic #2—Undermine Your Enemy. Start it today.

Right. He could do this.

To rev himself up, he thought of his toughest undercover assignments. If he could maneuver criminals and thugs and the underworld, he could certainly handle one high-bred young house stager.

What to do? How best to undermine her without really hurting her feelings?

He plotted. He schemed. He connived and came up with a kind yet devious plan. He would goad her into causing her own demise.

Nick took a trip to the souvenir shops on Seawall Boulevard and after striking out in several stores, finally found what he was looking for. Satisfied with his purchase, he had it gift wrapped. Then he hurried back to Nana's and found Delaney standing on the back porch, looking sumptuous in a red tank top and a blue-jean skirt, and all the underhanded subterfuge just flew right out of his head.

Delaney had given herself a good talking to after what had happened the previous day, and convinced herself she could indeed work around Nick Vinetti without succumbing to this charms. Donning her mental armor, she arrived at Lucia's house with a professional smile plastered on her face.

She was pleasantly surprised to find that Nick had tiled the kitchen and done a superb job at it too. The man was skilled with his hands, she'd give him that. She bragged on him, but not too enthusiastically. She didn't want to give him any ideas. Didn't want any repeat of yesterday's familiarity. Happy to have another thing ticked off her to-do list and encouraged by the progress they were making, Delaney decided to accelerate her plans. Painting was next on the agenda, and she ambitiously aimed to get two bedrooms done that day.

An hour and a half later, they were deeply into painting the bedroom Lucia had used as a library. They'd already completed the first coat on three walls and were working on the final one.

She and Nick stood next to each other, not speaking, just painting. Surprisingly, in their work, the silence felt uncomplicated and easy.

Then Delaney went and spoiled the peace by noticing they were painting in tandem—starting high and then pulling downward in slow, easy strokes. Her stomach dipped at the realization they were operating in total sync.

The rhythm was hypnotic. Sexual. Almost like foreplay.

Dip, brush, sweep, dip, brush, sweep.

Disconcerted, Delaney broke the pattern. She stopped painting and lifted the tip of her brush from the wall. She waited—for what she could not say—hand hovering, paint dripping. Splat. Splat. Splat. Onto the plastic drop cloth.

Nick stopped painting too and looked over at her, his bold stare caressing her intimately.

The sharp crackling of erotic current running between them raised the hairs on Delaney's arms. She shifted her gaze to the wall, pretending to assess the paint job.

"It looks good," he murmured, but he was not studying the wall. She could feel the heat of his gaze on her face. He was looking at her. "Real good."

His words echoed in the empty room.

Real good.

Closing her eyes, she willed herself not to shiver, then quickly opened them again. "Uh-huh."

He reached out and took the paintbrush from her, his

fingertips barely grazing her skin, and then balanced her brush, along with his, over the top of the paint can.

"You thirsty?" he asked.

She nodded and noticed perspiration had plastered his cotton muscle shirt against his toned chest. She was sweating too, but it wasn't from the summer heat. She could smell the salt air blowing in on the cool breeze. Hear the sounds of seagulls in the distance, calling to one another above the neighborhood noises. A car chugging up the street, children playing tag in the alley, a dog barking in the yard next door.

He disappeared for a minute and then came back with two ice-cold beers. He twisted off the tops, tossed them onto the drop cloth, and walked back across the room. His limp was barely noticeable. He handed her one of the longneck bottles.

It was cold and damp in her hand, and Delaney realized she'd never drunk beer directly from the bottle, only in an iced mug, and even then, only twice. Beer, Honey was fond of saying, was a middle-class beverage and best left for the middle class.

Without ever taking his eyes off her, Nick tilted his head and took a long swallow from his bottle.

Her gaze tracked from his lips to his throat. She watched his Adam's apple work and this time she did shiver.

Anxiously, she shifted her attention away from him, looking for something else to focus on. She surveyed the paint job.

It looked fresh and white and...

Bland.

All the personality of Lucia's house was being whitewashed.

"What's the matter?" Nick asked, coming up behind her. He was standing so close she could feel his body heat.

"You were right." She crossed her arms over her chest.

"In what way?"

"The room looks so generic. Like it could be in any house in America."

"I thought that was the point. It's what you said would help the house sell better."

"It is."

"But you want more."

"I want the house to sell for Lucia."

"Is that the real reason?" he asked. "Or are you just more comfortable playing it safe?"

She looked at him. There was challenge in his eyes.

"We could take the paint back," he continued. "Get another color. You could give your creativity full rein and not worry about what some upscale yuppie buyer wants in a vacation home. You could really do this house justice if you just allowed yourself to shake things up."

He was tempting her, egging her on, but the truth was she wanted to do it. Wanted to use Lucia's house as a canvas to create a bit of magic.

"We could do a Tuscan theme," Nick suggested. "Reflect Nana's heritage."

"But the research I've done tells me..."

"Screw research." He took her by the shoulders and turned her around to face him. He placed his hand over her heart. It thumped erratically. He was the devil, pure and simple.

"What does your heart tell you?" he whispered.

"I can't be selfish about this."

"The right person will find the house charming."

"But your grandmother needs to sell the house as soon as possible."

"Wouldn't it be better if the house went to someone who could love it the way my grandparents did? Someone who could appreciate all the love that went into it?"

It sounded so good. She wanted to believe it was possible. She wanted to let go. To take a chance. But she was also afraid.

"Hang on," he said. "I've got something I want to give you. I was going to give it to you later, after you finished the house, but I think it might be better for you to have it now."

"You bought me a gift?"

He pointed a finger at her. "I'll be right back."

Puzzled, Delaney watched him leave the room. She heard the back door creak open and then slam closed again a few minutes later.

Nick was back. Holding a pretty pink box wrapped with red ribbon.

He'd bought her a present. She was touched.

"Here. Maybe this will help you decide."

She untied the ribbon, lifted the lid. There, nestled in tissue paper, she saw his hula doll. Stunned, she raised her head and met his gaze. "Oh, Nick, I can't accept this. Your mother gave you Lalule to help you deal with your grief."

"It's not Lalule," he said. "I bought you your own hula doll. She's to remind you that when life gets too bland and predictable, you need to shake things up."

Delaney took the hula doll out of the box and gently thumbed her hips. The doll shook and shimmied.

Shake it up.

She looked at the white walls.

Shake it up.

She thought about what she wanted, but it was hard trying to figure out exactly what she did want. She'd spent so many years pleasing everyone else. Delaney had forgotten how to express her own desires.

Shake it up.

She looked at Nick and put the doll back in the box. She wasn't convinced shaking things up was the smart way to go. "Thank you. I'll treasure this."

"So what's your decision?" he asked. "Do we keep on painting white? Or do we make another trip to Lowe's and exchange the paint for something exciting?"

"I want to help your grandmother sell her house."

"Forget about that for a moment. If you could do anything with this house, what would you do?"

"I'd go for it. I'd make this place special. I'd make magic."

"Look out, Lowe's, here we come." He laughed and the sound warmed her from the inside out. Nick reached over, took the box from her hand, and then walked over to set it on the windowsill along with his beer.

He turned back to her, grinning his cocky grin, eyes glistening with the same out-of-control impulses that were simmering through her blood. He took a step closer. She did not move away.

Nick took another step and then another.

Her heart pounded.

He reached out a hand.

She stopped breathing.

His thumb came down to rub the tip of her nose. "Smudge of paint," he explained.

She exhaled heavily.

"If we were in a romantic movie," Nick said, "this would be the point where I'd kiss you."

"But this isn't a movie."

Their gazes fused.

"No."

"And you're not going to kiss me."

He leaned forward until his lips were almost touching hers. "No."

"That's very good," she said, "because I'm engaged to be married."

"I know. I've seen the rock. It's big enough to choke a two-headed Clydesdale."

She smiled. "It is rather ostentatious, isn't it?"

"From a cop's point of view, it's dangerous. You might as well wear a neon sign that says, 'Rob me.' You're just asking to have your finger cut off for that thing." He reached over and picked up her left hand. "And I'd sure as hell hate to see any harm come to that hand. Whenever you're in an unsafe area you should turn your ring around to the palm side and close your fingers around it."

He turned the ring to demonstrate. Closed his hand over hers. Over her engagement ring. His touch shook her. Fully. Completely. Upside down and inside out.

"Chopped-off fingers are not romantic," she said. "It isn't even remotely like something Tom Hanks would say to Meg Ryan. You are not making my knees weak."

"Good," he murmured and looked her straight in the eyes. "Because mine are weak enough for the both of us."

Now *that* was romantic.

"You *do* want to kiss me," she said. "Admit it."

"Woman," he answered softly, "you have absolutely no idea how much."

A thrill blitzed down her spine. His warm breath tickled her skin. He smelled so good Delaney could scarcely remember her own name, much less Evan's.

You can't let Nick kiss you. You mustn't let him kiss you. This cannot happen.

She raised her hands and clutched them together in front of her chest, building a barrier between them. It was weak, but it was all she could come up with.

"Please...," she whispered, meaning to add "don't," but her throat was so tight and his eyes were so dark and she was caught up in the strange magic surging between them.

He reached for her hand again and he turned the ring back where it belonged. Back where they could both see that she was spoken for and could not forget it.

"If you didn't have the ring on your finger..." His eyes flashed a promise of the wonderful things that could happen if she were unattached.

"But I do."

He nodded, took a deep breath. "Yeah."

"It's an engagement ring," she said, not really knowing why she said it. "Not a wedding ring. Not yet."

"Marriage is supposed to be for a lifetime," Nick said. "Like with Grampa and Nana. The vows don't read, 'Until some guy you like better comes along.' "

Sympathy tugged her heart. He was thinking about his ex-wife. What was her name? Oh, yes. Amber. She could tell by the way he screwed his mouth up tightly, absent-mindedly rubbed his injured knee, and stared off into the distance. Delaney wanted to make things better for him. She wanted to take away his pain.

It was the only excuse she could come up with for what happened next.

She was acutely aware of a very important line being crossed, but she couldn't seem to stop herself from crossing it. The question was, how far across that taboo line was she willing to go?

Delaney touched Nick's shoulder.

He looked at her and their eyes wed.

She felt everything all at once.

It was like an earthquake rocking her chest. Lust and chemistry. Longing and yearning. Guilt and loneliness. Hunger and sadness and hope. It fell in on her, heavy and warm and too much, too soon.

What had she gotten herself into?

His gaze was hot. Lightning that lingered.

The look made her lips tingle.

Neither of them moved.

He cupped his palm under her chin and tilted his head, his eyes never leaving hers.

She stiffened. Wanting him to kiss her, but scared, scared, scared of where it might lead.

He dropped his hand, backed up.

No, something inside her whimpered.

Compelled by a force she couldn't understand or explain, Delaney stepped forward. She just knew that she had to kiss him or die, but it wasn't in her nature to act so boldly. She was accustomed to finding roundabout ways to meet her needs. She couldn't bring herself to initiate the kiss, but she could make him kiss her.

Wantonly, Delaney slipped her fingers through the belt loops of his blue jeans and held on tight.

He arched his eyebrows, making sure he understood what she wanted.

She swallowed, moistened her lips. Nodded.

His eyes lit up and a smile tipped his mouth. It was like watching a drawbridge drop. And behind the door of the fortress, hidden beneath the tough-guy image, Delaney spied a center of tenderness she'd never imagined.

"Aw, Rosy," he murmured and lowered his head.

Her pulse danced, light as the sunshine dappling the freshly painted walls.

The kiss was quieter than she thought it would be, languid and deep, a slow opportunity to taste and smell and feel. A chance to settle, by layers, into a dreamy ease. The teasing of his tongue against hers brought a helpless response so acute, she felt faint, like she was falling.

Delaney locked her fingers in his hair and made him kiss her harder, deeper and harder still.

The taste of him!

Like returning home from a long, arduous journey. Recognizing every part of him with her lips and hands and body and yet at the same time he felt fabulously foreign—and strangely familiar.

While the world shrank down into the minute width of mouths, she opened herself up to possibilities as yet undreamed. She was completely disarmed. With any other man the quick intimacy and astonishing sensuality would have appalled her, but with Nick everything was different.

Her lips shuddered against his mouth and her body molded to his. His hands roved over her back and she strained into him, her breasts crushed against his chest. Instantly, she experienced a sense of peace and safety. In Nick's arms, she felt special.

And that very sensation scared her.

In her need to put some magic in her life, was she grasping at straws? Was she mistakenly reading something into this kiss that wasn't really there? Was she confusing passion for something substantial? How could she begin to compare the history, companionship, and compatibility she shared with Evan to this explosive, red-hot rocket of sensation with a man she'd only known for a little over a week?

Delaney dithered, caught between doubt and desire.

She did not like this push-pull of emotions. For years, she'd been living life on autopilot, melding with her mother's wishes, putting on a pleasant face, getting through life by putting things in soft focus. She did what felt safe.

But the power of Nick's kiss drove home the fact that she'd done so at the price of her vitality and aliveness. That's what scared her most. This arousal of aspects of herself she'd always chosen to ignore.

"I'm sorry, I can't do it. I wanted you so badly I thought I could ignore my conscience, but I can't." She splayed a hand against his chest and pushed him away.

"Because of your fiancé," he said, fingering her engagement ring again. "That you love. But not in the right way."

She nodded.

"Leave him."

"You're talking crazy. We don't even know each other."

"Forget about me. Leave him for your sake. For his sake. You can't marry this guy if you want me that badly."

Panicked, Delaney pressed a hand to her forehead, still tingly from where his lips had branded her. It was true, but it was not that simple. "I've been dating Evan since I was sixteen. We were high school sweethearts. I've never been with anyone else but him. You're just..."

"Just what?" Nick pulled back, his eyes glinting darkly in the light. "Exactly what am I to you, Delaney?"

"Just something to get out of my system."

There was no mistaking the hurt on Nick's face. Without another word, he turned and walked away.

"I've done a terrible, terrible thing," Delaney told Tish and Jillian and Rachael early the next morning as they struck the warrior pose on side-by-side yoga mats at a chic, women-only gym in downtown Houston.

"You?" Tish, who was positioned on Delaney's left, tipped her body into perfect alignment. "What did you do? Eat dessert with your salad fork at your mother's latest dinner party?"

"I'm serious, Tish."

The teasing expression on her friend's face changed. "What's wrong?"

"There's a guy."

"A guy?" Jillian said from Delaney's right.

"What did she say?" asked Rachael, who was on the other side of Jillian. She was having trouble hearing over the Eastern-flavored music.

"She met a guy," Jillian relayed.

"But she already has a guy. She's engaged." Rachael broke her form to lean around Jillian and glare at Delaney. "What are you thinking?"

"I know." Delaney's legs wobbled as she struggled to hold her pose. Trust Rachael to be the voice of her conscience. "I'm a horrible, horrible person."

"You're not horrible," Tish said. "You're human."

"Trust me. I'm horrible. You haven't heard the worst of it," Delaney said.

"What's the worst of it?" Jillian dared.

"It gets worse?" Rachael groaned.

"I kissed him. No, he kissed me. No, we kissed each other. Oh, I don't know what happened. I'm so confused." Delaney pushed away a stray strand of hair that had fallen out of her ponytail and into her face.

All three of her friends lost their poses as they turned to stare at her. Delaney looked straight ahead, keeping up the pose, keeping up appearances.

"What?" Rachael gasped.

"Naughty girl," Tish said.

"I didn't believe you had it in you." Jillian shook her head. "Way to go."

"Don't encourage her," Rachael snapped. "This is serious. Delaney has broken her vow to Evan."

"Lighten up, Rach. They're not married yet," Jillian said. "She just had to get it out of her system."

"That's exactly right. That's what I told Nick." Delaney nodded.

"Evan's the only guy she's ever been with," Jillian said. "Cut her a break. It was just a little kiss, right, Del?"

Just a little kiss? That was like calling the Grand Canyon a little crack in the ground.

"I feel terrible about it," Delaney said. But not so terrible that she could wish it never happened.

"Up dog," the yoga instructor called out as the music changed tempo, becoming more languid. They all made an attempt to follow her command.

"Okay, so you kissed him. It's not the end of the world." Tish stretched her spine upward.

"It wasn't just a kiss," Delaney confessed.

"You slept with him too?" Jillian, who never sounded scandalized, sounded scandalized.

"No, no. It was just the best damn kiss of my life."

"She's cussing," Rachael said. "Delaney hardly ever cusses. He's got her cussing now." She frowned deeply. "Who is this guy?"

"Up dog," the instructor said again.

Everyone dipped their heads down and stuck their butts in the air, stretching their hamstring muscles.

"Breathe deep, class."

Delaney drew in a deep, upside-down breath. "That's the problem. He's the grandson of the woman I'm doing the renovations for, and I can't avoid him because he's the one who's filling in for my crew since Lucia can't afford them."

"Oh, my God," Tish said. "It's that gorgeous undercover cop, isn't it? When I was at Lucia's house filming I thought I detected a vibe between you two." To Rachael and Jillian, she said, "He really is hot. You should see him. He's got the tightest butt that's just begging to be pinched."

"Tish!"

"I'm just saying." Tish shrugged and tilted her head toward the ceiling.

"There's vibes now?" Rachael exclaimed, clearly upset. "You're all vibey with the guy, Delaney?"

"And muscles out to here," Tish waxed rhapsodically and measured off a thick chunk of space behind her own bicep.

"Shh." Delaney frowned at her.

"Evan's got muscles," Rachael said.

"Not like these." Tish's eyes rounded in appreciation. "Evan has run-of-the-mill, work-out-on-the-weekend muscles. Nick's got oh-my-god-he-could-have-been-a-cover-model muscles. I bet anything his abs are equally amazing. What are his abs like, Del? Can you bounce a condom off them?"

"I don't know what his abs are like," Delaney cried, embarrassed by the attention they were drawing. Most everyone in the class had stopped striking poses and was staring at them. "I haven't seen him naked."

The music picked that moment to shift into another song, and for one brief second the only sound in the room was Delaney yelling, "Naked."

"Ladies," the instructor said sternly, "if you're not going to concentrate on yoga, could you please leave the room so that the rest of us who want to relax and enjoy our exercise can do so?"

"Let's get out of here," Jillian said, yanking up her yoga mat. "Who's for coffee?"

"Delaney is wrecking her life and you're thinking about coffee." Rachael shook her head.

"Maybe she's claiming her life, not wrecking it," Tish said.

"Oh, yeah, like what you did with Shane?" Rachael asked. "Maybe you're not the most qualified person to be giving Delaney relationship advice."

Delaney saw Tish freeze at the mention of her ex's name. Although Tish denied it, they all suspected she was still in love with her ex-husband. "That was really cold, Rachael."

"Ladies," the instructor said sharply and pointed at the door.

Chastised, they gathered up their yoga mats and trooped out into the hallway.

Eyes flaring, Rachael faced off with Delaney. "I can't believe you're doing this to Evan. He's such a nice, caring man. Why would you do this to him?"

Rachael was asking her the same thing that Delaney had been asking herself ever since Nick kissed her. It was wrong. So very wrong. She knew it. Regretted it and yet she still wanted to kiss him again.

"Hey," Jillian said, hopping to Delaney's defense. "Evan took off for Guatemala just before their wedding, and he was the one who came up with that celibacy thing. What did he expect her to do?"

"Unlike some people," Rachael said pointedly and glared at Jillian, "I thought Delaney could control her hormonal impulses."

"You calling me a slut?" Jillian challenged. "Is that where this is going?"

"If the stiletto fits..."

Delaney's pulse leaped as she realized the consequences of her actions on her friends. It distressed her that they were fighting over her. This wasn't just about her. She'd involved them and upset them, and now she had to step in and make things right before either Rachael or Jillian said something they couldn't take back.

She stepped between them. "Please, you guys are my best friends in the world. Don't do this to each other. Rachael is right, Jillian. I shouldn't have kissed Nick."

"You shouldn't be marrying Evan is what you shouldn't be doing," Jillian said. "No matter how nice and caring he is, he's wrong for you, and your heart knows it even if your head doesn't."

Delaney thought of Nick, whom she had known for only a very short time. There was chemistry there, yes. Lots of it. But what did they have in common beyond the attraction? Absolutely nothing. She tried to imagine him fitting in with her high-society world and failed miserably.

Then she thought of Evan, whom she had known her entire life. He was the man who'd been there for her during the bad times. He'd held her in his arms when her sister died. And when a bully at school made fun of the way she looked, Evan had punched him out, defending her honor. She and Evan were so much alike. They came from the same world. Knew the same people. Liked the same things.

She twisted her engagement ring on her finger. How could she throw away the history they had, the security Evan offered, for physical lust and sexual attraction with Nick?

And there was the issue of her mother.

At the mere thought of having to tell Honey she'd decided not to go through with the wedding, Delaney felt physically sick.

She couldn't. She wouldn't. Jillian was right. Nick was just something to get out of her system. This need for magic, for something special, was a childish impulse. Her experimentation had already caused discord between her friends. She had to stop this daydreaming and wishing for something more before it ruined her life and hurt those she loved.

Tish touched her arm. "You okay, Del?"

Delaney forced a smile. "I'm all right, or I would be if you guys would stop sniping at each other. I never meant to cause trouble in our little group. I just value your support so much, I had to tell you. Please, forgive me for dumping my problems on you."

"There's nothing to forgive," Tish said.

"I'm sorry too," Jillian apologized. "I'm far too reactionary at times."

"Group hug!" Rachael held out her arms.

Grinning, they all came together for a hug.

"Now," Jillian said, "let's go for coffee. I'm buying."

They walked over to the nearby Starbucks and Tish fell into step beside Delaney. "So, what *are* you going to do about Mr. Hard-Body Cop?"

Delaney sighed. "There's only one thing I can do."

"You're going to break it off with Evan?"

"No!" She stared at her friend, and then lowered her voice. "Of course not. I'm going to have to tell Lucia I can't stage her house."

"But what about the *American Home Design* contest and your own dream of taking your business out of the realm of your mother's friends and controlling destiny?"

"For now," Delaney said, "I've got to let that dream go. For the good of everyone involved, I simply can't trust myself around Nick."

Chapter 12

"What are we going to do?" Lucia asked Trudie as they pushed their shopping cart through the handy little community grocery store located two blocks from Trudie's doorstep. Just before they'd walked out the door, Delaney had called with the bad news she was resigning as Lucia's house stager.

"I'm telling you, Luce, you're worrying for nothing. Delaney is a Pisces. Nick is Scorpio. They're one of the most compatible matches in the Zodiac. Trust me on this."

"Not to offend you, Trudie, but I don't have much faith in astrology."

"That's fine, but what about your faith in the whammy? You do believe in that, don't you?"

"I don't know what the problem is," Lucia fretted. "Delaney said she didn't have enough time to do the house justice with her impending wedding plans. She never said a word about Nick. But I know that's the real issue. But what if she's telling the truth and she's simply overwhelmed?"

"She's only overwhelmed because the whammy has her rattled and she doesn't want to tell you she has the hots for your grandson, especially since she's engaged to someone else. She doesn't want you to think badly of her."

"But how are she and Nicky ever going to get together if she's not going to help me sell my house? And besides that, now who's going to help me sell my house?" Lucia turned their cart down the cereal aisle. "I knew we should never have meddled."

Trudie took a box of Lucky Charms off the shelf and tossed it in the cart. "It's not meddling when it's kismet."

Lucia fished the box of sugary cereal out of the cart and handed it back to Trudie. "You're as bad as Leo with the sweet tooth. Get the All-Bran."

Grumbling under her breath, Trudie put the Lucky Charms back and replaced it with bran flakes. "Happy now?"

"No, not at all. I'm worried about Delaney and Nick. I'm worried about selling my house."

Trudie waved a hand. "You worry too much."

"You don't worry at all."

"And that's what makes us such good friends. We balance each other out. Can I get some fruit roll-ups?"

Lucia sighed. "Go ahead."

Trudie scampered to the fruit roll-ups and brought a box to the cart. "You want Delaney back as your house stager?"

"Of course I do. Didn't I just say that? But how can we get her to come back?"

"We're going to have to meddle. Oh, and you might have to tell a little white fib or two."

Lucia desperately wanted to see her grandson happy. He deserved the same kind of happiness she'd known with Leo. She wasn't so sure of Trudie's interfering, but she didn't know what else to do. If Delaney married the man she was engaged to, Lucia knew the young woman would live to regret it.

She'd been there herself. She understood the pressure to comply with her family's wishes, especially if you were the kind of girl who took great care not to hurt people. If it hadn't been for Leo boldly taking matters into his own hands, she would probably be living in a hovel in Tuscany, waiting for Frank Tigerelli to get out of prison.

Lucia couldn't stand by and watch Delaney make a terrible mistake. Her gaze locked with Trudie's. "So what do you have in mind?"

Nick was caulking the front windows of Nana's house when he looked up to see Trudie's corvette pull into the driveway with his grandmother riding shotgun. Nana climbed gingerly from the low-slung sports car and then marched toward him, looking like she used to look just before she stuck his nose in the corner for bad behavior.

Uh-oh. Something was up.

He laid the caulking gun down on the window ledge and cocked a disarming smile. "Hey, Nana."

"Don't you 'Hey, Nana' me, young man." She glowered darkly and shook an index finger under his nose. "What did you do to that girl?"

"What girl?"

"Don't play dumb," Nana snapped.

Surprise widened Nick's eyes. His grandmother rarely lost her temper, but when she did, she got really steamed.

"I know what you're up to, young man."

His shoulder muscles bunched in defensive protest. "I'm not up to anything."

"Flirting with Delaney to chase her off so I can't sell the house. She called me up and quit today."

He felt a mix of relief and regret. The regret startled him. He had nothing to feel sorry about. "Is that what she said? That I was flirting with her?"

"Delaney has too much class and respect for other people's feelings to say that. She laid all the blame on herself. But I know the real truth, mister. Don't forget who raised you."

"I didn't chase her off," Nick mumbled and ducked his head. Nana had a way of making him feel seven years old all over again.

"You can't fool me, Dominic Vincent Vinetti. You've done it before."

"Done what before?"

"Ran off a perfectly nice young woman because you were getting too close, feeling too much, and couldn't deal with it." Her eyes sparked angrily and she reached over to snap the head off a dead bloom on the rosebush beside him.

Nick gulped.

"Yes," she said. "I know about your tactics. Probably more than you know yourself. For instance, I know you're at least fifty percent responsible for what happened between you and Amber. Maybe even more than fifty percent."

Now that was a low blow. Nick narrowed his eyes. "Amber left me. On our honeymoon. To run off with another man."

Nana sank her hands on her hips. "And why was that?"

Fear slid down his spine. Nick clenched his jaw, dropped his gaze, and picked up the caulking gun. "I've got to get this caulking done before it rains."

"That," Nana crowed. "Right there. That's why Amber left you."

"What? Amber left me because I like to caulk?" Was his grandmother losing it?

"Don't play dumb."

"Maybe I am dumb."

"Humph. You run away from your feelings, that's what you do."

"I married Amber, didn't I? How could I run away from my feelings if I married her?" he growled. "And look what happened."

"You married a woman you *knew* would break your heart. You damn well did it on purpose. Subconsciously, of course, but still purposefully."

His mouth dropped open and he stared at his grandmother, bewildered by her accusations. She *was* losing it. "Think whatever you want to think," he said, not knowing how else to respond. He'd never seen his grandmother like this and didn't know what to make of it.

"You're terrified," she accused. "Scared to death that if you really let yourself love a woman who truly deserves your love, she'll end up dying on you the way Dominique died on your father."

Nick studied the window casing, trying to ignore his grandmother, who was now systematically snapping the heads off all the dead rose stems and slinging them viciously to the ground. Hmm. Looked like he'd missed a spot with the caulk.

"Stubborn," Nana muttered, and he heard the crisp snap of another dried bloom being broken off.

Nick dabbed a white bead of caulk into the spot he'd overlooked, cocked his head, studied his handiwork. Nice.

"Arrogant." Snap, snap.

Let's see. There were three more windows in the front.

Would he have enough caulk? Or would he need to make another run to Lowe's?

"I swear you're just like your grandfather. He would rather putter around in the garage than express what he was feeling."

"What are you taking about? He kidnapped you from your wedding. That sounds like he was expressing his feelings to me."

Nana waved a hand. "Grand gestures came easily to him, it was the quiet moments—the moments that count to a woman—where he froze up. I loved your grandfather with every beat of my heart, Nick, but he was so stubborn. He never told me about his heart condition. Arrogantly, he wanted to shoulder the burden alone, spare me the worry." She snorted and then tears sprang to her eyes. "I never knew he was dying. He robbed me of the special conversations we could have had. The extra moments we could have savored. The ones your father and mother got to share."

Awkwardly, Nick wrapped his arms around his grandmother and she sank her head against his chest. He didn't know how to deal with Nana's tears. He patted her shoulder, his own emotions a tight clot in his throat.

Nana pulled back, dabbing at her eyes. "I'm sorry. I shouldn't have broken down on you like that."

Rattled, Nick ran a hand through his hair. "Um...it's okay."

"I shouldn't have gone off on you either. It's just that I want you to understand how you're sabotaging your chance for happiness."

"Yeah?" The question came to his lips even though he hated to ask it. "How's that?"

"All you've got to do is stop denying how you really feel."

Nick sucked in a deep breath. The heat of her gaze warmed his cheek. "You wanna know how I really feel?"

"Yes."

He opened his mouth, but he couldn't say the words. Couldn't tell her how betrayed he felt because she was selling the house out from under him. Couldn't tell her why he'd felt so compelled to chase Delaney Cartwright away.

"Well?"

Anger sent his pulse throbbing through his veins. Fear tightened his lungs. Denial squeezed his stomach. "Never mind," Nick mumbled, turned on his heels, and walked away.

Before he reached the corner of the house, he heard his grandmother muttering, "Men. Hardheaded as cement. Every last one of them."

Lucia and Trudie caught Delaney as she was leaving the office that afternoon. The minute she saw the two elderly ladies, her heart sank. Via the telephone it had been difficult enough to quit the job, but to reject Lucia to her face would be next to impossible.

"Lucia, Trudie, it's so good to see you," Delaney greeted them in the parking lot of her office. The silver Acura sat three spots away from the front door, taunting her. If she'd just parked a few feet closer, she would have already been driving away when they pulled up. "Were you in the area and decided to drop by?"

"No, no." Lucia beamed. "We made a special trip just to see you."

"It's over fifty miles," Trudie said. "And my driving's not what it used to be."

"You can say that again," Lucia chimed in. "We were

lucky to make it here alive. She almost hit a seagull. Twice."

"Pesky creatures," Trudie muttered.

"I was just leaving for the day," Delaney said, hoping that might deter them.

"We brought cannoli," Lucia said and held up a paper bag smelling deliciously of baked goods. "I made them myself."

"They're an especially tasty batch," Trudie said. "I had two on the drive over."

"That's why you almost hit the seagulls. Eating and driving don't mix."

"It's your fault. You're too good of a cook."

Delaney bit back a sigh. "Would you ladies like to come into my office?"

"We would love that." Lucia smiled. "Thank you."

Delaney took out her keys, opened the office back up, and ushered the women inside. "Have a seat," she said, inviting them to sit down on the love seat while she took the plush-cushioned chair positioned beside it.

"Nice office," Trudie said. "Informal, cozy. I like it."

"Thank you." Delaney smiled and braced herself for what she knew was coming next. "How can I help you, Lucia?"

Lucia reached across to take Delaney's hand in hers. She looked her in the eyes. "Come back, stage my house. I don't know what I'll do without you."

Delaney took a deep breath to bolster her courage. "Like I said when we spoke over the phone, Lucia, I should never have agreed to take on your project in the first place. Not with my wedding so close. I just have too much to do. I apologize for any inconvenience I might have caused you. I have the name of another house stager I can recommend."

"This is about Nicky, isn't it?" Lucia wasn't pulling any punches. "You can tell me the truth. He likes you. I can tell, but I promise he won't get out of line with you again. It hurt him so badly last year when Amber cheated on him on their honeymoon. He would never do anything to cause your fiancé to suffer like that."

"Lucia..."

"If being alone with Nicky is the only thing that's worrying you, we can take care of that."

Delaney paused. She still wanted to renovate that house. Still hoped to get on *American Home Design*. But she couldn't do that if she had to work alone in the house with Nick. She simply couldn't trust herself to keep her hands off him.

"This is very important to me," Lucia said lowering her voice. "Because you see..." She let go of Delaney's hand and splayed her palm across her heart.

"What she's trying to say," Trudie interjected, "is that her ticker isn't in the best of shape. She wants to get the house sold and settled before... well, you know, she kicks the bucket."

Delaney scooted to the edge of her chair. "You're sick? Lucia, why didn't you tell me?"

"She's proud," Trudie said.

"Please, Delaney," Lucia whispered. "Finish the house. Trudie and I will be there every day to act as chaperones. We promise you that."

"But is that good for your heart? Shouldn't you rest?"

"Doc says it's good for her to get out. Stay busy. She just needs to avoid any emotional distress. Right, Luce?"

Lucia nodded. "Please?"

When she presented it like that, how could Delaney say

no? "Under the circumstances, of course I'll finish the job for you, Lucia."

"Oh," Trudie said. "One other thing. You can't tell Nick about her heart condition. He doesn't know."

Delaney captured Lucia's gaze. "Doesn't he deserve to know?"

Lucia looked uncomfortable. "It's just that he's had so much to deal with over the past year. I thought it best to keep it from him for now."

Delaney didn't agree, but she had to respect Lucia's wishes. "I won't say a word to him about it," she promised.

"That," Lucia said to Trudie as they left Delaney's office, "was completely underhanded. I feel like such a liar. I just had a physical two weeks ago, and the doctor told me I had the heart of a thirty-year-old."

"It worked though, didn't it? Pretend heart problems get 'em every time. How do you think I con my kids into coming home for the holidays?" Trudie winked. "Now it's all up to the whammy."

Nick sat at the Sandpiper, an outdoor seaside bar near the entrance to the amusement park, his injured leg propped on an adjacent stool, nursing a longneck bottle of beer and idly watching a game of beach volleyball featuring bikini-clad coeds. He wished he could stop thinking about Delaney and what Nana had said to him.

He had chased Delaney off—fully, intentionally. Not because she was staging his grandmother's house, like he told himself, but because he was terrified of his growing feelings for her.

And he had done the same thing with Amber, albeit subconsciously. Nana had him pegged.

It was a painful thing to face. His denial. The way he'd been sabotaging himself. He was still doing it. Allowing himself to be attracted to a woman who was engaged to marry another man, knowing he stood no chance with her.

"You're one sick puppy, Vinetti."

"Excuse me?" the bartender said. "Need another beer?"

Nick waved him away. He didn't want the one he was drinking; he'd just needed to get out of the house and away from the renovations and Nana's on-target assessment to clear his head. "I'm good."

The guy nodded, swiped the bar with a towel, and slipped a bowl of cocktail peanuts in front of him. Nick reached for a handful, then stopped with the peanuts halfway to his mouth with he spied an elderly woman with a patch over one eye amble up to the bar.

He sat up straight.

Was this the woman he'd promised Delaney he would investigate and had completely forgotten about? Just his luck, the one-eyed carny woman drew herself up on the bar stool beside him, slanted her head Nick's way, winked, and said, "Buy an old gal a drink, handsome?"

Nick was painting the shutters on Lucia's house the next morning when Delaney drove up. She didn't see any signs of Lucia's car, and for one breathless moment when she looked across the lawn at him, she almost panicked and drove away.

He must have sensed her hesitation, because he looked up from his work and gestured her over.

Lucia had promised Delaney she would be here and she trusted her to keep her word. She could handle being alone with Nick until Lucia arrived. It wasn't like she was going to rip his clothes off his body and have her way with him on the front porch. But even as she thought it, she pictured it. What in the heck was wrong with her?

Putting the smile she'd perfected in charm school on her face, she strode up the sidewalk.

"Delaney," he said when she reached the porch.

"Nick."

"I've got some news for you."

Worry gripped her. What kind of news? Had he found out about Lucia's heart condition? Had something bad happened to Lucia? "Yes?" she asked and laced her fingers together.

"You remember that matter you asked me to check out for you?"

"What matter?" She was so busy worrying, his words didn't fully register.

"The patch-eyed woman from the amusement park."

"Huh?"

"You asked me to find out who she was."

"Oh, right, yes, yes."

"I should have followed up sooner, but we were so busy with the house that it slipped my mind."

"That's okay." Truthfully, it had slipped Delaney's mind too. "What did you find out?"

"All I learned is that she hasn't been working at the amusement park long, and in fact, she's leaving town soon."

"Where's she going?"

"Pensacola."

"Is that all?" Delaney curled her fingers into her palms.

"I asked a PI friend of mine to do a little more digging. See if he could find out where she came from. I'll let you know if he finds a connection to your mother."

"Any clues as to why my mother would be meeting her?"

"No idea."

"I'm sure it's nothing. Now that I think back on it, I was probably mistaken. I don't see how my mother could have a secret life where she slipped off to islands to visit carnivals." She laughed.

"I'm sure you're right about that."

"It's preposterous, really. Maybe we should tell your friend not to bother." Delaney tried not to notice how delicious Nick looked with the morning sun glinting off his muscles. She swallowed. "Thank you anyway. I appreciate it. I'll give you a check so you can pay your friend for the trouble he's already gone through."

"Don't worry about it. He owes me a favor. I'll just give him a call and tell him you decided not to persue the matter."

"Thanks," she said again.

They looked at each other.

"We should talk about what happened the other day," he said. "I'm sorry about my behavior. I was out of line."

"So was I."

"I can promise nothing like that will happen again."

"It's okay. I talked to your grandmother. She and Trudie are going to come over every day and act as our chaperones."

"That's pretty pathetic. We're adults, and we can't be trusted in the same room alone together."

"Things just got out of hand."

"I apologize for kissing you," he said. "But I don't regret it. It was bound to happen."

"I'm sorry if I hurt you. I'm sorry I said you were just something to get out of my system. The way I said it made it sound like you didn't matter, but you do matter and that's precisely the problem. You're a good person, Nick, and you deserve a woman who's free to love you, wholly, completely. In another time, another place..." She let her words trail off.

"Yeah." He nodded, but did not look at her. Restlessly, he ran his hands down the sides of his jeans. "It would be a lot easier if this was just an itch that needed scratching."

That was the hell of it. Underneath the guilt, her heart was breaking from the desolation of knowing she would never again feel the pressure of his lips against hers. If he had just been something to flush from her system, she wouldn't have felt such shame. But the kiss they'd shared held too much meaning to dismiss as a simple hormone rush.

"So we understand each other?" She looked deeply into his eyes. "Nothing more can ever come of this."

"Never," he croaked.

Chapter 13

Since she couldn't shake things up with Nick, Delaney shook things up by decorating Lucia's house in a Tuscan style. Lucia heartily approved and her input was invaluable. She told Delaney stories, reminiscing about her childhood in Tuscany, describing the countryside, the food, the people. Through her narrative, Delaney fell in love with a country she'd never seen, but soon felt as if she knew by heart. It sounded like a magical place, and she hoped someday to visit.

Her creativity took on a whole new facet as she explored aspects of color and lighting, texture and dimension, that she'd never before explored.

Most of the walls they painted using Venetian plaster technique. It was time-consuming, but the results were well worth it. In the kitchen, they installed new appliances, replaced the Formica countertops with Italian tile, and refurbished the cabinets. Delaney selected Roman shades as window treatments for the rooms. They added crown molding for visual flair, installed scroll casing around the doors, and exchanged the small baseboards for wider ones. They put in rounded archways and atmospheric lighting.

Lucia and Trudie helped out in what ways they could—refilling paint trays when they ran low, handing Nick tools as he worked to repair leaky pipes, making lunch, tending the flower garden.

Other members of the family put in appearances when possible, mainly on weekends, pitching in wherever they were needed. Delaney loved being around when the whole group got together. Even when they were arguing, the Vinettis had fun together. Teasing and disagreeing, laughing and squabbling and loving one another in ways Delaney envied.

Throughout the whole restoration project, Nick and Delaney kept a respectful distance from each other. Making sure they never accidentally touched or brushed up against each other, which was sometimes difficult in the confines of the small rooms. But even though it was possible to maintain their physical distance, it was almost impossible to keep from bonding emotionally.

Nick was a passionate man, yes, but he managed to retain his cool when things went wrong. Delaney admired that about him. He had a tolerance for the tedious and a willingness to start over from scratch if a project wasn't working out. His patience surprised her. She hadn't expected it.

Besides tales of Tuscany, Lucia told Delaney stories of Nick and his siblings when they were growing up in this house. How Nick had gone through an *Untouchables* phase when he was six—dressing up like Eliot Ness complete with suit, tie, hat, and plastic tommy gun. Even then, he was a cop in the making. She told of how he climbed up the chimney one Christmas to see if he could find Santa. And how he slid down the banister, crashed into his sister, and knocked out her front baby tooth.

On the long Fourth of July weekend, the Vinetti clan returned for one final big push on the project. It would be the family's last holiday in the house on Galveston Island, and no one wanted to miss it.

For four days they worked and joked and ate and drank. Teased and cried and laughed and sighed. At times it was something of a madhouse with all the activity. But miraculously, on the final day almost all of the renovations had been completed. Delaney and Nick would be left with only touch-ups and strategic decorating before the house was ready to display. Delaney's job was almost done, and oddly enough, she found herself feeling as nostalgic for the house as the rest of the family.

"I'll see you after the Fourth," Delaney told Lucia as she got ready to leave for the day. The family was standing in the kitchen, admiring how well it had all turned out. All except for Nick. He'd disappeared somewhere, and Delaney had to force herself not to look around for him.

"You're not coming to our barbecue tomorrow?" Lucia asked, disappointment in her voice.

"My mother..." Delaney waved a hand. "She has this event she sponsors for the Houston Symphony every year. I'm expected to attend."

"Can you get out of it?" Gina asked. "The party won't be the same without you."

Delaney's heart squeezed, and for some weird reason she felt like crying. "I always go."

Trudie clicked her tongue. "Tsk. Such a shame. You haven't lived until you've had Fourth of July with the Vinettis."

"We have fireworks," Zack said.

"And homemade ice cream," Jack added.

"And watermelon," lanky, teenage Tony threw in. "It's a blast."

She wanted so badly to say yes, but from the time she was little more than a toddler, Delaney had been attending the annual Fourth of July Symphony Under the Stars bash her father funded and her mother orchestrated. And all that time, she'd wished for the simple pleasure of backyard barbecues and fireworks.

There's no law compelling you to go to that symphony event. Tell Lucia you'll come and deal with Mom later. It was Skylar's voice whispering in the back of her head, urging her to misbehave.

"We'll miss you," Gina said.

Delaney smiled gently. "There's over two dozen people spending the night in this house; I seriously doubt I'll be missed."

"You underestimate yourself," said a deep voice from the doorway. "The party won't be the same without you."

Her pulse spiked. She looked over to see Nick standing there with an enigmatic look in his eyes.

"You want me to come?" Delaney murmured, unable to take her gaze off him.

"I'm just saying you'll be missed." His tone was grave, and he broke their eye contact.

Delaney's breath hitched in her lungs.

"Don't pressure her," Lucia scolded. "If she's got a previous engagement, she's got a previous engagement."

"I'd love to come to your barbecue, Lucia," Delaney surprised herself by saying. "I've been attending that boring symphony thing for as long as I can remember. I can skip one year."

"Really?" Lucia's face brightened so significantly,

Delaney knew she'd made the right choice. If Honey got upset with her for skipping the event, she could just lump it.

"Really."

Her announcement to Honey that she wasn't going to the symphony turned out to be amazingly anticlimactic. Her mother seemed very distracted about something, and while she expressed displeasure over Delaney's absence from the program, she didn't badger her the way she'd expected. So it was with a light heart Delaney arrived at the Galveston Island house at midmorning on the Fourth. But when she got out of the car and headed up the sidewalk, arms laden with grocery sacks filled with offerings for the barbecue, her legs started to quiver.

She spied Gina and her husband, Chuck—partially hidden by an overgrowth of bougainvillea along the fence—kissing like teenagers. Chuck's hand tenderly cupped Gina's bottom, and her arms were entwined around his neck.

The sense of jealousy-tinged sadness that swept over Delaney was so intense it almost brought her to her knees. Would Evan be pulling her in the bushes for a passionate kiss after they'd been married for ten years?

He doesn't do that now, why would he do it in a decade? muttered Skylar's annoying voice again.

Mentally, Delaney shook herself and tore her gaze from the amorous couple. What was the matter with her?

"Need a hand with that?"

And then there he was, coming up the sidewalk behind her, the source of all her internal distress.

Nick Vinetti.

Looking as if he was the answer to all her most

subversive fantasies, in his tight white T-shirt and black shorts.

He'd replaced his knee brace with an Ace wrap and his limp was barely discernible. He looked very strong and incredibly handsome, and Delaney was feeling as if she possessed the moral resolve of a jellyfish.

Suddenly she wished like hell she hadn't come.

"Here." Nick reached out and plucked the two heaviest plastic bags from her hands. His fingertips brushed against her skin and heat rushed to her cheeks.

She was achingly aware of every nuance between them. His manly nutmegy scent collided with the delicate lavender of her own perfume, producing an intoxicating clash of woodsy and floral. The sharp differences in their bodies—his sinewy muscles versus her supple softness. The emotional vastness of the very short distance between them—the tips of her sandals almost touching the toes of his sneakers.

"Where's your brace?" Delaney asked, fixing her gaze on his knee so she wouldn't have to meet his eyes and find out if he shared the same awareness of her that she did of him. She didn't know which thought scared her more. That he felt it too, or the possibility that he didn't.

"I don't need it any longer."

Helplessly, her gaze was drawn up past his hard-muscled thigh, to his narrow hips, to the flat of his belly barely hidden by his thin cotton T-shirt.

She raised her lashes and slanted a coy glance at his face and was caught in the trance of his bemused smile.

He lowered his head.

He's going to kiss me!

The thought set off a fire alarm in her head. *No!*

Please let him kiss me.

She lifted her chin, held her breath, eyes locked with Nick's, and waited. "Don't you dare kiss me, you scoundrel," she said, sounding exactly like a woman who desperately needed to be kissed.

From behind her, she heard Gina and Chuck giggle, and thankfully that broke the spell.

Delaney sucked in air and held up the remaining sack in her hand. "Meat. For the barbecue. Needs refrigerating."

Oh, gosh, how pathetic. He'd so rattled her that she couldn't even speak in complete sentences.

With that, she hurried past him, grateful that she was almost finished with the house and would soon be far away from the temptation of Lucia's maddeningly mesmerizing grandson.

Nick would have kissed Delaney and broken all the promises he'd made to her, if Gina and Chuck hadn't come strolling from the bougainvillea bushes with self-satisfied smirks on their faces.

It was a good thing they were there, he told himself as he frowned at his sister and her husband lounging against the fence, arm in arm. Otherwise, there was no telling what he might have done.

Then, unable to keep himself from watching her, Nick turned his head and enjoyed the view of Delaney's hips swaying as she hurried toward the house.

He thought about how her cheeks had turned red when he'd touched her while reaching for the grocery sacks. He grinned. Aw, Rosy. She disappeared around the side of the house, headed for the back door that the family used, and his grin widened.

Delaney was astute. He was a scoundrel. And he wasn't

proud of it. But he wasn't ashamed of it either. Okay, he was a little ashamed, but only because she was engaged to his doctor.

But what if she wasn't engaged to Evan Van Zandt?

She is, so stop thinking about it, he rebuked himself.

It was easy to say, but not so damn easy to do. Because ever since he'd kissed her, Nick hadn't been able to think of anything else.

By midafternoon the food was ready and everyone had assembled. The backyard picnic table was laden with food. Barbecued chicken, grilled Italian sausages, and hamburger patties. There was potato salad, cole slaw, corn on the cob, and baked beans, along with cold macaroni salad, an assortment of cheeses, antipasto, and tomato bruschetta. Dessert was a bountiful selection of fresh fruits, homemade brownies, and tiramisu. Two ice cream freezers churned batches of homemade peach ice cream. There was lemonade for the children and iced tea or cold beer or chilled white wine for the adults.

Nick, Delaney noticed, was in rare form. Playing with the kids, charming his sisters-in-law, guy-talking with his brothers, his cousins, his father, and Chuck. He surprised her. She thought he'd be gloomy today, on this last Vinetti family holiday in Lucia's house where they'd all shared so many memories.

The food was delicious, the company even more so. They lingered long over the meal, until the kids started begging to go swimming. Everyone pitched in to get ready—the women putting away leftovers and cleaning the kitchen while the men packed up the cars with coolers and blankets, fireworks, lawn chairs, beach towels, and a boom box. Even Trudie and Lucia went along for the trek to the secluded beach outside the Galveston city limits that only the locals knew about.

Delaney soon found herself—toes dug into the sand—sitting under a big beach umbrella. She watched the kids shriek gleefully as they ran through the surf, chased by Nick, Chuck, and Nick's brothers Richie and Johnny. Vincent was manning the boom box, causing the teenagers, who were too cool to play in the ocean with the younger kids, to roll their eyes and groan when he put in a CD of the Beach Boys.

Then, for absolutely no reason at all, a lump rose to Delaney's throat, forcing her to swallow back the salty taste. She was happy. Why the sudden urge to cry?

From childhood, she'd been trained to control her emotions, to repress her feelings, deny her impulses. She'd been taught that appearances were paramount, and she should conduct herself based on what others thought of her.

Growing up rich and privileged, Delaney realized, was like living on an island with other people who were exactly like you. The lifestyle imposed upon children of the wealthy and powerful entailed certain duties and conditions unknown to the rest of the population. In high society there was no blending into an anonymous background—which was one of the reasons Honey had been so strict with her. Delaney had been required to watch every step. No one trod easily on the emotions of others where money and manners mingled. This need for caution, this intricate caretaking, resulted in an inbreeding of the spirit. Too much held in. Too much regret. Too much silent brooding.

And she wanted out.

But she wasn't going to get out if she married Evan. He was too much like her.

The thought twisted her stomach.

Is this really about Evan? she had to ask herself. *Or your attraction to Nick?*

Her gaze tracked back to the man frolicking in the surf with his nieces and nephews, and it was her heart's turn to twist. His shirt was off and he was silhouetted against the backdrop of ocean and sunset, aglow in the ending day. Orange rays of light licked his body. Every muscle was ripped, rock hard, and clearly defined.

One look at him and she could feel the simmering chemistry. In her lungs. In her throat. Tight around her wrists like shackles. Light as a breath. Thick as blood.

He must have felt the heat of her gaze, because he turned his head and like a proud, regal wolf stared at her.

Delaney squeezed her eyes shut, and in that pop of difference between the setting sun on the horizon and the darkness behind her lids, she experienced the strangest sensation of falling down a long, black, empty tunnel. Her eyes flew open and she curled her fingers around the arms of the lawn chair to ground herself. Blinking, she glanced around. Vincent was lighting tiki torches, and his brother, Phil, was starting a campfire. Somebody's mom was dishing out mosquito repellent. But no matter how hard she tried to find something else to look at, time and again she found her eyes drawn back to Nick.

Honestly, even if she weren't engaged to Evan, she and Nick didn't stand a chance as a couple. They were simply too different. He was rugged and streetwise; she was pampered and polished. He valued directness and honesty, and she'd spent her life putting a perfect spin on reality. Gingerly, she reached up to finger the bridge of her nose—living a lie, pretending to be a beauty when she was not. Face it, she was insecure and he was self-confident. He was bold and she was timid. She could not view Nick as a way out of her circumstances. He couldn't rescue her. He was just a guy with problems of his own. Like it or not, she was engaged to another man.

Don't fill your head with dreams of him, she warned herself.

Nick's brother Johnny's wife pulled up a lawn chair beside Delaney. Her name was Brittany, Delaney remembered, and she was holding her new baby daughter in her arms. She was a slender woman about Delaney's age, with an elfin face and long dark hair she kept pinned back with a thick barrette. "Mind the company?"

"Not at all." Delaney shook her head.

Brittany tossed a receiving blanket over her shoulder and modestly began nursing her daughter. Delaney's attention drifted back to the shoreline, her eyes hooked on Nick.

"Gorgeous, huh?" Brittany said.

"What?"

"The Vinetti men."

She couldn't deny that. "Yes."

For a minute the only sounds were the rush of the surf, the Beach Boys singing about their little Deuce coupe, and the baby suckling.

"You're engaged to be married, right?" Brittany said after a long moment.

"Uh-huh." Delaney glanced over to find Brittany studying her speculatively.

"So how come you're not with your fiancé today? Wait, that was rude; you don't have to answer that."

Delaney smiled. "It's okay. Evan is in Guatemala." She told Brittany about Evan's medical mission to Central America.

"He sounds like a great guy."

"He is."

"Nick knows you're engaged, right?"

"Yes. Why do you ask?"

"We're all crazy about him, you know. He's a great uncle and a terrific cop and an all-around good guy. After what Amber did to him..." Brittany paused a moment to reposition her baby. "Well, we're pretty protective. The last thing we want is for Nick to get hurt again. He's been through a lot, what with his knee and being forced off the job and everything else that's happened."

"I understand."

"Do you? Do you really?"

Delaney met Brittany's gaze. "What are you trying to say?"

"The way Nick looks at you when you're not looking at him..." She trailed off again.

"What way is that?" Delaney felt her body tense, and she curled her fingernails into her palms.

She shrugged. "I dunno, sort of wistful and sad. It worries me and Johnny."

"I can assure you, Brittany, I have no designs on Nick."

"And Nick knows that?"

"Yes, he does."

Brittany blew out a breath. "Okay. Just wanted to make sure. Because we all really like you, but Nick, you know, he's family. Nothing is more important than family loyalty. Right?"

"Right," Delaney echoed, suddenly feeling incredibly out of place. It was time she said good-bye and left the Vinettis to their celebration. She looked around and realized she was going to have to ask someone to drive her back to her car. Why hadn't she driven herself?

At that moment, Brittany's five-year-old son, Logan, came running up, soaking wet and grinning. "Mama, can we shoot off some Black Cats now?"

"Only if your daddy or Uncle Nick or Uncle Richie or Uncle Chuck helps you with them."

Logan zoomed over to Vincent, who was sitting on the tailgate of Nick's pickup truck with Lucia and Trudie, changing the Beach Boys to Ira Gershwin.

Nick came trotting up after Logan. Droplets of water caught in his dark, curling chest hairs glistened in the waning sunlight. Delaney looked up at him and he looked down at her, and immediately she understood why Brittany had come over to warn her off. The look in Nick's eyes was undeniably hungry.

He flopped down on the ground dangerously close to Delaney's sand-dusted toes.

Up the beach some other picnickers had already brought out their fireworks. Kids twirled sparklers spewing yellow, red, and green heat into the gathering twilight. Fireflies had gotten into the act, blinking on and off among the dunes, Mother Nature competing with man-made pyrotechnics.

"That looks like such fun," Delaney said, drawing up her knees to her chest and resting her chin on them as she watched the sparklers dance and sizzle.

Nick lay propped up on his elbows. "You've never played with sparklers?"

"Always spent my Fourth at the symphony. They have a magnificent fireworks display after the concert."

"You never, ever shot off any firecrackers of your own?"

She shook her head.

"Now, that's just shocking." Nick grinned. "You've been so deprived."

"Tell me about it." Delaney grinned back.

"Would you like to correct that oversight?" He arched one eyebrow speculatively.

"What? Shoot off fireworks?"

He got to his feet, held out his palm. "Come with me."

She looked up at him.

He nodded encouragingly. "Yes?"

Swallowing hard, she committed herself by taking his hand.

He closed his fingers around hers and hauled her from the lawn chair. Brittany watched them with narrowed eyes and a disapproving expression on her lips that made Delaney quickly glance away.

Nick's hand was firm but gentle. A warm sensation of sweet security washed over her. *You are important to me,* his grip seemed to say. *I will take care of you.*

But she didn't need to be taken care of. She'd been taken care of all her life. Everyone telling her what to do, how to think, what to believe, and she'd complied with their wishes. What she really needed was someone who would challenge her, urge her to grow. A tender tether, not a ball and chain. Bonded but not bound. Could Nick be all that?

You're reading too much into this. He's just leading you to the fireworks. Stop overthinking things and enjoy the moment.

Sensible. Now, if only she could heed her own advice.

With his fingers loosely laced through hers, Nick guided her to the back of the pickup where Vincent was doling out small doses of fireworks from a large cardboard box to the excited children.

"We'll start with sparklers," Nick told Delaney. "They're the least intimidating."

Just as he said that, Zack lit off a Black Cat a few feet away, and the loud bang caused Delaney to jump and Brittany's baby to start crying.

"Go on down closer to the water with your dad," Vincent instructed his grandson. "And be careful not to burn yourself with that punk."

Nick retrieved a box of sparklers and a couple of punks from his father, took Delaney's hand again, and walked her down to the edge of the Gulf.

He handed her a sparkler. Then he lit the punk with a match and once it was going, touched the punk to her sparkler.

There was a quick hiss, and then a magical sizzle of light as the sparkler sprang to life in her hands.

"Oh, oh!" Delaney gasped. "It's going, it's going. What do I do? What do I do?"

"Circle your wrist," he said.

"What?" She was so disconcerted by the fact she was holding a sparking, spitting fire stick, she couldn't get what he was trying to tell her.

"Like this."

Nick reached around her, his bare chest grazing her back, his damp swimming trunks pressed against her hip as he slid one hand down her arm to her wrist and encircled it with his big, masculine fingers. He moved her hand in a circle. The sparks showered into a sweeping arc, decorating the night air.

This was fun!

She giggled as Nick changed the circles into zigzags, and then into figure eights, blurring the sparks into one smooth, rapid ride of light until it sputtered and died.

That's when she realized she was holding a spent but red-hot metal stick, and Nick was still pressed up close against her. She could feel the heat of his breath fanning the hairs on the nape of her neck. Delaney turned her head and peeked at him from behind lowered lashes.

A full moon had risen, bathing the shore in a soft white radiance. Nick's eyes were alight with a rarefied glow, the smile at his lips beatific. He had a passion about him. A sense of adventure. A childlike wonder when it came to play. He had what she longed for. The ability to let go and enjoy life.

Idly, she wondered if this was what his face looked like when he was having sex. Totally absorbed, blissfully engaged. That irreverent thought caused her whole body to tingle.

This was serious trouble.

Nick's lips brushed softly against her temple. She felt the erratic rise and fall of his chest, knew his breathing was as labored as her own.

Then the sky lit up with fireworks.

She and Nick turned in unison to see the Vinetti family gathered around as Vincent set off rockets. They were laughing and joking and hugging and talking.

Nick's arm went around her waist and Delaney's heart was pounding so hard she could barely hear the Roman candles screaming toward the stars in an explosion of color.

And in that moment, she knew she was going to miss the entire Vinetti clan in general—and one special Vinetti in particular—something awful.

Chapter 14

Once the renovations had been completed, Tish came back to tape the "after" video for the *American Home Design* contest, and they mailed it off just in time for the deadline.

But now Lucia's house had been on the market for a week, and no one had shown the slightest interest in it.

"No problem," the real estate agent Margaret Krist insisted. "It's only been seven days."

But Delaney couldn't stop worrying. The potential buyers that Margaret ushered through complained the house was too brightly colored, or too provincial, or not elegant enough, or too themed.

Delaney feared she should have listened to conventional wisdom and painted the walls white, with chic but generic decor. She shouldn't have listened to Nick. She shouldn't have tried to shake things up. Her experiment had failed.

Lucia told her not to worry, that they just hadn't found the right buyer who could really fall in love with the place.

Unfortunately time was running out for Lucia, and Delaney felt responsible.

The impulse to buy Nana Vinetti's house herself was strong, but how could she? She was marrying Evan, and he would never go for it. Not even for investment property. A house this old would require a lot of TLC. Something he had neither the time nor the inclination to pursue.

The third week the house was on the market, Delaney started to sweat. Another week and Lucia would be closing on the condo. But she couldn't close on it until her home had sold. Determined that her friend would not be left high and dry, Delaney took matters into her own hands and began contacting her mother's friends, telling them about the fabulous island home for sale. But the women in her mother's circle weren't impressed with Galveston. They had second homes in Florida and California and Hawaii and beyond.

She'd run out of options.

Glumly, she sat in her office, trying to figure out what more she could do, when the telephone rang.

"Ms. Delaney Cartwright?"

"This is she."

"This is Winn Griffin from *American Home Design*."

"Yes?" Her voice went up an octave as her grip tightened around the receiver.

"I'm pleased to inform you that your entry of Mrs. Lucia Vinetti's Galveston Island home has won second place in our contest."

Excitement shot Delaney to her feet. "Really?"

"You and Mrs. Vinetti will share the twenty-five-thousand-dollar second prize, and the video you submitted will be featured on the next installment of *American Home Design*."

"That's amazing. Thank you, thank you."

"The renovations you did on the home were charming.

Your entry really captured our judges' imaginations. Tuscany meets Queen Victoria. Brilliant work."

She wasn't the one with the brilliant idea. It had been all Nick's doing. Shake it up, he'd told her, and he'd been so right.

"You're a truly talented designer, Ms. Cartwright, and I'm sure this exposure will skyrocket your house-staging business."

"How soon will we get the money?" she asked, thinking that the money would be enough for the down payment on Lucia's condo.

"It takes six to eight weeks to process payment through our accounting firm."

That was too bad. The money wouldn't arrive before Lucia was due to close on the condo.

Maybe this time Lucia would accept a loan from her. She'd tried to get her to borrow the down payment from her before, but Lucia's fierce pride would not let her take Delaney's money. Perhaps knowing that the money was coming to her eventually would sway Lucia's thinking. Especially since she had that heart condition.

She'd told herself she would worry about that later. Right now, she had good news to share. Lucia's house was going to be featured on *American Home Design.*

The Vinetti clan along with Delaney and Tish gathered at Lucia's house for an *American Home Design* watching party.

Nick hadn't seen Delaney since they'd finished the house, just a few days after the Fourth of July party.

The minute she walked through the door, everyone was on their feet to greet her, welcoming her like part of the family.

She looked elegant as always—expensive and classy in a beige skirt cut from some kind of soft flowing material that made it look like water parting when she moved. Her top was simple, black and sleeveless, showing off her well-toned arms and smooth, creamy skin. The minute she saw him, her soft green eyes crinkled along with her perfectly straight nose and she smiled slightly, shyly.

And Nick couldn't take his eyes off her.

That smile was a missile launched straight into his heart.

It was over, he realized. After tonight he would probably never see her again.

Nick was going to miss her more than he'd ever thought possible. She'd brought lightness into his life at a time when everything looked dark and dismal. She'd made him believe in possibilities again, even though she was way beyond what he had any right to fantasize about.

He fought the feeling. Fought it hard. He didn't want to fall in love again. Couldn't fall in love again. Not with a woman who was marrying another man.

It was easy enough to avoid Nick in a room crowded with people, but Delaney couldn't seem to stop her gaze from straying over to him throughout the broadcast of *American Home Design.* He caught her studying him a couple of times. She would duck her head and will the heat not to rise to her cheeks. She didn't want anyone else noticing what he could do to her with just one meaningful glance.

When the first-, second-, and third-place winners of the contest were announced, the room broke into applause. The program ran the video of the third-place winner first. It was a house built among the trees near the Oregon coastline, and then they went on to Delaney's entry.

"Great video footage," Gina told Tish.

"Great house decorating," Nick's brother Richie said.

"It was a great idea to go with the Tuscan style, Nick," Delaney said, her eyes on him. "I'm glad you nixed the stark white."

He met her gaze with his intense stare, and she couldn't stop herself. This time she did blush.

The television show went to commercial before the final winner was announced, but the Vinettis had already seen the winning home. Everyone was talking at once. Someone broke open a bottle of champagne. Someone else muted the television and turned on a recording of Italian love songs. Lucia brought a tray of antipasto into the room. Zack and Jack trailed behind her with another tray of mini-pizzas and finger sandwiches made from prosciutto and provolone.

It was officially a party.

Delaney avoided Nick and Nick avoided Delaney.

They stayed at opposite sides of the room, both pretending not to notice that they were noticing each other. Restlessly, he prowled his corner, shooting quick, searing glances at her from time to time.

His leg was almost healed. She hadn't seen him limp in a long time. She was glad for Nick. He'd be returning to work soon, and that should make him happy. He deserved to be happy.

Except that he did not look very happy.

He looked tormented, and she had the most awful realization that she was the cause.

Unnerved by the black look in his eyes, Delaney escaped into the kitchen to see if Lucia needed any help. The older woman was standing at the stove stirring a simmering pot of marinara sauce that smelled like Tuscan heaven.

Lucia turned to smile at her and slipped an arm around her waist. "Delaney, I can't thank you enough for what you've done for me and my family."

A warm glow of affection for Lucia filled her up. "You don't have to thank me. It's my job."

"It's more than a job and you know it. The amount of love you poured into this house is exceptional. You've taken the heart of this place and made it bigger than anyone thought it could be. You're an artist, and I'm so pleased you chose my house as your canvas."

"I only hope that by expressing my creativity I didn't ruin your chances of selling the house. It got us on *American Home Design*, yes, but it doesn't achieve your ultimate goal."

In the distance, below the noisy hubbub of the Vinettis' celebration, the phone rang. A few seconds later Gina came into the kitchen wagging the cordless in her hand. "Delaney, it's for you."

She took the phone. "Hello?"

"Delaney, I've got fabulous news," Margaret Krist, the real estate agent, exclaimed.

"What's up?"

"We've had a bid on Lucia's house. The potential buyer saw *American Home Design* and they just have to have it so they called me on my cell phone. Get this, they offered fifty thousand dollars over the price we were asking before the program aired."

Emotion overcame her—relief, happiness tinged with a dose of sadness that it was over. "That's wonderful news."

"Oh, that's not all."

Delaney could feel the excitement in Margaret's voice. "How much better can it get?"

"My phone has been ringing off the wall with clients

wanting you to stage their houses. Check your messages. I'm sure you've received a lot of phone calls as well. This is it, Delaney. Your career has just been made. All your dreams are coming true."

Delaney looked through the archway from the kitchen into the living room, saw Nick playing with Zack and Jack, and her heart just sank. Margaret was wrong. There was one dream she knew would never come true.

"Thank you, Margaret," she said. "I'll let the Vinettis know." She hung up the phone and broke the joyous news to the family. The crowd let out a shout of happiness.

She found herself deposited breathless and laughing in the kitchen right next to Nick, who looked moody and disgruntled. She reached out to touch his arm.

"We did it," she said. "We restored your grandmother's house and got an offer just in time for her to close on the condo."

Nick hardened his jaw. She saw the emotion play across his face. Sadness, regret, anger.

Was he mad at her? She didn't understand. "You're not pleased?"

He didn't say anything. He just removed her hand from his arm, got up, and walked out the back door.

Now this was ridiculous. She was tired of his moodiness. She knew he'd been through a lot. But enough was enough. He needed a good, swift kick in the seat of his pants. He'd lost a lot, yes, but the man seemed to have no idea what he had. And she was going to give him a piece of her mind.

Delaney went after him.

He was already climbing into his pickup truck.

What was his problem? Her hurt and rejection turned to fury. How dare he spoil his grandmother's party?

Determinedly, she followed, yanking open the passenger door and hopping inside as he started the engine.

"Where do you think you're going?" he snarled.

"With you."

"You're not invited."

"Too bad." She thrust out her chin and folded her arms over her chest. "I'm going anyway, I..."

"Get a clue; I don't want you here," his deep, belligerent voice cut her off, his face looking like a volcano about to erupt. She half expected to see plumes of smoke rising out of his ears. He was steamed, and as far as she could see he had no excuse for his behavior.

"I'm not leaving until you talk to me."

"If you don't get out of here, be forewarned, woman, I can't be held accountable for my actions."

"What's the matter with you?" she scolded. "You're acting like a butthead."

Some of the family had come out on the back porch and were staring at them as they sat in his truck.

Nick swore loudly, put the pickup truck in reverse, and blasted out of the drive.

"What's your deal?"

He shot Delaney a visual bullet with enough power to arm a dictator-toppling death squad. Nick gripped the steering wheel so tightly she feared it would snap off in his hands. Grinding his teeth, Nick was headed for Seawall Boulevard, his brow furrowed. He did not speak a word.

Delaney shrank back against the seat, uncertain what to do next.

They drove in silence, past the main drag, away from the cluster of lights toward the secluded beach where the family had picnicked on the Fourth of July. He took the sandy road too fast and the truck bottomed out.

Delaney clutched the seat belt with both hands, hanging on for dear life. They bumped out onto the beach. There was no one else in sight. Nick pulled up on the hard-packed sand just short of the water, shut off the engine, and got out.

He went around to the passenger side and flung open the door. "Out," he commanded.

Her eyes widened. What was going on here? He was so forceful, so masculine. It both scared and thrilled her.

"You're going to leave me here?"

"You wanted to come, you wanted to hear this, well get out of the truck and listen."

"Why couldn't we have had this discussion while we were driving?" She glanced nervously around the dark, empty beach. "Or back at your grandmother's house?"

"Because I needed to move." He fisted his hands and paced the sand. "Because I'm so filled up with . . . with . . ."

"Rage?"

"Jealousy."

"Jealousy?" she squeaked. It was not what she expected him to say.

"Jealousy," he confirmed. "We're sitting in my grandmother's living room, watching your ideas on television, and then the phone rings and we find out you've sold her house."

"I thought that's what you wanted. What we all wanted."

"No," Nick shouted. "I wanted to be the one who took care of her. But you . . . you . . . come into her house, into our lives, and you changed everything."

"It was your idea to decorate the house in a Tuscan theme. I wanted to do it in something simple and chic. I wanted to make it look like some house from a glossy magazine. You're the reason her house sold, not me. You have no reason to be jealous."

He jammed his fingers through his hair in frustration. "You don't get it, do you?"

"No, I don't." She sank her hands on her hips and watched him stride back and forth, back and forth, a caged animal desperate to break free.

He stopped pacing and came over to glare at her. "I'm jealous of that ring you have on your finger and of the man who put it there. I had to sit across the room from you tonight, watching you, wanting you, being so proud of you, and knowing I can't have you. You fit in so well with my family. It's like you belong there more than I do. And every time you looked over at me, smiled in my direction, it was ripping my guts out."

His words were ripping her apart too.

"I tried the very best I could to control myself," he said. "And whether you realize or not, you've been toying with me. Flirting and confiding in me, but then using that damn diamond ring as a shield from getting close." He ground out the words.

Was it true? Had she been leading him on? It wasn't a pretty thought. She reached out her hand to touch him. "Nick, I'm so sorry, it was never my intention to lead you on."

"Don't touch me," he threatened. "If you touch me, I'm going to lose it. I've been hanging on by a thread ever since we kissed, and I can barely keep my hands off you."

Silence strummed the heavy salt air, stretching between them vast as the ocean.

She felt sorry for him. And for herself. They had met at exactly the wrong time in their lives. She was spoken for and he, on the rebound, hurting from his knee injury and his grandfather's death, couldn't really trust what he was feeling for her.

Nick was an intensely physical guy cursed with a strong moral compass. He wouldn't let himself act on his desires. No matter how difficult it was for him to keep them in check. She understood then why he'd gone into law enforcement. The attraction such a dangerous job held for a man like him. To Nick, the combination of a job that let him move and breathe and the justice it meted out would be the best possible career.

It would be wrong to touch him now. So very, very wrong. Compounding the problem. Making things worse.

Helpless, unable to hold herself back, she reached up and ran her fingertips along his jaw.

"You're playing with fire, Delaney." His eyes were dark and deadly. "I'll burn you up."

A hot rush of overwhelming desire surged through her. Her knees trembled. "Burn me," she cried.

He cupped her chin in his palm. "Be very careful what you ask for, Rosy."

"Nick." His name slipped past her lips on a sigh.

He captured her mouth without a moment's hesitation, fast and deep and hot.

Her lips parted for his. Eager and excited.

He splayed one hand against the back of her head, stabbing his fingers through her hair and hauling her closer.

They were chest to chest and she could feel his heart leaping against hers, quick and thrilling.

The reckless wildness startled Delaney. The stunning intensity of her feral need. Raw nature. Their passion was a brewing hurricane, threatening to roll ashore and decimate everything in its path.

How she wanted to ride out the storm! To let it overtake her, bring her down. Ruin her.

She wanted him here and now. Nothing else mattered.

All she knew was that nothing in her life had ever felt so right.

Sighing, Delaney sank against him, swept up in the feel of his calloused palms against her bare arms, the force of their tangling tongues and raspy breaths. Who would have guessed they'd be so hot together? The cool heiress and the fiery cop.

His lips trailed from her lips to her cheeks, to her forehead, to her temple where his mouth rested quietly against her throbbing pulse. The sweetness of the gesture in the wake of that fever-pitched kiss left her breathless and trembling.

She couldn't think, could barely remember her own name. The civilized part of her brain was numbed with lusty hormones. The animal part took over. Claimed her. Each and every sensation in her body dominated by the rough, decadent touch of him.

"Take me," she whispered.

Nick needed no more invitation than that.

He pushed her into the sand, not caring that it was damp. He was as hard as a man could get and growing harder by the second. His heartbeat spiked. It was a sudden kick in his chest, a vigorous thudding in his groin.

Any doubts he might have had about what he was doing vanished in the hazy heat of the moment. He forgot that she was engaged. Forgot that they were on a public beach where anyone could come upon them at any moment. He was consumed by a hunger so elemental it transcended everything else. He felt it to his soul, this wanting. He'd never felt anything quite this intensely.

She made him feel so real. So alive. He hadn't realized how shut off he'd become.

And when she slipped her arms around his neck and

drew him closer still, the pupils of her eyes widening darkly, he surmised she was just as startled as he was by the power of this thing between them.

He'd grown so cynical over the years and he thought he was immune to these kinds of feelings, especially after Amber. But here he was aching with the need to explore her fully, to burrow his way deep underneath her perfect facade.

Blindly, without purposeful thought, Nick trailed his fingertips over the nape of her neck and leaned his head down to kiss the throbbing pulse at the hollow of her throat. Her silky skin softened beneath his mouth and a tight little moan escaped her lips.

His hand crept from her neck and down the hollow of her throat to her breast heaving with each inhalation of air. A simple but lingering touch that escalated the intimacy between them and felt extremely erotic.

The air smelled of electricity. The ocean crashed loudly with the darkness of his deed. Stealing another man's woman. Time hung, suspended as they looked into each other's eyes.

Nick could not fully comprehend the hold Delaney had over him. She made him want to chuck all his values and morals and just do what felt good. He was a lost soul, vanquished by her kiss. Nick could think of nothing else but being melded with her in any way that he could.

She rocked her pelvis against him, lithe and graceful.

Blood dove through his body, pouring out from his heart and pooling into his crotch, setting his erection in stone. He closed his eyes, grappling for some semblance of control, but it was nowhere to be found.

He kissed her again, his clashing tongue hot against hers, enjoying the glorious taste of her.

She shivered in response, a tremor quaking through her slender body. He pulled his lips from hers and ran his tongue over the outside of her ear and she shuddered even harder.

Her quick intake of breath, low and excited, in the vast openness of sea and sky, ignited his own need, sending it shooting to flaming heights.

She lightly bit his chin.

The feel of her teeth against his skin rocketed a searing heat to all of his erogenous zones and he groaned. God, she was one helluva woman, willing to walk out on this limb with him.

Nick's lips found hers again and as they kissed, he raised a hand to touch her breast.

Her nipple poked through the material of both her silky lace bra and her silk top.

His thumb brushed against her hard little button and she responded by wrapping her legs around his and sliding her bottom against his upper thigh. The feel of her panties against the leg of his jeans was highly sensuous.

When he bent his head to gently suck at her nipple through her shirt, she gasped and clutched his head to her.

This wasn't good enough. He had to touch her bare skin or go insane.

Sliding his hand up underneath her shirt, he unhooked her bra from behind and set her breasts free. She moved against him, mewling softly. Her usual reticence was gone, replaced by a stark hunger that shoved his libido into overdrive.

No way could he resist the mounting pleasure, nor the sweet little sound slipping past her lips.

And yet, even as he succumbed, he couldn't help thinking that he was pushing her into this, no matter how eagerly she responded. He wanted her. But not like this. He wanted her to come to him once she had faced the problems in her life and untangled herself from Van Zandt. He didn't want their joining to spring from his anger or jealousy. Or from her desire to please him. He wanted her to want him unequivocally, with all her heart and soul. He would play second fiddle to no other motive.

"We've got to stop," he gasped, wrenching his mouth from hers. "I can't do this. I won't do this. You belong to someone else, and I won't violate your commitment. It's wrong and we both know it."

She drew in a shuddering breath. "Nick, no . . . please . . . don't stop. It feels too good."

"I made a promise to you. We can't do this." He shook his head. "Not as long as another man's ring is on your finger."

Delaney got home around midnight, her clothes damp and filled with sand. Her mind in turmoil, her soul filled with a dark roaring, like a house in a hurricane. Buffeted by a destructive force she could not control.

Thankfully, her parents were in bed. No Honey to deal with. No need to explain the wild, desperate look she knew was etched into her face.

Delaney undressed in her bathroom and stared at her reflection in the mirror, felt the cool tile beneath her feet. Who in the world was this woman? She was morphing into someone she no longer recognized.

Tonight, she'd almost been unfaithful to Evan. Delaney would never have believed herself capable of such a thing. Of violating her most basic principles. She shuddered to think what would have happened if Nick hadn't had the moral courage to put on the brakes.

Searchingly, she raised her fingertips and traced the outline of her lips, raw and aching from the imprint of his mouth. Trying desperately to make sense of the emotions commanding her.

The map is not the territory, she thought. It was a piece of paper marked with symbols and lines, a representation of a place. *You are here.* But when you were actually there, the space around you did not look like the map drawings. There was undocumented terrain and surfaces not captured. There were scents and sounds and tastes and textures no map could denote. There were secret alcoves and gradient shadows and varying shades of light and hue.

On the outside, Delaney's external map was a glossy image—perfected by scalpel and etiquette, but her internal map of reality was distorted by her changing values and beliefs. By the filters life as a Cartwright had placed on her sense of self.

What did she want?

Where did she fit?

Who was she really?

Unable to answer these disturbing questions, she blocked them out and hopped into the shower, eager to wash away her sins.

She turned the water as hot as she could stand it and let it roll over her in heated waves, but no amount of steaming water could drown her guilt. When the water finally ran cold, she got out of the shower, dressed in silk pajamas, and climbed into bed.

Her mind kept going back to Nick and what had occurred on the beach. She tried to barricade her heart against him. To tell herself these feelings weren't important. That hormones couldn't be trusted, but she knew it was all a lie to salve her aching soul.

The phone, which was a private line into her bedroom, rang. She checked the caller ID. Out of area. Who was calling so late? She picked up the receiver.

"Hello?"

"Delaney, it's Evan."

Guilt rushed her. Guilt, guilt, and more guilt, combined with a strange sense of relief and gratitude. Thank heavens he had called. She needed so badly to hear his voice. So desperately needed for him to bring her back to the values she had almost thrown away in the heat of passion.

"Evan, it's so good to hear your voice. I'm so happy that you called." She crossed her legs into a semi-lotus position.

"It's not too late to be calling? Did I wake you?"

"No, no."

"I've missed you so much, Delaney," his voice cracked with emotion.

"I've missed you too." And she had missed him, in her way, missed that he hadn't been here to stop her from making a huge mistake.

"I was thinking about you tonight," he said. "I think about you every night and all through the day."

"I think about you too."

"I can't wait to see you. We've got so much to discuss."

"When will you be home?"

"A week from Sunday."

"I can't wait."

"Neither can I." She heard the smile in his voice. "Remember when we were kids, when we were each other's best friend?"

She swallowed hard. "I remember."

"I wish we were still friends in that same way."

"But we are still best friends," she protested.

"No, we're not. You have Tish, and I...I have my work," he said.

Delaney's heart pounded with hope. "Is there something bothering you, Evan? You sound different somehow."

"No, no, not at all," he denied. "Just thinking about how long we've known each other and how very much I love you. I do love you deeply, Delaney. You do know that."

Oh, dear God, the guilt was ripping her apart. "I know."

"You're a very special person."

"Not so special," she said, fresh pins of guilt pricking her.

"Very special," he disagreed. "You believed in me when no one else did. My parents didn't want me to be a doctor, remember? They wanted me to follow Dad into the oil business. You alone encouraged me to follow my dreams. You were the one who told me I'd make the best doctor in the world. You remember that?"

"I remember."

"I owe my success to you."

"You don't. You did all the hard work. I was just your cheering section."

"And I love you for it. You matter to me. You matter in my life. Being with you makes me happy."

"Oh, Evan." She sighed.

They were the magic words. He couldn't have said anything that would have convinced her more that she was doing the right thing by marrying him.

"I better go," he said. "Surgery around here starts at five a.m. I just needed to hear your voice, touch base with you. Everything okay there?"

"Fine, just fine."

"And the wedding plans?"

"Perfect."

"With your mother handling the arrangements, of course they are. I love you."

"I love you too," Delaney whispered. *Even if it's not in the way you deserve.*

But it was going to be okay, she convinced herself. He needed her. She mattered to him. Ultimately, that's what she needed most. No chemistry, no sparks, not that certain magical something.

Because it was easier for her to pretend that what they had was enough rather than risk her security on the outside chance that she could have it all.

Chapter 15

Nick tried not to think about Delaney while he sat in Evan Van Zandt's waiting room, but it was like a drowning man trying not to think about oxygen. She was in his brain, in his blood—like a virus he couldn't shake.

To distract himself he picked up a copy of *Texas Monthly* and leafed through it, only to find an article about high-society summer weddings and there, smiling back at him from her engagement photograph, was Delaney. Evan had his arm around her waist, and they both looked so happy it was all Nick could do to keep from ripping the page out of the magazine and shredding it into a hundred little pieces.

Instead, he tossed the magazine aside, got to his feet, and began to pace. Hell, even if she wasn't already engaged to his doctor, there was no way he and Delaney could have a future together. She got her picture in *Texas Monthly,* for crying out loud. She was cool, she was rich, and she was beautiful. He was hotheaded, middle class, and scarred in more ways than one.

"Mr. Vinetti," the nurse called from the doorway. "Dr. Van Zandt will see you now."

Nick clenched his jaw. He couldn't do this. Couldn't walk in there, look at Van Zandt's smiling mug, and not ache to coldcock him for running off to Guatemala and causing this whole mess in the first place.

It's not his fault, it's yours. You kissed Delaney when you knew she belonged to someone else. If you get your heart broken, you're responsible. No one else.

"Mr. Vinetti?" the nurse called again, and he followed her into the back offices.

Five minutes later, Nick was on the examination table, stuck in that damn yellow paper gown again, when Evan Van Zandt strode through the door. He looked tanned and lean and happy. Apparently, Guatemala agreed with him.

Van Zandt plopped down on the rolling stool and scooted over to the exam table. "How's the leg?"

"Improved."

"That's good to hear. Let's have a look." Van Zandt flipped up the corner of the paper gown and prodded Nick's knee. "How's that feel?"

"Doesn't hurt," he said. "A little sensitive to pressure, but no real pain."

"Excellent, excellent, and the swelling is gone. You really took my advice to heart. Nice progress." Van Zandt nodded, then rolled back over to the counter where he made some notations in Nick's chart.

Don't ask him about his trip. Don't ask about his upcoming wedding. Don't ask about Delaney. Get your release form and get the hell out of here.

"How was Guatemala?" Nick asked.

"Oh, terrific, wonderful." Van Zandt put down his pen and an expression came over his face that could only be described as transformational. "I've never felt so alive. We were in the wilds of the jungle, doing primitive surgery on children, most of whom had never even seen Americans. We were changing lives. These kids had horrible deformities, and when we were finished with them they looked normal. Their families were so grateful. I've never experienced anything like it."

The way Van Zandt was looking now was the way Nick felt whenever he thought about Delaney. If Van Zandt preferred getting off on his God complex to being with Delaney, in Nick's opinion, he was seriously delusional.

"There was this one little fella..." And Van Zandt was off, regaling him with the specifics of his trip.

Nick shifted uncomfortably on the table and indulged Van Zandt's riff for several minutes. Finally, he couldn't take it any longer. "What does your fiancée think about all this?"

"Oh, well, you know, I just got in late last night and I was so exhausted, to tell you the truth, I haven't had a chance to see Delaney."

"You haven't seen her since you got back?" Nick couldn't believe it. If he'd been gone from Delaney for six weeks, he'd immediately run to her house, sweep her into his arms, and make love to her all night long.

"I know, it sounds odd, but she's busy preparing for the wedding, and I'm busy catching up with my patients, and we've known each other since we were little kids. It's not like the crazy, can't-get-enough-of-you breathless kind of love that you see in the movies. Ours is a quieter, more mature relationship."

"Don't you think you deserve the breathless kind of love?" Nick surprised himself by asking. It was all he could do to keep from smashing his fist into Van Zandt's clueless face.

Van Zandt looked startled. "But that's not love. That's just a romanticized version of lust."

"Have you ever felt it? That breathless variety."

Van Zandt moistened his lips. "Well, no."

"That's what I thought."

Their gazes met and Nick saw a flick of doubt in Van Zandt's eyes and it made him feel stronger. "Can I go back to work?"

"What?" Van Zandt blinked.

"You'll sign my release form? Let me get back to work?"

"Yes, sure." Van Zandt shook his head. "I've got the form right here. A man does need his work."

A few minutes later, after getting dressed and settling up his bill, Nick found himself on the sidewalk outside the building. The same place where Delaney had first thrown the tarp over him—the release form clutched in his hands.

Scrawled in Van Zandt's strangely legible hand were the words, *Mr. Vinetti may return to full active duty.*

He looked at the form and an arrow of sadness pierced straight into his heart. He'd gotten what he'd come here for. How come he didn't feel the least bit happy about it?

The packages arrived like swarms of locust. Everyone in Houston, it seemed, was eager to curry favor with the Cartwrights by sending Delaney and Evan wedding gifts.

Now that she no longer had Lucia's house to worry about and had closed her office until after the honeymoon, Delaney was stuck opening wedding presents and writing thank-you notes. Honey oversaw the operation like General Patton reviewing his troops. Delaney sat at the kitchen table, glumly wielding a calligraphy pen while her mother opened the day's arrivals.

"That's the sixth food processor you've gotten," she sniped. "Doesn't anyone follow the wedding registry?

How difficult is it to go to Neiman's online and type in your name?"

"It's okay, Mother," Delaney said. "I don't mind exchanging them."

"I think it's just inconsiderate."

"You have to realize not everyone stresses over proper etiquette the way you do."

"Etiquette? I'm talking common courtesy."

Delaney sighed. "Just let it go."

"Excuse me?"

"Let it go, Mother. Stop trying to control everything."

"I'm not. I just think it's—"

"You are."

Honey drew herself up. "Well, what's wrong with trying to control things in order to have the best outcome?"

"It's my wedding. I should have some say in it."

Honey sat down beside her and reached out and took her hand. "I just want this to be the most perfect wedding ever. You deserve it. I can't tell you how much it means to me and your father. We love Evan so much. And you know how I've dreamed of this day. Especially since I never got to do this for Skylar."

Her mother's eyes misted with tears, and she fumbled in the pocket of her linen suit for a crisply starched and pressed monogrammed handkerchief. She dabbed carefully at the corners of her eyes, taking care not to smear her makeup. "How I wish your sister could be here for this celebration."

Seeing her normally composed mother tear up wrenched Delaney's stomach. In a flash, she was thrown back seventeen years to the day when they first heard the news that Skylar had been killed. It was the first time she'd ever seen her mother fracture, cracking like an egg, collapsing sobbing onto the floor.

Delaney had vowed then and there to do everything in her power to make everything all right. To do what it took to be the perfect child, to make her mother smile again. She packed down her anger, packed down her own desires, and devoted her life to being good. Her mother had taught her it was not okay to assert herself, and she'd lifted the lesson to virtuoso status.

The defense mechanism had served her well.

Following her mother's advice had transformed her from a chubby, unattractive, socially awkward child into a thin, pretty woman with lots of friends. But now, as she stood on the verge of marrying Evan and entering a life not of her own making, Delaney couldn't help feeling it had crippled her too.

All these years, what she longed to hear was that her presence mattered. That she was as important to her mother as Skylar had been.

But she'd never heard it.

Instead all she'd heard was that it was not okay to be who she really was, to assert herself.

Her mother put the handkerchief away and forced a bright smile. "Enough regrets. Since the other bakery we were using inconveniently went out of business on us, Sunshine Bakery graciously agreed to stand in at the last minute. They just e-mailed a picture of the cake they've specially designed for you based on the specifications I sent them. I think you're going to love it." Honey reached inside the portfolio she carried stuffed with wedding details and passed her the computer printout. "The other bakery's going out of business turned out to be a blessing in disguise."

Disappointment stole over her as she studied it. Delaney had wanted a traditional wedding cake with lots of tiers and roses and beading made of frosting.

This three-tiered cake was simple, sleek, and smooth. While it was stylish, it had no personality, no heart.

"Isn't it perfect?" Honey looked at her expectantly. Delaney knew what she was supposed to say; she was supposed to echo "Perfect."

But her success with Lucia's house gave her courage. She moistened her lips and met Honey's eyes. "Mother, I'm not sure this is the right one for me."

"Of course it's the right one. I know you think the wedding cake is a bit plain, but darling, it's simple and elegant. All those colored flowers and excess layers and cream frosting you wanted looked so trailer park."

"I'm not speaking of the cake."

"No?" Honey tilted her head. "Is there something else you wanted to weigh in on?"

For years her mother had been able to quell her with a single look that said, *I'm disappointed in you.* Delaney saw the awakening of that look now. One wrong word, and Honey's face would shift into full-blown disapproval.

"The wedding..." Delaney swallowed. *Come on. You can do this. Tell her the truth. Tell her you're not sure you're really ready to get married.*

"Yes?" Honey crossed her arms over her chest, warning her with her change in body language.

The childhood fear that her mother would no longer love her if she expressed an opinion dogged her.

Don't let her run over you. Say it.

"I'm not sure...August is so hot, and...while I love Evan to death, I'm not sure he's the right one for me."

"Young lady," Honey said and sternly pointed a finger at her. "Enough with the cold feet. It's time to grow up. You are *not* postponing this wedding again. The last two postponements have already cost your father in the neighborhood of twenty thousand dollars. He doesn't complain because he loves you, but I will not tolerate another postponement. You are marrying Evan Van Zandt on August fourth at three p.m., and I will not hear another word about it."

"It's time," Skylar told her that night, "to play your trump card. Mother might have issued an edict about your marriage to Evan, but you can still rattle her cage enough so she'll have to let you wear the veil."

Delaney, who had been growing more and more upset as the wedding plans progressed, was susceptible to Skylar's words. She climbed out of bed and as she made her way to the closet, she bumped against the dresser where she'd installed the hula doll Nick had given her.

The hula girl wildly shook her hips, and darn if she didn't appear to be winking.

Shake it up.

She flung open the closet door, took out both the consignment shop veil and the one her mother had bought for her at Bergdorf's. Using great care, she sat down at her vanity table, snapped the label from the Bergdorf's veil, and painstakingly stitched it into the hem of the veil Morag had tatted three hundred years ago.

As she worked, Delaney felt the power of the veil suffuse her. On this one thing, she would have her way. She might not get the chapel she'd hoped for or the wedding cake or the invitations or the dress or the groom of her choice, but by God she would wear Morag's veil. One way or the other she would have some small bit of magic in her life.

After she finished sewing the label in the veil, she crept downstairs to the closet where Honey kept the wrapping paper. She put the veil in a Bergdorf's box and then went back to her room to print off a note from her computer. Delaney racked her memory for the name of one of Honey's Philadelphia relatives and could only recall one. A great-aunt Maxie whom she'd never heard from nor met. Delaney had no idea if the woman was even still alive or not, but at this point she did not care. The note she typed read:

> To Delaney—so sorry I cannot attend the wedding. Please accept this veil in lieu of my presence. Wear it in good health—Your Great-Aunt Maxie.

Pleased with her handiwork, she wrapped the veil in elegant gift-wrapping paper, adorned it with a lavish bow, and sneaked back downstairs to put it with the stack of presents yet to be gone through sitting on the dining room table. She couldn't wait to see the look on her mother's face when Delaney opened that veil in the morning.

Honey could not believe Delaney was trying to back out of the wedding a third time. Children could be so ungrateful. No matter how much you did for them, it never seemed to be enough. They criticized and complained and generally behaved in a disagreeable manner.

She was going to take the high moral ground and forgive her daughter. Cold feet was an unpleasant affliction. Not that she could empathize. Marrying James Robert had been the best thing that had ever happened to her. She'd never had second thoughts. Even years later, when he'd developed a drinking problem. She knew you had to take the good with the bad.

Delaney was just nervous. That was all. Everything

would be fine as long as Honey did not allow her to consider postponing as an option. This wedding was happening. Honey would not be embarrassed again.

"Mother," Delaney told her at breakfast, "I want to apologize for my behavior yesterday. You were right and I was wrong."

Honey smiled. There now. That was the daughter she knew and loved. "It's all right, darling. I really do understand that this is a stressful time for you."

"Will you help me go through the gifts that arrived since yesterday? I want to keep abreast of the thank-you notes."

"Absolutely." Honey beamed. Yes, this was what she'd been wanting from Delaney. Full participation in the process. Honey retrieved the embossed stationery she'd had printed up just for the wedding and her Mont Blanc pen and joined her daughter in the dining room.

The packages that had arrived in the previous day's afternoon deliveries were stacked beside the boxes they'd already opened and gone through. Honey pulled out her list and settled at the table to write down who had given what while Delaney unwrapped the packages. She brought her orange juice with her from the breakfast table. It rested on a coaster to her left.

"Oh," Delaney said after she'd pulled the wrapping paper off the first gift. "It's in a Bergdorf's box."

"Who's it from?" Honey asked, picking up her glass of orange juice for a sip.

"I don't know. Let me see if there's a card in the box." Delaney lifted the lid and took out a wedding veil.

No, not just a wedding veil, but that hideous consignment shop wedding veil Honey had found under Delaney's bed. The one she'd hidden in her own closet.

She felt the blood drain from her face. What was going on here?

"Isn't it beautiful? And it has a designer label," Delaney said, shooting Honey a cool, calculated gaze.

"Who... sent it?"

"There's a note right here. 'To Delaney—so sorry I cannot attend the wedding. Please accept this veil in lieu of my presence. Wear it in good health—Your Great-Aunt Maxie.'"

Maxie. The name she'd never expected to hear again.

All the air left Honey's lungs. The glass of orange juice slipped from her hand and crashed to the tile, splattering her white slacks like a Jackson Pollock painting.

"Goodness, Mother, are you okay?"

Honey met her daughter's gaze, and she couldn't believe the cunning expression she saw there. It was as if Delaney was channeling Skylar.

"Fine," she managed to whisper. What was going on?

"Wasn't that sweet of Great-aunt Maxie?" Delaney clutched the veil to her chest. "I simply have to wear this veil at the wedding. I'm sure you won't mind if we return the veil you bought me. Right, Mother?"

"Right," Honey croaked.

And that's when she realized it was the beginning of the end of her life as she knew it.

On Thursday evening, at the Orchid Villa retirement community, Trudie and Lucia threw Delaney a bachelorette party.

Still flying high on her victory with the wedding veil, Delaney brought it with her to the party.

Everyone oohed and aahed over it as they passed it around. Then Tish told them about how wishing on the veil was supposed to make the deepest desires of your heart come true. Then, of course, everyone wanted to try it on and make a wish. As if it were a birthday cake or a falling star or a wishing well.

Delaney cringed as it was passed from head to head. "Please, you guys, I promised the lady I bought it from that I wouldn't wish on the veil."

"You promised you wouldn't wish on the veil," Jillian pointed out, just after she wished to win an important court case she was in serious danger of losing. "We didn't."

Delaney wrung her hands. "It still feels wrong."

"You don't seriously believe in it?" Tish said and then wished to get out of debt, before passing the veil to Rachael.

"The issue isn't whether I believe in it or not, but the fact that I promised Claire Kelley."

"But like Jillian said, that was your promise, not ours." Rachael settled the veil on her head.

"*Et tu,* Rachael?"

Rachael shrugged. "I wish for a grand romance."

"It's not Aladdin's lamp, you guys."

"We know. We're just having fun." Trudie accepted the veil from Rachael. "I wish to find a red-hot stud in my bed," she said, then passed it to Gina, who wished to get pregnant.

That brought an "aah" from everyone assembled.

Everyone except Lucia.

Lucia met Delaney's eyes. She was the only one who appreciated the power of the veil. When Gina passed the veil to her, Lucia said, "I wish you would all respect Delaney's wishes."

She got up and said to Delaney, "I'm just going to put this in Trudie's bedroom so no one else is tempted to monkey with fate. Don't forget it when you leave."

Delaney smiled gratefully at Lucia.

"Okay," Trudie said, rubbing her palms briskly together. "Who's up for Jell-O shooters?"

"I'm in," Tish said.

"Me too," Jillian chimed in.

"None for me." Gina patted her flat belly. "Chuck and I are working on giving the twins a little sister."

"I'm the designated driver," Rachael explained. "I'll have to pass as well."

"Delaney?" Trudie coaxed. "It's your next to last night as a free woman. Gotta shake things up and cut loose."

"No Jell-O shooters," Lucia said, coming back from the bedroom. "Until everyone has some food in their stomachs. There's Stromboli in the kitchen."

They all crammed into the kitchen, and soon they were laughing and talking and eating and drinking and doing Jell-O shooters and telling worst-date horror stories.

"I went out with a guy who, instead of going in for a good-night kiss, licked my face." Jillian shuddered.

"Ugh!" everyone shouted in unison.

"A guy took me to the movies, and when I came back from getting popcorn, he was necking with the woman sitting across the aisle from us," Gina said.

"What a pig." Rachael shook her head.

"Sex addict," Jillian diagnosed.

"Anyone wanna talk brushes with celebrities?" Trudie asked.

Lucia sighed. "Trudie had sex with Frank Sinatra when she was eighteen, and she's just dying to tell the story to a fresh audience."

"No kidding?" the younger women exclaimed. "Tell us, tell us. What was old Blue Eyes like in bed?"

"First let's set the stage. Anyone for poker?"

Five minutes later they had Sinatra on the stereo. Trudie was dealing Texas Hold 'Em, and Tish was passing around a bottle of peppermint schnapps because they'd run out of Jell-O shooters. Everyone seemed to be having a great time.

In Delaney's estimation, it was a pretty cool bachelorette party and she was glad no one had hired a male stripper. That would have been so embarrassing.

But then halfway through the game, there was a knock at the door. "Get that for me, will you, Jillian?" Trudie asked.

Jillian pushed back from the kitchen table just as another knock sounded.

"Houston PD," came a rough, masculine voice. "Open up in the name of the law."

Delaney's heart leaped.

And when Jillian opened the door to reveal a very buff masked man in a police uniform, for one crazy second Delaney thought it might be Nick.

The minute he walked over the threshold, her hopes were shattered. "We've had reports of disturbing the peace."

"Please, Officer Goodbody," Trudie said. "Don't arrest us. We're having a bachelorette party."

"Well, why didn't you say so?"

In an instant someone killed Sinatra and put on stripper music and Officer Goodbody whipped off his Velcro pants. "Who's the bride-to-be?"

Delaney good-naturedly endured the striptease and to please her friends pretended to like it. But the thing was, the fake cop made her think about the real cop in her life.

Nick's not in your life.

Her heart hit the floor. Sadness filled her, and she had to force herself to keep smiling as Officer Goodbody waggled his groove thing. She missed Nick so much.

What would it be like? she wondered. If it was Nick she was going to meet at River Oaks Methodist Church on Saturday afternoon instead of Evan?

Inside her head, wistful longing warred with loyal duty. Sexual chemistry duked it out with steadfast stability. Desire versus dignity.

She couldn't take it anymore. "Excuse me," Delaney said, got up from the table, and left the room, leaving Officer Goodbody looking surprised.

"Hey, what gives with her?" he asked. "Don't she wanna see the finale?"

"You can show us," Delaney heard Jillian say as she hurried into Trudie's bedroom, looking for solitude so she could collect her thoughts.

The minute she walked into the room, she saw the veil stretched out on Trudie's bed, looking more magical than ever.

Wish on me, it whispered to her. *Make the deepest wish of your soul come true.*

Delaney paced Trudie's small bedroom, casting frequent glances at the veil.

You can't wish on the veil. You promised Claire Kelley.

But it was a promise Delaney couldn't keep. The veil was her only way out. The single salvation left to her. She knew no other way to get out of the marriage that should have been so perfect and yet loomed like a total disaster. She had to rely on the magic of the veil. She had to believe.

With trembling hands, Delaney put the veil on her head.

"I wish...," she whispered, drawing in a deep breath, inhaling courage. "I wish to get out of this marriage."

Immediately a strange tingling spread over her scalp and her entire body grew hot.

She felt it once more, that wavery suspension of time that she'd experienced the first time she'd touched the veil and she'd had the vision.

The one where she was marrying Nick.

She saw it again. In minute detail.

Dizziness spun her head. She had to sit down hard on the edge of Trudie's bed to keep from falling.

"I wish to get out of this marriage," she said again, stronger, more certain this time.

"Do you really want to get out of it?" a voice asked.

Delaney's eyes flew open and she saw Trudie standing with her back pressed against the closed door.

"Yes."

"So why don't you just call it off?"

"I can't. Evan is so good. I've known him since we were kids, and I don't want to lose his friendship. Plus there's my mother. She'll be crushed. And the money my father has spent." Delaney shook her head.

"It's better than spending a lifetime married to a man you don't love."

"I don't know how to tell them so they'll hear me. No one really listens to me." *Except for Nick,* she thought. "I've spent most of my life letting people push me around, bending to their will, going with the flow to avoid confrontation. I can't stand the thought of hurting someone's feelings to their face."

"Too bad you don't have a Leo to come rescue you from the altar the way Lucia did."

"Yeah," Delaney echoed. She could wish all she wanted, but she knew Nick wouldn't come save her. He had too much integrity to steal another man's wife. "Too bad."

"You could hire someone to kidnap you."

Delaney looked up. Possibilities raced through her. If she hired someone to kidnap her from the wedding, then her family would have to listen to her. It was dramatic. It was bold. And Delaney saw it as her only way out.

"Remember my nephew Louie?" Trudie said. "You met him when you staged my house."

Louie had been a little rough-looking, with lots of piercings and tattoos, but he'd seemed like a nice enough guy. "Yes."

"For the right price, he'll kidnap you."

Chapter 16

Someone was beating on his front door.

Nick pulled himself from slumber, squinted at the clock on his bedside table, and groaned. Who in the hell had the audacity to show up on his doorstep at three o'clock in the morning? One of his brothers? A cousin?

Growling his displeasure, Nick threw off the covers.

"Coming, coming," he called out, searching in his closet for the bathrobe he hardly ever had the need to wear. Even though his knee was almost completely healed now, he didn't want to push it and move too quickly too soon. "Hold your horses."

He ambled to the living room, turned on the front porch light, and looked through the peephole to find Trudie Klausman, dressed like a twenty-year-old party girl in a belly-baring tank top and a short skirt that showed off her wrinkled knees and with sparkle glitter on her face, swaying in the night air. At first, he thought something must have happened to his nana.

Terrified, Nick yanked open the door. He stared Trudie in the eyes and realized she'd been drinking.

Horror squeezed his heart as another thought occurred

to him. Holy shit, what if Trudie was here for some kind of perverted, middle-of-the-night, Mrs. Robinson booty call?

Nick gulped. "Um, hello, Mrs. Klausman."

"Nicky, we've got an emergency situation on our hands." She rushed into his apartment.

Dear God in heaven, she *was* here for a booty call.

"Emergency?" The word came out high and squeaky, the way it did when he was thirteen and his voice was changing.

She wrapped her hand around his wrist and Nick stopped breathing. "I've got a very dire problem, and you're the only one who can solve it for me."

Nick had had a few booty calls in his life, but none he'd ever had to turn down before. He didn't know how to go about deflecting his grandmother's best friend without hurting her feelings.

"Mrs. Klausman... I...," he stuttered. "I'm very flattered, but . . but..."

Trudie gave him an odd look and quickly let go of his hand. "Oh, my God, you thought I came here for a booty call."

"No, no."

"Don't lie." She shook her finger under his nose. "And just because you are one handsome devil doesn't give you the right to assume that just because I'm an ex–Vegas showgirl and that I had a little too much to drink and I'm wearing something sexy, that I would want to have sex with you. You're far too young for me, and besides, your grandmother is my best friend. What do you take me for? A complete hussy?"

Mortified, he ducked his head. "Trudie, I'm truly sorry."

"If Delaney didn't need your help, I'd turn around and walk right out of here."

Nick's head shot up. "Delaney needs help?"

"I've done something kinda illegal and I'm having second thoughts, but Delaney was so desperate to get out of this wedding tomorrow, she asked me to hire my nephew, Louie, to kidnap her from the chapel."

Delaney wanted out of her marriage to Evan Van Zandt? Hope was like a gift, sprung in his chest, resurrecting the feelings he'd tried so hard to bury. "You're kidding."

"Do I look like I'm kidding?" Trudie glared and sank her hands on her hips.

No, she did not.

"Delaney's planning on standing Evan up at the altar?"

"In the most dramatic way possible. Poor girl, she's such a people-pleaser. Can't bear to hurt her fiancé's feelings, can't sum up the courage to face her overbearing mother. She feels backed into a corner with no way out. That's why I offered to contact Louie for her. She's such a good-hearted person, but she's never learned to stand up for herself."

"She's stood up to me a few times," Nick said, recalling the arguments they'd had. The time she flipped him the bird.

"Which is why you're so good for her. You inspire her to be more. You let her speak her mind and don't squelch her. You don't put her in a box or up on a pedestal. You actually like it when she's not perfect. You give her the freedom to be herself. You're exactly what she needs."

"Did you contact Louie already?"

"Yes."

"Has money exchanged hands?" Had a crime already occurred?

"I don't know. Delaney was on her way to meet him when I left her."

Nick blew out a breath and shoved a hand through his hair.

If what Trudie said was true and Delaney wanted out of the marriage so badly that she'd hired Trudie's nephew to kidnap her from the wedding, it meant she didn't have the courage to tell Evan the truth.

It must also mean she finally recognized platonic love was not enough to sustain a marriage.

While he admired Delaney for not going through with the wedding when she knew it was wrong, he was disappointed that she was taking the easy way out. And he wasn't going to let her get away with it. He was going to make her face up to her feelings.

"Call up your nephew," Nick told Trudie. "Tell him his services are no longer required."

"But if Louie doesn't kidnap Delaney from the chapel, she'll end up married to Evan. And you of all people should know how miserable it is to be married to the wrong one."

"I'll handle it. Just call off the kidnapping."

"Oh," Trudie exclaimed, her eyes flashing with excitement. "Are you going to do for Delaney what your grampa Leo did for Lucia? Are you going to whisk her away and save her from marrying the wrong man?"

"No," Nick growled. "She's spent most of her life looking for a magical solution to her problems. Rescuing is not what she needs. What I'm going to do is be there to make sure that Delaney saves herself."

The members of the wedding party and their families gathered outside the River Oaks Methodist Church for the wedding rehearsal. Delaney had driven over with her parents, and she regretted the decision. Her mother's constant nit-picking of every little detail had given her a headache.

"Don't worry, it'll be over soon." Evan smiled and squeezed her hand. "Your mother means well."

"I've got to get something for this headache," she said. "I think there's some ibuprofen in the glove compartment of the Caddy. Go on in, I'll be right behind you."

Head throbbing, Delaney headed back out to the parking lot, angling for her mother's Cadillac. It wasn't just her mother's nit-picking that had given her the headache, and she knew it. Guilt was the thing pounding through her veins. She didn't want to go through with this wedding, but she didn't have the courage to tell Evan to his face. She had written him a long note, explaining how she felt and begging his forgiveness. She still hadn't figured out how to handle her mother.

Delaney thought about all the people she was going to hurt and felt physically ill.

She plunked down in the front passenger seat of the Caddy. The humidity plastered her panty hose to her legs. She wouldn't have worn them, but her mother insisted. Apparently in Honey's book it was gauche to go barelegged to a wedding rehearsal.

After resting a moment to let the nausea subside, she popped open the glove compartment and rummaged around until she found the ibuprofen. She pulled the bottle out, and a crumpled-up note fell out with it.

What was this?

Delaney unfolded the note, read what was written there in stark black block letters.

She let out a gasp and plastered her hand over her mouth. Her mother had been lying. At last, she knew the reason her mother had gone to meet the patch-eyed woman at the amusement park on Galveston Island.

Honey Montgomery Cartwright was being blackmailed.

What she didn't know was why.

"Invitation, sir." The security guard posted outside the River Oaks Methodist Church held out his palm and waited expectantly for Nick to paper it with a wedding invitation.

But he didn't have one.

"No invite?" The guard arched an eyebrow.

"No."

"Sorry." The guard moved to block the door. "Without an invitation you don't get in."

A few people were still trickling in from the parking lot, but they were rushing as if late, flashing their invitations to the security guard, then slipping inside through the heavy wooden door. The sun beat down hot, pooling sweat under the collar of the only suit Nick owned. The suit he'd bought for his grandfather's funeral.

"You don't understand," Nick said. "It's imperative I get in. The bride is about to make a huge mistake."

"If you ask me, anyone who gets married is making a huge mistake." The guard shook his head. "Can't go in."

The sounds of the wedding march began. He had to get in there before it was too late. Louie wouldn't be showing up to kidnap Delaney as she expected, and if Nick wasn't there to intervene, he feared she'd just go ahead with the ceremony.

"I have to get in there."

"You want me to call the cops?"

"I am the cops."

"Prove it."

Grinding his teeth in frustration, Nick fumbled in his pocket for his badge and shoved it in the guy's face. "Now get the hell out of my way."

"Jeez, fella, why didn't you just say you were a cop in the first place?" the guard grumbled and stepped aside.

Nick tore into the building.

The contrast from the bright sunlight to the darkened interior of the church had him blinking. Disoriented, he stood in the entryway while his eyes adjusted.

Flowers invaded the foyer, filling his nose with their fresh summer scent. He heard the rustling of clothes, the muted coughs of the spectators, and the wedding march. The song was already half over.

The doors leading into the chapel were thrown wide. He hurried toward them and saw Delaney on the arm of a man he presumed was her father, moving toward the altar.

Instinct had him wanting to shout her name, but he would wait for the right moment. When the minister asked if there were any objections, that's when he would say his piece.

He looked around for a place to sit, but he was out of luck. The chapel was crammed to the rafters. This shindig was costing her father a boatload of money. Boy, was he going to be upset when everything blew up in his face.

But probably not as upset as Evan Van Zandt was going to be. Nick actually felt sorry for him. He knew what it was like, getting dumped by the woman you loved.

Heart clogging his throat, Nick went to stand against the back wall, watching the proceedings with a surreal feeling of detached anxiety. It was as if he were in a dream, knowing he was dreaming but unable to wake up. What if, when the time came, he shouted out his objection but no one heard him?

Goose bumps broke out on his arms. He was too far away. He needed to move closer. Nick started creeping around the back of the church, picking his way past the other attendees who'd been too late to find a seat, all the while craning his neck to follow what was going on up at the altar.

Delaney looked absolutely, totally stunning in that white dress and wedding veil.

Nick stared at the veil. When she walked, it looked as if a hundred white butterflies were fluttering up around her. She looked like magic, pure and perfect. And he wanted her with the same seven-year-old fervency he had wanted his mother not to die. If he didn't stop her from marrying Van Zandt, he feared his heart would never, ever recover.

Delaney's father put her hand in Van Zandt's and stepped back to take a seat in the front row.

Nick stopped making his way around the side of the packed pews, every muscle in his body tensed as he heard the portly minister say, "Dearly beloved..."

But that was as far as the man got.

A loud noise, like someone tripping over tin cans stacked high behind the exit door to the left of the altar, drew everyone's attention in that direction.

The minister paused.

The exit door flew open and a man dressed in black jeans, a long-sleeved black button-down shirt, black boots, and a black ski mask came tumbling out. He looked as out of place as a chunk of charcoal in a basket of marshmallows.

The guests heaved a collective gasp.

Anger shook him. Dammit. Trudie must have forgotten to cancel her nephew, Louie. Either that or she hadn't trusted Nick to get Delaney out of this mess of her own making. That was a fine state of affairs. Now what was he going to do?

Before Nick had time to formulate a plan, Louie was at the altar waving a gun around. He hoped like hell it was a prop gun, because if it wasn't, whenever he got his hands on Louie he was going to make him sorry he ever agreed to this fake kidnapping.

Poor Van Zandt looked scared out of his wits. He was trembling and blinking and just standing there impotently letting it all play out. If Nick had been up there, he would have charged the guy.

So charge him anyway. Put a stop to this nonsense.

Nick ran.

But some woman had her purse in the aisle and he tripped over it. His knee crumbled. He cursed but immediately got back up.

Louie was already dragging Delaney out the exit. The crowd was on their feet, everyone following after them.

The mob bottlenecked at the exit door, and Nick knew it was time for another plan. Ignoring the pain shooting through his knee, he did an about-face and headed back in the direction he'd come, dodging the guests surging forward.

Somehow, he made it out to his pickup just in time to spy a white delivery van careering out of the parking lot with Louie at the wheel.

Nick started his engine, popped the clutch into gear, and sped off after them.

The nondescript white delivery van roared from the church parking lot. Jim Bob Cartwright stared after it, his mind numb. "Someone call 911. My daughter's been kidnapped!" he intended to shout to the clump of tuxedoed crowd gawking at him, but his throat squeezed so tight he could not speak.

Honey wrapped her hand around his wrist. "We've got to get out of here, James Robert. Right now."

"No, no," he gasped and clung to her arm. "Must call police. FBI. Delaney's been kidnapped."

Honey lowered her voice. "Listen to me. We can't call in the authorities."

Jim Bob stared at her, uncomprehending. "What?"

"We can't call the police."

Was his wife afraid of public embarrassment? The vein at his forehead throbbed suddenly, violently. He let go of her, stepped back, and fisted his hands. Was Honey actually worried about how this was going to reflect on her? Was she more concerned about appearances than her daughter's safety?

Disgust sickened his stomach. "Why in the hell not?"

"Please, James Robert." Her eyes beseeched him. It had been a very long time since he'd seen her this vulnerable, and it scared him. "Just take me home."

"No, no. We have to call the authorities. Someone just kidnapped our daughter."

"We *can't*." Fear drew her mouth tight, creased the fine wrinkles around her eyes. She looked haunted, hunted.

"What is it, Honey? What's wrong?"

"I know who took Delaney."

He watched her—confused, nervous, heart pounding. Beneath his tuxedo, sweat plastered his shirt to his back.

Honey hitched in a fragile breath that sounded strangely like the frantic beat of hummingbird wings. "And I know why she took her. She took her because of me."

"She? It was a man who kidnapped Delaney."

"Hired thug."

"What?"

Honey swayed and Jim Bob was afraid she would collapse. Instinctively, he circled his arm around her waist. "Are you all right?"

"This heat. Get me out of here."

"We have to call the cops," he said. "I'm going to call the cops."

"No." Her voice was soft, yet shrill.

He ignored her protest, turned to the crowd around them. The longer they waited, the farther Delaney got from them. "Does anyone have a cell phone I can use?"

A half dozen people thrust cell phones at him, but before Jim Bob could grab one, Honey tugged him in the direction of their car, her fingernails digging into his skin.

He balked, digging his heels into the pavement.

"James Robert," she said through gritted teeth, "don't buck me on this."

He studied her face, regal, proud, well preserved yet suddenly looking every bit of her fifty-three years. This was the first time in years he'd seen her looking so unguarded, so full of pain and hunger and desperation. She was a mystery to him. Always had been and he feared she always would be.

"I'm tired of tiptoeing around you, Honey," he growled. "Tired of pretending we don't have a big problem with our marriage. Tired of kowtowing and trying to please you. It's impossible. Nothing pleases you."

"Stop," she hissed, shifting her gaze to the gawking crowd gathered behind them.

"Why? Afraid of a little public embarrassment? Is that it? You'd rather save face than save your daughter?"

Honey's cheeks blanched so pale Jim Bob thought she

might faint. He felt like an utter shit and rushed to sh
his arm around her once more.

His wife rested her head against his shoulder, pressed her lips against his ear, and whispered hoarsely, "We can't call the cops because I'm being blackmailed."

"You're not Trudie's nephew," Delaney exclaimed to the man who'd snatched her from the chapel.

"Surprise, surprise."

"Where's Louie?"

"I dunno. Who's Louie?"

"You're not working for Trudie?"

"No."

"I think you've abducted the wrong bride."

"No, I haven't." He pulled a piece of paper from his front pocket. "Delaney Lynn Cartwright. That's you, right?"

"Pull this van over right now and let me out of here," she commanded in her best imitation of her mother.

"Sorry." He shook his head, thick with dark, shaggy hair. "No can do."

"You're kidnapping me for real? This isn't some prank?"

He eyed her in the rearview mirror. "What do you think?"

How had this happened? What was going on? "Who in the hell are you?"

"There's no need for you to know my name."

"So what am I supposed to call you? Here, kidnapper, kidnapper, kidnapper?"

He laughed. "Cute, but it's not going to work. You ain't getting my name."

"Maybe I'll just call you Little Dick," she said, feeling

a million miles away from her old self. In spite of being kidnapped, she was feeling spunky and relieved. This guy didn't know her. She could say anything. Be anyone. It was a surprisingly freeing thought.

"Hey!" he snapped. "Five and a half inches is average-sized!"

"Little Dick."

"Stop saying that."

"Why? What are you going to do? Kill me?"

"Not if you don't give me a good reason. Word to the wise, calling me Little Dick is bordering on a good reason."

"You're right," she said. "Excuse me. My bad manners."

How ridiculous! Here she was, apologizing to a kidnapper. It took a lot to totally shake off a lifetime of indoctrination in proper etiquette. Although, she doubted Emily Post had penned anything on kidnapping protocol.

"Where are you taking me?"

"It's a surprise."

"I don't like surprises."

"Too bad."

"Remove these handcuffs," she demanded and then added, "Please."

"Nope."

"They're hurting my wrists."

"You'll live, princess."

"Let me go. I'll pay you."

He didn't answer.

"I have money."

"It's not just about that."

"No? What else is it about then?"

"Not my place to tell you."

"Are you an enemy of my father? Is this some business deal gone awry?"

"Nope." He sounded too damn casual. "Now be a good girl and just sit back and relax."

Oh, God, this guy really was kidnapping her for real. What were the odds of someone plotting to kidnap her on her wedding day? The exact same day she'd already hired someone to kidnap her? Impossibly high and suspiciously coincidental.

Suddenly the kidnapper sped up and Delaney was thrown backward onto the floorboards again. Real terror struck her then. Hard and coppery-tasting.

"What is it? What's going on?"

"Some asshole is chasing us."

"Where?" Delaney twisted around and tried to peer out the back of the van, but a dirty window and the lace veil blocked her view. She'd wished on it for a way out of her impending marriage and she'd gotten her wish, but certainly not in the way she had expected.

What was it Claire Kelley had said? You get your most heartfelt wish, not necessarily the thing you wished for most. Maybe this was cosmic punishment for wishing on the veil when she'd promised Claire she wouldn't.

She crawled to the back of the van with an unformed plan for escape, her handcuffed wrists held out in front to brace herself in case she fell over again. The progress was slow because the train of her dress kept wadding up underneath her. She would shuffle forward a bit, stop, pull the nest of collected material out from under her knees, and shuffle forward again. Just as she reached the back window, the nut job behind the wheel swerved crazily and she went down, weeble-wobbling into the side of the van.

"Drive like a human being," she hollered. "My parents won't pay you a single dime if I'm dead."

The word "dead" echoed in the empty confines of the

van, and for the first time the true reality of the situation struck Delaney.

"He's trying to cut me off," the kidnapper whined.

Hope vaulted into her chest. Was it someone from the wedding party out to save her? Could it be her daddy? Was it Evan? Oh, dear, how could she ever look her fiancé in the eyes again once he learned she'd hired someone to kidnap her? "Who's trying to cut you off?"

"Some son of a bitch in a red Ford pickup truck. Friend of yours?"

That tenuous hope blossomed into full-blown optimistic joy. Her heart sang.

Nick!

But how could it be Nick? He hadn't been invited to the wedding. He didn't even know where it was being held.

He's a cop, he could figure it out.

But why would Nick be after her?

Her mind spun a crazy fantasy worthy of *The Graduate*. Nick had come to rescue her from an ill-conceived wedding in the tradition of Leo and Lucia. Only to discover she'd already hired Louie to take her hostage. Except that had gone haywire, and now she was being spirited away by some unknown kidnapper. What the hell kind of wish-fulfilling magic threads was the veil made out of?

She had to get a look out that window and see if it was indeed Nick. Delaney finally made it over to the back window for a peek outside just as the red pickup truck pulled into the left lane beside the delivery van. All she could see was the bumper.

Bummer.

"The red truck," she called to the driver, "can you see the dashboard?"

"Lady, it's taking all my concentration to keep us from getting run off the road."

"Look in your side-view mirror. Can you tell if there's a hula girl shimmying away on his dashboard?"

"I can't tell. Hold on. I see something. Yep, there's a hula girl shaking it up on his dashboard. Mean something to you?"

Hello, it was her Nick! Shaking things up.

Her insides knotted with emotion. She felt giddy and scared and happy and surprised and so many other things she couldn't even name them all.

The right front and back tires of the van veered off the road and rattled along the shoulder. Delaney ended up toppling over again. At this rate, she might as well stay on the floor until Nick got her out of this mess.

The van was making ominous noises, tires thrumming against the uneven asphalt. The smell of tar melting hotly in the August sun burned her nose. Delaney's mouth tasted of dry anxiety. Her knees and elbows stung from carpet burn. The driver was twisting the van to and fro, trying to outrun Nick.

Fear spun her head. Her heart slammed her blood through her veins as rapidly as a six-piston pump.

"This bastard's crazy!" The driver accelerated. "Hang on, I'm gonna cut across the freeway, and it ain't gonna be pretty."

The van swerved dramatically. Car horns blared. Tires squealed. Delaney shrieked before the van ever slammed the concrete median separating the southbound lane from the northbound lane.

The impact jarred her teeth as they bumped over the barrier. Her heart stilled suddenly and her chest felt tense and cold. She was going to die like this. Handcuffed.

Wearing an outrageously overpriced wedding dress that she'd chosen for her wedding to a man she didn't love in the right way, while she secretly longed for another man. A different man.

Her heart stirred restlessly. The very man who was risking his life to come after her. Closing her eyes, she prayed Nick would have sense enough not to follow them over the median.

"He's still coming after us."

No, Nick, no, she thought, but could not contain her elation. He was coming after her. No concrete median or big-city traffic was going to stop her brave, daring cop.

"Holy shit!"

"What, what?" Delaney's eyes flew open. She struggled toward the back window again, desperate to see what was happening. An eighteen-wheeler's horn blared. Brakes screamed.

"Your boyfriend in the red pickup... holy shit..."

"What is it, what is it?" she cried.

But the loud noise of metal smacking metal said it all.

"He just wiped out."

Chapter 17

After an SUV sideswiped his bumper, Nick battled physics to keep the pickup truck on the road. He squeezed the steering wheel in a death grip and his right leg quivered from the adrenaline rush and quick tromping from the brake to the gas pedal.

Cars swerved, drivers flipped him off. He spied a couple of people with shocked expressions on their faces, grabbing their cell phones, no doubt phoning 911.

Good. He could use all the help he could get.

In the meantime, he was hell-bent on catching up with the bastard in the white van who'd taken off with Delaney before the vehicle disappeared from Nick's sight. His heart was willing; his pickup truck, however, was made of weaker stuff. The tires shimmied as he turned on his blinker and guided the clattering vehicle into the middle lane. His muffler had been knocked loose in the impact, but he had no time to worry about it.

Delaney needed him.

His pulse pumped hard and fast. Who had taken her hostage and why?

Why? Well, her father was one of the richest men in Houston. That was motive enough.

Nick's cop mind wasn't buying it. The kidnapping was too much of a coincidence, what with Delaney already hiring her own abductor. There had to be another connection, something important that he was missing.

But he couldn't think. His emotions were strangling him, pushing him forward, stamping out caution and common sense. He was ready to fight. To battle anyone who got in his way. He was getting Delaney back.

He tromped on the accelerator, anxious to close the widening gap between him and the white van. In the distance, he heard the sound of sirens. He didn't slow down. Nothing was going to keep him from his woman.

His woman?

What the hell was that?

Nick's chest tightened. Okay, he was ready to admit it. He felt possessive of Delaney.

Up ahead, the van took the exit ramp. Nick tried to coax more power from the pickup, pushing the gas pedal to the floor, but nothing doing. The engine rumbled ominously. Nick swore.

He changed lanes, swerving around a slow-moving Caddy, and followed the van off the freeway.

There was a traffic signal up ahead turning from yellow to red. The van never slowed, just sailed right through the intersection, accompanied by a cacophony of honking horns.

"Dammit, Delaney," he muttered, cursing because he knew no other way to deal with the intensity of his feelings. "Hang in there, babe, I'm coming, I'm coming."

But just as he declared it, the pickup sputtered and died right in the middle of the crossroads.

* * *

Honey made James Robert take her home before she would tell him the truth. But even once they were there, she realized it was the hardest thing she would ever have to admit. She had no idea how to explain to her husband that the woman he'd been sleeping beside for thirty-four years had never really existed. That she'd been living a lie, that their marriage was a sham.

They'd sent the maid home and turned off the ringer on the phone. The neon numbers on the answering machine blinked wildly. Twenty-seven messages. Everyone wanting to know what had happened to Delaney. Honey wondered if any of the calls were from Evan, but she didn't have the energy to think about him. She had enough problems on her hands. Evan and the Van Zandts would just have to wait.

James Robert sat on the leather sofa in the living room while Honey paced in front of him, still wearing her stiff, uncomfortable mother-of-the-bride dress and high heels. *Tap, tap, tap,* went her shoes as she moved back and forth, top teeth sunk into her bottom lip as she tried to decide how to begin.

"Just tell me," James Robert said. "Why are you being blackmailed?"

Honey cleared her throat and glanced over at him. He looked at her with haunted eyes, pleading for her to deny everything. But her past had finally caught up with her. It was time for the truth. He deserved the truth. Even if afterward he told her he wanted a divorce. That he never wanted to see her again.

Her heart cleaved. This was a mess of her own making and she knew it. The rubber had smacked up against the road. Time for the truth.

"I'm not who you think I am," she said at last.

James Robert blinked. "I don't get it."

"I'm not Honey Montgomery."

"What are you talking about?"

Fear of losing everything in the world she loved cemented her throat. She shook her head. "I...I..."

"If you're not Honey Montgomery, who are you?"

She took a deep breath and spoke the name she hadn't said aloud in over thirty years. "My real name is Fayrene Doggett."

"I don't understand. How? Why?"

Honey sat down across from him, hands clasped in her lap, shoulders razor-straight the way she'd taught herself to sit. She wanted to duck her head to look away, but that wasn't her style. She might be a liar and a fraud, but she wasn't a coward.

James Robert's eyes searched hers. He looked bewildered, confused, but not judgmental or angry. That would change. When he learned how she had deceived him, discovered who she really was deep inside.

"Let me get this straight. You're not in the social registry? You're not a Philadelphia blue blood?"

"No."

He didn't say a word—just studied her intently, as if she were some alien pod person who'd kidnapped his wife. In a way, she was. Honey wished he'd yell at her or curse or slam his fist into the expensive coffee table imported from Germany. But he did not.

The lie, her admission, his shock, her betrayal, cohered into a thick, dark wall of emotion and tension, vibrated the bleak air between them.

Honey spied the slightest quiver in his hands and her own body quaked in response.

The long moment of silence stretched between them. Sweat beaded on Honey's upper lip in spite of the air-conditioning cooling their vast home to a balmy seventy-five degrees. She noticed how the lines around her husband's eyes had deepened with the years. How the loss of their daughter had etched pain into his face. She wanted to reach out to stroke his cheek, but she didn't dare. She didn't deserve to touch him. Not after what she'd done.

"Well?" James Robert prompted. "Just who the fuck are you, Fayrene Doggett?"

His rough language made her cringe, but she reveled in it. Ah, there it was. The anger. The emotion that meant he still cared, that he hadn't given up on her completely. "I was born the daughter of carnival workers," she began, and it hurt so much to say those words she thought her lips must have cracked.

"Carnies?"

"Yes," she whispered.

James Robert snorted and dragged a palm down his face. "That explains your violent hatred of carnivals. I always wondered about it."

His response seemed so incongruous to Honey that she almost laughed. Except nothing was funny.

"So how did you get from there to here?" he asked, anger growing in his eyes. A chill chased over her, raised goose bumps on her arms.

"We moved in caravans from town to town. It was a rough life. My parents were essentially grifters, con artists. I was forced to pickpocket and beg for money. From the time I was very small, I dreamed of a better world. I would cut pictures from magazines and paste them in a scrapbook. I promised myself one day I would escape. I would become a great lady. I would live in a beautiful house and have a loving family and lots and lots of money. Everything would be perfect and then I could finally be happy," she said.

Tears pressed at the back of her eyelids, but she blinked them back. After so many years of disciplined self-control, she had no idea how to just let them fall. How to show her vulnerability to the man she loved more than life, but had never been able to share her true self with.

Her mind scalded with the thought of all she'd hidden from him. She felt strangled, weighted down, burdened by her lies. A great hopelessness washed over her. How could she ever expect him to forgive her? How could she ever forgive herself for cheating them of the closeness they could have had?

But if he'd known you were from carny stock, you'd never have had a chance with him at all.

Her husband stared at her, unmoving, hands clenched atop his thighs. She could see him processing what she had told him, trying to understand. But he could never really understand. His life had been blessed from the beginning. Charmed. James Robert had no idea what it took to crawl up from the gutter.

Nervously, she cleared her throat. This was a good sign, right? That he was even hearing her out. That he hadn't already thrown her from the house?

"I never even finished high school," Honey admitted. "My parents never stayed in one place long enough. But wherever we went, I found the local library and I read and read and read. Reading was my escape from reality. The safe haven I ran to when things got ugly. I took the GED when I turned seventeen and scored one hundred percent on the test."

Her hands trembled. She was afraid to look him in the

eyes, but she couldn't stand not knowing what was in his eyes. The look on James Robert's face was empty, unmoving. Honey's soul ached. He hadn't thrown her out yet, but the potential was there.

"My father had a heart attack that same year." She smoothed her fingers over the skirt of her dress, ironing out wrinkles that weren't there. "We were in Philadelphia then and my mother couldn't handle it. Her drinking spiraled, she started dating a really rough character and dabbled with drugs. They fought all the time." Honey swallowed. She had blocked the details from her mind so long ago. It was difficult to call them up again. "It was ugly. I tried to get my mother to leave him, but she was too deep into alcoholism to drag herself out, and I was terrified her boyfriend was going to turn his violent temper on me if I stayed. So I ran away."

Guilt and shame suffused her as the truth spilled out of her. She told him all the things she should have told him years and years ago. She talked and talked and talked and when she was done, she sank back against her expensive leather couch, drained and exhausted.

She peeked over at James Robert, who hadn't moved a muscle during her recitation. She wanted him to take her in his arms, kiss her gently, and tell her it was all right. The past was over, and he loved her no matter who she was. But she couldn't hope for that. She didn't deserve his forgiveness.

"I'm sorry you suffered," James Robert said, but his tone was devoid of emotion. He sounded flat, dead inside.

Honey lifted her chin. Always the fighter, always the survivor. Never give up, never surrender. He didn't ask her what happened next, but she told him anyway. "I survived. I went to a homeless shelter and they got me a job as a live-in companion taking care of a wealthy elderly woman with Alzheimer's, who'd been a recluse for years."

"Abigail Montgomery," James Robert said.

"Yes. She had no immediate family left. Her only child, a daughter named Honey, had died years before in a skiing accident in the Alps."

"So when did you decide to assume the daughter's identity?" He spit out the words. His jaw muscles clenched tight.

"It was never a conscious decision. She'd call me by her daughter's name and when I tried to correct her, she'd get upset. It was easier to humor her and let her call me Honey. In the beginning Abigail had her days where she was more lucid than others, and even when she wasn't lucid about the present, she still remembered her debutante days. She taught me the ways of high society. How to speak. How to act. Proper etiquette. The right way to do things. She was lonely and enjoyed my company."

Honey stared off into the distance, remembering who she used to be and the path she'd taken to become who she was now. "As Abigail's condition worsened, she started calling me Honey all the time. She'd kept her daughter's clothes and gave them to me to wear. It was easy to pretend I was her daughter, who'd been living abroad for some years and had returned home to care for my ailing mother. It took little effort to fool the boy who delivered the groceries or the mailman or the local pharmacist. Remember, by this time, I was walking the walk and talking the talk of a woman raised in the lap of luxury."

"And Abigail," James Robert said, "because of her condition and her lack of immediate family, was no longer active in her social circle. I'm guessing her friends had long ago abandoned her, so it made it easier for you to pretend. There was no one to ferret you out as a fraud."

"That's right."

His gaze hardened. "So you formed a plan to become Honey Montgomery, and you started trolling the University of Pennsylvania campus, looking for a rich husband. You knew Abigail's gravy train wouldn't last forever."

"No, no," Honey denied. "It wasn't like that. On the one day I had off from caring for Abigail, I took a class at the university. I was interested in an education, not getting married. Marriage was the last thing on my mind."

"I find that hard to believe." His eyes were cold, unfeeling. "Coming from a liar like you."

Real fear pushed bile into her throat. She curled her fingernails into her palms. She was losing him. He wasn't going to forgive her. But she couldn't fault him. She'd done an unforgivable thing.

"And the day I met you?"

She sat up straighter. "That was the day I killed Fayrene Doggett, and Honey Montgomery was resurrected from the grave. I knew that a man like you, from a rich, successful family, could never love a common carny pickpocket like me. I became what you needed me to be, James Robert."

"I guess you're pretty lucky Abigail Montgomery died when she did, or you wouldn't have been able to fool me for long. If we'd stayed in Philadelphia, I would have eventually found out the truth. Unless, that is, you killed her."

Honey gasped as if he'd slapped her. "Do you actually believe that of me?"

"How would I know? I have no idea who you really are."

"I'm not capable of murder." Her voice quivered, half with anger, half with fear.

"I didn't think you were capable of lying and cheating your way into marriage, either, but apparently I was wrong. I always knew you were one determined woman.

That you never let anything stand in your way. It was one of the things I admired most about you." He gave a rough, humorless laugh.

"I'm not denying that Abigail's death, two weeks after we met, made my deception much easier. And the fact she left me a small inheritance gave credence to my story that medical bills and bad investments had wiped out the family fortune."

Honey felt the familiar ache of loss and loneliness deep within her heart, a void that plunged straight through to her soul. A single tear slid down her cheek. Wet and hot. She didn't swipe it away, just allowed it to roll until it dried at her chin.

"You tricked me into marriage. You were the one who insisted on a quick elopement." Resentment was etched into every corner of her husband's face, and she couldn't think badly of him for it. He had every right to his resentment, his anger, his hatred for her and what she had done.

"I did it only because I loved you so much," she murmured.

He made a harsh, unforgiving noise. "You irrevocably altered the course of my life, without my knowledge, without my permission. You cheated me."

"Please," she begged for his understanding, even though Honey Montgomery Cartwright never begged. "I couldn't bear the thought of living without you, and I knew if you found out who I really was, your family would pressure you to dump me."

"You're probably right about that." His eyes were cold as flint, the look in them striking her through the heart. The gulf between them loomed impossibly wide. And she realized there was no bridging this canyon. There was no going back.

"And you would have done it because you had a hard time standing up to your family, James Robert."

"Just like Delaney does," he said.

The mention of their daughter's name brought them out of their muddled past and back into the room, back to the reality that their daughter had been kidnapped from the chapel on her wedding day. Honey wanted to reach over and touch her husband's hand, but she was so terrified he'd shake off her comfort. She couldn't bear that.

"You've lived in fear all these years. That the world was going to discover your dark secret. That's why you were so insistent on things being perfect. That's why you pushed the girls the way you did. Everyone was watching. You couldn't risk a misstep, nor could your children."

"Yes," Honey admitted.

"Lying turned you into something you're not, into someone you're not. I've watched you change over the years, and I never understood why you did the things you did. At times I felt like you were doing your best to push me away."

Her husband was right. She had pushed him away with her demands of perfection. She'd known she was pushing him away, forsaking intimacy for secrecy. Honey thought of all the love she'd missed, all the joy she'd negated. In her desperate need to forsake her past, she'd hopelessly maimed her future.

Despair seized her. Turned her inside out as the world as she knew it flipped upside down. And nothing would ever be the same again.

"And now," she whispered, "I'm being blackmailed by my own mother. She saw my picture with Delaney in *Society Bride* and demanded twenty thousand dollars or she was going to the police. I paid her off."

James Robert got up from the couch.

"Where are you going?" Honey asked, nervously lacing her fingers together.

"To phone the police."

Terror gripped her. "You can't. If you call the police everyone will find out about me."

He stared at her. "Keeping your secret is more important than our daughter's life?"

"No, no, of course not. It's just that I'm sure my mother is behind this kidnapping. She won't hurt Delaney. We can pay her off and still keep things quiet."

Hatred flared in his eyes. "Good God, woman, you can't keep living this lie. It's over. Everything is over."

Honey closed her eyes. He was right. She'd been hiding and lying for so long, her values had gotten completely screwed up. Her eyes flew open. Mentally, she braced herself. "Call them."

James Robert reached for the phone, turning on the ringer at exactly the same moment it rang. He picked it up. "Hello."

Honey sank her teeth into her bottom lip.

"Evan," James Robert said on a sharp intake of breath.

Hand splayed over her chest, she got to her feet and went to stand beside her husband. He had a short, one-sided conversation with Evan that she couldn't decipher, then he hung up and turned to look at her.

"Delaney left Evan a note."

Honey blinked. "A note."

James Robert pursed his lips and glared at her. Honey felt his rage all the way to her bone marrow. "I guess it was a good thing you didn't let me call the cops."

She frowned. "I don't understand."

"Seems our daughter was desperate to get out of the marriage, but because of you and your inflexible demand for perfection, she had no idea how to tell us she didn't want to marry Evan. Congratulations, you officially pushed her over the edge."

Misery lay like granite in Honey's stomach. "What are you saying?"

"Delaney hired someone to take her hostage."

Nick had been in a car accident racing to rescue her. He could be hurt. He could have been killed.

Delaney felt a shock of fear and dread unlike anything she'd ever experienced before. The white-hot pain of sorrow rocketed into her heart, so intense she thought she was going to be sick.

She had to get out of this van. Had to get to Nick. She had to make sure he was unharmed. Had to let him know how much she loved him.

Because she did love him. Loved him so much she could scarcely breathe.

She had loved him from the moment she'd seen him in her vision that evening in Claire Kelley's consignment shop. She just hadn't known it then. But there was no denying it. They were fated. He simply could not die.

Please, God, she prayed. *Please, let my Nicky be okay.*

How to get out of here? How to get away from this kidnapping creep? What she needed was a plan.

But she had nothing.

Do what you do best, Skylar's voice whispered in the back of her head.

What was that? She wasn't brave or bold or intrepid. She wasn't particularly smart or cunning. Most of her life she'd been motivated by the need to live in harmony with those around her. She'd preferred blending in to rocking the boat, to accommodate others and put her own needs on hold.

She had nothing that could help her out of this fix.

You've got empathy. It was Skylar's voice again. *And you're patient and nonjudgmental.*

Okay, she could do that. Pretend to be on the side of her kidnapper.

Delaney heard sirens wail from somewhere in the distance behind them. Her heart jumped into her throat. Nick!

Do something! Now!

"Whew," Delaney said as calmly as she could and tentatively raised her gaze to meet the eyes of her kidnapper in the rearview mirror. "Thank heavens we shook him."

The man behind the wheel narrowed his eyes suspiciously. "Whaddya mean?"

"The guy in the red pickup was my bodyguard. I'm so glad he's out of the picture. You have no idea what a pain in the neck it is having your every move monitored."

"You kiddin' me? I've been in the pen, girlie. You're the one with no idea what it's like to have your every move monitored for real."

"I'm sorry. I had no idea. You're right. It's completely inappropriate for me to compare my pampered life to prison."

"Damn straight."

"It'd be really awful if you had to go back there."

"I'm never going back."

"Well, you might. Kidnapping is a felony."

"I ain't getting caught."

"You might."

"I'm not going back to jail," he said stubbornly.

"I bet it's hard," she mused. All the while she was talking to him, Delaney was edging up the floor of the van toward the seat that separated her from the driver. Getting him to talk was one thing, but she needed a better plan. Needed to shake things up, but at the right moment, when it would do her the most good. "Starting all over again after prison. Is that why you turned to kidnapping?"

"Pays better than working at Wal-Mart."

"What did you do for a living?" she asked. "Besides kidnapping, I mean. Before you went to jail."

"I'm a barker at the Whack-a-Mole on Galveston Island," he said proudly.

Ah, now she knew why he looked familiar. Was that how the kidnapping had come about? He'd seen her at the amusement park and recognized her as a Cartwright?

"You like that work?"

"Outside, near the ocean, no boss. What's not to like?"

Closer, closer. She was just a few inches from the back of his seat, although she wasn't quite sure what she was going to do once she got there. Her hands were cuffed. It wasn't like she had a whole lot of options.

She scooted forward. Her veil fell across her face, blurring her vision with a curtain of lace.

And then she knew what to do.

In a soothing voice, she coaxed the driver to talk, while the seconds ticked away and they drove farther and farther from where Nick had crashed his pickup. It took everything she possessed to keep herself from acting immediately. If she was going to be successful in her escape attempt, she had to time things right.

He turned on his blinker and changed lanes. Up ahead lay a freeway ramp. She couldn't let him get back on the freeway. Her plan would be far too dangerous to execute on the expressway.

The time was now.

She was positioned directly behind the driver. With her

cuffed hands she reached over her head, while simultaneously rising up on her knees. Briefly, her eyes met those of her kidnapper in the rearview mirror at the very same moment she flipped the long veil up over his head.

The guy swore, swerved violently. The van shot back across the lane they'd just left.

He batted at her veil.

The van rocked.

Delaney fell back on her butt.

The van bounced hard up onto the curb.

He cut the wheel tight, brought the van down on the road with a solid smack. The jarring impact caused the back door to swing open. Hot air rushed in.

A horn sounded and Delaney looked up in time to see a delivery truck headed straight for them.

She screamed. The kidnapper twisted the steering wheel, sending them careening around a corner and up over a second curb.

Delaney somersaulted across the floor of the van, and the next thing she knew she was free-falling out the door.

Chapter 18

While Delaney was tussling with the kidnapping Whack-a-Mole barker, Nick pumped the foot feed and twisted the key in the ignition. He grunted with relief when the engine fired up again.

He took off after her, not knowing for sure where the van had gone. It might be back up on the freeway by now, completely out of reach. That thought fisted his gut. No, no, he wasn't that far behind them. He'd only lost a few seconds, maybe a minute, but no longer. He had to believe they were still on this access road.

Resolutely, Nick goosed the ailing pickup and ignored the rattling and groaning noises coming from the rear end. Lalule shook on the dashboard, urging him onward.

He sped over the rise in the road, eyes desperately scanning the area in search of the white van.

Then he saw something that stopped his heart. The van, maybe eight blocks ahead of him, spinning around a corner with the back door flapping open.

In horror, Nick watched as the woman he loved fell out onto the pavement.

*   *   *

Ouch. That was going to leave a bruise. Delaney lay on the ground, breathing hard as she watched the van disappear in a blinding blur around the corner.

She heard the squeal of brakes and the sound of tires sliding in gravel. She felt pebbles pelt her skin. Delaney pushed herself up, winced against abrasions on her palms.

A car door slammed.

She shook her head and the veil fell to one side. She saw someone running toward her.

Nick! He was all right!

Delaney had never seen a more welcome sight. She grinned in spite of cuts and scrapes.

He was at her side, picking her up, dusting her off, his face knitted with concern. "Are you all right? Are you okay?" He sounded breathless and scared.

"Fine, fine. How about you?"

"I'm okay."

"You sure?" She touched his face, needing proof.

"Are you sure?" His brow furrowed with concern.

"What in the hell is going on with Trudie's nephew? Why did he run from me? When I get my hands on that punk..."

"That wasn't Louie," she said.

"Then who the hell was it?"

Delaney shrugged. "Your guess is as good as mine."

Nick stared her in the eyes and felt such a surge of gratitude, he couldn't even speak. Ignoring his weak knee, he scooped her into his arms and carried her to the pickup, even though she protested the entire way.

She looked okay, kept demanding he put her down so she could walk, but he wasn't taking any chances. He held her tightly against his chest and maneuvered toward the passenger side of his truck. Her hair was pressed against his nose. She smelled like sunflowers, and she was trembling like a fawn abandoned by its mother.

His heart jerked hard. If that kidnapper had hurt her in any way, shape, or form, he would strangle him with his bare hands in a crime of passion. He put her in the truck, snapped the seat belt around her, and realized he was trembling too. She could have been killed. He could have lost her.

Taking a deep breath, Nick walked around to the driver's side and got in beside Delaney. He sat there a moment staring out across the hood of the pickup. He couldn't look at her. If he looked at her and thought about what could have happened, he would lose it completely.

Nick Vinetti didn't cry. Not when his wife left him. Not when he hurt his knee. Not when his grandfather died. The events of the past fifteen months were all knotted up inside him. One little chink in his armor and the dam would burst and he would bawl like an infant.

And that little chink was sitting next to him, looking as vulnerable as Bambi and twice as cute.

They were both breathing raggedly, sliding down off the adrenaline high. She was staring straight ahead too, as if trying to reconcile her own emotions. Cars were chugging slowly past, curious rubberneckers staring through their tinted windows at them, trying to guess at their story. They must have made a sight. A handcuffed bride and a limping man in a black suit more fit for funerals than weddings.

No one could guess this.

Once he'd collected himself, he got on his cell phone, called the Houston PD, alerted them to the kidnapping, and had them put out an all-points bulletin on the white delivery van.

"Where to?" he asked and started the engine.

"Away from here."

"Back to the chapel?"

"No!"

"To your parents' home."

"Definitely not."

"To your fiancé?" He said this last part with difficulty and dread.

"Evan is no longer my fiancé."

"No?"

Instead of answering his question, she held up her cuffed wrists. "Can you help me out of these?"

"I believe I can help you with that." Nick leaned over her lap to dig in the glove compartment for the spare handcuff key he kept stowed there. He was acutely aware of her, and from the way her body tensed, he knew she was just as aware of him. He unlocked the cuffs and straightened in the seat as she rubbed her wrists.

Delaney dumped the handcuffs on the dashboard beside Lalule and slipped off her veil. She carefully folded it up and settled in on the seat. Amazingly, the veil appeared no worse for the wear, although her dress was stained with dirt, tar, and grass.

"Does Evan know he's no longer your fiancé?" he asked, determined to know the answer.

Delaney nodded. "I left him a note where he would find it after the ceremony. I explained why I took the easy way out and had Louie kidnap me. Except, of course, it wasn't Louie."

"That's because I told Trudie to cancel Louie."

She jerked her head around sharply to pin him with those sea green eyes. "Why did you do that?"

"For one thing, you were involving Trudie's nephew in a crime."

"What's the crime? I was having myself kidnapped."

"Filing a false police report. Wasting government agency funds to search for you. Remember the brouhaha over Jennifer Wilbanks, the runaway bride?"

It fully hit her then, what she'd done. How she'd been unable to deal with her problems head-on. She'd cheated, taken the easy way out. Delaney uttered a bleak laugh, but nothing was funny. "I'm just like her, aren't I?"

Nick reached across the table to touch her hand. "Don't feel ashamed. Your family sort of cornered you into it."

"That's no excuse. I was a coward."

"Don't be so hard on yourself. You're not a coward so much as someone who hates to hurt other people's feelings. You let their needs come before your own, and then you feel trapped by their expectations and don't know how to get out of it."

He knew her so well. Better even than Evan, who'd known her all her life. It was as if he could see past the glossy surface her mother had polished and honed to the real Delaney beneath.

"Still, it was such a dumb thing to do." She dropped her face into her palms. "What must you think of me?"

"Everyone makes mistakes, and I'm sure from the time you realized your kidnapper wasn't Louie that you were feeling pretty punished by yours."

This didn't sound like a cop talking. He was making excuses for her, acting like someone who cared. Delaney held her breath. She didn't dare hope he cared as much for her as she did for him. A pall of tension hung in the air as they gazed at each other.

"But if you canceled Louie, then who kidnapped me?" Delaney asked. "Maybe more important, why?"

"That's the big question."

Puzzled, they looked at each other.

"It could have been a real kidnapping," Nick said. "You are an oil heiress."

"But that's awfully coincidental," she said. "Unless..."

"Unless what?"

"Unless the kidnapper is involved with the same person who's been blackmailing my mother. He did work as a barker at the Whack-a-Mole booth at the Galveston amusement park."

"You figured out that she's being blackmailed?" Nick didn't look surprised.

Delaney stared at him. "You knew?"

"I didn't know for sure, but I can guess why."

All the blood seemed to drain from her body. Her skin felt at once icy cold and blistering hot. "Why's that?"

"Because your mother isn't Honey Montgomery Cartwright."

Jim Bob Cartwright sat on a stool in a dark, dank-smelling bar not far from the oil refinery his family had owned and operated for three generations until economics had forced them to join forces with corporate America. He was a figurehead these days. No real power. His seat on the board of directors was little more than a commitment to the contract he and his brothers had signed. Jim Bob still made lots of money, but he had no real duties, no real influence in the company his grandfather had built. Without the Cartwright name, he was nothing.

Not even a good husband.

The place was almost empty. A couple of barflies hung off the other end of the bar, engrossed in a golf tournament on television. The jukebox was playing a Dwight Yoakam song.

Jim Bob stared at the double shot of Crown Royal he'd ordered. Stared and licked his lips and thought of Honey.

Correction. *Fayrene.*

He gritted his teeth as fresh rage swept over him. He closed his fist around the shot glass. How could she have deceived him so thoroughly? Everything they'd built together had been based on a lie.

His stomach roiled.

He loved her so damn much, but how could he love her? He didn't even know who in the hell she was. Fuck, but he felt like crying. His wife was a stranger, and his daughter had arranged her own kidnapping simply because she hadn't been able to tell him she didn't want to go through with her wedding.

Both his wife and his daughter had hidden their secrets from him. He'd failed them both. Failed them spectacularly. Jim Bob hadn't felt so alone since he'd given up drinking.

He eyed the beautiful amber liquid, and then lifted the whiskey to his lips. The smell of it was like an old, familiar friend. How easy it would be to swallow it back, allow it to take him under.

It's not the answer. Remember your vow of sobriety. Remember the night you swore it?

Until he took his dying breath, Jim Bob would remember the day he'd hit rock bottom.

It was the first anniversary of Skylar's death, and the Dallas Cowboys had been scrimmaging the Buffalo Bills in the Super Bowl. Honey had planned a memorial service for eight p.m., and the Wildcatters bar was hosting a Super Bowl party with two-for-one whiskey shots.

He hadn't purposely chosen the Super Bowl over his daughter's memorial service, but the thought of putting himself through more emotional pain had overwhelmed him. He'd stopped by Wildcatters after leaving the office, intent on one shot of liquid courage before heading home to change into the black suit and tie Honey had laid out for him that morning.

A handful of his drinking buddies had been at the bar, rowdy and well on their way to getting drunk. He'd been jealous of how happy and pain-free they looked, and he wanted to join them in that blessed state of oblivion.

One shot of Wild Turkey had turned into two and two into three.

The next thing he knew it was almost eight o'clock, and the Super Bowl was starting and he was too drunk to drive. Guilt and grief had burned inside him. To kill the feelings he'd had another shot and then another.

But it couldn't drown out the image of Honey standing at the front of River Oaks Methodist Church waiting and waiting and waiting for him to appear. In a whiskey-soaked stupor, he'd called a taxi.

He arrived at the memorial service ten minutes before nine and stumbled into the church in his khaki Dockers, plaid western shirt, and scuffed cowboy boots.

The altar was still set up with candles burning, pristine white lilies, and a big color poster from Kinkos with Skylar's picture on it. But the pews were empty. He dropped to his knees at the altar. The smell of the cloying lilies, reminding him too much of the day he'd buried his precious baby, turned Jim Bob's stomach.

Where was everyone?

You're too late; they've already gone home.

But he knew Honey wouldn't leave Skylar's portrait behind. She had to still be here.

Then he heard the sound of muted voices somewhere

in the distance, and he remembered about the reception Honey had put together.

Staggering to his feet, he swayed a moment, fighting off the nausea, and then lumbered to the rectory.

He pushed open the door and stepped inside.

Everyone was dressed in black. They stopped talking the minute they spied him, his family and friends sizing him up with barely disguised disdain.

"Jim Bob." His brother Lance had come toward him, but Jim Bob shoved him aside and barreled straight for his wife.

He would never forget the look of horror that crossed Honey's face. It was as if someone had doused everything she owned in gasoline and set a blowtorch to it. Grief and disgust and embarrassment and fury flashed across the face she normally kept pleasant and controlled.

"My precious baby's dead," he wailed and fell against her, hoping she'd gather him up in her arms and hold him close. But she had not. "I'll never love anyone the way I loved her."

He sank to his knees, clutching the hem of her skirt in his hands. He'd cried, pathetic and maudlin, clinging to Honey as she tried her best to retain her dignity. She was the most stoic woman he'd ever known, and he was jealous of her ability to detach herself from her pain.

Jim Bob had looked up to see chubby little Delaney standing in the corner staring at him, her thumb in her mouth at age eight, her eyes wide as quarters. Shame engulfed him.

And then he'd thrown up all over Honey's shoes.

The next morning he'd joined AA and hadn't had a drink since. Hadn't even come close.

Until now.

Temptation coaxed. *Drink it. Everything's changed. Honey's not who you thought she was. Your marriage is a sham. Your daughter doesn't trust you to keep her confidences. You've no real purpose. Come on. Slide back inside the bottle.*

Hand trembling, he touched the rim of the shot glass to his lips. The smell of the whiskey was nauseating now.

He gulped, opened his mouth.

And set down the shot glass. He couldn't do it. He couldn't cross that line, couldn't throw away his hard-won recovery.

Just then, his cell phone rang. He pulled it from his pocket, flipped it open, saw it was Honey calling.

He didn't want to talk to her. Not when he was sitting so close to temptation.

But she wouldn't stop ringing him. Not even when it forwarded to voice mail. She just hung up and called again. Four times, five, six.

What if it's about Delaney?

He knew he had to answer. He pushed the talk button. "Yeah?" he said gruffly.

"Jim Bob," Honey said, startling him by calling him by his nickname. In the whole thirty-four years of their marriage he couldn't recall a time when she'd called him Jim Bob. The sound of her voice, desperate and scared, wrinkled his heart. "Please, you've got to come home right away. I just received the ransom note. My mother's threatening to kill our daughter if we don't pay her ten million dollars."

Chapter 19

"What do you mean my mother isn't Honey Montgomery Cartwright?" Delaney blinked at Nick.

"We need to go someplace more private for this conversation," he said. "It's not the kind of thing you discuss sitting on the side of the road."

She met his gaze. The serious look in his eyes scared her. "That bad, huh?"

"It's probably going to rock your world."

She considered the implications of that. "Let's go to Galveston. Get away from the city. Sit on the beach and get rip-roaring drunk on umbrella drinks."

They didn't talk on the drive to the island. But Nick stretched his right arm out across the seat palm up, and Delaney rested her hand in his. He squeezed her fingers lightly, comfortingly. They held hands and watched Lalule dance and by the time they reached Galveston, Delaney was feeling somewhat better, even if anxiety over her mother's identity was sitting squarely in the middle of her chest.

"Where to from here?" Nick asked. They couldn't go to Lucia's. The house was in escrow.

"I need someplace quiet where I can think."

"I know just the place."

He took her to a quaint little bed-and-breakfast close to the beach but a little out of the way of the usual tourist crowd. "I'll get you a room for the night," he said. "Until you can make up your mind what you want to do."

"Thank you." She smiled at him.

The proprietor of the B&B, June Harmony, was a plump middle-aged lady with a mischievous smile and an unexpected mane of glorious auburn hair that curled halfway down her back. She immediately assumed they were married from the way they were dressed and showed them to the honeymoon suite. After the woman gave them the usual welcoming spiel and details about the B&B, she turned to Nick and asked, "Where's your luggage? I'll send my husband, Henry, to bring it up to you."

"Luggage got lost," Nick explained.

"Well then." June winked. "I'll just leave you two alone to settle in."

"Why don't you take a shower," Nick said. "And try to relax while I head over to one of those souvenir shops on the seawall and pick us up shorts and T-shirts."

It was as if he'd read her mind. "Thank you."

He leaned over to kiss her lightly on the cheek. It was the sweetest kiss she'd ever gotten, but it upped her anxiety. If he was being so sweet, what he had to tell her must be bad indeed. "Be right back."

Nick left and Delaney shed her bedraggled wedding dress. Just looking at it lying in a heap on the floor made her feel wistful in a way she'd never quite felt before. It was a sadness tinged with relief and regret, concern and longing. Part of her wanted to pick up the phone right now, call her mother, and tell her everything. But another part of her, the rebellious part she'd hidden for years, needed to hear what Nick had to say before making any phone calls or drawing any conclusions.

She got out of the shower and wrapped herself in one of the thick terry-cloth robes provided by the B&B. BRIDE was embroidered across the pocket in maroon stitching. The matching robe said GROOM.

Pulling a comb through her wet hair, Delaney walked to the French doors leading to the balcony. She opened them up and a draft of sultry Gulf breeze blew back the thin white sheers. The sound of the water lured her out onto the little terrace barely large enough for two chairs and a bistro table.

On the bistro table sat two champagne flutes, a metal bucket filled with ice and a bottle of champagne. A note card propped against the bucket said: "To the Happy Couple, complimentary champagne to start your new life in style. Best wishes, June and Henry Harmony."

For no good reason Delaney's eyes misted and that sad, wistful feeling blocked up her chest again. She might not be part of a happy couple, but she was ready to start her new life in style. She pocketed the comb, picked up the bottle.

She'd just poured herself a glass of champagne when Nick returned, carrying a paper bag and wearing rubber flip-flops. She looked at his bare toes sticking out from under the cuff of his suit pants and smiled.

"Those dress shoes were killing my feet."

"Still," she said. "I'm betting they're not as bad as stilettos."

"You got me there." He grinned. "Hey, champagne."

"Compliments of June and Henry. I thought a drink was in order, considering the serious discussion we're about to have. Pour yourself a glass while I change."

She took the sack he passed to her and went into the bathroom to change out of the robe. He'd bought her a form-fitting, spaghetti-strap pink T-shirt, white denim shorts, and a pair of pink-and-white flip-flops. When she sauntered back to the balcony, she felt her cheeks warm as his eyes raked boldly over her body.

He too had changed into a T-shirt and shorts. His knee wasn't wrapped, and for the first time she saw the network of purple-red scars. She sucked in her breath, startled by the extent of his injury.

His eyes tracked the direction of her gaze. "Ugly, huh."

"No." She shook her head. "Not ugly. Vulnerable."

"Great. Just what every guy wants to hear." He plunked down onto one of the chairs and self-consciously pointed his knee away from her. She found his embarrassment touching.

"You don't have to hide from me."

"Better sit down." He waved at the chair beside him and ignored her last comment. "We've got a lot to discuss."

She drained her champagne, poured herself another glass, and slid into the chair next to him. They watched the tourists walk along the seawall for a few minutes, then Delaney took a deep breath and plunged in. "Okay," she said. "What's this about my mother not being my mother?"

"She's your mother. She's just not Honey Montgomery."

"I don't understand how that can be." From the moment he'd first told her that, she'd been trying not to think about it. The idea was so ludicrous she couldn't really wrap her head around it.

"Her real name is Fayrene Doggett. She's been pretending to be Honey Montgomery."

"I find that hard to believe. How can she possibly be someone else?"

"Identity theft is not indigenous to the computer age."

"There's got to be some kind of mistake."

"I'm afraid not. I have proof. Birth records. Fingerprints. The real Honey Montgomery's death certificate."

"May I see it?"

"It's back at my apartment. I know you told me to stop investigating, but my PI friend had already collected the information and I knew I couldn't leave it alone."

Delaney pushed her hand through her hair. How could her mother not be who she thought she was? What about all that high-society, blue-blood stuff Honey had drilled into her head? How could it all be a charade? "But that means she's been living a lie for thirty-four years."

"That's right."

She glanced at Nick. His eyes were full of understanding and compassion. That look, along with the second glass of champagne, caused her to feel a little dizzy. "Do you think my father knows?"

"I'm guessing he doesn't."

She could barely comprehend that her mother had been living a lie. All her mother's rules, her proper code of conduct, had been based on big fat lies. For years she'd been toeing a false line. Trying to live up to an image that was exactly that and nothing more. An image. An illusion. She felt totally betrayed. Her mind spun in turmoil.

Pushed by anxiety, fear, and confusion, she reached to pour another glass of champagne. Nick closed his hand over hers. "You don't need any more of that. It's not going to change things."

His fingers rested across the knuckles of her left hand, and they both ended up staring down at Evan's engagement ring on her finger. Delaney took it off and slipped it into her pocket, and then she raised her head and met

Nick's eyes. "There's no other man's ring on my finger now."

Desire glazed his eyes. He reached up to cup her chin in his palm. "You need time," he said. "To sort out your feelings. I won't take advantage of you when you're so susceptible."

His thumb brushed her bottom lip and she shivered. "Nick," she whispered softly. "Nick."

He leaned in close. "Yes."

They hung there, leaning over the table, staring into each other's eyes, his thumb on her lip, his hand on hers, Delaney's heart beating crazily in her chest.

If he didn't kiss her she would come unraveled. He had to kiss her. He was the only solid thing she could trust, the only sure thing in her life right now. Everything else was quicksand under her feet.

"Nick."

"Delaney."

He took both his hands and interlaced them with hers on the table, his body heat radiating through her. The act of joining hands was highly underrated, she decided, as the current of possibility flowed between them, electrified.

His gaze searched her face and she searched his. Her heart just bloomed big as roses in springtime. Looking into his eyes she forgot about her parents, about her mother's true identity, about Evan, about the wedding, about everything.

Nick had so many layers she had yet to peel back, so many things about him she did not know. The edges of his mouth were angular and unyielding, but she knew his lips were soft. The contradictions in him were exciting. She felt as if she was teetering on some great chasm and he was her only ally.

She was caught up in the moment and the sweet vortex of Nick's dark eyes. With a groan, he pulled her to her feet, took her from the table to the balcony railing, and then his mouth was on hers, tasting of champagne and raw vulnerability.

Who was he trying to kid? Nick was as susceptible as she. Maybe even more so. He was the one who'd been hurt in so many ways. She was merely confused about her place in the world. He had a lot more at stake than she did.

His kiss was tender, almost reverential. Delaney wanted wild and impudent, but she would take whatever he was willing to give. For almost two months she'd been fighting the attraction, and now she was finally free to give in, let passion sweep her away.

Ah, yes, this was what she craved. Sexual oblivion.

His hands were at her back, smoothly sliding down her spine. She arched into him. He didn't close his eyes and neither did Delaney. They stared into each other, searching deeply and both finding what they were looking for.

Acceptance.

Delaney couldn't stop looking at him. She felt like the bride off a cake topper, but instead of going home with the perfect plastic groom, she'd tumbled off the cake and fallen into the arms of a very sexy bad boy. She told Nick this and he laughed.

She liked making him laugh.

"There goes the bride," he said ruefully. "But this time it's into my arms instead of away from them."

He undressed them both, slowly, seductively. First came her top. Then his T-shirt. Followed by her shorts and his. Her bra was a showstopper. He groaned softly at the sight of her breasts and had to dip his head to kiss first one and then the other before he could continue with the undressing. Delaney felt a hot flush rise to her cheeks at his careful attention.

"Ah," he said and traced a finger over her blushing cheek. "There's my Rosy."

Nick kicked off his flip-flops and then knelt before her in his underwear. He kissed her navel and sent a jolt of awareness angling straight for her crotch. She fisted her fingers in his hair and gasped when he took her white lace panties between his teeth and pulled them down the length of her legs.

She shuddered against him and he buried his face in the triangle of her hair.

"Get out of your underwear," she commanded.

He obeyed, whipping off his briefs. Delaney stood before him totally naked.

"I know you have trouble believing this, but Delaney, you are so beautiful." He breathed in a reverential sigh.

When he said it, she did feel beautiful. He made her feel beautiful with the way he looked deeply into her eyes. Without taking his gaze from her face, he held out his hand and led her to the bed.

The sweet magic of the moment of their first time together made her heart ache. In her head, she heard music. Soft and low. Irish music. The music of the veil. Morag's song. It was low and lyrical and haunting.

He looked at her so long and deep she thought he must have heard it too—the sound of Celtic harps and flutes binding them together.

It occurred to Delaney her wish had come true. She'd wished on the veil, wished to get out of marrying Evan and she had.

Nick lay down on the bed and pulled her gently on top of him, holding her close, smiling into her face. She curled into him. He made her feel cherished, treasured. He made her feel like she mattered.

He touched his lips to hers. Time spun away from them, ceased to exist. Such exquisite tenderness.

Delaney had thought she wanted raw sex but this was so much better. Ten times better, this leisurely journey of discovery. Touching each other softly, lingeringly, finding the spots that made each other wriggle and wiggle.

He held up his palm. "Press your palm against mine."

She did as he asked, and she could feel the powerful strum of energy flowing between them. Their hands were fused, and it was as if there had been no other before them, nor would there be any others after.

Magic. There was no other word for the sensation she was feeling. Unbelievable magic.

Except she was a believer—fully, completely, unequivocally. In the veil, in Nick, in magic.

He kissed her and then his lips slid down her throat to her breast. He kissed each nipple, then after a time began to suckle them with his mouth as his hand crept to the apex between her legs. Gently he pushed her legs apart and began to do amazing things with his fingers, finding tantalizing spots she never knew existed.

He kept touching her there and tenderly nibbling her nipples, and the next thing she knew she was moaning softly and slipping toward oblivion. Lost in the wonderful moment of discovery.

Slowly, he drew his fingers up the sensitive underside of her arm and took her hand in his. She watched transfixed as he brought her knuckles to his mouth, kissed each one separately, then opened her hand and moved his tongue in small circles around her palm.

"You taste so good," he murmured.

Delaney shivered.

Nick propped himself on his elbow and looked down at her, eyes shining with emotions she couldn't name.

Heat filled her cheeks and then abruptly embarrassed, she felt her old self again, nervous, aiming to please, but terrified of falling short of his expectations. She reached for a pillow and pulled it over her face.

Nick grabbed one corner of the pillow and tugged at it. "What are you doing?"

Delaney clung to the fluffy rectangle of goose down. Wrapped both arms around it. Buried her face in it.

"Stop hiding behind the damn pillow," he growled. "I want to see your face when you come."

"I can't...I don't want you to see me like this."

"Like what?"

"You know, with my mouth all twisted up and my eyes rolling back in my head. I don't want you to look down and think, 'Good God, I never noticed before, but when she's in the throes of an orgasm she's got the tackiest double chin.'"

"Come on, I'm a guy."

"Meaning what?"

"I would never think that."

"You wouldn't?" She uncovered one eye to peek at him.

"No, I'd be thinking, 'God, I love the way her tits jiggle when she wriggles.'"

"Really?" She lowered the pillow and peered up from behind a thick strand of hair that had fallen across her face. "Should I put my bra back on while we have sex? You know, so I don't jiggle so much?"

"Good grief, woman," he exploded. "I love your jiggling breasts and orgasm chin. I want to see your face while we're making love. I want to see what I'm doing to you and I want you to see what you're doing to me. That's what intimacy is all about. Sharing what's going on between us, whether we look good doing it or not. Stop being so self-conscious. You'll never fully enjoy sex until you do."

She relinquished her grip on the pillow. Nick sailed it across the room.

"There now," he said. "No more hiding from me."

She stilled and looked up at him and her heartbeat stalled.

His mouth came down hard on hers and she tasted the yearning on his lips, the urgency on his breath. Delaney's body responded with a craving so intense it stunned her.

Whenever she was around him her perfectly structured control just shattered. She didn't fully understand why, but around him she felt freer, more like the person she was supposed to be. But letting go of the old Delaney was pretty darn scary, no matter how much she wanted to let go.

Even though he'd chased after her, Nick hadn't promised her anything. He offered her nothing but his loyalty and his help facing her family.

Was it enough? Could she just surrender to him, make love to him, without any expectations? Without any need for everything to be perfect? She wanted to, but she didn't know if it was really possible.

Shake it up.

The phrase drifted into her head. Shaking it up meant letting go of everything. Of her fears. Of her old self. Of the way she'd always believed things were supposed to be. Her old world was gone forever, it was time to adapt to new situations and circumstances. Time to live in the present.

Her ache for him was undeniable, and she just stopped resisting.

She didn't need any promises. All she needed was Nick.

His calloused hands moved down her shoulders and her body came alive with pleasure. She whimpered helplessly into his mouth as he kissed her.

"That's right, Rosy, just let go," he said, giving her permission to do the one thing she'd been dying to do for years and years and years but hadn't known how until now.

Until Nick.

Surrendering to the moment, she became the Delaney that she was always supposed to be. Boldly, she pulled his bottom lip into her mouth with her teeth. The feel of their colliding mouths curled her toes.

This was the magic she'd been missing.

She'd been so placid for so long, not rocking the boat, letting herself be swept away by her mother's dominant personality, that she'd been unable to express her repressed will.

But Nick's blunt directness gave her the permission to discover what she needed.

Firmly, he tilted her chin up with his thumb and index finger, snaring her so he could thrust his tongue deeper inside her. He pressed his body closer until she could feel him everywhere. With each bold stroke of his tongue, he dared her to resist him, challenging her to deny what they both wanted so desperately. His kiss taunted, punishing her for provoking him.

Even through the haze of their mind-soaking arousal, there was no denying that she provoked him to levels to which he'd never before been provoked. Intensity rose off him like heat off the desert sand. His biceps nearly quivering beneath her fingertips. His hips pressed into her as if he would never let her up off this bed.

Desire ignited, hot as gasoline, and surged through her veins, snatching her entire being on an upswell of yearning.

He kept kissing her, doing these absolutely amazing things with his tongue.

Her breasts ached, heavy and taut, eager to feel the caress of his fingers, to construct memories she would never forget. If this was the only night she spent with him, Delaney would remember it forever. They might be fated for only a hot, quick fling, but this joining would stand out as one of the greatest points of her life.

For better or for worse, she was going to make love with Nick Vinetti, and she knew without a doubt that it was going to be the most splendid sex of her life.

Her abdomen melted into a steamy puddle of hungry lust, and the most feminine part of her clenched in a desperate cry for release.

As if reading her mind, Nick pushed her legs apart with his knee and leaned forward until his erection branded her skin. The head of his penis thrust firmly against the throbbing head of her clitoris.

Delaney could not have prevented her hips from arching upward if a tornado had blown the roof right off the building, swept them over the rainbow and into Oz.

Nick groaned, his lips vibrating against her mouth. He broke their kiss, trailed his lips down to the underside of her jaw, and nipped her skin just hard enough to send a jolt of powerful need straight through her entire body.

While planting more erotic love bites along her throat, he ground his pelvis against hers, in long sinuous strokes that let her know she had not been mistaken about his potency.

He kept up the steady rocking, driving her deeper and deeper into the savage wanting that was changing everything she had ever known about herself and what she was capable of.

She reached up and pressed a palm to his chest, intending on restraining him until her mind caught up with what her body was doing. But instead of putting on the brakes and telling him she needed more time, that this was moving too fast, her head was reeling, she felt the wild pounding of his restless heart.

He was as crazy for her as she was for him.

I'm responsible for this, Delaney thought in awe. She'd never caused Evan to react in this manner, and she felt as giddy as if she'd drunk a whole bottle of champagne by herself.

She couldn't get over how wonderful he looked—firm biceps, taut abs, manly shoulders, tousled hair. Or how powerful she felt. It was freedom of the most delicious kind. With Nick, she didn't have to gauge her response and adjust accordingly. She didn't have to pretend. She could just be.

His eyes were open wide, and he was staring at her as if she was the most incredible thing he had ever seen. The look made her blush. She felt the hot flush.

"Rosy," he whispered. "Oh, Rosy, don't be embarrassed with me."

"But that's just it," she whispered. "That's the glory of it. I'm not, I'm not."

"So why are you blushing?"

"Because," she said, "all my life, I've tried to be perfect and fell far short of my goal. But then you came and I stopped trying to be perfect and now, when I look into your eyes and see the way that you see me, I finally feel perfect at last."

Tears misted his eyes and he swallowed hard. "Damn, Rosy, that was some speech."

The pounding thrust of their lust had slipped a bit, but in its place came a softer, kinder desire. She still wanted him, oh, yes, with a need that would not be denied. But there was something deeper too. Something more than lust and hunger and wanting.

There was love.

Big and rich and true.

She didn't know if either of them was ready to say it, but she felt it to the depths of her soul. He didn't have to say it. She knew.

Happiness erupted from her lips in a giggle.

He kissed her again, swallowing her giddy sound. She tasted her joy on his tongue.

They danced together in a ritual as old as time, moving in perfect union, their bodies pressed close, smoothly, in tandem.

A heated calm seeped through Delaney's body as she experienced a blissful sense of homecoming. A wondrous peace unlike anything she'd ever known.

She understood the mystery of creation, recognized the cosmic connection between herself and Nick. They were one soul, one entity. His eyes latched on to hers and she could not look away. Did not want to look away.

They climaxed together like that, locked in each other's embrace.

And in that moment, two souls became one.

Chapter 20

They spent the entire weekend holed up in the room with only brief forays down to the beach. For two glorious days they made love. In the bed, on the floor, in the bathroom in front of the mirror, and even on the terrace late one night.

At times their lovemaking was sweet—a romantic seduction in the bathtub, complete with bubbles and candles and expensive champagne. At other times, it was hungry and fierce and raw—they tore at each other, animals unable to get enough. After one such session, they came up for air and Nick glanced around the room.

"We knocked two seascapes off the walls." He grinned. "I think we broke the glass in the frames."

"Oh, my." She grinned back and drew the covers to her chest. "Seven years' bad luck."

"No, no, that's mirrors."

"Better check the bathroom. The way we were going at it, we could have knocked the mirror off the wall too."

"You were amazing." Nick was lying facedown in the pillows. He reached a hand over and trailed his fingertips over her belly. His touch raised gooseflesh on her arms.

She couldn't believe the way he made her feel. As if the very air they breathed was special.

She sat up, pushed back a strand of hair that flopped across her face. "Oh, dear."

"What is it?"

"There's scratches all over your back. How did they get there?"

His laugh was deep and rich. "You clawed me."

"I did?"

"You don't remember?"

"I remember feeling all shook up."

"Yep." He grinned up at her. "You were wild, out of control."

"I'm sorry."

"Don't apologize. I loved it."

She leaned down and gently pressed her lips to the scratches she'd inflicted upon him in the throes of desire. She would never have thought herself capable of such passion. It renewed her excitement.

When she finished kissing the scratches she kept going, tracing her lips down the curve of his spine to the high, tight mound of his bottom. Once there, she bit down tenderly on a nice chunk of butt.

"Watch out, woman, you're playing with fire."

"Promises, promises," she teased. "We've already made love twice today."

"Are you questioning my stamina?"

"Stop bragging and back it up."

Quick as a cobra, he flipped her over. She giggled as he grabbed her around the waist and tackled her to the mattress. "There's two more seascapes on the wall. Wanna go for double or nothing?"

Looking into his eyes, a thrill so rich and true she

would never be able to express it filled her up. He kissed her and they were off again. Riding the crest of their passion.

They woke again at dawn on Monday morning, locked in each other's arms. He leaned in to kiss her.

"No, no, morning breath." She put a hand over her mouth.

"I don't care. I want to share everything with you, including morning breath."

"That's yucky."

"That's life, baby."

He kissed her, then pulled back laughing. "Okay, so maybe it's a little yucky."

Teasing each other, they filed into the bathroom to brush their teeth. They stood side by side, naked in front of the mirror, making silly faces at each other. Delaney felt lighter, freer, than she'd ever felt in her life.

She realized with a start that she had never been naked in the bathroom with a man before she'd been with Nick. How had she managed to get to the ripe old age of twenty-five without such intimacy?

Nick wandered back into the bedroom and flicked on the television. It was the first time they'd had the TV on all weekend. He channel surfed, looking for the morning news. And stopped cold when he saw Delaney's face flash across the screen.

Uh-oh.

He thumbed up the volume.

"Delaney Cartwright has been missing since she was kidnapped from the chapel on her wedding day," said the News 4 anchorwoman. "Police departments all across the country have been looking for her. This morning we have stunning new revelations in the case. We go now to our correspondent, Joe Sanchez, outside the main precinct of the Houston Police Department."

Delaney came running in from the bathroom, her toothbrush still in her mouth, wearing nothing but her underwear. Since they'd been holed up together, she'd stopped flatironing her hair and it curled around her face. Nick said it made her look like an erotic sea nymph and she liked the sound of that.

"New revelations," she mouthed around the toothbrush. "What new revelations?"

"Kelly," Joe Sanchez addressed the anchorwoman. "Here's what we've learned. James Robert Cartwright, Senior VP of Cartwright Oil and Gas, and his wife, Honey Montgomery Cartwright, received a ransom note asking for ten million dollars or their missing daughter will be executed."

Delaney pulled the toothbrush from her mouth and waved it at the TV. "They can't execute me," she shouted. "I'm not being held hostage."

"Your parents don't know that," Nick said quietly and the full extent of his words hit her like a slap.

Guilt took hold of her then, sharp and raw. What a horrible daughter she was. She hadn't thought about her parents or Evan from the moment Nick kissed her on the balcony. She imagined how frantic they must be and recalled how crushed they had been after Skylar's death. She thought the note she'd left for Evan would ease their minds, let them know she'd gone off on her own.

The taste of shame filled her mouth. She'd wanted to punish her mother for lying, for deceiving her all these years, but this was too cruel. How thoughtless she'd been. How selfish.

Nick loosely hooked his elbow around her neck and

drew her against his chest and whispered, "Don't browbeat yourself."

"In a stunning revelation," the newscaster continued, "Honey Montgomery Cartwright revealed that she was being blackmailed by her biological mother and that her real name is Fayrene Doggett. Thirty-five years ago, she assumed the identity of a dead woman. For over three decades, Fayrene Doggett was posing as a Philadelphia blue blood. The scandal has rocked Houston high society, and the police have put out an APB on Paulette Doggett Wilson and her stepson Monty Wilson, who are suspected of holding Delaney Cartwright hostage. Their fingerprints were all over the ransom note."

Delaney's mouth dropped open and she sat down hard on the floor. "Mother went public? She admitted she's Fayrene Doggett? She'll be drummed out of the society that means so much to her. I can't believe she confessed."

"She did it for you," Nick said.

Her mother had come clean in order to get her back. Letting go of her too-high standards, telling the truth, risking everything for Delaney. Guilt and shame mixed with sadness and concern inside her. There'd been too much pain and misunderstanding on both sides of the fence. It was time for open and honest communication between mother and daughter.

She looked up at him, tears streaming down her face. "Take me home, Nick. Take me home."

As Nick drove Delaney up to the security gate of the mansion she called home, he felt decidedly out of place.

Delaney told him the security code and as he punched it into the keypad, he wished he could disappear. The driveway was crammed with unmarked police cars. Nick recognized the Feds when he saw them, standing guard outside the house. Before he even stopped the pickup, they were running toward him, guns drawn.

He got out with his hands up, identifying himself.

The FBI yanked open his truck door and pulled Delaney out. They ushered her inside the house, while another batch of agents surrounded him. Nick stood watching Delaney go, and he'd never felt more like an outsider in his life.

"Delaney!" Honey swallowed her daughter up in the tightest embrace she'd ever given.

The last two days had been a living hell. Right in front of the FBI, she and James Robert had fought and cried and argued and slammed doors and relived the day Skylar had been killed. But he'd stayed and they'd fought it out. Then they'd talked in a way they hadn't talked in years, if ever. Honey didn't hold back. She told him all her secrets, her fears, her terror of losing him. Letting down the guard she'd held up so high for so long wasn't easy.

When they could argue no more, James Robert took her in his arms, kissed her tenderly the way he'd kissed her in the early days, and told her he forgave her, but that for them to go forward, she was also going to have to forgive herself.

That was the hard part. Letting go of thirty-five years of self-recrimination and guilt. But she was trying her best.

Honey kissed her daughter's face over and over. They were both sobbing and apologizing profusely. Delaney for running away from her wedding, Honey for keeping a lifetime's worth of secrets and lies.

The FBI debriefed Delaney at her parents' home and

then went off to find Paulette and her stepson Monty. Honey would eventually have to deal with her blackmailing mother face-to-face, but for now, her only concern was her daughter.

"I'm so sorry," she told Delaney. "The way I raised you was wrong. In trying to keep anyone from finding out that I was living a lie, I forced my fears and anxieties onto you. I emphasized perfection, because I couldn't afford to slip. I demanded too much from you and Skylar. I know that now, and I'll go to my grave regretting what I did to you."

"No, Mother," Delaney said. "I don't want you to have regrets. You were strict, yes, but you taught me a lot. And now that I understand where you came from and why you did what you did, it makes it easier to accept your flaws. I forgive you, Mother, and I only hope you can forgive me for hiding out from you for two days. I was just so angry when Nick told me your real identity. I couldn't believe you'd kept such a dark secret for so long. I mean, if you weren't who you said you were, then who was I? I needed time to sort it all out. I should have called you. It was so wrong of me to let you worry, fearing I was dead."

And then she told Honey about how Nick had rescued her from the kidnapper.

"Where is he?" Honey asked softly. "I'd like to meet the man you're in love with."

"Who says I'm in love with him?" Delaney's eyes widened.

"You can't hide it, sweetheart. It's in your face. You look the way I felt when I first met your father."

"I guess he wanted to give us our space," she said.

Honey reached over and squeezed Delaney's hand. "I'm so happy you didn't marry Evan. And I'm sorry you felt pressured into a wedding. I'm so glad that you knew better than I did and stuck to your convictions, even if your methods were a bit unorthodox."

The maid appeared in the dining room where Honey, Delaney, and James Robert had congregated. "There's a visitor at the door to see Delaney," she announced.

"Nick!" Delaney cried. She was up and out of her seat. She ran down the hall, threw open the door.

"Hello, Delaney," Evan said. "May I come in?"

Somewhere in the back of her mind, she'd known this moment would come; she'd just hoped it would be later rather than sooner. But here was Evan, and from the look on his face, he wasn't going away until he'd had his say.

"Evan," she said.

"Delaney." His eyes were tinged with sadness, and she just felt awful. "I'm glad to see you're all right."

She ushered him over the threshold. "Come on in."

He followed her inside and then they just stood awkwardly in the foyer, avoiding looking each other directly in the eyes. It hurt her to realize how she must have hurt Evan. He'd been her best friend for as long as she could remember.

"Evan," she started, "I'm so—"

"Shh." He raised an index finger. "Don't say it. You don't have to apologize to me."

"Yes, yes, I do. I'm so ashamed of the way I treated you. Arranging my own kidnapping." She shook her head. "It was cowardly."

"It's all right. I understand. In fact, I'm glad you had the courage to dump me at the altar. Granted, your methods were a bit unorthodox." His laugh was shaky.

"You were glad?"

"Yeah." He smiled ruefully. "I didn't want to marry you either."

Flabbergasted, she stared at him. "Then why didn't you just say something?"

"Why didn't you?"

Good question. "Because we were perfect for each other, everyone said so."

"Same here."

"Why did you ask me to marry you in the first place?" she asked.

"Because my family was pressuring me to get married, to give them a grandchild. It's a drawback to being an only child born late in life. Your parents fear they'll die before they'll get to see their grandchildren. I wanted to make them happy, and you're one of the finest women I've ever known. But after going to Guatemala, I realized I love that kind of primitive medicine. I want to move there, live there. I want to make a real difference in those children's lives. And I do love you, Laney—"

"But not in the way we both deserve," she finished the sentence for him.

"Yeah." He pressed his lips together tight.

Tears misted her eyes. He was a good man. Just not the man for her.

"I was looking for the magic that was missing between us," he said. "And I found it in Guatemala."

Delaney smiled. Tears were in his eyes too. "I understand completely."

They looked at each other and then burst out laughing, as tears slid down their cheeks.

"Friends?" Evan stuck out his hand.

She took it. "Friends."

He reached out and gently touched her cheek in a sweet brotherly gesture that she cherished but did not yearn for. "You're an amazing woman, Laney. I hope you know that, and I hope you find the same kind of happiness in your life that I've found in Guatemala."

"I've already found it," she said.

"Good for you." Evan kissed her on the forehead and then he was gone, leaving her feeling a little startled by his admission and a lot relieved. She was also stunned by what she suddenly realized about herself.

All this time she'd been looking outside for the answer to what was missing from her life. And here it turned out the magic had been inside her all along. Afraid of her own power, she'd hidden it, covered up beneath a fake facade, a false image. By trying so hard to please others, she'd denied her true essence.

Nick alone had seen her potential. He was the one who had shown Delaney her real self.

And she loved him for it.

Now all she had to do was tell him exactly how she felt.

It was a media circus around the house for the next few days. Delaney kept expecting Nick to call her, but he never did. She knew he'd gone back to work and she supposed he was too busy to make contact, and that he was trying to give her some privacy.

But when a week went by and he still hadn't called her, she began to worry.

She called Lucia and was distressed to learn not only had Lucia not heard from Nick, but that the buyer for her house had backed out of the deal and it was back on the market.

She called his cell phone. No answer. Same with the home phone.

She had to face facts. He was screening his calls and didn't want to talk to her. Heart breaking, she came to the awful conclusion their time together hadn't been as magical for him as it had been for her.

In the past, she might have accepted defeat, but no longer. She'd been through too much. She'd learned how to speak her mind and tell people what she wanted. Sure, she might get rejected, but wasn't it better to get rejected than to never express your opinion, never get what you really want, and always settle for second best because you were afraid to speak up?

She picked up the phone and called Lucia again. Delaney had a plan.

That night, Delaney dreamed of Skylar. She was wearing the same black baby-doll-style KISS T-shirt and faded blue jeans that she'd worn to the concert on the day she'd died. She was also wearing the wedding veil and carrying a pink suitcase.

"So what's up? You eloping with a KISS roadie or something?"

"Witty," Skylar said, "but no. I just dropped by to say so long."

Delaney sat up in bed. "So long? What do you mean?"

"I got my wish."

"What?"

"I wished on the dream version of your veil on the same night you wished on it, and well, the deepest desire of my soul came true."

"What did you wish for?"

Skylar gave her a wistful smile. "You can't guess?"

"You wished for me to find true love?"

"No, you had that covered."

She met her sister's eyes and saw tears shining there. "For Mother's secret to come out?"

"Not exactly."

"What exactly?"

"I wished for you to be able to let go of the past—to let go of me. I was happy to be here for you, in your dreams, Delaney, since I couldn't be here in the flesh, but you don't need me anymore. You've confronted your demons, faced off with Mother, and found your true self. You don't need me anymore. And that's a good thing."

Anxiety gripped her. She'd been dreaming of her sister almost weekly for the last seventeen years. What would she do without her? "But I don't want you to go!"

"It's okay. It's time to embrace the future, embrace your new life with Nick, and you can't do that with me hanging around."

"Skylar," her voice, brittle with tears, cracked open.

"Adios, little sister." Skylar leaned over and kissed her forehead. "Never forget I'll always love you."

And with that, her sister picked up her pink suitcase and was gone.

A week later, Nick was moping in his truck on the beach at Galveston Island where he and Delaney had almost made love, listening to sad country-and-western songs. Going to Delaney's home, seeing how she really lived in opulence and glamour, had brought out the fact that he was pipe dreaming if he thought he was ever going to fit in with a woman like that. No matter how down to earth she seemed.

He took a pull off his soda and tried to tell himself that everything was going to be all right. That they'd had a good time together, and it needn't be anything more than that. But deep down inside he knew it was a lie. He loved Delaney as he'd never loved another.

Finally, he understood why Amber had left him for

another man. With Feldstein, she'd found the magic that was missing in their relationship. The magic he thought he'd found with Delaney.

But now he wasn't so sure. Would love and magic be enough to bridge the chasm between their upbringings? He feared it would not.

Despair consumed him.

He reached up to start the engine and accidentally hit Lalule. She hula danced.

Shake it up.

What on earth had compelled him to let down his guard and let her get so close to him? Why had he told her about his mother? Why had he given her a hula doll of her own?

From the minute Delaney had tarped him outside Evan's office, he'd known she had the potential to hurt him bad. He hated feeling like this—all soft and mushy. He wanted his hard outer shell back, wanted his cynical cop attitude back.

It was too late for regrets. He'd fallen in love with Delaney, but she was out of his league, out of his reach.

There was a knock on his window and Nick almost jumped a foot. He looked up and saw Trudie standing there, a deep frown on her face.

He rolled down the window. "Jesus, Trudie, you about scared me to death."

"What are you doing out here feeling sorry for yourself?"

"I'm thinking," he said.

"Well, your grandmother is looking for you. She just found a new buyer for the house, but she wants your approval first."

"She didn't want it before, why is she suddenly interested in my opinion now?"

"Don't be a putz," Trudie said. "Get over to the house."

Grumbling, Nick drove over to Nana's. Lalule did the hula.

Shake it up.

Damn that hula doll.

He parked in the driveway of the house he'd grown up in and his chest tightened. He hated that he was losing both Delaney and his home too.

"Nana," he called as he went up the steps, house keys in hand. He turned the key in the lock, pushed open the door. "Nana? What's up?"

The smell of lasagna was thick on the air. Damn, but he was going to miss the smell of this house.

He went to the kitchen.

And stopped dead in his tracks.

There at the stove stood Delaney. Wearing nothing but high heels and an apron.

What was this?

She turned to smile at him. "Welcome home, Nick."

"What do you mean, welcome home?"

"I'm your grandmother's new buyer."

Damn if his smile didn't spread all the way across his face. "You're kidding me."

"Nope. Unfortunately, this house is just a little bit too big for little ole me. I was hoping that maybe you could help me fill it with children."

"Why, Delaney Cartwright," he said. "Are you proposing to me?"

"Why yes, Nick Vinetti, I think I am."

And that's when Nick Vinetti knew all was right with the world.

Epilogue

The winter issue of *Society Bride* declared the double wedding ceremony of undercover cop Nick Vinetti to successful business entrepreneur Delaney Cartwright—and oil tycoon Jim Bob Cartwright to Fayrene Doggett—the "must crash" nuptials of the season.

Texas Monthly decreed that following on the heels of her daughter's faked kidnapping from her wedding to Evan Van Zandt, the outing of Philadelphia blue-blood Honey Montgomery Cartwright's true identity was nothing less than a Texas-sized scandal.

The *Houston Chronicle* dubbed it the best water-cooler gossip of the year.

Bouquet clutched in her hand, Fayrene walked down the rose-petal-strewn garden path in the backyard of her daughter's home on Galveston Island. Accompanied by the traditional Wagner's wedding march and escorted by Nick's father, Vincent, Fayrene wore a simple pale blue dress and the happiest smile on her face. When she got to the makeshift altar, she stopped and turned to wait for her husband and daughter to come down the cobblestone walkway behind her.

The backyard was packed with friends and family. Tish was recording it all on video. Jillian and Rachael were bridesmaids. Lucia and Trudie sat in the front row, beaming like the conniving matchmakers they were. Chalk up another one for the whammy.

The wedding march ended and the band struck up the Cars' tune "Shake It Up."

Jim Bob was dressed in a Texas tuxedo—tuxedo top, blue jeans on the bottom, and shiny new cowboy boots. Honey would have had a hissy fit over such lax wedding attire. Fayrene, however, thought he looked adorable.

Delaney wore an off-white gown and the wish-fulfilling consignment-store wedding veil that had foretold this very day. She looked to the altar where Nick stood to the right of her mother, patiently waiting for her. He looked stunningly handsome in his own Texas tuxedo. She'd never seen a more glorious sight.

Her father shifted his weight. "You sure you want to do this, princess?"

"Positive. How about you?"

Jim Bob looked to his wife. "I've never been more sure of anything in my life."

"Me either. Let's go then." She didn't even wait for her father to take the lead. Delaney was already hurrying down the aisle, pulling him along with her. She couldn't wait to marry Nick. Couldn't wait to start the next chapter of their lifelong romance.

When they got to the altar, her father put her hand in Nick's, then he stepped over to his bride and looped his arm through hers. The minister stepped forward to renew the vows between her parents.

"You look so beautiful," Nick whispered. "I'll never forget this day for as long as I live."

Their eyes met and Delaney's heart soared. She didn't hear the minister's words to her parents, didn't smell the scent of the sea on the air, didn't see the crowd surrounding them. She only had ears and nose and eyes for the man standing beside her.

He was gazing at her with eyes so bright she thought she might stop breathing. This, then, was nirvana. Happiness enveloped her so completely she lost awareness of everything but him.

In that moment, true courage was born in her. She was not afraid of anything. Not with Nick.

For most of her life, she'd lived in the illusion of the perfect world, shielding herself from pain and the uncertainty of taking risks. But through knowing Nick, she'd learned to say "yes" to what she wanted and "no" to what she didn't.

She'd come full circle and now she was back where she's started, but totally changed. She was a fully realized person now. She could see clearly all the ways in which she'd held herself back, let her mother run her life. And she could see it in her friends too. Tish, who was afraid to admit she loved her ex-husband. Jillian, who was terrified to love altogether. Rachael, who fell in love too easily. She wanted desperately to help them all.

Her heart swelled with the exquisiteness of everything she'd learned, with the sweetness of her journey. And as the minister joined her and Nick together, Delaney knew what she must do to help her friends.

The band played "Shake It Up" again as they went back up the aisle accompanied by applause. Tish had taken up a crouching position at the end of the back of the last row of folding chairs. She started to stand up as Delaney and Nick walked up, but ended up bumping her head on the corner of the gift table.

"Son of a..." Tish started to swear, realized she was recording, and clamped her lips closed.

"Wait." Delaney placed a restraining arm on Nick's hand. "There's something I need to do."

He stopped, waited patiently. He would always be there for her. She knew it as surely as she knew her own name. "Do what you have to do."

Delaney reached up, took the veil from her head, walked over, and handed it to Tish.

"What's this?" Tish asked.

"Be careful what you wish for," Delaney said, gazing happily at her new husband. "Because you're going to get your soul's desire."

"Huh?"

Delaney left her friend staring with puzzlement at the wedding veil and went back to Nick. He took her hands, kissed her tenderly, and then just before family and friends descended upon them, Delaney caught sight of someone standing at the far corner of the backyard.

Claire Kelley.

Her eyes met Delaney's,

Claire nodded at Tish, winked, and then she was gone.

And in that whisper of a second, Delaney realized the truth of the universe. The magic of the wedding veil had been inside her all along. Faith—in herself, in love—was what had activated it.

With that, she took Nick's hand and walked into her brand-new life.

Once Smitten, Twice Shy

This book is dedicated to my parents,
Fred and Maxine Blalock, who lost two children
but never lost their faith or love in each other.

Acknowledgments

No one writes a book alone. It feels like it sometimes, all those hours spent in front of a computer wrestling with the words, but if it weren't for the following people propping me up, I wouldn't be able to make the magic happen.

To my husband, Bill, who takes care of all the domestic details so I don't have to worry about any of that and who loves me unfailingly. I'm the luckiest person on earth.

To my editor, Michele Bidelspach, who gently nudges me in the right direction.

To my agent, Jenny Bent, who keeps my spirits up when the publishing business closes in.

To the people of my hometown, from Jay, Melinda, and June at the post office who smilingly accept my numerous packages to Leah Western at Freedom House to Linda Bagwell at Weatherford College, I'm blessed to know you all. Thank you for all your support over the years.

Chapter 1

From behind his high-end designer sunglasses, Secret Service agent Shane Tremont scanned the crowd gathered for the groundbreaking of the Nathan Benedict wing at the University of Texas campus.

His elbows were loose, his breathing regular, his stance commanding and self-confident. The perimeter had been secured. The crowd controlled. His Sig Sauer P229 357-caliber pistol nestled comfortably in his shoulder holster, freshly cleaned and loaded, along with a full capacity of ammunition clips stowed in the holster pockets and a bulletproof vest molded against his chest.

Although Nathan Benedict, the President of the United States, was being honored at his alma mater, he wasn't attending the ceremony. In Nathan's place was his twenty-two-year-old daughter, Elysee, who'd been entrusted with clipping the ceremonial ribbon in her father's absence.

Everyone loved sweet-natured Elysee, and it was Shane's job to guard her life with his own. His nerves might be relaxed, but his muscles were tense as coiled springs, cocked and ready for action.

The sky was clear and blue and balmy—the perfect

mid-October afternoon in Texas. He was acutely aware of the political protesters. They carried signs scrawled with anti-Benedict sentiment. The Austin police held them at bay behind the picket line several hundred yards from the groundbreaking site.

Potential assassins, all of them. From the smiling young mother with a towheaded toddler in her lap to the elderly man leaning on a cane, to the trio of cocoa-skinned, dark-haired men gathered at the periphery of the crowd.

Shane narrowed his eyes and took a second look at the three men. They fit a profile that was politically correct to ignore, but he was Secret Service. Political correctness didn't figure into it. A whiff of Al-Qaeda and his adrenaline kicked into hyperdrive. He touched his earpiece and quietly mouthed a coded message that sent another Secret Service agent closer to the trio. Better safe than sorry.

"Everything okay?" Elysee laid a hand on his elbow.

"Yes, miss."

"Miss? Getting formal on me, Agent Tremont?" Her eyes twinkled.

"We're in public. I'm on high alert." He resisted the urge to smile.

"The crowd looks pretty tame to me."

"Protesters lined up on the sidewalk."

"Ubiquitous," she said, "I'm surprised. Usually there's more."

"It's because it's you here and not your father. Few are eager to protest a true lady."

"Why, Agent Tremont." A soft smile touched her lips. "What a gentlemanly thing to say."

He gave her a conspiratorial wink and her smile widened.

"Your tie's crooked," she said and reached up to give

his plain black necktie a gentle tug, then passed the flat of her hand over his shoulder. "There now. Spit-polish perfect."

"What does that mean?" he teased.

"I don't know. Just something my mother always said to my dad when she hustled him out the door each morning."

Shane and Elysee and her entourage were standing on a small platform suspended over the site of the groundbreaking. A fat yellow backhoe, along with several other heavy construction vehicles, sat with their engines powered up and running, ready to get to work as soon as Elysee sliced through the thick scarlet ribbon.

Some committee had decided a ballet of earthmoving equipment would be more cinematic than Elysee shoveling dirt. Although in the end, cinematography had turned out to be a nonissue. A devastating category four hurricane had just crashed ashore along the South Carolina coastline, pulling news crews eastward. Other than a few print journalists, the groundbreaking ceremony was devoid of the usual media brouhaha.

Shane swung his gaze back to the President's daughter. He had been assigned to her detail for the past thirteen months and in that time they'd become close friends. The relationship between a bodyguard and his protectee bore many similarities to that between a psychiatrist and his patient. Elysee told him things she couldn't tell anyone else. He listened, sympathized, and kept his mouth shut.

The intimacy had created a special connection. Shane liked her, even though she was seven years younger than he. This unexpected emotional bond wasn't something his training had fully prepared him for.

Elysee was petite and soft-spoken, with earnest opinions and tender sensibilities. She loved fully, completely, and without reservation, although men were always breaking her heart.

Shane couldn't understand why she hadn't become hardened or cynical about love. Her capacity to pick up her crumpled spirit and move on with the same degree of hope, trust, and optimism impressed him.

He thought of his ex-wife and his own heart—which was finally, finally starting to mend—swelled, testing the tentative seams of its emotional stitches. Two years divorced and thoughts of Tish still made him shaky. He'd loved her so damned much and she'd disappointed him so deeply. No pain had ever cut like Tish's secrecy and betrayal.

Many times over the past twenty-four months he'd tried to convince himself that he hated her. His anger was a red-hot flame he held close to his chest and stoked whenever his mind wandered to tender memories. But he couldn't hate her. Not really. Not when it counted.

Thing was, no matter how hard he tried to suppress his weakness, in the dark of midnight, he found himself longing for Tish and all that they'd lost.

He still ached for the feel of her curvy body nestled against his. Still longed to smell the spicy scent of her lush auburn hair. Still yearned to taste the rich flavor of her femininity lingering on his tongue. Even here, in the brightness of the noonday sun, surrounded by a crowd, he felt it.

Dry. Empty. Desperately alone.

The tip of his left thumb strayed to the back of his ring finger, feeling for the weight of the band that was no longer there. He swallowed past the unexpected lump in his throat.

Head in the game, Tremont.

Shane clenched his jaw to keep from thinking about

Tish. Channeling all his attention onto safeguarding Elysee. This was his life now. Without a wife. Without a real home. The job was the only thing that defined him. He was a bodyguard, a protector, a sentinel. He was descended from war heroes. It was in his blood. In his very DNA.

The University of Texas chancellor stepped to the microphone and made a speech about Nathan Benedict and the dedication of the new Poli-Sci wing in his honor. Then he introduced Elysee.

A cheer went up. She *was* a crowd pleaser.

Elysee smiled and cameras clicked. An award-winning high school marching band that had been recruited for the event struck up "God Bless America." Shane's eyes never stopped assessing; his brain never ceased analyzing.

An assistant handed Elysee a pair of scissors so outrageously large that she had to grab onto them with both hands. Laughing, she raised the Gulliver-sized shears. Whenever she smiled, Elysee was transformed. Her bland blue eyes sparkled and her thin mouth widened and she tossed her hair in a carefree gesture. For one brief moment she looked as beautiful as any runway model.

Elysee snipped.

The thick red ribbon fell away.

The backhoe dipped for dirt at the same moment the bulldozer's blade went to ground and the road grader's engine revved.

The crowd, including the protesters behind the picket line, cheered again and applauded politely. Nearby, the backhoe operator was apparently having trouble with the equipment. It moved jerkily as its bucket rose. Elysee was perched precariously close to the platform's edge.

The backhoe arm swung wide.

In that instant Shane saw pure panic on the backhoe

operator's face and realized the man had lost control of the machinery. The bucket zoomed straight for Elysee.

Shane reacted.

He felt no fear, only a solid determination to protect the President's daughter at all costs.

But it felt as if he were moving in slow motion, his legs locked in molasses, his arms slogging through ballistics gel. He lunged, flinging his body at Elysee.

He hit her with his shoulder. She cried out, fell to her knees.

Spinning, Shane turned to face the earthmoving equipment, hand simultaneously diving for his duty weapon at the same second the backhoe bucket sluiced through the air, slinging loamy soil.

His arm went up, gun raised.

The bucket caught his right hand, yanking him up off the platform. He heard the awful crunch, but the pain didn't immediately register. He was jerked from his feet. He tried to pull the trigger, not even knowing what he was shooting at, just reacting instinctively to danger. He'd kill for Elysee, if that's what it took.

But his fingers refused to comply. What the hell was wrong with his fingers? Shane frowned, puzzled.

The driver looked horrified as his gaze met Shane's. He was dangling from the bucket right before the operator's eyes as the man frantically grabbed levers and fumbled with controls.

Distantly, Shane heard Elysee screaming his name. Was she hurt? In pain? Had someone gotten to her? Was she being kidnapped? Was the runaway backhoe all a ruse to deflect attention from hostage takers? The questions pelted his mind, hard as stones.

People were running and screaming, rushing in all

directions, ducking and dodging, tripping and falling. He feared a stampede.

Shane swiveled his head, trying to locate Elysee in the confusion. Why couldn't he feel the pistol in his hand? Dammit, why couldn't he feel his hand?

"Elysee!" Her name tore from his throat in a guttural growl.

The backhoe arm slung Shane up high, and then slammed him down hard onto the cab of the earthmoving vehicle.

Metal contacted with bone.

Pain exploded inside his skull, a starburst of bright searing light.

Then his vision went dark as he tumbled toward the hardpacked ground and slumped into the inky-black tunnel of unconsciousness.

Chapter 2

Affluence attracts affluence.

Tish Gallagher repeated her mother's favorite mantra to herself as she wriggled into the skirt of a fifteen-hundred-dollar gray tweed Chanel suit. Her potential client was a banker and quite conservative.

After a quick peek into her closet, she added a lavender silk blouse to the ensemble. The color complimented her deep auburn hair. She removed four earrings from the multiple piercings in her ears, leaving only a single pair of simple gold studs. She clipped a strand of pearls around her neck and then donned the jacket and four-inch, open-toed, lavender-and-gray Christian Louboutin stilettos. Because, hey, an artistic girl's just gotta wear *something* whimsical.

Although it was mid-October, the weather in Houston was still in the upper eighties and dastardly humid. But Tish knew La Maison Vert, the upscale French restaurant where she was meeting Addison James and her daughter, Felicity, kept their dining room chilled like fine champagne. Hence the long-sleeved tweed jacket. This job was very important. She couldn't afford to shiver throughout the interview.

As she studied herself in the full-length mirror mounted on the inside door of her closet, Tish spied the price tag dangling from her sleeve. "Uh-oh, that won't do."

Since her divorce, she'd lived in a one-bedroom garage apartment behind a lavish manor house in the old-money section of River Oaks. The apartment had once served as maid quarters and its 1950s décor, with black-and-white tiled floors and foam green appliances, held a certain kind of retro charm. Not to mention that the six-hundred-dollar-a-month rent was a salve to her strained budget.

The elegant neighborhood was quiet. The only drawback to the apartment was that her bedroom had to double as her office. Consequently, everything was always in disarray. Cameras hung from hooks on the wall, a bank of editing monitors vied for space on the bedroom furniture, and papers and files were stacked on the floor.

A search for the scotch tape amid the disorganized, overflowing room finally turned up the dispenser, lurking beneath a tote bag on her computer desk, but not before she almost knocked the bookend off.

Her fingers traced over the weighted statuette of a little girl with a pail of water in her hand. The bookend had been carved from the burl of two banyan trees that had twined and grown together.

Her ex-husband, Shane, had bought the Jill half of the Jack and Jill bookends for her at a rummage sale while they were on their honeymoon. She'd fallen in love with the bookend the moment she'd seen it, although Shane had tried to discourage her from getting it because it was just one lone bookend. But she'd wanted it so much, he'd used Jill's singleness as a bargaining chip to get the price down.

Seeing how happy the bookend made her, he'd promised he would search the Internet and haunt garage sales until he found the missing Jack and reunited him with his Jill.

An empty feeling settled in her stomach. That was another promise Shane hadn't kept.

Tish shook her head, shook away Shane. Water under the bridge.

She peeled off a strip of adhesive tape and carefully taped the price tag up inside the sleeve of her suit jacket so she could return it to Nordstrom's for a refund on her credit card once her meeting was over.

Then, she took another spin in front of the mirror. Yes. She exuded money, polish, and sophistication. Never mind that deep inside she still felt poor, tarnished, and from the wrong side of town. "Please, please, let me get this job."

Her car payment was two months overdue and she'd been eating Ramen noodles at every meal for the past two weeks. She was hoping to procure a down payment from Addison so she could zip it to the bank before the check she'd written for the stilettos ended up costing her thirty bucks in overdraft protection.

For five years now she'd been struggling to get her fledgling business off the ground. She was a damned good videographer and she knew it, but she couldn't seem to catch a break. She wasn't one to give up on her dreams, but at some point didn't prudence step in? When did common sense shout that your dreams were going to destroy you and you'd better let go of them before you lost everything that was important to you?

Like Shane.

Tish winced and bit down on her bottom lip. The love of her life. The man she'd foolishly allowed to get away. But she wasn't going to think about him. Not today, dammit.

Sometimes, in spite of her best attempts to look on the

bright side of life, it felt as if everything was slipping, spreading, festooning headlong into a disaster she could neither name nor predict. Her throat tightened and she shook her head against the dark, creeping thoughts.

No, no. She wasn't the sort to dwell on unhappy things. Onward and upward. That was her motto. She was just about to shut her closet door when she caught sight of the wedding veil in her peripheral vision.

The three-hundred-year-old veil was carefully folded and sealed in a special bag. Her best friend in the whole world, Delaney Cartwright, had given Tish the veil for good luck after her own wedding the previous December.

Tish remembered the day they'd found the veil in a tiny consignment shop. Delaney had immediately fallen under the spell of it, but Tish had been skeptical. Then the mysterious shopkeeper, Claire Kelley, had told them a fantastical tale about the veil that Tish did not believe.

Still, it had been a compelling fable and she recalled it with clarity. For some reason, the story had stuck with her.

Once upon a time, according to the legend, *in long-ago Ireland, there lived a beautiful young witch named Morag who possessed a great talent for tatting lace. People came from far and wide to buy the lovely wedding veils she created, but there were other women in the community who were envious of Morag's beauty and talent.*

These women made up a lie and told the magistrate that Morag was casting spells on the men of the village. The magistrate arrested Morag, but fell madly in love with her. Convinced that she must have cast a spell upon him as well, he moved to have her tried for practicing witchcraft.

If found guilty, she would be burned at the stake.

But in the end, the magistrate could not resist the

power of true love. On the eve before Morag was to stand trial, he kidnapped her from the jail in the dead of night and spirited her away to America, giving up everything for her love.

To prove that she had not cast a spell over him, Morag promised never to use magic again. As her final act of witchcraft, she made one last wedding veil, investing it with the power to grant the deepest wish of the wearer's soul.

She wore the veil on her own wedding day, wishing for true and lasting love. Morag and the magistrate were blessed with many children and much happiness. They lived to a ripe old age and died in each other's arms.

Claire Kelley had gone on to claim that whoever wished upon the veil would get their heart's deepest desire.

Delaney had believed. She'd wished upon the veil and ended up finding her true love in Houston Police Department undercover cop Nick Vinetti.

Tish was truly happy for Delaney, but magical wedding veil or not, she wasn't sinking all her hopes into happily ever after. She'd thought she'd found true love with Shane, and look what had happened. The old familiar misery rose up in her, the misery she'd struggled for two long years to exorcise.

She took the veil from the bag and fingered it, wrestled with the idea of making a wish. It seemed silly.

But what would it hurt? Even if you don't believe?

Good point. Tish slipped the veil from the hanger. The lace felt strangely warm to the touch.

Tentatively, she settled it on her head and examined herself in the mirror. The design was constructed of tiny roses grouped to form a larger pattern of butterflies. The veil was so white it was almost phosphorescent.

Her scalp tingled. Her pulse quickened. There was something undeniably magnetic about the veil, even to a die-hard cynic.

"I wish," Tish said out loud. "I wish, I wish, I wish..."

Her voice tapered off. Oddly, the veil seemed to shimmer until it looked like butterfly wings were fluttering all around her.

Eerie.

She swallowed hard. Goose bumps danced across her forearms. "I wish to get out of debt. I wish I didn't have to struggle over money. Oh hell, I'm just going to come out and say it. I wish for my career to skyrocket into the stratosphere and I'll become rich beyond my wildest dreams."

Instant heat swamped her body. The tingling at her scalp intensified. Her lungs felt at once both breathless and overly oxygenated.

She almost ripped off the veil, but something held her back. She stared into the mirror. Stared and stared and stared.

The looking glass blurred.

She'd skipped breakfast that morning. Was that why she was feeling weak and a little dizzy?

Tish blinked, shook her head. Her reflection swept in and out, her mirror image fading before her eyes as if she were in a slow, dreamy faint.

A face appeared. Indistinct at first. Fuzzy.

A man's face.

Not just any face, but a familiar one. A face she loved. Joy, full and unexpected, filled her heart.

"Shane," she whispered breathlessly. "Shane."

And then she could see all of him. He was dressed the way she'd seen him last, in his Secret Service black suit, white shirt, and black tie. Her man in black. Even through his clothes she could see the steel of his muscles and she knew that beneath the tailored material his body was ripped, perfectly defined.

His jaw was clenched, his brow furrowed. Some who did not know him might think him angry. But she knew that look. She saw it in the edges of his mouth, the corner of his eyes. He was in pain.

"Tish, I need you. I'm lost and I can't find my way back. Help me, Tish, help me."

Mesmerized, she reached out a hand to touch him, but her fingers met the hard surface of the looking glass.

Tish gasped as if she'd been splashed with cold water.

The vision vanished.

She stumbled backward, her temples pounding, eyes wide with awe and terror. She was back in her bedroom, back in the closet, gaping at the mirror, struggling to breathe.

The cursed veil lay on the floor at her feet.

Her stomach pitched. Her knees swayed. Impossible.

She stared into the mirror, but nothing was there except her own frightened reflection. Tish couldn't explain what had just happened, but her body hummed and ached with raw energy, rattling her to the very core of her soul.

"Holy shit," she exclaimed. "Shit, shit, shit. Today of all days, I certainly didn't need this."

Consciousness filtered in by degrees.

First, Shane detected sounds. Distant, muted. He tried to make sense of them, but when he concentrated too hard the fog in his head thickened.

Squeaky wheels on a rolling cart. Voices dark and soft. A rough scratchy kind of noise, like Velcro pulled apart. He heard a steady blipping. A heartbeat. Was it his?

Where was he? What had happened? Was he dead? Was this hell? He tried to think, but his memory was a curtain, heavy and black. It hurt too much to think. His brain burned. He willed himself back down from where he'd climbed. Willed the pain away and slept once more.

Time passed.

During his second swim up from unconsciousness, his nerve endings swarmed with feeling, buzzed with pain. *Fuck-o-fuck*, his head hurt like there was a steel beam jammed through it.

And his hand. What in the hell had happened to his hand?

Then a wisp of memory was there. Tenuous as a broken spiderweb. Free-floating and sticky. Something bad had happened. He didn't know how long he'd been out, but his body identified the minutes, hours. Days? Surely not weeks. Please, God, not weeks.

His skin ached. His joints were stiff. He tried to move, but his mind did not seem connected to his limbs.

Move your hand, he commanded, but he didn't want to move it because he knew it was going to hurt like seven levels of hell. He gritted his teeth. He concentrated, but he could not feel his fingers respond to his brain's demands.

Open your eyes.

Nothing.

The air smelled foreign—like hard plastic mattresses and sterile sheets, like powdered eggs and stale blood. The thick earthy scents made him want to gag. What were these smells? Where was this place? Why couldn't he move?

He found no answers to these disturbing questions. Abject despair propelled Shane to dive back into the pool of darkness, seeking solace in the oblivion of drugged sleep.

* * *

All the way to the restaurant Tish's mind kept drifting back to the vision she'd had in her closet and the awful feeling that something bad had happened to Shane.

"You're imagining things. Shane is perfectly fine," she told herself, but her gut didn't believe it.

Tish nibbled a thumbnail, then forced herself to stop. Chipped nail polish would not earn her any brownie points with Addison James.

At an intersection, she missed the green light and had to sit through the red. Shriners made their way through traffic, soliciting donations from passing motorists. Tish dug in her purse for change. She only had a ten-dollar bill. She rolled down her window and waved the ten. The man in a tasseled fez thanked her for her donation just as the light changed and she zoomed off.

She pulled into the parking lot of La Maison Vert, gathered up the things she needed for her presentation, and rushed inside. The hostess escorted her to a back table where Addison and her daughter were sitting.

"You're three and a half minutes late," Addison said coolly, glancing at her Rolex. "Not an auspicious beginning."

"My deepest apologies for keeping you waiting." Tish slid into her seat feeling as if she was already behind the eight ball.

After they'd eaten and the dishes had been cleared away, Tish set up her DVD player in the middle of the table and ran the wedding montage she'd put together to showcase her work.

Addison was nodding and Felicity was smiling, and Tish thought she might be close to winning them over.

Don't do anything to screw this up.

If she were selected as the James-Yarobrough

videographer—following on the heels of documenting Delaney's wedding to her dreamy hunk of a husband—Tish would be in with the elite of Houston's crème de la crème. And all her money problems would disappear.

"So when's the big day?" she asked Felicity.

"Next June."

"Good thing you're starting early. I book up quickly," Tish fibbed and hoped God wouldn't hold the little white lie against her. Sometimes in this business you had to stretch the truth to get what you needed, and Tish badly needed this wedding.

"We're starting right on schedule." Addison James pulled a checklist from her purse. "Nine months before the wedding, book the videographer," she read.

Tish kept smiling. Clearly, Addison was one of those by-the-book people. Just like Shane. Tish didn't do well with sticklers.

Beggars can't be choosers; you need this job.

"If we hire you," Addison asked in a snotty tone, "will you be three and a half minutes late for the wedding?"

"No, no, of course not. I'll be there hours before the wedding," Tish promised.

"Mom," Felicity said. "I really like what Tish has shown us. She's got a way of drawing out people that makes for great video. She's the sixth videographer we've spoken to and I like her presentation the best."

"What have I taught you?" Addison chided.

"Never act in haste," Felicity replied dutifully.

"That's right. We've got four more videographer interviews scheduled."

Their waiter approached the table. "Dessert, ladies?"

"None for me," Addison said. "I have a size-six mother-of-the-bride dress to fit into."

"I'm fine," Felicity said.

"Could you just bring us the check?" Tish asked.

"Most certainly." The waiter scooted off after the check.

"What are your rates?" Addison steepled her fingertips and slanted Tish a calculating glance.

She quoted a price that was slightly higher than her stiffest competition's. She based her fees on another one of her mother's mantras, *If you want people to think you're the best, charge like you're worth it.*

The waiter brought the check and Tish gulped at the total. Praying she wasn't over her credit limit, she pulled out her Visa card and handed it over to him. He disappeared to run her card.

"That's more than your competitors charge," Addison commented.

"Do you want the best? Or the most affordable? I can understand if budget restrictions knock me out of the running." Tish reached across the table to turn off the DVD player and hoped her strategy would cause Addison to rise to the occasion rather than get up and walk away.

"I'm not going to pretend I don't appreciate a bargain, but when it comes to my daughter's wedding, we want only the best."

"And that's what you'll get if you hire me." Tish stashed the DVD player in her briefcase. Yes, okay, it was an egotistical thing to say, but she could back it up. She was damned good at her job. Why let false modesty sell her short?

"Mother, I really want Tish to video our wedding," Felicity wheedled.

Addison shot her daughter a quelling glance and said to Tish, "You put together a very compelling video. It's the best we've seen. But there are other considerations. I also want to make sure you're of upstanding moral character. Last year, my friend June hired a videographer who turned out to have a criminal record. He got access to their security code when he came over to interview June's daughter and during the wedding, his accomplices burglarized their home."

"I can assure you, Mrs. James, I don't have a criminal record. But feel free to run a background check on me if that would ease your mind."

"Ms. Gallagher"—the waiter came back to the table looking distressed—"I'm afraid your credit card has been declined."

Tish tried to make her face a blank slate as she inwardly cringed. She couldn't let Mrs. James see her sweat. Smiling back the huge lump of trepidation in her throat, she said, "There must have been a mistake. Can you run it through again, please?"

The waiter shifted his weight. "I've been told by the credit card company to cut it up."

He pulled a pair of scissors from his pocket. Right in front of Addison James, the conservative banker with concerns about Tish's moral character, he chopped the card neatly in half.

Humiliation sank its fangs into her. Her heart lurched. The waiter was killing her lifeline. Tish kept the smile plastered to her face and pulled another card from her wallet. "Here, try the MasterCard."

"Yes, ma'am." He left her murdered Visa behind and trotted off with the MasterCard.

"There's got to be some sort of mix-up," Tish said. "I'll call my credit card company as soon as I get home and find out what's going on here. I hope it's not identity theft."

Addison shot her a judgmental look. Tish felt the deal slipping away.

The waiter returned a moment later, shaking his head, her MasterCard in one hand, scissors in the other.

Not again! Fear struck her then, hard and vicious. How on earth could she be over the limit on both credit cards? It wasn't possible. Maybe someone *had* stolen her identity.

Snip, snip went the scissors. The desecrated MasterCard fell into pieces beside the Visa.

She felt fractured, disjointed, as if she, the real Tish, was separate from the woman who did dumb things like this. It was a feeling that dwelled in the fringes of her consciousness, a ghost of something she'd never been able to pinpoint. A feeling that she could never be whole, no matter how hard she struggled to integrate herself. It was a desolate sensation and made her want to run out and buy something expensive.

"What next?" the waiter asked. "Where do we go from here?"

"I'll pay for the lunch," Addison James said icily. She took out her wallet and counted out the correct amount of cash to cover the bill.

A deep silence fell over the table after the waiter departed. Tish worked up the courage to look Addison in the eyes. "I'm deeply sorry for that. I'll reimburse you."

Fury drew Addison's brows down tight in a disapproving frown and her lips thinned out. "What kind of business professional does something like this? Invites clients to lunch and tries to pay for it with not one, but two maxed-out credit cards?"

The air leaked from Tish's lungs. She couldn't breathe, could hardly speak. "I...I..."

Addison pushed back her chair and got to her feet. "Come on, Felicity. We have somewhere else to be."

"Please, wait." Tish put a hand to the woman's wrist.

Addison glowered at Tish's arm. The price tag had fallen out of her sleeve and was dangling there for everyone to see.

"You were planning on returning that suit after you wore it, weren't you?" Addison accused.

The deal was lost. No point lying at this juncture.

"Yes."

"You are so pathetic," Addison hissed. "Talented perhaps, but pathetic. Until you can pull your life together, stop shooting for the stars."

Reeling, Tish watched her meal ticket, daughter in tow, sweep out of the restaurant. Feeling as if her arms had been amputated, Tish fumbled for the pieces of her massacred credit cards and stuffed them in the pocket of the suit that she had to return to Nordstrom's for a refund.

Loser.

She raised her head and saw people were watching. Peeved with herself, she glared at an owl-eyed woman at the next table staring at her as if she had the avian flu.

Embarrassed but proud, Tish raised her head, pushed back her chair, and got to her feet. At the same time a waiter, zigzagging around tables with a big tray of butter-slick crawfish balanced over his head on the palm of his hand, zipped past.

The leg of Tish's chair clipped his ankle.

The waiter stumbled. His tray slipped. The crawfish attacked—pelting Tish's suit with red, buttery bits of seafood hail.

Horrified, she gasped.

"Oh, gosh, ma'am," the waiter apologized as he brushed

crawfish from her clothing. He lifted his head and met her gaze. His eyes narrowed, his lips curled. "Oh, it's you," he said out loud, and then under his breath he muttered, "deadbeat."

Tish's cheeks burned and her heart pounded. She wanted to throw back her head and bawl. This wasn't the waiter's fault. She was in a mess of her own making.

Again.

Accusing eyes scalded, judging her.

Flicking a crawfish off her lapel, she gathered up her briefcase, slung her purse over her shoulder, and strode from the restaurant. Shame tasted like heated aluminum foil in her mouth—hot, sharp, and metallic.

She dug her car keys from her purse and pressed the alarm button to locate her Ford Focus in the overflowing parking lot. No reassuring *chirp-chirp* indicated her car door had been unlocked. She hurried to the area where she remembered parking, hitting the alarm button a second time.

Nothing.

Tish was certain she'd been in this section of the lot. But an SUV sat where she thought she'd parked. Maybe, in her humiliation over what had just happened to her inside the restaurant, she was mistaken.

She retraced her steps. Yes, she was almost one hundred percent sure this was where she'd parked.

Clearly not. Your car isn't here.

She stalked up and down the aisles, the humid Houston heat causing sweat to pool under her collar. Her stilettos were made for showing off, not for walking, and her toes throbbed beneath the leather straps. She felt a blister forming. The heels kept sticking in the heat-softened asphalt and Tish stumbled twice. Where was her car?

Dread, sudden as lightning in a cloudless sky, struck her. Someone had stolen her car!

She dug into her pocket for her cell phone and turned it on. Just as she pressed the 9 of 9-1-1 an image rose in her mind. She recalled the stack of unpaid bills on her kitchen table.

There'd been a letter or two from the finance company threatening to take back her car if payment wasn't made soon. She thought of the phone calls left on her answering machine that she hadn't returned.

And she realized the awful truth. Her car hadn't been stolen.

It had been repossessed.

Chapter 3

Elysee Benedict was in love with love. She adored the heady rush of early romance—the kisses, the long, lingering glances, the surprise gifts, and the undivided attention. Her mother, Catherine Prosper Benedict, God rest her soul, had instilled in Elysee the staunch belief of happily ever after.

When she was young, her mother would occasionally take her out of school early on the pretext of a dental appointment. Instead, they would slip off to the matinee and watch romantic movies, eating popcorn from the same box and giggling like best girlfriends over handsome movie star heroes. Elysee loved those surprise outings in the darkened theater with her mother.

When she was ten, Catherine passed on her dog-eared copies of romance novels with muscular, longhaired men on the covers. Reading the stories had made her heart beat faster and she yearned for a romance of her very own.

When she was eleven, her mother was diagnosed with terminal bone cancer. "I'm not going to be around to see you fall in love and get married," Catherine had told her. "So you must listen to me now."

"Yes, Mama."

"True love is out there for you, Elysee, if you just believe it."

"I believe," she vowed, believing as only a young child could.

Her mother squeezed her hand. "Don't give up until you find him."

"But how will I know when I meet the right one?"

"You'll feel it." Her mother laid her hand over Elysee's heart. "Deep down inside here."

"What will he be like?"

"He'll be kind and strong and he'll fight for you and he'll protect you, even if it means he must give up his own life to save you, and he'll be your very best friend."

Six months later her mother was dead and Elysee's longing to find her true love was stronger than ever. The problem was, she saw love everywhere, in any masculine face that smiled. She went through crush after crush, each time feeling it deep within her heart, each time thinking, *It's him. He's the one.*

"She's too much like her mother," she'd once heard her father tell her nanny, Rana Singh, not long after Catherine had died. "Head in the clouds, mind filled with silly romantic notions about life. I don't know what to do with her."

Much to her father's consternation, at twenty-two she'd already been engaged three times. Elysee had been on the front page of too many tabloids, their ugly headlines burned into her brain.

First Daughter's First Romance Fizzles.

Elysee Benedict: Fickle Princess or Lonely Teen?

Beau Number Three Breaks Heart of Prez's Only Child.

Yes, okay, she'd made a lot of mistakes, picked the wrong kind of men, gone for flash over substance.

Shane Tremont, however, was different. For one thing, he was older. For another thing, her father liked and respected him. And there was the fact he'd saved her life, just as her mother had said her true love would do. Quiet, strong, steady Shane.

She'd stayed at his bedside from the beginning. Her father had tried to talk her out of it, but she insisted on being there when he woke up. He'd been her bodyguard for over a year and while she'd always thought of him as a good-looking man, she'd never considered him in a romantic way until he'd sacrificed himself for her.

Before that, well, he'd scared her just a little with his tough masculinity. In the past she'd favored polished, soft-featured, erudite men, and Shane certainly wasn't that. But seeing him in that hospital bed, with those tubes coming out of him and his head wrapped in bandages, he'd looked so lost and vulnerable she'd wanted to scoop him into her arms and cuddle him. He wasn't so big and tough and scary after all.

Elysee realized what she felt for Shane was different from what she had felt for her other three fiancés. This was a quiet love, a soft love, a mature love. This was the kind of love her father told her she needed, and she'd begun to realize that this was what true love must be—a deep, abiding friendship grown stronger through sacrifice and devotion.

So what if there was no electricity? No sparks. That was the point. Chemistry had led her down the wrong path before, caused her to make foolish choices. Sometimes, she missed her mother so much, it was a physical ache. She wished Catherine was here to confirm her belief that Shane was indeed The One. True friendship was the ingredient that had been missing from her other love relationships.

Elysee sat at Shane's bedside day in and day out. Willing him well, willing him to love her back the way she was coming to love him. And if she squeezed her eyes closed and concentrated really hard, she could feel it deep inside her heart.

Yes. Shane Tremont was indeed her true love. Now all she had to do was convince him of it.

•

"Häagen-Dazs is not the answer," Tish's best friend Delaney scolded her as she pried the empty cup of what had once contained coffee-flavored ice cream from her hand.

"Creamery-ista," Tish said to the woman behind the counter at the Häagen-Dazs kiosk in the Galleria mall, "I'll have another round. This time serve up a double scoop of Dulce de Leche."

Delaney shook her head at the woman and narrowed her eyes. "Don't make me stage an intervention, Tish Gallagher. Put down the sample spoon and step away from the Häagen-Dazs."

Tish gripped the spoon tighter, anxiety clotting her throat. She knew her friend had her best interests at heart. She also knew gorging herself wasn't an antidote. She'd screwed up big time and now here she was, trying to drown her sorrows in high-fat premium ice cream.

Two weeks had passed since the incident with Addison James. Two miserable weeks dodging bill collectors and begging rides to work from friends and neighbors. Her cable service had been shut off for nonpayment and she'd had to cancel both her Netflix subscription and her broadband service.

She'd been without television or online access since her car had been repossessed. She'd nixed her morning trip to Starbucks and stopped picking up newsstand copies of *People* and *Entertainment Weekly* to read during her treadmill workouts. Hell, she couldn't even go to the gym because she was behind on her membership dues.

Tish felt isolated, cut off. She had no idea what was going on in the world. For the last two weeks she'd spent her leisure time listening to mournful CDs and leafing through old photo albums, trying to figure out where things had gone so wrong. Addison James was correct: She *was* pathetic.

Stop whining, commanded the voice in the back of her head. *You're not a whiner. Pull yourself up by the bootstraps.*

But the straps were gone off the proverbial boots and she had nothing left to pull herself up by. She was divorced from a man she was still in love with, her car had been repossessed, she carried over eleven thousand dollars in credit card debt, and she hadn't been on a date in six months. Young and single in the city was not what television cracked it up to be.

"Give me the spoon." Delaney waited, palm outstretched.

Biting down on the inside of her cheek to keep from crying, Tish put the tiny pink plastic spoon in her friend's hand.

"Thank you." Delaney tossed the spoon in the trash. She took Tish by the elbow, propelled her past Victoria's Secret and The Gap to a wooden park bench underneath a trellis of fake yellow roses positioned beside a cement mermaid fountain. "Sit."

Tish sat.

"Why don't you let me loan you some money?" Delaney pulled a checkbook from her Prada purse. "To tide you over."

"Friends shouldn't borrow money from friends."

"What kind of friend would I be if I let you flounder?"

"A smart one."

"Tish, stubborn pride won't help you."

"I'm the idiot who dug myself into this hole. It's not your problem."

"But you ran up the credit cards getting your business going and surviving after your divorce. Those are extenuating circumstances. I know you're going to come out on top in the end."

"Most people would tell me to get a real job, to stop pipe dreaming."

It's what she'd been telling herself, too. But she hated so badly to give up on her dream that she'd ignored the mound of debts piling up and simply prayed it would all go away.

"I'm not most people and you know that I understand. Getting your own business up on its legs isn't easy." Delaney did understand. She had her own house-staging business, but she also had a trust fund.

"Maybe some people aren't meant to have their heart's desire," she mumbled, thinking of Shane.

Delaney patted her hand. "You're just in a down cycle. You're a fabulous videographer, Tish. If you can just hang in there, your career is going to take off big time. I know it."

"I appreciate you, Delaney." Tish shook her head. "But I can't let you bail me out of this." The same stubborn pride that had kept her from asking Shane not to walk out the door clutched her tight as a closed fist.

"Why not?"

"I've got to do this on my own," Tish said, knowing she was tripping over her pride, but not knowing how to get out of her own way. "But thank you."

"So what do you plan to do?" Delaney asked softly. She tilted her head and Tish felt the heat of her gaze.

"I'm going to get a real job. Two if it comes to that."

"And how are you going to get to those jobs with no car, and no money or the credit rating to buy one?"

There was the major kink in her plans.

"Well," Delaney said, putting her checkbook away. "If you won't take my money, at least let me loan you a car."

"How are you going to get around?"

"My parents have a spare car I can borrow."

"No, it'll be too big an inconvenience."

"I don't expect you to have to borrow it for long, because I'm going to put a bee in the ear of every dowager with a marriage-minded daughter in River Oaks and tell them what a wonderful videographer you are."

"You didn't much like it when your mother helped your business."

"That's because my mother was trying to meddle in my life. I'm your friend. I don't want to control you or tell you what to do. I just want to help. It hurts my heart to see you in distress."

Her friend's kindness was too much. Tish felt tears pushing at the back of her eyes, threatening to flow down her cheeks. Aw, damn. She wasn't a crier. She was tough. She prided herself on it.

Delaney reached over and hugged her. "Everything is going to be all right. I promise."

When Delaney said it, Tish could almost believe it. But there was a small ugly voice inside her that kept whispering,

Who do you think you are? Daring to dream big dreams? You don't stand a chance. You're just like your mother. Every time you get something good you ruin it.

Like your credit rating.

Like Shane.

Two years later and the pain still washed over her, fresh as the day he'd walked out—the day she'd let him go forever. It was the biggest mistake of her life. She knew it now and she'd known it as she was letting him slip away. Something in her weird psyche kept thinking that if he loved her, he would understand her. That she shouldn't have to say anything. He should just *know* what she was feeling. But he hadn't known and he'd left because she could not tell him how much he meant to her. And she could not forgive him for not being there when she needed him the most.

Delaney jangled her car keys. "The Acura's yours for as long as you need it."

Swallow your stupid pride for once. Take her up on this.

She'd been unable to fix her marriage, but maybe she could fix her career. Humbled, Tish held out her palm, and closed her fingers around the keys. What else could she do? "Thank you."

"There's more, isn't there? Something else is bothering you."

Tish felt strange talking about the wedding veil, about the odd vision she'd seen and her irrational fear that Shane was in some kind of trouble. Two weeks had passed and she still couldn't forget what she'd viewed in the mirror. She'd been too afraid of what she would see to put the veil back on again.

"It's safe. You can tell me anything."

"Do you really think your wedding veil has magical powers?" Tish whispered. "Do you really believe in all that wish fulfillment nonsense?"

"You had a vision." It was a statement, not a question.

"How did you know?"

"It's what happened to me in Claire Kelley's consignment shop, the first time I touched the veil."

"How come you never said anything?"

Delaney shrugged. "How do you admit something like that?"

"Point taken." Tish stared across the mall unseeingly, thinking about her disturbing vision.

"You saw the face of your true love, didn't you?"

"No."

"No?" Delaney arched an eyebrow.

"I saw Shane. And I got the awful feeling he was in trouble. Tell me I'm just being silly. It's stupid to think the veil has some kind of magical power, right?"

Delaney shifted on the bench. She looked uncomfortable. "I'm not sure how to answer that. In my vision I saw Nick and then when I met him in person I knew instantly he was the man I was supposed to spend the rest of my life with, even though I was engaged to Evan at the time."

"No fantasy man for me. Just Shane."

"Do you think your mind could have created the vision as a smoke screen for your problems? That you're projecting your fears onto Shane so you don't have to face what's going on in your own life?"

"Maybe."

"It's time to let go of Shane." Delaney's eyes were kind. "You've been holding on to the possibility that he would come back. It's been two years. He's not coming back, Tish."

"I know," she whispered. "We were too different. The

maverick wild child and the stalwart soldier. But the deal is, whenever we were good together, we were really, *really* good. Shane connected me to a part of myself I didn't even know existed. He grounded me. Made me feel secure in a way I never felt before or since. When I was around him I felt like more. You know?"

Delaney smiled with understanding. "I do know."

"I screwed it all up, Delaney." Tish's breath hitched.

"There are two sides to every story, Tish, and it seems to me that Shane doesn't know how to forgive. And if he couldn't forgive you for being human, how could he have truly loved you unconditionally? We all make mistakes. Shane's mistake was letting his anger rule his heart."

Tish wanted to cry, but she'd learned a long time ago tears were a weakness she couldn't afford. Delaney was right.

It was time to let go.

The next time Shane surfaced things seemed brighter, lighter. Was that sun on his face? Had someone opened a window?

A soft touch squeezed the fingers of his left hand. A woman's hand. His heart leaped with hope.

"Tish," he whispered, barely able to push his wife's name across his dry, cracked lips.

"It's Elysee." Her voice was quiet, reassuring.

Disappointment locked him in a stone fist. It wasn't Tish. "Elysee?"

"I'm here. Open your eyes. Open your eyes and look at me."

He wanted to look at her, but it wasn't as easy as she made it sound. His eyelids lay heavy as gold medallions. Stubborn. Hanging on to the darkness.

Slowly, he managed to force them open and he saw Elysee Benedict sitting at his bedside, her fingers clasped around his. There was a forlorn expression in her gentle blue eyes that he'd never seen before.

He noticed something else. His right hand was bandaged like a mummy, his whole arm cradled in a sling that slipped over his neck, and it hurt. Throbbing, blinding pain blunted from his fingertips, up through his wrist. He gritted his teeth and forced himself to ignore the pain. He was Secret Service. He knew how to accomplish it.

Elysee sucked in a breath through the cute little gap in her front teeth. "I'm afraid that I have bad news."

"Wh...?" His mouth was so damned dry, his tongue was glued to the roof of his mouth. "What happened?"

"You don't remember?"

He tried to shake his head, but movement hurt too much. "No."

"The groundbreaking at the University of Texas?"

His memory was foggy. He frowned, trying to call up the scene.

"You saved my life." The smile on her face was wistful, but warm. The sight of it caught him low in the gut. He felt as if he'd stumbled in from a frigid blizzard and she was a hot, crackling fire welcoming him home.

"I did?"

"You did. And I've been here with you ever since."

"How long?" Shane tried to moisten his lips with an arid tongue.

"Thirteen days."

"Thirteen days?" It seemed impossible. How could he have checked out for so long?

"Almost fourteen, actually."

The news flattened him. He felt at once both restless

and leaden. "You've been here with me for two weeks? But you have duties, appointments, and responsibilities."

"All canceled. Nothing is as important to me as your recovery."

"It's not necessary."

"Shane, you're not only my bodyguard, but my friend. I'm staying."

She looked so fiercely loyal that he had to smile even if it hurt.

"You gave us quite a scare in the beginning," she went on. "When the backhoe bucket hit you, it caused your brain to bleed. You had surgery."

Her voice went softer and he could tell by the tears swimming in her eyes that he'd been close to death. The realization didn't frighten him, but her emotional reaction did.

"Surgery?"

"They shaved your head. All that beautiful dark hair." She sighed.

He reached up a hand to touch his scalp. It was prickly with hair stubble. He'd been burred before. In the Air Force. In boot camp. He didn't care about the hair. His fingers crept to his right temple, the spot that ached, and he found the raw seam of stitches four fingers long.

"I hate to be the one to have to tell you this, but that's not everything." She smoothed the bedcovers with her fingers, and she couldn't meet his gaze.

He laughed. He didn't mean to laugh at her. It just came out. "No?"

"Your hand."

His chest tightened. She didn't have to say it. He guessed. "Yeah?"

"It was crushed by the backhoe. They managed to save

your hand, but it's very doubtful you'll ever regain full use. You're probably going to have to give up protective detail for a desk job."

He couldn't absorb that information. Not now. Not yet. To hear the news that he could no longer be a Secret Service agent on protective detail was more than he could handle at the moment. So he refused to acknowledge it. If he didn't acknowledge it, then how could it be true?

"How are you?" He tightened the fingers of his good hand around hers. "Are you doing all right?"

"Unscathed except for skinned knees when you knocked me down and a little worn out from this bedside vigil. Otherwise A-okay." She canted her head, smiled wryly.

His memory finally flashed and he saw himself pushing Elysee to the platform as the backhoe bucket descended. "And the backhoe operator?"

"He's fine, too."

"No," Shane said. "I mean why was the bastard trying to kill you?"

Elysee gave a gentle laugh. "He wasn't trying to kill me. He'd been up all night because his wife had been giving birth to their first child, but he didn't tell his boss he was sleep-deprived because he wanted to be at the groundbreaking to meet me. He just made a mistake. Pushed the wrong levers, then panicked and kept pushing them."

"You could have been killed."

"But I wasn't, because of you."

The tenderness in her eyes separated his heart from his chest. He felt it free-falling straight to his feet.

"You saved my life," Elysee whispered, her cheeks pinking. "You saved me, Shane. At great personal cost to your own safety."

He'd done his job. Elysee was safe. That's all that mattered.

"I called your parents," she said. "I thought they should know."

"Are they here? In Austin?" His parents were supposed to be on an around-the-world cruise celebrating his father's retirement. They'd been looking forward to this trip their entire lives. He hated to think that they'd been forced to cut their travels short because of him.

"No, I downplayed your injuries. I hope that's okay." Elysee looked anxious. "I remembered you told me how important this trip was to them and I knew you'd hate being responsible for ruining it. I felt a little guilty myself. If you hadn't been rescuing me, you wouldn't have gotten hurt."

"You did good," he said. "Thank you."

In that moment, in that serious exchange of glances, he felt as if he'd known her his entire life. Her calm energy was as comforting as a kitten's purr. He already knew her so well. She was predictable, safe. He liked that about her. With Tish things had always been exciting and electric, but keeping up with her boundless energy had taken constant effort. Elysee was effortless.

"Thank you." Her eyes glistened.

His ego inflated. To think she was looking at him, a scarred war dog, with such adoration and respect. Heady stuff. Was their friendship growing into something more?

It was a scary thought. This wasn't smart, these budding feelings he was having for her—he hadn't been involved with anyone since Tish. Right now, he was feeling pretty damned vulnerable.

Shane thought of Tish again. Wild and rebellious and passionate. Never a dull moment. Life with her had often mimicked an episode of *I Love Lucy.* Madcap, adventuresome, filled with irrepressible spirit. She'd been like a lit firecracker in his hand. Sizzling hot and ready to detonate.

And explode she had.

Their marriage had been the collateral damage.

Shane had learned the hard way that blistering passion was bound to blow up in your face. He'd followed his heart and not his head and it had nearly ruined him.

Elysee was Tish's polar opposite. Not a risk taker at all. It had made guarding her easy and being friends with her even easier. Being married to a woman like her would be serene. And right now, nothing seemed more appealing than serenity.

Shane closed his eyes, unable to keep them open any longer. Waking up, jogging his memory, learning that his skull had been cracked and his hand had been shattered had taken a toll.

He felt the gentle brush of Elysee's lips against his cheek. "That's right, darling," she whispered. "Sleep."

Darling?

The word befuddled him, but he was already sliding away, unable to make sense of why the President's daughter was kissing him and speaking in terms of endearment.

Chapter 4

Tish usually got over the blues by going shopping, but this time, shopping had caused her blues. How was she going to get over that?

At ten o'clock in the morning, she sat in Delaney's Acura outside the Galleria. She wanted to go in and buy a new outfit to cheer herself up, but she was broke. Completely tapped out. Ninety-seven dollars and fifty cents was all she had left in her savings account; there were no groceries in the house and no new wedding gigs in sight.

October was a slow month for weddings. She'd planned to make ends meet by taking the gray tweed suit back and living on her credit card until she had another wedding to photograph. But the suit had been ruined, her credit cards ruthlessly massacred, and her car repossessed.

Unless she could manage to sell a few of her used clothes on e-bay, she was royally screwed. And seriously regretting having closed out her Macy's account after paying it off with the money she'd earned from videotaping Delaney's wedding.

Go in. Go shopping. With ninety-seven fifty you could buy an accessory, or an autumn blouse, or a new pair of jeans.

E-bay. She'd do it tonight. In the meantime, the mall beckoned.

Tish opened the car door and swung her legs to the asphalt.

She poised there, half in, half out of the car, taking stock of her life and the mess she'd made of it.

Stop thinking. Just go shopping. Remember what Mom always taught you. Affluence attracts affluence. You wouldn't have met Delaney if you hadn't been following Mom's hard-and-fast rule.

Tish had met her best friend during college when she'd pledged Phi Beta Kappa at Rice University and had blown her entire IRS refund on a new wardrobe to look the part, with money originally earmarked for tuition.

She and Delaney had ended up rooming together, and if it hadn't been for Delaney feeding her and sharing her textbooks, Tish wouldn't have made it through. Even with Delaney's help, a night job, and the scholarships she'd received, Tish had barely finished college.

Promising herself that she was only going to window-shop, Tish climbed out of the car and headed inside the mall. Nordstrom's was having a sale. She felt the immediate squeeze of excitement. This wasn't just any sale, it was a fire sale—everything except new arrivals was listed at the lowest prices of the year.

Adrenaline streamed her down the aisles. Fossil watches normally priced at seventy-five dollars and up were marked thirty percent off.

Her heart beat faster.

Lingerie was slashed forty percent. Since she had no one to wear sexy lingerie for, Tish skipped over to the next department.

Shoes. Omigosh, shoes!

Sixty percent off! Designer names. Stilettos and pumps and sandals and boots. Red and blue and black and tan.

Blood rushed through her ears. She felt breathless, faint. A sixty-percent-off sale on expensive designer shoes, and she was dead broke.

Not dead broke. You have ninety-seven fifty.

Tish paused. It wouldn't hurt just to try on a few pairs. Sixty percent off for great shoes. How often did one find a deal like that?

But you have no money and no credit cards.

She walked into the shoe department. Women were grabbing shoes, elbowing each other out of the way. The display racks were a mess. Shoes and shoeboxes were scattered everywhere. Harried salespeople ran to and fro, trying to find missing slippers for disgruntled Cinderellas. After circling the area a few times, Tish found an adorable pair of red Stuart Weitzman sandals.

And they were in her size.

Hands shaking, she took the sandals, sat down in an out-of-the-way area, and slipped them on her feet. They fit like a dream. She got up and walked around. Like walking on whipped cream. She was already halfway in love and she had the perfect red cocktail dress to go with them.

She went back to her seat and nervously lifted the box. They were regularly two hundred and fifteen dollars. She was lousy at math, but she thought she might just have enough.

Clutching the shoes to her chest, she waited in line for the cashier.

Put them back, Tish; this is insane.

She turned to get out of line, but then she thought of the shoes, how cute her feet looked in them. How they made her feel like a princess.

You've got six boxes of Ramen noodles in your pantry. You can hit a couple of happy-hour free buffets. Maybe you can call up an old boyfriend or two and see if you can finagle dinner. The shoes are worth it.

She thought of how it had felt when the waiter chopped up her credit cards, when Mrs. James walked out on her, when she'd discovered her car had been repossessed.

"Next," the cashier called out and Tish realized the woman was talking to her.

She hesitated.

Go ahead. You can always return them.

Tish stepped up and slid the shoes across the counter. She'd let fate decide. If the total came to more than ninety-seven fifty, well, it was out of her hands.

"Ninety-three seventy-two," the cashier said.

Feeling as if she'd just won the lottery, Tish grinned and ran her debit card through the card reader. But just as she punched in her debit code and the machine accepted it, the cahier said, "All sales are final. Absolutely no refunds."

Panic gripped her. She had shoes she did not need and less than four dollars in her checking account.

That's when she knew she'd hit rock bottom.

Hello, my name is Tish Gallagher and I'm a shopaholic.

Every night he was in the hospital, Shane dreamed of Tish. Whether it was the painkillers or his head injury or the combination of both he didn't know, but he just couldn't seem to peel his ex-wife off his subconscious mind.

He dreamed of the way she'd looked when he'd walked out the door, her mouth pressed into an unyielding line unable to say the words he needed to hear. Her jaw clenched, but her eyes begging him to forgive her, begging him to understand, begging him to stay.

But he'd just kept going. If she couldn't learn to ask for what she needed from him, he couldn't continue to try to read her mysterious mind. Now he realized how stubbornly stupid he'd been, how fragile Tish was, in spite of the toughness she projected. He'd wounded her. She'd wounded him. They'd stupidly wounded each other.

Then he'd wake up and look over at Elysee, his dear friend who would touch his good hand, murmur words of reassurance. She looked so serene. He came to expect her, looked forward to opening his eyes and seeing her face. A smile from Elysee sent his demons running for the shadows.

Three weeks he had been stuck in the hospital, enduring a series of tests, undergoing therapy, recovering from surgery. Elysee had steadfastly refused to leave his bedside for any length of time.

Her new bodyguard turned out to be his old partner Cal Ackerman. Cal lurked in the hallway, waiting patiently, watching for danger. Doing Shane's job while he was stuck in the bed.

Wounded. Infirm. Weak. He hated it.

The doctors had told him it would take several months of physical therapy for him to regain partial use of his right hand. They'd told him he would never have full range of motion. He couldn't make a fist, couldn't even hold a spoon. And although there would be no long-term damage from his head injury, he still had headaches. He felt as raw and vulnerable as he had during his first week at boot camp.

"You're being released tomorrow," Elysee said. "And you're going to need a place to recuperate."

"I'll be fine at home," he said, although he'd been dreading the thought of staring at the bare walls of his apartment, having no one to talk to, no place to go except physical therapy three times a week. He realized then how narrow his life had become since the Secret Service had promoted him to protective detail.

"I've spoken to Daddy," she said. "He's agreed the best place for you to recover is at our ranch in Katy."

"I appreciate the offer, Elysee, but this isn't your problem."

"You saved my life." She sounded hurt. "I thought we were friends.

His eyes met hers. She *was* hurt. "I'm sorry," he said gently. "I can't accept."

"I'll be at the ranch with you," she said. "You shouldn't be alone."

"You can't put your life on hold for me. You have duties in Washington. Your father needs you."

"Daddy understands that you need me more."

The dynamics in their relationship had shifted. He'd gone from protector to patient and he didn't like it. He wasn't the man he used to be and he didn't know how to find his way back.

"Elysee, I just don't think it's the best idea."

"Don't make me pull rank on you." She grinned. "I could have your Commander-in-Chief give you a direct order."

He thought again of his sparse, lonely apartment back in Georgetown, and then he looked into Elysee's eyes.

"Please," she said. "Do it for me."

In the back of his mind something was jangling, but his thoughts were still so jumbled he couldn't put a name to it. Too much damned Percodan. He had to lay off the stuff, blinding headaches or not. Because the tender way she looked at him both worried him and drew him to her.

He didn't know how it happened exactly, but Shane found himself saying what he feared wasn't in his best interest. He said the words for her, because she seemed to need to hear him say them. He said them for himself because he didn't want to be alone.

"Yes, okay, I'll recover at your father's ranch."

Five mornings later, Shane and Elysee ate breakfast in the dining room at her father's sprawling ranch house in Katy, with a handful of servants and her new bodyguards hanging around. Shane felt odd as a panda strolling up Broadway, sitting across from Nathan Benedict's daughter reading the *Washington Post* in his pajamas and bathrobe. Elysee leafed through her magazines, trying to catch up on the back issues she'd missed while nursing him through his recovery.

For one thing, the role reversal didn't fit. He should be guarding her, taking care of her, not making idle chitchat over cereal and cantaloupe. For another thing, he wasn't a pajama and bathrobe kind of guy. Nowadays, he preferred sleeping in the buff.

He used to be the sort who snoozed in his BVDs, but Tish had broken him of that habit. When they were married, he never knew when he would awaken to find her tugging at the waistband of his boxer briefs with a come-hither look in her eyes and making impatient get-naked noises at the back of her throat.

"Even though Hurricane Devon took top billing on the day of the UT groundbreaking," Elysee said, "we still managed to make page ten of *People* magazine. Look, here's a picture of you in the hospital."

She held up the magazine for him to see. Sure enough, there was a picture of him sitting up in the hospital bed, head bandaged, IV snaking from the back of his hand, looking like hammered dog crap. He had no idea when the photograph had been taken or who had snapped it.

Something else in the photograph caught his eye and caused Shane's chest to tighten. Elysee was sitting at his bedside, gazing at him with an expression of pure adoration. Cautiously, he shifted his gaze from the page to meet her frank stare from across the table.

She smiled, then ducked her head.

His lungs chuffed against his constricted chest. It wasn't his imagination. She was infatuated with him.

Shane gulped. Oh, shit. He didn't know how to feel about this discovery. The truth was it felt pretty damned nice being here with her, knowing how much she respected and admired him. Knowing he respected and admired her just as much. It was flattering.

It's hero worship is what it is. Don't let your ego swell out of control, Tremont.

"Omigosh," Elysee gasped and splayed a hand against her heart.

"What is it?"

"It's my old nanny, Rana." Elysee held up the magazine again, showing him a photograph of a woman in her early forties who looked to be of East Indian descent. The woman's eyes blazed intensely. Her mouth was set in a serious expression. The headline read DEATHLIST TARGET.

"What's that all about?" he asked.

Elysee scanned the article. "Rana is a key player in a group called WorldFem that helps women in Third World and Middle Eastern countries escape honor killings at the hands of their families. Now she's being targeted herself for bringing shame on her country! Oh, this is terrible. What is wrong with people?"

It was a philosophical question Shane couldn't begin to answer. "This woman used to be your nanny?"

"Yes, when I was very small, for the couple of years my parents lived in London. Rana cared for me while my mother was getting her graduate degree at Oxford. She taught me how to speak Hindi. Then later, after Mother died, Dad hired her again while he was governor of Texas. She was with us a little over three years then, from the time I was eleven and a half until I turned fifteen."

"You speak Hindi?"

"Well, not fluently, but I can get by."

"I'm impressed. I didn't know that about you, Elysee. Who knew you were such a woman of mystery?"

"I know what you're trying to do." She smiled. "Thanks for that."

"Thanks for what?"

"Trying to get my mind off Rana's grim plight. I've got to speak to Dad, see if he'll throw some political muscle around and get the heat off Rana."

"You know next year is an election year."

"Meaning what?"

"Your father has to be careful what causes he champions if he wants to get re-elected."

"What's more important? Rana's life or winning an election?"

Shane raised his palms. "Hey, I'm on your side. I'm just pointing out your father's advisors might discourage him from wasting political energy on this issue."

"Well, he's got to do something. We just can't stand by and let whackos with crazy ideas kill Rana because she's trying to save women held down by an archaic system."

"You know it's more complicated than that."

"God." Her eyes flashed. It was the first time he'd seen her look so passionate. Her verve both surprised and delighted him. "I hate politics."

"You definitely should talk to your father. I was just pointing out it might not be a slam dunk."

Elysee closed the magazine. "I've got to get my mind off this. Nothing I can do until Dad comes to the ranch tomorrow. Why don't we take a walk in the garden this morning before your physical therapy session?"

"Sure."

"The chrysanthemums are in full bloom. I'd like you to see them. My mother planted the flowers before she died." Her voice saddened.

They finished their breakfast and Elysee waited patiently when he almost lost his balance getting up from the table and had to pause a moment. Since the surgery, if he moved too quickly he got dizzy. Damn this cursed weakness. He bit down on his bottom lip to keep from letting loose a string of foul words.

"Easier than yesterday," she said brightly.

If Tish were here, she would tell him it was okay to swear. She would probably even get the ball rolling with a few choice words of her own. Shane smiled, thinking about it.

"That's how I like to see you." Elysee tucked her arm through his. "With a nice big grin on your face."

When he looked at Elysee he saw all the ways she wasn't his ex-wife. Her hair was mousy brown; Tish's deep auburn. She was thin, petite; Tish busty and tall. She was quiet and thoughtful; Tish was energetic and spontaneous.

Something stirred inside him. Not desire, but something just as compelling for a man who was feeling vulnerable. Contentment. Around Elysee he felt content.

She maneuvered him out the back door. They picked their way across the patio, up and over the wooden deck, past the gazebo and down the walkway leading to the gardens. Once he was in motion, Shane's muscles relaxed and his joints loosened. His feet grew more self-assured over the cobblestones. No more dizziness.

The top of Elysee's head came to his chin and the smell of her gentle shampoo crowded his nose. Lavender. It had been his grandmother's favorite perfume. Tish preferred spicy fragrances. Like cinnamon and anise and ginger—exotic, sharp, and memorable.

Strangely, a lump formed in his throat. Damn injury brought his emotions too close to the surface. Shane swallowed back the bitter lump and clenched his jaw.

The late October weather had finally cooled from the intense dog-day summer heat. It had rained the night before and the damp morning breeze felt good against his skin. Fall flowers were in full flush. Pink and orange and rust-colored. Elysee leaned over to pick a flower. She straightened, the bloom held to her nose, and took a deep breath. "Smells like autumn."

The eastern sunlight dappled through the languid limbs of willow trees and cast Elysee's face in an ethereal glow. Looking at her, Shane's chest tightened again.

She was so delicate, so fragile. Her soft blue eyes looked the way clouds felt. He found himself thinking crazily—*cumulus, stratus, cirrus*—and he had an irresistible urge to comb his fingers through the wisps of her flyaway hair. For the briefest of moments the sunlight tinged her hair auburn and she looked vaguely like Tish.

His eyes must have given away his impulse because she gave him a little smile and her gaze hung on his lips.

"Shane," she whispered and dropped the flower blossom. "Shane."

He leaned forward, surprised by how calm he felt, how utterly at peace. No raw passion. No disturbing chemistry. No volatile boom-boom of his heart like the first time he'd kissed Tish. Nothing except tranquil serenity. His lips brushed her mouth.

She kissed him back, tentatively curling one hand around his arm.

Safe, he thought. Safe and simple and comforting as mashed potatoes. Elysee would never max out his credit cards behind his back. She'd never challenge his authority, or question his motives.

The kiss was nice and sweet and reliable. Nothing to complain about. Everyone liked mashed potatoes.

But the minute the kiss was over and he caught the puppy-dog-in-love look in Elysee's eyes, Shane realized he'd just crossed a very important line that he hadn't meant to cross.

Chapter 5

The following day, the President arrived at the ranch for a weekend-long stay. Nathan Benedict was a tall, lean man, as aloof as his daughter was welcoming. He was fiercely intelligent and a moderate Republican who commanded respect from both parties. He was a man of few words, but when he spoke, everyone listened. Some compared him to Abraham Lincoln.

Shane's admiration for him was second only to his admiration for his own father and grandfather. Whenever he was in Nathan's presence, he felt as if a great honor had been bestowed upon him, but he was nervous as well, afraid that he wouldn't live up to the President's standards.

The dinner conversation was restrained. Nathan sat at one end of the table, Elysee down the length of the table at the other end, and Shane in the middle, feeling decidedly displaced. He should be outside the doorway with Cal, not dining on roasted chicken and tomato aspic with the leader of the free world.

He was especially self-conscious about his table manners. The physical therapist had insisted he use his right as much as possible, but not tonight. As awkward as eating with his non-dominant hand was, it was preferable to anything his injured paw could accomplish. He ate slowly, carefully, aware of each bite. A silence fell over the table and he realized that Elysee was studying him.

And that Nathan was watching his daughter watch Shane.

He shifted uncomfortably in his seat and put his fork down.

Elysee coaxed a few stories from her father about his trip to China, but ultimately she was the one who carried the dinner conversation. Toward the end of the meal, she brought up Rana Singh and what she'd read in *People* magazine.

"Dad, you've got to do something to get Rana off that death list."

"Sweetheart." Her father smiled at her kindly. "The fact that she's been featured in *People* has effectively guaranteed her safety. If she were murdered, everyone would know who was responsible."

"So? It doesn't stop them from killing their daughters, their wives, their granddaughters, their nieces over their illogical sense of honor."

"Elysee, all of that takes place in other countries. Rana lives here, in the U.S."

"But she goes overseas to help those women. Evil men could kill her then and the U.S. couldn't touch them."

"Then Rana's just going to have to stay in the U.S."

"Well, what about those other women? If Rana's not helping them, then who will? Can't you do something? It's a horrifying practice."

"Agreed, but making moral and religious policy in other countries is beyond my scope."

"But you're the President of the United States! How can it be beyond your scope?"

"We had a similar conversation when you were thirteen and I was governor and you thought it was unfair that you had to pay adult prices at the movie theater, but you weren't allowed to vote, drink, or drive a car."

"It's not the same thing at all. You're comparing Rana's life to the price of a movie ticket?"

"You're taking it out of context, Elysee. What I'm saying is that I'm not the president of the world."

"Well, you should be."

"My opponents might disagree with you there."

"You might not want to help, Dad, but I've got to get involved with WorldFem."

"Be mindful of your position. You have a lot of influence. You must choose your causes with care."

"Exactly. What's the point of having influence if you can't effect change?"

"Just proceed with caution."

"I'm not a child, father. I understand my responsibilities."

Nathan frowned, but said nothing. Father and daughter exchanged a meaningful look. Shane couldn't help wondering if the President was thinking about Elysee's broken engagements and the men who'd taken advantage.

She pushed back from the table. "If you'll excuse me, I have a bit of a headache. I think I'll go to bed early."

"Good night."

Elysee paused at the door, and looked at him over her shoulder. "Shane?"

"Shane and I have a few things to discuss in private," her father said.

"You're not going to fire him off my detail just because he got hurt, are you?"

Was he? It was Shane's greatest fear.

"No, no, of course not. It's just the first time I've had a chance to speak with him in person since the incident."

"Oh. Okay." Looking appeased, Elysee left the room.

Nathan Benedict pushed back his chair, nodded at Shane. "A brandy in the study?"

"Sure." He didn't usually drink, but when the President of the United States suggested you take a brandy in the study, you took a brandy in the study. Shane followed Nathan past Cal Ackerman, standing sentry in the hallway.

He had the feeling his old buddy had been eavesdropping on their dinner conversation. It was a complication of the job, being privy to high-placed secrets but having to pretend that you didn't hear or see anything you weren't supposed to.

They exchanged glances, but Cal's face was unreadable. Shane wished he could change places with his former partner. He wanted his old role back. This strange new one didn't fit.

"Shut the door," Nathan said.

Shane entered the study behind him. He closed the door with his left hand, and kept his right hand tucked in his pocket.

"Let's see the hand."

"Excuse me, sir?"

"Your hand. I heard it was crushed. That you'll never be able to use a gun again."

"That's just one doctor's opinion." Shane shrugged.

"Let me see the hand," Nathan repeated.

He didn't want to comply. Was the man trying to humiliate him? Or use his injury as a reason to dismiss him, even though Benedict had promised Elysee he wouldn't?

The thought angered him. His eyes locked with the President's. "What for?"

"I want to see what you were willing to sacrifice for my daughter."

It was an odd statement. It effectively diffused Shane's anger, but not his embarrassment. Slowly, he pulled his hand from his pocket and thrust it under Nathan Benedict's nose. He steeled his jaw, hardened his feelings.

"Can you make a fist?"

Shane bent his fingertips as far as they would go. His mangled paw wouldn't even make a good talon. His fingers felt stiff as concrete and almost as cold. They ached, but then again, they hadn't really stopped aching since he'd awakened from the coma. What good was a Secret Service agent who couldn't pull a trigger?

"They had to fuse the metacarpals in your hand." Nathan said it as a statement, as if he had already talked to Shane's doctors.

"Yes."

"You took a blow to the temple as well, survived a brain bleed without any lasting damage."

"That's what I've been told."

"You saved my daughter's life." Benedict headed for the wet bar in the corner of the room.

"I did what had to be done." Self-consciously, Shane eased his hand back into his pocket.

"You're a hero." Benedict poured the brandy and turned back to him. He extended the brandy snifter toward Shane's left hand.

"I'm not." How could he be a hero when he couldn't even make a fist? "I was simply doing my job."

"It's more than that."

"Beg your pardon?" What was the man getting at?

"Your job is your identity. I know all about you, Tremont. I know your grandfather was killed at Normandy on

D-day and your father is a decorated Vietnam POW. I know you saved a fellow recruit from friendly fire during boot camp maneuvers. Heroism is in your blood. I also know that you've had some sadness in your life and that your marriage broke up because of it."

As a Secret Service agent on protective duty in the White House, he knew he'd undergone the most extensive of background checks. He just hadn't realized how extensive. If the government knew the reasons his marriage had ended, then they knew everything there was to know about Shane Tremont.

"What's your point?" Shane asked bluntly.

At this juncture, he felt he had nothing else to lose. Elysee might believe her father wouldn't cut him loose from protective detail because of his injury. Shane, however, harbored no such illusions. He was useless as a bodyguard, at least until his hand was fully functional again.

If that ever happens.

He swallowed hard. No. He wasn't even going to entertain that thought. He would recover. Fully. Completely. He was determined.

Benedict took a sip of his brandy, but never took his eyes off Shane. "My daughter's in love with you."

Shane was bowled over. It wasn't what he'd expected to hear. "I'm aware of that, sir."

"Elysee told me that you kissed her."

He tensed. Where was this conversation headed? He'd done it. He'd kissed her and he wasn't a liar. "Yes, sir."

"Why?"

"It felt like the right thing to do at the time." Shane tried to gauge the President's reaction and was surprised when he nodded.

"Do you have tender feelings for her?"

"I'm very fond of Elysee. We're good friends."

"I'm aware of the psychological bond that develops between a bodyguard and the person he's protecting," Benedict said. "Especially when the bodyguard saves the protectee's life."

"What exactly are you trying to say, sir?" Shane took a swig of the stout brandy. It burned his throat as he swallowed back the biting mouthful.

"I respect you, Tremont. But more than that, I like you. You're honorable and straightforward. You don't pull any punches, but you can be trusted to keep your mouth shut."

"Thank you, sir."

"With someone like you, I wouldn't have to worry that Elysee would be taken care of," he said.

"No, sir," Shane said. "You have no worries on that score. I'd protect Elysee with my dying breath."

Yeah? And how are you going to do that with a useless hand?

"And you've proven it." Benedict kept nodding. "She couldn't do any better than to marry a man like you."

Marry?

Shane's gaze flew to Nathan Benedict's face. This was the first time such a notion had crossed his mind, but he felt that any man would be damned lucky to marry Elysee.

"Until now, she's been picking these spineless peckerheads who are just interested in her because of who she is. But I don't have to tell you that. You've been her bodyguard for over a year. You know."

"Yes, sir."

"Then she gets her heart broken when her flash-in-the-pan boyfriends realize they'll have to sign a pre-nup agreement leaving them with nothing if they divorce her. Or they discover what it's really like living in the public eye and find out they're never going to be stars just because they've glommed on to her. But you, you're different. You really care."

"I do care about Elysee, sir." And he did. But just how deep did his feelings run? He was startled to realize how much he did care. It didn't compare to what he'd felt for Tish of course, but he never wanted to feel that kind of chaotic madness again.

Benedict polished off his brandy with a long gulp; for the first time Shane realized the man was as nervous as he was. "Have you ever considered getting remarried? I know this sounds strange, but I'm worried about my little girl. I was forty-eight when she was born and I'm not going to be around forever. I'd like to see her happily married to a good man who'll do right by her."

"Sir, I..." Shane didn't know what to think, much less say.

Nathan Benedict held up a hand. "Elysee loves you and you're fond of her. You already know how easy she is to get along with. You kissed her. That means something."

Did it? Shane stroked his chin.

"Whatever you decide, you have my undying gratitude for saving her life. If you hadn't gotten between her and that backhoe..." Nathan let his voice trail off and Shane saw his eyes glisten with emotion. "You're going to be compensated for that. And I want you to stay here at the ranch until your doctors release you from their care."

"What about my job as Elysee's bodyguard?"

Benedict shifted his weight and didn't meet Shane's eyes. "I don't see how you can continue being her bodyguard, knowing she's in love with you. But if you regain full function of your hand, we'll find another protective detail for you."

"And if Elysee and I were to get married? What then? What kind of work would I do?"

"How would you feel about heading up the Secret Service? Marshal Vega is retiring next year. The position has a lot of power. You'd be effecting policy, in charge of all my personal security, my life," Nathan Benedict said with his unerring ability to read people. He'd figured out what motivated Shane most—the desire to protect and serve.

"Elysee is a wonderful girl."

"She is."

"Give it some thought, Shane. I'd be honored to call you son."

He looked at the President and a feeling he'd never wrestled with came over him. He felt flattered and intrigued, honored, and yet he didn't want to be given a job he hadn't earned just because he'd married the President's daughter. He also didn't want to marry Elysee simply because it was the easiest thing to do.

"I have to be honest, sir. I have no idea how I truly feel. About Elysee. About the job. About myself." He indicated his injured hand.

"I understand." Benedict nodded. "You've got a lot to think about."

"Yes," he said. But deep within, Shane heard a soft voice whisper, *This is it. This is the way to let go of Tish forever.*

The next afternoon, Elysee took Shane horseback riding around the perimeter of the ranch. The kitchen staff packed them a picnic lunch and the day was all blue sky, cool breeze, and autumn wildflowers in full bloom.

They ate their lunch beside the lake, dining on chicken salad sandwiches, carrot sticks, and fresh fruit. Elysee talked animatedly about how she wanted to get involved with WorldFem. He could see the caring in her eyes, knew her heart ached over the injustices. They were so much alike in that respect. Both of them focused on making the world a better place, though each in their own way.

"What a team we could be," she said. "Going around the world, fighting for women's rights. I'd give speeches, visit women in need, head charity drives, raise funds, and you could be there to watch over me. Making it all possible. If only I could convince my father that I know what I'm doing and that with you at my side I wouldn't get taken advantage of."

"Elysee," he said softly, "I'm afraid I can't be your bodyguard."

Alarm spread across her. "How come?"

He laid his right hand on the picnic blanket between them. "I can't protect you, not with this."

"You're going to get full function back. You're dedicated to your physical therapy and you've got the right mental attitude," she encouraged.

"I'm trying my best, but I have to face the reality that no matter how hard I try, it might not ever happen. Besides, it's more than the hand."

"You're quitting? But why would you walk away from a job you love?"

"It's not that simple."

She leaned forward, bracing her chin in her palm. "Explain it to me."

He thought of his conversation with her father the night before. He thought about how lonely he'd been for the last two years. How much he'd loved being married until the worst had happened for him and Tish. How he'd like to have that kind of happiness back again. It was time to release the past and move on. And Elysee, the one he was closest to, was the perfect person to do it with.

"I can't continue being your bodyguard, under the circumstances."

"What circumstances?"

He didn't know what he was going to say. He hadn't planned it, hadn't even made up his mind for sure until the words were out of his mouth.

"Elysee Benedict, would you marry me?"

"What?" She blinked, looking completely caught off guard.

"Would you marry me?" he repeated.

Elysee squealed, knocking over the picnic basket on her way into his lap. She hugged his neck and rained kisses upon his face. "Yes, yes, yes!"

Shane blamed circumstances—his injury, their forced proximity, the beautiful autumn day. He blamed his job, his role as her hero. He blamed the way her eyes, blue as a robin's egg, promised to ease the loneliness he hadn't realized ran so deep. He blamed the earnestness on her face, her sweet scent, and her open honesty that made him want to tell her everything.

But most of all, he blamed himself. For missing being married so badly he wanted to do it again, and for failing Tish so spectacularly that he felt a burning need to make some kind of amends. He was crossing all kinds of boundaries, violating oaths, breaking taboos. Bottom line of the bodyguard's code—never, ever get emotionally involved with the person you're protecting.

What had he done?

"Elysee," he said, and then stopped. How did you go about taking back an impromptu marriage proposal? "Listen to me a minute, sweetheart, I..."

"I'm calling Daddy!" she cried and whipped her cell phone from her pocket. "I can't wait to tell him the good news. He really, really likes you. Oh, Shane, I'm so happy."

He looked down into her face, her eyes brimming with joyous tears, and his heart stilled with confusion and tenderness and a strange sort of peace. He liked taking care of people and Elysee let him take care of her. That was important for a man. To feel needed. It was something independent-minded Tish had never understood.

This was suddenly too real.

Tell her it was a mistake. Tell her you didn't mean to ask her to marry you just yet. Tell her you jumped the gun, spoke too soon. You don't even have a ring.

But he couldn't. She looked so happy and making her happy made him feel good. This was the right thing to do. No second-guessing. He'd made his decision and he was sticking with it.

"Daddy," Elysee bubbled into the phone, "guess what? Shane and I are getting married!"

And that's how Shane Tremont, middle-class boy from small-town America, found himself engaged to the President's daughter.

Chapter 6

Tish was sitting cross-legged on her couch, staring at the new Stuart Weitzman sandals propped on her coffee table and feeling like a binge eater who had just downed two boxes of double-stuffed Oreos, when the telephone rang.

She let it ring.

What if it's a job?

Forcing a smile so the caller couldn't tell she'd over-indulged on shoes two days ago and had the grand total of three dollars and seventy-eight cents in her checking account, she picked it up, answering with the name of her business. "Capture the Moment Videos."

"Tish Gallagher?"

"Yes. How may I help you?" Tish uncoiled her legs and sat up straight.

"Amber Wilson gave me your name. You videotaped her wedding and she can't stop raving about how great you are."

"Thank you." Her spirits soared on the praise.

"I'm getting married this Christmas Eve and while I know it's rather short notice, I'm on the hunt for the best videographer in Houston."

"You've found her," Tish said with a smile.

"My name is Elysee Benedict—"

"Whoa, wait a minute. *The* Elysee Benedict?"

"That's my name." There was amusement in her voice.

"Elysee Benedict? As in the President's daughter?"

"Well, yes, but I'm going to have to ask you for complete confidentiality."

Tish couldn't believe it. The daughter of the President of the United States was calling?

Her bravado vanished and she was left breathless. This was the opportunity of a lifetime. If she snagged this job, she was set. All the fame and fortune she'd been dreaming of would fall right into her lap.

"Totally. Zipped lip. Tick a lock. Throw away the key."

Elysee laughed. "I'm interviewing videographers this afternoon at my father's ranch in Katy. Are you available to drop by, say, three o'clock–ish?"

"Absolutely." Tish would have found a way to go to the moon for Elysee Benedict. She couldn't believe it. The President's daughter.

"I'll tell security to expect you. Just check in at the front gate and they'll direct you around."

Several hours later, Tish arrived at the Benedict ranch, her heart filled with hope. She had changed outfits several times before deciding to go with a Bohemian style reflecting her personality—fresh, creative, fun. She wore a multi-colored circle skirt made of crinkle cloth with an expensive but simple turquoise V-neck tee. She put earrings in all four piercings in each ear, piled on the bracelets, and finished the ensemble with turquoise ballet-style slippers. She felt a hundred times more comfortable than in the Chanel suit she'd worn to meet Addison James.

After making it past the security checkpoints, Tish found herself standing on the front steps of a sprawling ranch house that put her in mind of Southfork, from the old television show *Dallas*. Her body tingled. She was here. At the Benedict ranch, about to have a meeting with the President's daughter.

A woman dressed in a simple black pantsuit and a stern expression met her at the door. "I'm Lola Zackary," she said, "Elysee's executive secretary."

"Good to meet you."

Lola ushered her into a sitting room furnished with polished antiques. "A female Secret Service agent will frisk you for weapons, ma'am."

The Secret Service agent came into the room and frisked her. The woman nodded at Tish's purse and the backpack containing her DVD player, video camera, and other equipment. "I'll need to look through your bags."

Tish surrendered her things and stood watching while the agent leafed through them.

"Take a seat, ma'am," Lola said when the agent had finished her job and left the room. "Miss Benedict will see you shortly."

Tish sat on a high-backed chair near the window and knotted her fingers in her lap. The minute the Secret Service woman had vanished from the room, doubts crowded in. They were the same doubts that had occasionally overwhelmed her in the middle of the night when she was married to Shane.

You're out of your element. Out of your league. For Pete's sake, you grew up on the south side of Houston. Who would want the likes of you?

But she'd come so very far from her early background and, excluding her problem with impulse shopping, she was a pretty decent person. She was loyal to her friends, volunteered at the local battered women's shelter a couple of hours a week. She was good at her job. But most of all, she genuinely cared about people.

"You're Tish?" Elysee Benedict came through the door with a warm, welcoming smile. She wore a simple pair of beige slacks and a black silk blouse that washed all the color from her skin. Her hair was pulled back with a headband. It wasn't a look that flattered her narrow face.

"You're too young to be getting married," Tish wanted to tell her, because she'd been Elysee's age when she'd gotten married. But instead she enthusiastically shook her hand and said, "Hi, I'm Tish."

"I love your outfit," Elysee said.

"Thank you."

"And such gorgeous hair." She gazed enviously at Tish's mass of corkscrew curls.

"It's an untamed terror, is what it is."

"Try working with this thin, fine mess." Elysee touched a poker-straight lock of mousy brown hair. "I'd kill for curls like yours."

"No one is ever satisfied with their hair. I bet Jennifer Aniston hates hers."

"Oh, I've met Jennifer," Elysee said.

"Really?" Tish widened her eyes. "She's my favorite actress."

"Mine, too."

"Is she going to be at the wedding?" Excitement made Tish's palms grow sweaty. She'd never thought that movie stars might be attending the ceremony.

"We're hoping to keep things fairly small. Two hundred guests. I don't have room for a celebrity list, plus it becomes such a security nightmare. Please, sit down." Elysee waved at the chair Tish had just vacated and took the adjacent seat.

Tish sat.

"So tell me a little about yourself." Elysee seemed so poised; but of course, growing up in the public eye, she'd received lots of coaching. Tish wished she'd had someone to coach her through the bumps in life.

Tish took a deep breath to calm her nerves. "I started my own wedding video business five years ago. I'm slowly starting to gain a reputation locally."

"No, no." Elysee shook her head. "Tell me about Tish the person. I already know you have gorgeous red hair and Jennifer Aniston is your favorite actress. I googled you so I know that you went to college at Rice. Are you married?"

"Divorced."

"That's a shame. I've gone through three broken engagements and while I'm not presuming to compare that to a divorce, I do know how painful breakups can be."

Tish wanted to tell her, *Honey, you don't know nothing until the love of your life ends your marriage on your first anniversary by walking out on you because you couldn't live up to his expectations*. Instead she said, "Three?"

"It's a lot, I know." Elysee shifted in her seat. "My father tells me I'm in love with love, and maybe I am. But my main problem has been that I have trouble sorting out the men who really like me for myself from those who want to be with me for who I am and what I can do for them."

Tish clicked her tongue in sympathy. "That's got to be rough."

"It is." Elysee smoothed imaginary wrinkles in the fabric of her slacks. "But that's the way it goes."

"How did you know this fiancé was a keeper?"

Elysee blushed. "For one thing, he saved my life."

"Literally?"

"Yes."

"That's a good start." Tish laughed. "At least you know he cares enough to put his life on the line for you."

Elysee leaned in and whispered, "He's my bodyguard."

"You're marrying one of your Secret Service agents?"

"Uh-huh."

"Just like Susan Ford?"

"Uh-huh." This time she giggled, absurdly happy. Tish remembered being that giddy once.

"How romantic."

"It is." Elysee reached over and touched Tish's forearm. "But the best part is that what I feel for him isn't the kind of crazy, off-the-wall, gotta-have-him-or-I'll-die kind of love like I had with the other three fiancés. It's a steady and strong and mature love."

"Um, that's good." Tish struggled to keep her opinion from showing. She would never have married Shane if there hadn't been such seething chemistry between them. For one thing they were just too different. For another, without chemistry, well, what was the point? You might as well just marry your best friend. If every time she'd looked at him her knees hadn't gone weak and the breath hadn't squeezed from her lungs, if her womb hadn't ached and her mouth hadn't yearned for his kisses, she would never have taken the risk.

Even now, she would occasionally wake up in the middle of the night still burning for Shane's touch. Her body still craved him with a certain kind of wildness she'd never felt for another man before or since.

Then again, she was divorced. Maybe Elysee was on to something. Maybe steady, sweet, and mature was the way to go.

They talked for over an hour, discussing everything under the sun before they watched Tish's wedding montage DVD. They just seemed to click—she and the President's daughter. And it was easy, without any of the tension and need to prove herself that Tish had felt with Addison James.

"Oh my goodness." Elysee laughed. "I love how you humanize the guests by catching them in vulnerable moments. The sleeping baby. The canoodling grandparents. The teens sneaking kisses in the rectory. The friends of the groom opening up about their feelings for their buddy as they tie cans to the getaway car."

Elysee's words sent a warm pool of pride sliding into her belly. Even if Tish didn't get the assignment, she would come away from this interview feeling much better about her work. "Thank you for saying so."

"My father's warned me against making snap decisions," Elysee said. "Three broken engagements by age twenty-two and all that, but Tish, I like you. I like your work. And I want to hire you as my wedding videographer. What do you say? Can you do it? Are you available for Christmas Eve? It's already late October so I know that doesn't leave you much time for production, but I have my heart set on getting married on Christmas Eve. It would have been my parents' thirtieth anniversary if my mother had lived."

Every dream she'd ever had was coming true. Not only would Elysee's wedding go a long way toward getting Tish out of debt, but also, once word got out that she was the videographer to the President's daughter, the telephone would never stop ringing. "Oh, Elysee, that's so sweet and romantic."

"You don't have to answer right away. I'm sure you've got a lot to think about. This assignment isn't going to be easy with all the security details and confidentiality issues. Would you like a day or two to think it over?"

"I suppose I shouldn't make snap decisions either," Tish said, "but I can tell you're going to be such a dream to work with and I can't imagine a greater honor than videoing your Christmas Eve wedding. I can rise to the challenges. I'd be honored."

Elysee clapped her hands. "That's so great. I'm so excited!"

"Right, right." Tish nodded. "Leading up to the wedding, I'll need several sessions with you and your fiancé, interviewing you on your childhoods, going through old family photo albums and scrapbooks. Talking with your family and friends to get a real sense of who you are and what your union is all about. I want to capture the spirit of you both. I spend a lot of time on research, but it pays off in the quality of your video. This is a once in a lifetime affair and we want it to be something you'll cherish and show your children and your grandchildren. I charge by the job, not by the hour, so you don't have to worry that the clock is ticking."

"Absolutely. That's exactly what I want. I'm so happy we're on the same page." Elysee grinned.

"Me, too."

"I want to introduce you to my fiancé. I don't think he'll have any objections, but since you will be working closely with him for the reception video, I want to make sure you guys click as well."

"Certainly." Tish nodded and prayed Elysee's fiancé loved her as much as Elysee seemed to.

"Could you stay for dinner?"

Dinner at the Benedict ranch or Ramen noodles in her apartment? Jeez, what a dilemma.

"I can stay."

"Excellent. Let me just get my secretary, Lola, to write you out a retainer check and we'll be good to go."

His physical therapy session had gone badly and Shane was in a foul mood. Determined to get the use of his hand back, he'd told the physical therapist, Pete Larkin, to challenge him. Larkin had been reluctant, insisting it was too soon, but Shane had been adamant.

And he'd failed miserably.

Not only had he been unable to complete the exercises, he'd ended up straining the muscles in his wrist and forearm as well, setting back his progress for days, and bringing on a fresh round of red-hot pain.

He'd suffered his defeat in stoic silence, but a dark cloud of anger gathered thickly over him. He hated being weak. And the therapy session had brought home an ugly truth.

He would never be the same again.

It was a disturbing realization that shook him to the very center of his masculinity. He had been a tough, strong man, with lightning-fast reflexes and deadly aim. But that was before the accident.

Who was he now?

What would he be if he couldn't be a bodyguard? His family history had indoctrinated him to be a hero. He'd never considered any other professional role. With these disparaging thoughts circling his brain he walked into the ranch house, telling himself he had to put on a cheery face for Elysee's sake. None of this was her fault.

"Honey, is that you?" Elysee's voice called to him from the sitting room.

He wanted to slide under the carpet and wait for his dark

mood to pass before facing his bubbly bride-to-be, but he didn't have that option. She caught him in the hallway, took him by the left hand and, chattering like a three-year-old at her birthday party, dragged him toward the sitting room.

"I've found our videographer. She's the most dynamic, creative, interesting person and I know you're just going to love her."

"If you love her..." Shane intended on finishing the sentence with "I'll love her," but when he saw the woman sitting in front of the window, his heart just stopped.

No, it couldn't be.

Elysee hooked her elbow around his arm. "Honey, this is Tish Gallagher. Tish, meet my fiancé, Shane Tremont."

Tish stared into Shane's eyes. Time evaporated and the years fell away.

Her face instantly went ice cold as blood drained from her cheeks. Her heart rate dropped and she heard the slow, loud *boom, boom, boom* of blood beating against her eardrums. Dumbly, she stood there, mouth hanging open. Unable to speak. Unable to move. Unable to breathe.

Shane looked different now—older, leaner, with a hollow cast to his cheeks—but wiser, and if possible, even more handsome than she remembered. His hair was clipped close to his head in a precision military cut. When they had been married, she'd coaxed him into growing it out, but she had to admit the very short cut suited him.

And then she saw the scar at his temple.

Tish felt a sharp, sudden pain in her own temple at exactly the same spot as his wound. He was hurt. He'd had brain surgery. That was why his hair was so short.

She thought of what Elysee had said about her bodyguard saving her life. The full impact hit her then. Elysee

Benedict's fiancé was her ex-husband. For one microsecond, her heart just stopped. She'd told herself that she was over Shane, that she was no longer in love with him. But one look into his eyes and she knew it was all a vicious lie she'd been telling herself—a fairytale falsehood to keep the demons at bay.

Her initial impulse was to turn and flee as far from this house and her past as possible. But running was a luxury she could ill afford. If she wanted to achieve her life-long ambition and pay off her maxed-out credit cards, she had to stick this out.

Silence stretched into the room. It seemed to go on forever, until Tish was almost convinced she'd been ensnared in some sort of cosmic time warp. His gaze was on her face and no matter how hard she tried, she couldn't tear her eyes away. What to do?

Her right hand fluttered to her throat. This would be a very good time to faint. Unfortunately she wasn't the fainting type. Shane, her Shane, was engaged to marry the daughter of the President of the United States.

Snap out of it. You can't let Elysee know who you are or you'll lose the job and with it, all your cherished dreams. So what if she's engaged to Shane? He doesn't belong to you anymore.

Tish swallowed hard and pasted an artificial smile on her face. Honestly, someone should nominate her for a frickin' Oscar. She cleared her throat, put her hand out, and stepped the short distance between them.

"Hello," she said. "I'm very pleased to make your acquaintance, Mr. Tremont."

Shane didn't smile, didn't take her hand. It was only then she realized he had his right hand tucked into the pocket of his trousers.

Why wouldn't he shake her hand? Oh, God, was he going to make a big deal of this and ruin her chances at the opportunity of a lifetime, just because they were once married to each other?

"I don't shake hands," he said. "An accident."

"Oh," she said, feeling relieved that she didn't have to touch him, but at the same time sorry not to feel the heat of his hand against hers.

"So you're the best wedding videographer in the business?" he said.

"Yes," she replied and proudly raised her chin. "I am."

They used to have fights over her business. He claimed she spent too much money on camera equipment while they were trying to get a fledgling household started. He'd wanted her to take a part-time job to pay for her overhead. She'd accused him of not supporting her artistic vision.

Ha, so there. I made it without you. She'd gotten good enough at her craft to bag the President's daughter's wedding.

Hell, Tish, he's one-upped you again. Shane's bagged the President's daughter and you're going to have to film the whole ceremony.

Misery crawled through her, but she'd be damned if she'd let him see how this development affected her. "Congratulations on your impending marriage," she said through clenched teeth.

"Thank you," he replied, sounding equally as tense.

"Did I tell you Shane saved my life?" Elysee interjected. She was gazing at Shane's face as if he'd created the sun.

"Yes, you did." Not surprising. He seemed to make a habit of rescuing damsels in distress and then asking them to marry him. "You sound like a real-life Sir Galahad, Shane."

Better watch out, honey. There's a real downside to these big burly guardian types.

"Oh, he is. Shane saved my life and now I've been nursing him back to health." Elysee stroked Shane's upper arm.

Yes, this story was sounding decidedly familiar. Tish thought of that first night she and Shane had spent together. How she'd tended the wounds he'd acquired in a bar fight while defending her honor. Far, far too familiar.

She suddenly felt sick to her stomach. "Um, Elysee," she said. "Is there a powder room I could use?"

"Oh, yes, sure, this way. Please make yourself at home."

Tish followed Elysee down the hallway, never looking back at Shane even though she could feel the heat of his gaze burning the back of her neck. She had to get by herself, calm down, and decide what she was going to do about this mess.

She stepped into the bathroom, shut the door, and took a deep breath. Stepping up to the washbasin, she dampened a washcloth and caught sight of her reflection in the mirror. Her throat was tight, her stomach even tighter as she assessed herself.

What had Shane seen when he'd looked at her? How had she changed over the course of the last two years? Was he sorry that he'd let her go? Or was he perfectly happy with sweet little Elysee?

Feeling short of breath and slightly disoriented, Tish closed her eyes. She pressed the damp cloth to her lips and then opened her eyes again.

Her mass of unruly corkscrew curls was longer now than when they'd been married, but they were still the same shade of burnished auburn. Thick ginger-colored lashes framed her kelly green eyes. Her peaches-and-cream complexion was still clear, but when she smiled she could see the faintest beginnings of crinkle lines around her mouth. Not old by any means at nearly twenty-six, but time was marching on.

People often told her she looked like a young Nicole Kidman, but she didn't think she was nearly that pretty. Her style was too funky and eclectic, from the four earrings in each ear to the henna tattoo scrolling around her upper right arm. Shane had liked her Bohemian flare, if not her Bohemian lifestyle. They'd been a severe case of opposites attracting.

And colliding.

Ha, that was the underassessment of the century.

A knock sounded on the door.

"Just a minute," she said.

"I'm coming in." The voice was dark, masculine.

Shane!

Her heart leapfrogged into her throat. She spun for the doorknob, determined to flip the lock and keep him out, but she was too slow.

Chapter 7

The bathroom door opened and Shane slipped inside. He reached behind him, clicking the lock in place.

Tish, who was already fumbling for the lock, ended up touching his hard, flat belly instead.

Electricity.

Hotter and quicker than ever. Lightning in a hail storm. It scared the hell out of her. She jerked her hand back at the contact. It gave her little satisfaction that Shane looked as unnerved as she. Being this close to him felt more dangerous than juggling fire.

"What are you doing in here?" she demanded. "You have to get out. What if I was using the toilet? You can't just barge in. We're divorced, remember?"

"We have to talk."

"Now? You want to talk now? Two years ago I wanted to talk, but you clammed up. Now you want to talk?"

"Yes, now."

"Where's little Miss Sunshine?" Tish tossed her head, trying to stall, trying to identify her emotions and figure out exactly how she felt without letting it show on her face.

"Elysee went to tell the cook to set an extra plate for you," he said.

"Aren't you worried what she's going to think when she catches us in here together?" Tish crossed her arms over her chest, both to stop her hands from trembling as well as putting up a barrier between them.

The room was claustrophobically small now with him in it. She'd forgotten just how masculine he was, with his big biceps and manly-smelling cologne.

"She's not going to catch us, because you're going to go tell her that while you're flattered by the offer, you just realized you have a scheduling conflict and can't serve as her wedding videographer," he said firmly.

"Don't you mean 'our' wedding videographer?"

He looked startled. "What?"

"You said 'her' wedding videographer. You're getting married, too. Shouldn't it be 'our' wedding videographer?"

"You're changing the subject."

"No, I'm not. I'm talking about *your* impending wedding."

"You're missing the point."

"But not the irony."

His eyes flared and her breath caught. She felt the old flutter in her chest. Divorced two years and with just one look he could still send her heart reeling.

But Shane had moved on with his life. He had someone else. A very nice someone else. Tish had absolutely no right to feel envious.

It sounded rational and well thought out. The problem was that her emotions weren't having any of it. She was jealous and angry and hurt. She wanted to throw back her head and howl for everything she'd let slip through her fingers. No, no, she wanted to run right out and buy the most expensive pair of shoes she could find.

What? You expected he would pine over you forever?

No, no. Yes.

Honestly, secretly, she'd always held on to the hope that some day, some way they'd find their way back to each other. When they'd both achieved their dream jobs and worked through their personal issues. How naïve was that?

If growing up with a mother who was always looking for love but never finding it had taught her anything, it was that happily ever after was nothing but a romantic myth. So why did she want so badly to believe in it?

Tish's eyes tracked over him. His shoulders were so broad they filled almost half of the wall behind him. Her gaze snagged on the scar running across his temple; unbidden fascination had her reaching up to touch it.

He grabbed her wrist before her fingers could graze his skin. "No," he said sharply, "no."

They stared into each other's eyes, both of them breathing hard. Her heart slammed against her chest, pounding erratically.

Kiss me! she thought, crazily, wildly. As if a kiss would fix everything. She tossed her head and pursed her lips, mentally daring him to do it.

He looked hard into her eyes, as if assessing the depth of her soul. Their lungs moved in tandem, drawing in great gasps of ragged air. There was such raw hunger in his eyes she couldn't help but gasp. The look was naked, completely without guile, a mirror image of her heart.

He cupped her face with his left hand, tilted her chin up to look at him. This time she did gasp. The harsh sound echoed in the tiny room.

Was he going to kiss her?

She held her breath and waited. If she were to lay her palm against his chest would she feel the wild thunder crashing under her hand? She looked into his eyes and knew if she lived to be a hundred she'd never forget the starving look in his eyes at that moment.

He *hungered* for her.

Shane did not kiss her. In fact, he raised his head, let out his breath in quiet exhalation. Disappointment smashed down on her like a windowpane shattering.

But his eyes blazed black as lump coal. Heated, sizzling, eating her up.

I can still make this man…burn, she thought, and a powerful thrill rippled through her.

You could kiss him.

No. No way. Tish wasn't going to be the one to step across that line. If he wanted her, he was going to have to be the one to come after her.

"Why did you pretend not to know me?" he asked, sliding his hands down her shoulders to her upper arms. "Why didn't you tell Elysee who you were?"

"What? And blow my chances for videotaping this wedding?"

"You're not seriously thinking of going through with this. You can't take this job and not tell Elysee who you are," he said.

"Why not?" She wrenched herself from his grasp. "I'm just trying to spare Elysee's feelings."

"And make your career." He clenched his teeth.

"What's wrong with that?"

"You haven't changed a bit," he said, bitterness tingeing his voice. A twist of panic went through her as his pupils constricted and his eyes darkened disapprovingly.

"What's that supposed to mean?"

"You're still hiding. Still keeping secrets."

She opened her mouth to deny it, but what was the point? He'd made up his mind about her. There was nothing she could say to change it. Instead she muttered, "I'm not the only one who keeps secrets."

Scowling, he drew himself up. "Is there something you want to say?"

Oh yeah. Things she should have said two years ago. But it was too late, water under the proverbial bridge and all that. They stood glaring at each other. The past was a brick wall between them that they couldn't climb over. They'd been at this impasse before. Unable to understand each other, unable to move forward.

"You're going to go back out there and tell Elysee who you are."

Defeat and despair crowded out any lingering hope. Not for the chance to videotape the President's daughter's wedding, but for the possibility that Shane still loved her in the same way she loved him.

"And if I don't?" Tish asked, challenging his authority.

Shane cocked his head and studied her face for a long moment. Same old Tish. She never accepted anything without question. It was one of the things he had always respected about her, but it had irritated him as well: her inability to put her faith in him.

Shane knew her distrust stemmed from the fact that Tish's father had taken off when she was a kid and that she'd rarely seen him after that. Men leave, she'd learned. Why should she trust him when he'd spectacularly reinforced that lesson when he'd walked out on their marriage?

He was sorry for it now. So damned sorry. His arms

ached to hold her. Lips burned to kiss her. There were no words, which was just as well. It was too late.

How had this happened? The day after asking Elysee to marry him, he found himself locked in the bathroom with the one woman who could still send his senses reeling and his heart thumping.

"Well?" Tish's chin trembled defiantly. "Are you going to tattle on me?"

"No," he answered quietly. "Because I know you'll do the right thing and tell her yourself."

"Bastard," she said.

"That's beside the point." He quirked an eyebrow.

She flashed him a smile, brief, but it was there.

He grinned. "God, Tish, it's good to see you again."

"You mean it?"

"I missed you." Why had he said that? It was true, but he was courting trouble.

"Really?"

"You find that so hard to believe?"

"Well, you are engaged to another woman."

"I'm just saying you look good."

"Thank you." Her earlobes pinked and she peered up at him from underneath those long auburn eyelashes. His heart knocked when he saw the vulnerability she struggled so hard to hide in those green depths. Her eyes narrowed, condensing the world to him.

Only him.

She raised a hand and nervously slipped her fingers through her hair, trying to tame the springy curls that defied taming. Her breasts rose and fell beneath the stretchy material of her turquoise V-neck T-shirt. She looked damned good in turquoise, the way it contrasted with her red hair—like springtime in Arizona.

Her fingers dropped from her hair in one long graceful movement and fell to the pocket of her purple hippie skirt. Her fingernails, he noted, were painted an avant-garde color of silver, as always, flaunting convention.

He wondered, not for the first time, why she'd ever married him. Look up "conventional" in the dictionary, he thought, and you'd find a picture of Shane Tremont.

His eyes fixed on her lips. Rich, ripe, painted the color of sweet raspberries. He held his breath. Waiting for what, he did not know, but he was sure waiting for something.

Tish pulled a small round red-capped pot of cinnamon lip gloss from her pocket, unscrewed the lid and dipped the tip of her index finger into the petroleum jelly laced with cinnamon flavoring. She lifted her finger, slick and glistening, and slowly traced the glossy residue over her bottom lip with the cool certainty of a woman who knew just what it took to keep her lips supple and ready for a kissing. She recapped the lip gloss and slipped it back into her pocket, and the startling sienna-colored smell of cinnamon floated toward him.

The overhead lamp slanted a shaft of light across her face, bathing one half in light, the other in shadow. He looked down at her, glimpsing something melancholy there. Old feelings—both good and bad—rose between them like soap bubbles, rainbow-prism shiny and fragile as a whisper.

A balance was struck, only for a moment, but enough to pull the air from their lungs in a simultaneous exhale.

His heart slunk back against his spine in shame. What in God's name had he been thinking to ever let her go?

You were hurting.

But so was she, and he'd selfishly let his hurt mean more than hers. She'd betrayed him, yes, but in the end, hadn't he ultimately betrayed her more?

He fixed on those lips. Lips he craved to kiss. Lips that called to him late in the middle of the night, in the dark of his dreams. He leaned forward. Not thinking, just wanting.

She didn't draw away.

Shane never took his eyes off her face, and then suddenly realized their noses were almost touching. She used to give him what she called Eskimo kisses. Whimsically rubbing her nose back and forth against his, until he begged her to stop because it made him want to sneeze. How he wished for one of those Eskimo kisses right now.

It would be so easy for him to kiss her, Eskimo style or otherwise. The most natural thing in the world.

He felt the heat of her skin, so warm near his.

So damned easy.

But he could not. Would not. Should not.

She flicked out her tongue, tracing it over the lips that her fingertips had just touched, making the lip gloss application moot. The gesture wasn't calculated. She wasn't trying for seduction. She was just anxious. He recognized the nervous way she hugged her elbows against her body. Unsettled, just as he was, by the chemistry that time had not erased.

They stared at each other with a stunned mix of surprise and affection and stark sexual heat.

It was still there. The old spark. The embers that had never gone out. Two years and they were still burning.

Hope blossomed.

They were still undeniably connected. And that connection was incredibly complicated. Guilt clutched his gut in a slippery fist. He had no right to hope.

Then a knock sounded at the bathroom door, severing the tenuous chain.

* * *

Gently, Elysee knocked on the door a second time. She prayed her plan was going to work. It might be unorthodox, but it was the only way she could know for sure that Shane was indeed The One her mother had promised. She'd mistaken men for The One when they were not. This time, she was taking a different approach.

"Tish? Shane? Are you guys still in there?"

The door wrenched open to reveal Shane standing there, Tish hovering in the corner just behind him.

Elysee put a perky smile on her face. "Hi, guys."

Tish raised her hand in a halfhearted, guilty-looking wave. She *should* be feeling guilty. She hadn't come clean about her relationship with Shane, but Elysee understood why Tish had lied and didn't hold it against her. She believed in giving everyone the benefit of the doubt.

Even her fiancé's ex-wife.

Besides, she liked Tish. A lot more than she had thought she would. She could see why Shane had married her. Tish was passionate and beautiful and talented. What she didn't know was why they'd broken up.

That was the reason she'd asked Tish to video their wedding. She wanted to see if Shane could have a civil relationship with his ex. Elysee also had an added agenda. She wanted to discover how to avoid the problems Tish and Shane had faced in their marriage. What better way to do that than to ask Tish herself?

Plus, Shane had never talked about his ex-wife. This was certainly one way to get him to open up and face his feelings about her and resolve them once and for all. This way, she and Shane could have a fresh start.

It might be rocky for a bit, until Tish and Shane ironed out their differences, but in the long run, Elysee was convinced hiring Tish to video their wedding was the best thing for all concerned.

"Hi," Shane said, but didn't meet Elysee's gaze. Was he feeling guilty, too?

A momentary panic gripped Elysee. What if Shane still cared about Tish? *If he still cared about her, he wouldn't have left her. Shane's a loyal guy.*

That idea made her wonder what Tish had done to chase him away. Had she cheated on him? She seemed to be a very adventuresome and passionate woman, with her snapping green eyes and sassy red hair.

Elysee's heartstrings tugged, and she smiled sympathetically at Shane. Poor baby. She was going to make everything all right in his world again. She glanced from Shane to Tish and back again.

"Did you two have a nice chat?"

Tish cleared her throat. "We've . . . er . . . *I've*, got something to tell you."

"Oh?"

"Shane's my ex-husband." Tish cringed as if waiting for a bomb to detonate.

"I know." Elysee grinned. "Isn't it great?"

"You knew?" Tish sounded stunned.

"You knew?" Shane echoed, looking bushwhacked.

Elysee shook her head at Shane. "You know that I don't hire anyone without doing a thorough background check. Of course I knew."

"And you hired me anyway?" A suspicious frown furrowed Tish's brow. "What's this all about?"

"I want us all to get along. Like Demi and Bruce and Ashton," she said. "Wouldn't that be great?"

Tish looked at her as if she was seriously delusional. Elysee supposed it might appear that way to her. She winnowed into the bathroom with them, threw one arm around Shane's neck and the other around Tish's.

"Call me naïve," she said, "but I think this is the emotionally healthiest thing we can do. So, are you still on board, Tish? Please know that we both want you here. Don't we, Shane?"

"We do?" Shane said it more as a question than a confirmation, but she pretended he was one hundred percent behind her.

Elysee operated on the assumption if you believed the best about people they usually lived up to your expectations. Well, except in the case of her three ex-fiancés—but those relationships hadn't worked out because they hadn't been The One. Elysee was a firm believer that everything happened for a reason.

"See." She beamed at Tish. "We're all in agreement. You're going to videotape our wedding and it's going to be fabulous. Now let's get out of the bathroom and go have dinner. I'm starving!"

Chapter 8

I'm in serious need of an intervention," Tish wailed to Delaney over the telephone.

It was after ten o'clock at night and it was really too late to call, especially since her best friend was a newly-wed and it was a Monday. But Tish was drowning deep in emotional quicksand and Delaney was the only one who would know how to pull her out of it.

"What's wrong?"

"There's a half-gallon of Blue Bell mint chocolate chip in my refrigerator and a very big spoon in my hand and I'm afraid of what will happen next."

"Don't do anything drastic. I'll zip right over."

Ten minutes later her doorbell rang. Dressed in one of Shane's old T-shirts, fuzzy yellow Tweety Bird slippers, and a purple chenille bathrobe, Tish shuffled to the door, the half-gallon of mint-chocolate-chip Blue Bell tucked in the crook of one arm. She flung open the door without even checking the peephole first, something she never did. *That's how depressed I am.*

"I brought reinforcements," Delaney said, "and they've all got spoons."

Tish had to smile at the sight of her two other close friends, Jillian Samuels and Rachael Henderson, standing on the porch beside Delaney. All three held up white plastic spoons.

Swinging the door wide, Tish sighed with relief at the cavalry and said, "Move your fannies in here now. I need all the help I can get."

They ended up piled in the middle of the king-sized bed she had once shared with Shane. Tish sat cross-legged in the center, with Rachael on her left, Jillian to her right, and Delaney right in front of her. Tish held the Blue Bell in her lap while everyone dug in. What good friends they were! They weren't about to let her get fat alone.

"So let me get this straight." Delaney licked a dab of mint-green ice cream dotted with chocolate off her upper lip. "Elysee Benedict hired you specifically because you *were* Shane's ex-wife?"

Tish nodded. "No kidding, you guys, the first daughter is a nutcase. She's impossibly nice. When I had to tell her who I was, it felt like I was a rabbit hunter looking down the barrel of a rifle at Flopsy Cottontail."

"I still can't believe your Shane is engaged to marry the President's daughter." Delaney shook her head. "How did that happen?"

"He was on her protective detail and he saved her life."

"Ah," Jillian said. "She's got him up on a pedestal. He's her hero."

"Which is perfect," Tish said, "because Shane has a desperate need to be a hero. It bodes well for their marriage. I'm happy for them."

"You don't have to lie to us," Delaney said. "Go ahead, dis the President's daughter. We won't tell."

"Do you think they could have your bedroom bugged?"

Jillian, who was a bit on the paranoid side, asked and eyed the corners of the room as if she were going to spy a radio transmitter recording their conversation and sending it along to the FBI.

"I'm confused. Why would the President's daughter want her fiancé's ex-wife to videotape their wedding?" Rachael interjected. Rachael was a sweet-natured kindergarten teacher, with dazzling green eyes, long-flowing blond hair, and creamy porcelain skin. She was the starry-eyed romantic of the group. If she couldn't understand Elysee's motives, no one could.

"Apparently, Shane would never talk about me to her." Inwardly Tish winced. It hurt to think that he disliked her so much he wouldn't even discuss her with his fiancée. "So Elysee had someone do a little digging into his background, learned my name, and found out I was a wedding videographer. She believes this will help me and Shane 'confront our baggage' as she put it over dinner, help us 'assimilate the trauma' of our marriage."

"Is she for real?" asked Jillian, an ebony-haired, black-eyed, street-savvy lawyer.

"Exactly," Tish said. "De-lu-sion-al."

"Maybe she's just trying to be very adult about the whole thing," Delaney said.

"Yeah? Like you would have hired Nick's ex-wife to videotape your wedding?"

"Oh, hell, no."

"See? That's what a normal woman would say. You know what else Elysee wants from me?"

Her three friends leaned in closer, spoons dangling above the mint chocolate chip.

"What?" they breathed in unison.

"Bedroom secrets."

"What!" her friends shrieked.

"Yep. She wants me to tell her what Shane likes." Tish took a deep breath. "She said they're waiting for the wedding night to consummate their relationship and she doesn't want Shane to be disappointed. Can you believe she's asking me for sex tips?"

Clearly scandalized, Rachael slapped a hand over her mouth and her eyes widened.

"It's always the mousy ones." Jillian shook her head. "Never trust the mousy ones."

"I used to be a mousy one," Delaney said.

"Case in point." Jillian raised a finger. "Who staged their own wedding day abduction, hmmm?"

"You've got me there," Delaney admitted with a big grin.

Last year, before she'd married Nick Vinetti, Delaney had been engaged to an old childhood friend. Because of the pressure of family expectations, she hadn't known how to get out of the wedding. In desperation, she'd ended up hiring someone to kidnap her. It had turned into a big media drama, but also into a spectacular happily ever after.

"That's gotta hurt," Rachael said, looking at Tish with sympathy. "Your replacement expecting you to pave the road for her that you had to stumble down."

Trust Rachael to ferret out the real meat of her emotions. Tish bit down on her bottom lip and thrust the mint chocolate chip away from her. "You guys do something with this, please, before I end up with ice cream intoxication and ten pounds of extra blubber on my butt."

Delaney whisked the ice cream away to the kitchen and Tish glanced around at her remaining friends.

"The thing of it is," she said, "I like Elysee. It's

impossible not to like her. And she and Shane just seem to go together. Far better than he and I ever did. They're both so calm and steady and they look so comfortable around each other. Like an old married couple. I can definitely see them making it to their golden wedding anniversary."

"Comfortable." Jillian snorted. "Like a sweater."

"Like wool socks," Rachael added. "Who wants to marry wool socks?"

"Being around them made me feel like a total disaster. I mean, Shane's not only moved on but he's going to be the President's son-in-law. It doesn't get any bigger than that, and meanwhile I'm still this stupid loser who can't manage her finances or hold on to the best thing that ever happened to her." Tish's voice caught.

"The reason you and Shane broke up runs much deeper than money problems and you know it," Delaney murmured as she stepped back into the room. "Don't keep beating yourself up for something that couldn't be prevented."

"You'll land on your feet. You always do," Jillian said.

Rachael rested a hand on Tish's shoulder. "You're still in love with him, aren't you?"

Tish nodded and instantly tears sprang to her eyes. Savagely she swiped them away. She didn't break down like this. She was tough. She'd survived her nomadic childhood. She should be able to skip blithely through a broken heart, particularly one two years in the making.

"What am I going to do, you guys? If I do a good job on this wedding, the dream I've been struggling to achieve for so long will finally come true. Plus, it will solve all my money problems. I don't see how I can turn it down. But I don't know how I can survive it emotionally."

"We'll stand by you, whatever decision you make," Delaney said. "We're always here for you."

Rachael shook her head. "You can't take this job. It would be pure mental torture. Seeing Shane happy with the first daughter, feeling his hand on yours every time he touches *her*."

"I think you have to take the job." Jillian was so tough and strong. She was Tish's hero. "It's the only way to prove you're over him."

"But I'm not over him."

"Then this will help you get over him. It's time to move on, Tish. It's been two years. Shane's found someone else. Let him go so you can be free." Jillian's words might be stark, but they were exactly what Tish needed to hear.

It was way past time to move on. And she could only do that by accepting reality. She had to experience the pain and allow herself to fall through it to the other side in order to be free.

Tish looked around at her three friends gazing at her with supportive sympathy. She was so lucky to have them in her life. "I'm going to accept the job," she said. "I'm going to see this thing through, make the best damned wedding video I've ever made, clear up my finances, and end up on top of the world."

"You go." Jillian grinned. "Don't let any man keep you down."

But even as she was declaring it, Tish wondered if she truly had the courage to make it happen. "Enough about me," she said. "I'm through whining. What have you guys been up to lately?"

Jillian had a cryptic smile on her face. "I'm moving to San Francisco for six months."

"What?" Delaney arched an eyebrow.

"Why?" Rachael asked.

"We'll be bereft without you," Tish said.

"I've got a golden opportunity I just couldn't turn down," Jillian rushed on excitedly. "I've been selected to be on the team of co-counsel with Belton Melville on the Nob Hill murder trial."

"No way!" Delaney leaped off the bed and gave a hoot of joy. "*The* Belton Melville?"

"It's going to be an amazing education for me, although I'm sure I'll just be doing research." Jillian beamed.

"This is that case where the ex–NFL football star stabbed his estranged wife to death in her boyfriend's backyard?" Rachael asked.

"Allegedly," Jillian said.

"Spoken like a true defense attorney," Tish said, and hugged her friend. "I'm so happy for you, but what are you going to do with your condo?"

"I've already leased it out."

"This is happening so fast," Tish wailed.

"When the time is right to move on, the time is right to move on," Jillian said and shot Tish a meaningful glance.

"I've got a little news of my own," Rachael said shyly.

"Oh?" Everyone turned to look at Rachael.

A grin spread across her cherubic face. "I've met someone."

"That's so wonderful," Tish exclaimed, and meant it. Rachael was a loving person, but she had such a Cinderella outlook on love. She was always getting her bubble burst when reality met fantasy. Her friend deserved someone nice.

"So tell us about him."

"It's too soon to say much," Rachael said. "Except he's sent me flowers every day since we met."

"How long ago was that?" Jillian asked.

"Just last week. See, I told you that it was too soon to

say anything, but you guys, he's so gorgeous." Rachael swooned. "Blond and broad-shouldered and with the most amazingly rippled washboard stomach."

"You've seen his stomach already?" Jillian teased.

"Don't jump to conclusions. He was washing his car," Rachael said. "But I have a very good feeling about this relationship."

"Then you're going to be needing this." Tish got up off the bed, went to the closet, and retrieved the antique wedding veil. She took it to Rachael and laid it in her arms.

"Oh," Rachael exhaled. "Don't you want to hang on to it?"

Tish shook her head, remembering the day she'd tried it on and made her wish. "I've no use for it."

"Thank you." Rachael held the veil to her chest. "I'll treasure it."

"Just remember what they say about making a wish on it," Jillian warned. "Be careful what you wish for—"

"Because you just might get it," they all finished in unison.

"Well, I think that's great," Delaney said. "We're all getting what we wanted. I got Nick, Jillian's got a fabulous job opportunity. Rachael's got a new man, and Tish is videotaping the President's daughter's wedding. Are we on top of the world or what?"

Yeah, Tish thought. *Or what?*

All her friends were slowly drifting away and she was facing the next several weeks, helping to make Shane's new marriage wonderful. That was the funny thing about being on top of the world. Nobody clued you in to the sacrifices it takes to get there.

Long after her friends had left, Tish lay in bed trying to sleep, but the past wouldn't let her be. Finally, at midnight, she threw back her covers and got dressed.

The past was a tombstone weighing on her chest, to the point where she could scarcely breathe. She had to find some release. Picking up her purse, she hurried out to the car Delaney had loaned her. Not even knowing where she was going or why, Tish began to drive.

Meanwhile, on the President's ranch in Katy, Texas, Shane couldn't sleep either. Dinner had been as surreal as a Fellini film. He'd sat sandwiched between his bride-to-be and his ex-wife, saying as little as possible while they made small talk about the wedding.

Tish looked so damned good. Every time his gaze landed on her, he felt a familiar tightness in his chest. It had taken everything he had in him not to ask Tish to leave. If she was courageous enough to stick it out, then he had to be courageous enough to let her stay. She needed this assignment.

As painful as it was going to be to have her around, he owed her this much. He also owed it to Elysee to uphold the promise he'd made to her. They were engaged. He had no business having feelings for his ex.

Not long after midnight, edgy, restless, and conflicted, he left his bed, got dressed and drove into Houston. He cruised past the house he and Tish used to own. A family lived there now. He hoped they were as happy in the place as he and Tish had been before the worst had happened.

A trip down memory lane; this was what he needed. A good review of what had gone right and what had gone wrong with his first marriage before he embarked upon the second. He didn't know where Tish lived now. That was good. The last thing he needed was to end up on her doorstep.

Instead, he found himself at Louie's Blues Bar on

Second Street near the edge of downtown Houston, just before the neighborhood turned seedy. Yuppies loved this place, with its mysterious atmosphere and top-notch musical fare. A flight of gray stone stairs descended into the belly of the club. Wailing notes from a woeful saxophone lured him down.

He'd been here before with Cal, when they were on assignment. With one long deep breath, Shane stepped over the threshold and was transported back three years.

He and Cal had been undercover in polo shirts and jeans, but Shane had felt strangely naked without his black suit and tie. At the time, they had been junior field agents bucking for the same promotion.

They'd had a serious competition going and Shane was determined to win. More than anything in the world, he wanted in on protective detail at the White House and the new promotion was another step toward that goal. He'd dreamed of it since he'd been an Eagle Scout.

To avoid getting clipped by a low-hanging entryway, they were forced to duck their heads as they entered a room lit only by blue neon lights. Both of them were big men, Cal just a shade taller at six-three to Shane's six-two. Although, at two hundred and three pounds, they weighed the same. Shane was twenty-six, Cal twenty-seven.

They'd traced a credit card identity theft ring to Louie's weekend bartender, a slender, rat-faced man known as Cool Chill. Cool Chill liked to pretend he was a young, urban gangsta. In reality he was thirty-three-year-old Euell Hotchkiss, who perpetually smelled of high-grade marijuana and still lived in his parents' converted garage.

But they didn't find Cool Chill behind the bar. Cool Chill, one of the waitresses had told them, was on supper break. They took a corner table and sat with their backs against the wall, assessing the situation and waiting it out until Cool Chill returned.

Cal ordered gin and tonic. Shane got a seltzer. He didn't drink on the job, didn't drink alcohol much at all. He leaned back in his chair, getting the lay of the land.

Shane knew the curvy redhead was trouble the second he spotted her.

She was everything he shouldn't want. But as he watched her undulate alone on the dance floor, swaying to a sultry rendition of an old Muddy Waters tune, his body ached for her.

This was bad.

"Check out the redhead," Cal said.

"Where?" Shane said, pretending he hadn't noticed.

"On the dance floor. By herself. God, she's a stunner."

He was obligated to take another look. After all, Cal had pointed her out.

What was her story? Who was she? Where was she from? Why was a gorgeous chick like her alone in a blues club on a Saturday night?

Shane was intrigued. Here was a woman who packed a sexual punch and every man in the vicinity knew it.

Cal nudged him in the ribs. "Is she a hottie or what?"

Or what. Hottie didn't begin to cover it.

"She's attractive," he said and took a sip of his seltzer.

Cal snorted. "You dead from the neck down, Tremont?"

Not hardly.

The guys in the band were watching her with the same horny expression in their eyes, particularly the long-haired trumpet player striving for the Chuck Mangione look with his cool cat hat and hip daddy beard. The musicians' lust for the redhead reflected exactly what Shane was experiencing. But then he felt a new emotion.

Jealousy.

It fisted inside him, hard and petulant.

How the hell could he be jealous over a woman he didn't even know? This wasn't like him. He wasn't usually easily distracted from his goal. In fact, he had received commendations for his ability to focus and get the job done under pressure.

Purposefully, he forced his eyes off the dance floor and scanned the rest of the smoky bar. It was still early in the evening and the place was fairly empty. He speculated that most of Louie's regular patrons were still out to dinner, and they wouldn't be wandering over to the nightclub for another hour or two.

That suited Shane just fine. The smaller the crowd, the easier they would be to handle if something went wonky. And with Cal for backup there shouldn't be any problems. The only fly in the ointment was Cool Chill's MIA status.

The band left Muddy Waters behind and slid into Beyoncé's "Crazy in Love." The tune drew a few more couples onto the dance floor. The redhead never stopped dancing, just changed tempo in time to the rhythm.

Shane's peripheral gaze locked on Red, even though he was fighting not to notice. Something about her ease with her own body, the way she danced all alone and didn't care that everyone was watching, stirred his admiration along with his spirit. He would never have been able to let go like that, shed his inhibitions. He was envious and lustful and jealous and deferential. He didn't like this mix of feelings one damned bit.

Head in the job, man; head in the job.

Great advice, but then he spied a thick-shouldered,

shaved-bald man treading across the dance floor toward Red. He was bigger than the bouncer lounging against the wall by the front door. Bigger even than he and Cal.

Shane forgot why he was in the bar. He rotated in his seat, eyes narrowing, alert for trouble.

Baldo said something to Red.

Asking her to dance?

She shook her head, stepped away from the bald man and kept boogying all by herself.

It's her prerogative to reject you, Baldo. Take the hint and keep moving.

But apparently Baldo wasn't going to take no for an answer. The massive man grabbed hold of Red's arm and spun her around.

There was no fear on Red's face, only spitfire anger. She snapped at Baldo, warning him off.

He didn't budge. Instead, he started arguing with her. She tried to jerk her arm away from him, but he held on tight. She was not a small woman, but next to Baldo she looked delicate as a porcelain doll.

That was all the provocation Shane needed to get involved, which wasn't like him. Not at all. He was the rational partner, the one slow to anger. The good cop to Cal's bad cop. He jumped up from his chair, pushing aside tables, knocking over beer bottles in his rush to the dance floor.

"Tremont," Cal called out sharply, but he didn't listen.

Shane knew better. He shouldn't be getting into a bar fight. Cool Chill could walk in any minute. He could blow his cover. And for all he knew Baldo could be Red's old man come to drag her home.

But he couldn't seem to stop himself. He slapped a hand on Baldo's shoulder. Up close the guy was the size of a tugboat. "Let go of the lady."

Baldo pivoted, snarling, "Fuck off."

Big the guy might be, but he was slow. Shane saw the punch coming long before the larger man finished making a fist.

Baldo took a swing.

Shane ducked just in time to hear air whoosh above his head. The swing would have knocked him out cold if it had made contact.

"Fight!" someone yelled.

Couples scattered from the dance floor like chickens fleeing a coyote. The trumpet player blew a sour note. A woman screamed, but he didn't think it was Red. She didn't seem like a screamer. At least not in a bar fight.

Fist cocked, Shane popped up and smacked Baldo dead on his jaw.

Turned out the dude had a glass chin.

Baldo's eyes glazed. His knees wobbled. He made a noise like a strangled bull and toppled face-first onto the concrete floor.

Shane figured he just might get away scot-free.

But he didn't count on Baldo being a pal of the band. Next thing he knew horns were flying and the microphone was screeching tortured feedback as it got knocked off the stage onto an amp. The lead singer came out of nowhere and punched Shane squarely in the eye.

He wasn't thinking of himself. He'd been in worse fights than this. Red was on his mind.

Where was she? He had to make sure she was safe.

He swiveled his head, but didn't see her. Good, maybe she got out of the building unscathed.

Someone grabbed him around the neck, locked him in a choke hold. Someone with deeply muscled arms. Someone very strong.

The bouncer?

The grip around his neck tightened. Where the hell was Cal? Some partner he'd turned out to be.

Shane couldn't catch his breath and his head throbbed. In his worry over the redhead he'd made a classic mistake. He'd forgotten to protect his flank.

"Let him go, you jackass!" Shane heard a woman holler.

Was it her? Was it Red?

He tried to turn his head to look for her, but between the pressure on his carotid and the smoke in the air, it was pretty nigh impossible to see anything more than the guy in the Chuck Mangione hat coming at him.

The trumpet player punched him in the breadbasket while the bouncer squeezed his neck so hard Shane feared his head was coming off. He gasped. Soon he was going to pass out.

Shit, where was Red?

That was the last thing he remembered until he came to a few minutes later. He was propped up beside the Dumpster in the back alley behind the nightclub. His lungs burned and his brain felt as if he'd had nails hammered through it.

Way to go, Tremont. No more undercover at Louie's for you.

His boss was going to be steamed and Cal was going to get his promotion. All over a woman he'd never even met. He drew in an aching breath trying to rouse the energy to get to his feet. Then he heard the crisp snap-snap *of stiletto heels clicking on asphalt. Gingerly, he raised his head and looked around.*

There was Red.

Standing in front of him, her gorgeous legs positioned

shoulder-width apart. The skirt she wore was extremely short, revealing a mile of coltish legs and creamy thighs. The stretchy material molded tight against her generous hips.

He was overwhelmed by the sight.

She met his stare openly, took his measure even as he took hers. No shrinking violet, this one.

Looking at her, he felt a sappy sloppy feeling light up his heart for no fathomable reason at all.

"Hey, there," she said and squatted beside him in the alley. She smelled like a spice shop, hot and zesty. She made him think of a brownie he'd once had that was made with smoked jalapeño peppers. Tasty, but fiery.

"Hey there yourself," he surprised himself by answering. By nature, he was not a flirtatious man, but something about her spurred changes in him. He was getting his first real eyeful of her up close and personal and definitely enjoying the experience.

"You make a habit out of this Sir Galahad thing?" That voice, vivacious and sultry as a tropical night, was as flat-out erotic as the rest of her.

Shane tried to shrug and ended up just wincing. So much for macho cool. "I hate to see women get pushed around by drunken jerk offs."

"I could have handled the situation, but thank you anyway. It was sweet."

Sweet. Hmph. He didn't want her to think of him as sweet. He wanted her to see him as her own personal Hercules.

Hercules. Right.

"I'm afraid," she said and tenderly ran a fingernail down his cheek, "you got the worst end of the deal."

He nodded. "Forgive the line, but what's a nice girl like you doing in a place like this?"

"Who says I'm nice?" She winked.

"You're out here with me. If you weren't nice, you would have ditched me."

"And leave Sir Galahad all alone? Not even a naughty girl is that cruel."

"So you're naughty? Is that the reason you come down to Louie's and dance by yourself?"

She touched the tip of her tongue to her upper lip. "Usually it's a safe place to come blow off steam."

*"*Safe*'s not exactly the word that leaps to mind." He jacked himself up higher against the Dumpster and held a hand over an aching rib, praying it was bruised and not broken. He flicked an apple peel from the cuff of his pants.*

"The bald guy was new. A roadie for the band. Normally no one bothers me."

"Ah. That explains it."

"Lucky for you, Louie is my ex-stepfather."

"Ex-stepfather?"

"My mother's second husband."

"How many husbands has she had?"

Red shrugged. "I lost count after three. Anyway, I convinced Louie not to call the cops."

"Kind of you," he mumbled.

She laughed and the sound of it lit him up inside. He was not a particularly humorous guy, but he had a sudden urge to spend the rest of his life trying to make her laugh.

"One small detail," she said. "I promised Louie you'd pay for the damages."

"Didja now?"

"It was that or the cops."

"Smart call."

"I thought it a fair exchange."

His cheek was cut and one eye was swelled shut, but he felt like the king of the universe because she was safe and here with him and her long red hair was trailing across his bare arm as she leaned forward. And kissed him.

Gently, on the forehead, but it was still the most erotic kiss he'd ever had. Then she held out her hand and tugged him to his feet. She led him to her car. Took him to her apartment. Tended his wounds.

She let him sleep in her bed with the condition that he promised to keep his hands to himself. Even with bruised knuckles Shane had found it a challenge to honor that promise, because no woman had ever turned him on the way she did.

All night he lay awake, watching her sleep. By morning, he had decided she was the woman he was going to marry.

And he didn't even know her name.

Chapter 9

What'll you have?" The smooth voice of the woman behind the bar at Louie's jerked Shane out of the past and back to the present. He blinked, reorienting himself to place and time.

"Club soda," he said.

"Heavy drinker," she commented dryly.

"Okay, add a splash of cranberry juice."

She laughed and turned to get his drink.

Shane pivoted on his barstool. The place hadn't changed much in three years. On a Monday night, without a band and this close to last call, the bar was empty except for hard-core drinkers. The bartender passed him the club soda and cranberry juice. Shane took a sip.

A hand clamped down on his shoulder. "Well, hell, look what the cat dragged in."

Shane turned his head to see Louie Browning grinning at him. They shook hands. "Hey, you old sonofabitch, you haven't aged a bit."

Louie plunked down on the stool beside him and waved a hand at their surroundings. "This place keeps me young. How you been?"

"Good, good."

Louie's gaze dropped to Shane's damaged hand. "Looks like things could be better. On-the-job injury?"

Shane resisted the urge to tuck his hand out of sight. He hadn't expected Louie to be here this late. A strained awkwardness quickly replaced his delight at seeing a familiar face. Louie was Tish's ally. Shane was on her turf. Why had he come here? What was he searching for?

"You talked to Tish."

"No." Louie shook his head. "Not lately. I just took a wild guess about the hand."

He hoped Louie wouldn't ask him any more questions. He didn't want to explain about this injury, about his job, about his engagement to Elysee, about what had happened between him and Tish. He drained his club soda and cranberry juice, put a ten-dollar bill on the bar, and got to his feet.

"You leaving already? What? I forget the deodorant or something?" Louie pantomimed sniffing his armpits.

Crap. How was he going to get out of having this conversation? "I just gotta go." He jerked his thumb in the direction of the men's restroom.

Louie nodded.

Shane hightailed it to the restroom. The place was empty. He sank his shoulder against the wall and took a deep breath. Briefly, he closed his eyes and thought again of the first time he'd come into this bar. The first time he'd laid eyes on Tish.

Coming to Louie's had been a bad idea. Why had he come here? He had to get out. He spun on his heel, pushed through the door, and stepped back into the bar.

Just in time to see Tish come skipping down the stairs, calling out, "Louie, I've come to pay back the two hundred dollars I owe you."

Shane blinked, froze in mid-stride, unable to believe what he was seeing.

No, no, she couldn't be here.

Tish stopped in the dead center of the bar as her gaze landed on him. "Shane," she whispered on an exhaled breath.

"Tish." He fisted his good hand.

Louie's Blues Bar on Second Street filled with loss and pain and Tish. Shane felt as if he was fighting for his very soul. Three years ago, on this same spot, they'd first met and started their inevitable dance toward destruction. Why had wretched fate drawn them together again? Both back to this place, on the same night, at the same time.

He looked at her and she looked at him and time shifted under their feet, the past and present morphing together in keen weirdness.

"Are you really here?" she asked.

"I'm here."

"But why?"

"I don't know."

Tish gave him a long searching look. A dozen different emotions flitted across her face like a slideshow from the past. For one brief second, he could have sworn he saw a tear in her eye, but no, it had to be a trick of the lighting. "Why aren't you at the ranch?" she asked.

"Couldn't sleep."

"Me either. Unless I fell asleep and I'm dreaming this. Am I dreaming you?"

"Maybe." He shrugged as if he wasn't unnerved. "You always were uncanny."

"Maybe we're both dreaming."

"Just a dream," he murmured.

Shane sensed rather than saw Louie, the sly old fox, as

he slipped around behind them and dropped two quarters in the jukebox. A couple of seconds later, Beyoncé began to sing "Crazy in Love."

Their song.

Was he just dreaming? Only one way to tell.

He stalked the short distance between them, reached out to her with his good hand. "Dance?"

Her eyes rounded, but she didn't take his hand.

"For old time's sake?"

"For old time's sake," she echoed and sank her palm into his.

He guided her toward the dance floor, knowing this was insanity, but once in motion, he was unable to stop.

One last spin around the dance floor. That's all it is.

But once he had her there, he didn't know how to proceed with his damaged hand. He slipped his good arm around her waist, but felt off balance with his right arm cradled against his side.

Why had he started this?

She read him, obviously sensed his anxiety. Gently, Tish took his right hand in her left, interlaced their fingers and raised their joined arms.

Her eyes met his. The mood between them burned intensely.

"It's our last dance," she said.

"Yes."

"So we should enjoy it." Her eyes were like daggers, sharp and glistening, stabbing him deep.

"Yeah." His throat was so tight he could barely force the word out.

They swayed to the beat, gazes welded. She sighed and the sound of her sigh, sweet and forlorn, seeped through him, unhinging coherent thought. And then she did something that unraveled him completely. Tish laid her head on his shoulder, buried her face against his neck.

His heart thumped. He tightened his grip around her waist. In that moment, she had him. He felt it. The deep pulse of sexual energy they'd always shared. The music hummed, vibrating the air, vibrating their bodies moving in faultless harmony.

"Shane," she whispered, her lips touching the bare skin over his collarbone.

Her vulnerable voice cut him to the quick. Chill bumps slipped down his spine. He dipped his chin, pressed his nose against the top of her head, breathed deeply of her distinctive fragrance.

They swayed past a revolving beer sign. It cast blue fingers of neon over them, bathing the moment in pathos. Her hot body was pressed against him. He could feel every line, every curve, causing him to think things he should not be thinking. Her cheek lay pressed against his chest, inciting in him an old desire that should best be ignored.

"Tish." Her name rolled from his tongue on a groan.

She pulled back and stared at him, studying his face, seeking answers to unspoken questions.

He met her gaze. He was sorry he had no answers to give.

She had eyes that were at once both sultry and mystical, eyes that held no slight amount of sorrow, tucked behind her brave smile. Her thick cascade of curly auburn hair tumbled down her shoulders like an angel's mane. The look she gave him shot straight through his heart and made it hard to breathe.

He blinked, dazed, even as a small part of him buzzed with the magic of holding her in his arms again. He stared into her eyes and she stared into his, and Shane just felt lost.

Around them in the almost empty nightclub stretched rows of tables, and the staff turned chairs upside down in a higgledy-piggledy thrust of legs. The yeasty smell of spilled beer rode the air. On his tongue, in his mouth, was the taste of everything he'd lost.

Tish splayed her palm over his chest. Her eyes went wide as his heart rate quickened. It shook him up.

The song ended. The jukebox fell silent. The bartender announced last call.

And just like that, the dream was over.

The next morning, Tish was out running errands, struggling not to think about what had happened at Louie's the night before or the significance of she and Shane both showing up at the bar at the same time, when her cell phone rang.

She pulled it out of her purse and flipped it open. "Capture the Moment Videos."

"Tish, it's Elysee."

Guilt, immediate and ruthless, squeezed her stomach. "Um...hi."

"Hi," Elysee bubbled. "There's a WorldFem luncheon today and I want to go. Shane's rattling around the house all by himself. I think he's a little down in the dumps because his physical therapy sessions aren't going well. If you're not otherwise engaged, I think this might be a prime time to start putting together the *Our Love Story* video for the wedding reception. You could get a head start on it and Shane wouldn't have to be by himself when he's feeling so low. But don't tell him that I told you he's bummed out. You know how proud he is."

That she did. "You want me to go to the ranch right now?"

"Please."

Aw, hell, she still hadn't sorted out her feelings from last night. The last thing she wanted right now was to come face-to-face with Shane. "Um, I'm in line at the drive-through at the bank."

"Well, after you finish that, of course."

"Okay," Tish agreed, because she didn't know what else to say. This check had to go into the bank today or she was screwed in a hundred different ways. She had no real choice. But once the check was cashed, there was no turning back.

The car in front of her moved on and she drove up to the teller window.

"Great," Elysee said. "Oh and by the way, we want you to come to DC next weekend to film our engagement party. Are you available?"

"Washington DC?"

"The one and only."

Tish Gallagher in Washington DC, filming the first daughter's engagement party? It was simultaneously a dream come true and a living nightmare.

Be careful what you wish for, Tish remembered Claire Kelley telling Delaney when she'd bought the veil. *Or you just might get it.*

"Um..."

"We'll pay to fly you there, of course. Put you up at the Ritz-Carlton."

Tish Gallagher from South Houston living it up at the Ritz in Washington DC? Just yesterday she'd been eating Ramen noodles and dodging bill collectors.

"And we're granting you exclusive video rights. Yours will be the only movie camera allowed into the party."

"Really? An exclusive of the first daughter's engagement? I don't know what to say, Elysee."

"Say yes. The party's on Saturday. Please don't tell me you have another wedding scheduled for next Saturday."

"No."

"Great, so you can do it?"

"Yes."

She thought of having to spend the afternoon at the Benedict ranch with Shane, looking through old photo albums, and felt sick to her stomach. *This is how Julia Roberts's character must have felt in* My Best Friend's Wedding. *Trapped into being nice to a woman she wanted to despise, but couldn't because she was just so darned nice.*

She stared at the phone, stared at the check, stared at the teller who was raising her eyebrow, waiting for Tish to make a move.

Taking a deep breath, she rolled down the window and did the irreversible. She handed the teller her deposit slip and the check.

It was official. Like it or not, she was committed to seeing this thing through.

"You're out of your mind, you know that," Elysee's secretary, Lola, told her as they entered the WorldFem meeting, Secret Service escorts leading the way. "Leaving your man alone with his ex-wife. It's insanity."

"They won't be alone. The ranch is crawling with people."

"Yes, but you won't be there to put a stop to any hanky-panky."

"There's not going to be any hanky-panky. Trust me, I know what I'm doing."

"Do you?"

Elysee wasn't going to let Lola's opinion rattle her.

She trusted Shane implicitly and odd as it might sound to someone else, she also trusted Tish. Whatever her faults, whatever the reason she and Shane had broken up, Elysee couldn't help feeling Tish had integrity.

"They need time alone to heal the old wounds without me peeking over their shoulders."

"If you say so."

Elysee chose to ignore Lola and any niggling doubts she might have of her own. She was very excited that the WorldFem conference was right here in Houston. When the organizers had learned she wanted to attend, they instantly made her a guest speaker. It was a last-minute invitation, so she hadn't prepared a speech. She intended to speak from her heart.

Being in the presence of like-minded women fired her up. There were several celebrities on the panel—including a famous actress, a cable news anchorwoman, and a late night talk show host's wife who'd been instrumental in drawing attention to the plight of women in Afghanistan long before the second Gulf War.

Toward the end of the conference, Agent Ackerman came over to whisper to Elysee. "There's a woman who wants to speak with you. She says it's urgent. A matter of life or death, but I don't advise you to see her."

"What woman?" Elysee asked.

Cal Ackerman pointed her out. She was waiting near the exit, dressed in a sari with a veil cloaking her face.

"I'll speak to her."

"For security reasons...," Agent Ackerman began, but Elysee cut him off.

"I'll speak with her in the limo. You can secure that easily enough and check her out before bringing her to me."

"Yes, Miss Benedict." He didn't seem happy about it, but a few minutes later Elysee and Lola were waiting in the back of the limousine. He brought the woman over, opened the car door, and she slid in.

Agent Ackerman started to get in as well but Elysee raised her hand. "You can wait out there."

His body stiffened in response and his eyes narrowed. He did as she asked, but he didn't look pleased.

"Hello," Elysee said to the veiled woman sitting across from her. "Do you speak English?"

The woman dropped the veil. "It is me, E-lee. Your Nana Rana."

"Rana!" Elysee threw her arms around Rana's neck and hugged her tightly. "Thank God you're alive. I saw your picture in *People* magazine and that's when I knew I had to get involved with WorldFem."

"I am so proud you are here." Tears streamed down Rana's face. "This is such a happy moment for me. To see you all grown up and passionate about human rights. Your mother would be so proud."

They both swiped at tears then. Lola extracted tissues from her purse and passed them around.

"Agent Ackerman said you needed to see me on a matter of life and death. Do you need me to hide you?"

"It is not my own safety that concerns me," Rana said. "I come to you on behalf of another."

"Yes?" Elysee leaned forward, eager not to miss a single word.

"The young woman's name is Alma Reddy. Her father is a cabinet minister in India. He was very distressed when she dishonored her family by secretly marrying an American student attending university in Bombay. The young man's visa was revoked and he was thrown out of India.

Alma's father demanded she renounce the young man and have the marriage annulled. Alma refused and her family has hired attackers to kill her. WorldFem managed to hide her, but we need to get her out of India. Her beloved husband lives in Texas, but we don't have the funds or proper entrance visa to get her into the U.S. Can you help?"

"How much money do you need?"

"One hundred thousand dollars."

Elysee sat back against the seat. "That's a lot of money."

"We must bribe many people. Pay hush money. Plus the route to smuggle her out of the country is an arduous one. There are many planes, trains, and boats she must take. She must change transportation modes often to ensure she is not followed. We must also hire a decoy and send her on a similar journey. Alma's father is ruthless. He has put a price on my head. This all must be kept as secret as possible. He has many spies, many eyes."

"I don't have access to that kind of money here, Rana. Since I'm not yet twenty-five I can't withdraw funds without my father's permission. I do have a safety-deposit box with antique coins left to me by my grandmother. They are worth at least that, but the safety-deposit box is in DC. I'm headed there this coming weekend for my engagement party. If you can meet me there, I'll give you the money on Saturday."

"Thank you, thank you." Rana kissed Elysee's hands. "You are an angel."

"I'll make sure you get an invitation to the engagement party. We can make the transfer there."

"She's playing you," Lola said after Rana exited the limo. "Want to bet you never see her or your money again?"

"Shame on you, Lola," Elysee scolded. "Rana was my nanny."

"And that precludes her from being a con artist?"

"You always think the worst of people."

"That's why your father hired me as your secretary. You need a counterbalance."

"Well, I don't care what you say. I'm giving her the money and I forbid you from discussing the matter with my father."

Lola shrugged. "Don't say I didn't warn you."

"Squeeze it. Push. Go for the burn."

Shane grunted against the grapefruit-sized rubber ball the physical therapist, Pete Larkin, had dropped into the open palm of his right hand.

Once upon a time, he could hurl a fastball sixty miles an hour. Those days were gone. Sweat beaded on his brow as he struggled to contract his fingers around the spongy ball.

I'm half the man I used to be, he thought, and tried not to feel bitter. He'd been doing his job for his President and his country. He couldn't complain when injury and painful rehab came with the territory.

What was he going to do if, no matter how hard he pushed, it didn't work? Would he be happy with Marshal Vega's job, running the Secret Service? Did he even want it? What in the hell did he want? He'd never had this kind of self-doubt in his life and it was troubling.

After ten measly squeezes, his throbbing hand forced him to drop the ball. Shane swore loudly.

"Don't get discouraged," Pete said. "You're making steady progress."

"Doesn't feel like it."

"You're distracted, dude. You're not focusing on the squeeze. You gotta focus."

Shane shook his head. He already knew that. After driving back from Louie's, he'd spent the remainder of the night tossing and turning, unable to get Tish and the impromptu dance he'd instigated off his mind. Hiring her as their wedding videographer had been a huge mistake.

Elysee was convinced working with Tish was the only way he was going to get her out of his system. Shane was determined to prove to Elysee that he had let go of the past and was ready to embrace the future with her.

But his fiancée was naïve. She didn't understand the complexities of marriage, how emotions lingered long after the legal bonds had been severed.

Shane remembered how it had felt being locked in the bathroom with Tish. The hairs raised on his arms just thinking about how close he'd come to kissing her. Even after being away from her for two years, she still affected him like no woman on earth. Hell, to be honest, the powerful pull she held over him was scary.

If you're so hot for Tish, why are you marrying Elysee?

Because he'd been down that road before with Tish and he knew exactly where it led. They were oil and water. No matter how hot the chemistry between them. Passion was a very dangerous thing and after Tish, he'd sworn to avoid it at all costs. The thing he had going with Elysee was much safer.

Since when have you opted for safe?

Shane stared down at his hand.

"You wanna talk about it?" Pete asked, casually curling twenty-pound dumbbells, making it look as easy as kneading bread.

"Talk about what?"

"What's got you tied up in knots?"

"Who are you?" Shane growled, wiping sweat from his brow with a gym towel. "Oprah Winfrey? Dr. Phil?"

"I'm just saying. If you need to talk, I got two ears and a quiet mouth. I know how to keep secrets."

"Nothing to talk about." Shane didn't like dissecting his feelings. He wasn't about to open up to a stranger.

"Still, it can't be easy. Going from the Secret Service agent in the background to center stage as the President's son-in-law-to-be. I can't imagine it. But things are just going to get worse, you know, when the media get wind of the engagement."

"Yeah," Shane mumbled. He'd already considered that.

And it would happen soon. The wife of the Speaker of the House was throwing a party for him and Elysee this upcoming weekend in DC to officially announce their engagement.

"Elysee hired my ex-wife to videotape our wedding," Shane confessed.

"No shit." Pete gave him a grin that said *you poor dumb bastard*. "Weird coincidence."

"No coincidence. Elysee hired her on purpose. She wants us to get along. Be friends."

"Dude"—Pete shook his head—"that's so screwed up. No wonder you can't concentrate on physical therapy. Your mental lifting is a helluva lot heavier."

Shane sank down on the weight bench. His knees seemed suddenly to be made of paper. His nerves poked like sharp spikes, sticking him all over.

His injuries had brought him close to death. Closer than he'd ever been. Was his mortality the problem? Was that what had him questioning everything? Was that what had him missing Tish? Was that what had him fearing that divorcing her was the biggest mistake he'd ever made?

Ah, there it was. The thought he'd been running from

all night long. It felt like a dash of ice-cold water in the face. Frigid and sobering.

"Forgive me, Tish," he muttered. "I was such a damn fool."

"You talkin' to me?" Pete racked the dumbbell.

"Yeah." Shane shoved his thoughts away. The damage was done. He couldn't turn back the clock. All he could do was make damn sure he didn't commit the same mistake with Elysee. He couldn't allow his relationship with his ex-wife to get in the way of their wedding. "Hand me those three-pound weights. It's time I moved on."

Chapter 10

Tish arrived at the ranch to find Shane behind a push mower with his shirt stripped off. She didn't know which was more unexpected. Seeing Shane mowing the President's lawn, or catching a glimpse of his incredible bare body.

She pulled to a stop in the driveway, slung the backpack that served as her camera bag over her shoulder and got out of the car, bumping the door closed with her hip as she went. Tish shaded her eyes and a rivulet of sweat slid down between her breasts—not because the weather was hot, but because Shane was.

Every chest muscle was perfectly honed and defined, ripped and rock hard beneath the silk of his skin. Her gaze slid over him, her mind remembering how firm and thick his skin had felt beneath her fingers. She remembered and ached to touch him again. His denim jeans hugged his hips, molded to his thighs. His dark hair glistened in the sunlight

She swallowed hard and felt the movement of her gulp track all the way down her throat, leaving her feeling dry and breathless. She'd never been so aware of his body.

Or of her own.

Her heart knocked against her rib cage. She moistened her lips, tasted cinnamon-flavored gloss.

This had to stop. She couldn't keep lusting after him, not if she was going to make it through the wedding in one piece.

Shane's left hand guided the lawn mower. His right hand balanced awkwardly against the handle.

Her gaze fixed on that damaged hand. Sadness for him, for them both, swelled inside her on equal par with her regret.

He saw her then, watching him. He killed the mower engine. His gaze lasered into her, sharp as a razor, burning right through her, causing her nipples to tighten underneath her shirt.

His expression was inscrutable, the cool countenance of a protector—a man who always needed someone to look after. That was why he was marrying Elysee; ultimately, it was the same reason he'd left *her*. She hadn't let herself need him. At least not in the way that he needed to be needed.

"What are you doing here?" he asked.

"What are you doing mowing the lawn?" She forced herself not to watch as a bead of sweat trickled down his bare bicep.

At first it seemed as if he might not answer; his mouth drew tight into a straight line. But then, as if forcing the words from his mouth, he said, "Bored out of my skull with rehab. I figured I'd have a go at the last mow of the season. There's something satisfying about putting in an honest day's work."

A hint of a smile quirked one side of his upper lip, and drew her attention to the fact that he hadn't yet shaved today. The sight of his beard growth made her shiver. She recalled exactly how it had scratched and tickled. Involuntarily, she arched her back; her breasts rose.

He sank his hand onto his hip, looking arrogant and dangerous. His grin widened.

No, no, she thought as her knees quivered, *not that damnable lopsided grin.* She thought of last night in Louie's bar, the dance they'd shared, the feelings that touching him again had conjured. Feelings she'd hoped she'd laid to rest.

Her lips craved to caress his mouth, to brush against his stubbled cheek; to lick the salt off his skin. But she couldn't. Shane no longer belonged to her. He was Elysee's man now, and she was just their wedding videographer. He was taboo and this feeling was forbidden.

Yet it thrilled her to the very core of her soul.

"You haven't answered my question."

The smile disappeared. His eyes darkened as his gaze flicked from her face to her body. She was wearing the same clothes she'd run errands in—a snug pair of jeans and a shirt that conformed to her breasts. He was definitely noticing.

"Elysee sent me." She held up her camera bag. "She thought it would be a good idea to start on the *Our Love Story* video for the reception."

"*Our Love Story*?"

"Well, your story. Yours and Elysee's."

"I'm not following."

"You know. I take photographs from both of your pasts, mix them together with pictures of you two dating, add your favorite love songs, headlines of the times, and meld all of it into a pictorial video of the story of your romance."

"Um...Elysee and I never really dated."

"What do you mean? You're getting married. How could you not have dated?"

"I was her bodyguard for over a year and then I saved her life. That's our love story."

It made perfect sense. Shane loved to save people and Elysee had needed saving. "Yeah, so when did you fall in love with her?"

"I don't recall you and me having all that many dates before we decided to get married."

"Look how that turned out."

"Tish," he said. An odd expression crossed his face.

"Shane." She tossed her head.

"I've known Elysee longer than we were married."

"Ouch." Tish pantomimed pulling a sword from her heart. "Want your blade back, Zorro?"

"You started it." He raked his gaze over her, his dark eyes narrowing.

They used to enjoy teasing each other with lighthearted banter. It had been the cornerstone of their relationship, back when things were good. Back before the very worst had happened. Tish caught her breath and forcefully shoved away the dark memory from her mind.

"I don't have time to stand here bickering with you," she snapped. She nodded toward the veranda where a row of heavy mesquite rocking chairs sat. "Get cleaned up and I'll meet you on the front porch and we'll go through your old photo albums."

"I don't have any old photo albums."

"I do," she said. "That's what's in my camera bag."

"Where did you get old photos of me?"

"Your mother gave me copies of your childhood pictures when we were married, remember? Plus, I did take a few of you myself. I'm a photographer, you know. That's what I do. Take pictures, make videos."

"As if that's something I could forget." His voice cracked. With sarcasm? Or another kind of emotion altogether? "And you kept photographs of me?"

"Yeah."

"Why?" He looked amused. It was not a reaction she'd anticipated. "I would have expected you to scissor my head off."

She shrugged, keeping it light. Trying to deny her heart had fallen forward against her chest. Trying not to think about all the other things she remembered about him. "Like it or not, Shane, you were a big part of my life. I'm allowed to keep your photographs if I want. You didn't get sole custody of the photos."

They stood staring at each other, only a few feet apart, both breathing in the heavy, still air thick with the scent of freshly mown grass. She knew they were being watched. Knew there were security cameras hidden all over the ranch and that there were servants and Secret Service agents within eavesdropping distance.

The knowledge only heightened her arousal. Tish desperately wanted to ask him if he'd kept any pictures of her, but she was too afraid of his answer to ask. If Shane said no, it would hurt her feelings and if he said yes, well, that might hurt even more. To think that he still cared. Even just a little bit.

Resolutely, she turned her back and picked her way across the lawn in her sandals, blades of damp St. Augustine clinging to her toes. She could feel the heat of Shane's gaze on her back and it was all she could do to keep from turning around, running right back to him, and flinging herself into his arms.

She sat down in one of the rocking chairs on the front porch.

A maid appeared from seemingly out of nowhere. "Would you like some lemonade to drink while you wait, miss?"

"Um, yeah, sure. Thanks."

It was weird, this presidential life, being waited on hand and foot. Living in a fishbowl. She wondered how Shane was going to like it.

Doesn't matter if he likes it or not. It's no concern of yours.

The maid returned with two glasses of lemonade and a plate of homemade sugar cookies. She set the refreshments on the round patio table positioned between the two rocking chairs and disappeared as silently as she'd come.

Tish sat sipping lemonade and gazing out at the red-and-white Hereford cattle grazing on the other side of the fence until Shane appeared ten minutes later smelling of sandalwood soap and shaving cream. He loomed over her, blocking out the sunlight.

Suddenly she felt a tiny splash of fear.

Calm down. It's all right. You've got absolutely nothing to lose. You've already lost it all.

The thought was strangely freeing. She took a deep breath, smiled up at him, and patted the rocking chair beside her. "Sit."

He sat down awkwardly.

"Lean over."

"Why?"

"Just do it."

"Why?"

"Why not?"

"What is it?"

"Some things never change. I see you're as argumentative as always."

"Me? You're the feisty one."

"Stop being difficult. You've got a smudge of shaving cream on your earlobe."

He didn't lean over, but she did, reaching out to wipe the spot of white shaving cream away. It dissolved against the heat of her thumb.

Shane sat back in his chair, angling his body away from hers, then picked up the lemonade and took a long swallow. She watched his throat muscles work and realized he was more nervous than she was, but he'd carefully arranged his features not to give himself away.

The Secret Service had taught him a lot of tricks, but she'd been intimate with this man. She knew him inside and out. The clues to his emotional landscape were easy for her to read.

He held his shoulders like a razor, stiff and sharp. He sat leaning away from her as if an accidental brushing of their skin would unravel him completely. A sweet sense of power rippled over her. This man was four inches taller than her and seventy pounds heavier, yet he was afraid of her. Tish almost laughed. Instead, she reached for the top album on the stack. "Let's see what we've got here."

"I don't..."

She pulled the album into her lap, cocked her head, and slanted him a sideways glance. "Yes?"

His gaze met hers and she felt it. That click. That lock. That old black magic.

One look in his eyes and she was jettisoned back in time to the moment that had sealed their fate.

Tish had never intended for him to be more than a fling. They were simply too different and she'd known it the minute she'd met him.

It was about sex.

Or that's what she told herself. That was how it started out.

The morning after she'd taken him home from Louie's was his day off. She asked him if he wanted to go to Galveston Island for the day and he'd surprised her by saying yes. They enjoyed the island, and neither of them wanted to go home. It was almost midnight when Tish suggested they walk onto the ferry and take a late night cruise.

"I don't know about that," he'd said, eyeing the sky. "Looks like rain."

She touched the tip of her tongue to her upper lip and gave him a wicked grin. "I don't melt. Do you?"

He smiled back. They were the only foot passengers on the ferry and there weren't even many cars. They climbed the stairs to the open-air deck. The wind was whipping and the waves were rocking and thick black rain clouds obscured the stars.

They found a little alcove between a support beam and the railing. Shane pulled her into his arms and crushed her mouth with his. It was the first time he'd kissed her, even though they'd been touching all day. And it was the most savagely wonderful kiss of her life. Full of sex and promise.

He pulled back from the kiss and shoved his fingers through her curls. "I love your hair," he murmured huskily. "Autumn on display."

She tasted rain on his lips, and that was the first time she realized it was sprinkling. She tasted her own desperate hunger for him. The intensity of her hunger was stark and startling. She yearned to be joined with him. Nothing less than full body contact would do.

Tish had never possessed much self-control, but around Shane, her willpower was nonexistent. The hold he had on her was mysterious and strong. He was not her usual type. Too darkly handsome. Too straitlaced.

But how she longed to undo those laces!

This whole thing was turning into a big game. Could she seduce him without losing her heart? It would be fun to try. And dangerous.

What if she fell for him? What then?

I won't fall for him, *she promised herself, but secretly, deep inside where she kept the truth well hidden from herself, she was halfway there already.*

His arms were around her and he pressed her spine into the side of the ferry. The rain picked up speed, falling warm and spiky against their skin. The wind caught the skirt of her short dress, whipping it around her legs. Brilliant lightning so white it hurt her eyes split the churning black sky with a single perfect hot-fingered fork.

In the stab of lightning, lash of rain, bluster of wind, there was no resistance, no logic, no regret. There was only pleasure. Great waves of sweet, intense pleasure.

"I've never done anything like this," Shane rasped after he pulled his mouth from hers and stared deeply into her eyes.

"Neither have I," she whispered back.

He looked like he didn't believe her. That sort of hurt her feelings.

"I haven't," she insisted.

"I'm not saying that you have."

"You think I'm easy. Because I like to have fun. Because I'm not interested in commitment." They'd already spent the day talking about those things.

"No," he'd said. "You're wrong. That's not it."

"What is it then?"

"Every time I look at you, I can't help but ask myself why me? Why would a stunning woman like you bother with a guy like me?"

No man had ever talked this way to her. He made her feel special. "What are you talking about? You're handsome."

He shrugged. "Not in a traditional way. I've been told I can be pretty scary-looking."

His eyes were deep-set, almost black. His eyebrows were thick and dark. His chin was strong and determined. He could look a little scary to the timid sort.

"I'm not a traditional girl."

"So I've noticed."

She smiled.

"Why are you here with me?" he asked.

Tish didn't have an answer. She couldn't say why she was attracted to him. She simply was. He stirred her blood in a way no man ever had. Couldn't that just be enough? Why did he need to analyze it?

If there was one thing that troubled her about him, it was that. His need to dissect everything.

"Just shut up and kiss me again." She slid her arms around his neck as the next crack of thunder shook the small ferry. The waves rocked against the boat in sensuous, rhythmic motions.

Raindrops splattered the deck, patterned their skin. Tish's T-shirt had stuck wetly to her chest, clearly outlining the contours of her bra.

"This is insanity," he said.

"Yes," she agreed, laughing loud enough to be heard above the wind.

The next charge of lightning was hotter than ever and

mind-jarringly close. The chance they could be struck by lightning was very real and very thrilling. This was the most erotic thing that had ever happened to her. She had a feeling the same was true for him.

He pulled her up tight against his chest, pressing her to his hard angles that promised so much enjoyment. She tilted her head to plant a kiss on his masculine chin.

Cupping a palm behind her head, he trapped her to him. He kissed her, thrusting his tongue deep inside her mouth, ironing his body flat against hers. She could feel him everywhere—her breasts, her pelvis, her knees. His taste was in her mouth. His smell, mingling with the rain, was in her nostrils. His breathing, rough and rapid, resonated in her ears.

Awareness sparked off them, sharp as the lightning decorating the sky. She gripped his hard-muscled back. His hips locked hers against the boat, holding her safe. He wasn't going to let her slip into the churning black waters.

But she couldn't trust him completely, no matter how tightly he squeezed her. For her whole life, there had never been anyone to catch her when she fell. Her father had taken off when she was a kid. Her mother, while well-intentioned, bounced from man to man, always looking for the one great true love that Tish had decided never to believe in.

She might not be able to trust him, but she wanted him right now more than anything else in the world.

Desire rolled like liquid fire through her veins, tugged her down on an upsurge of sexual need. Tossed her heedlessly, mindlessly toward a destiny she couldn't fathom but lusted after.

He was a stranger. She barely knew him. Maybe that

was the reason she wanted him so badly. Attraction to a stranger was always more exciting than the familiar.

The waves rocked the ship, rocked her pelvis into his. Tish moaned soft and low. She swayed into him. She had no self-control. She couldn't stop her hips from rubbing against his; not even if the ship were sinking could she stop.

Their clothes hung heavily from their bodies, sodden with rain. The weighted sensation added to the intrigue.

Tish wanted out of her clothing. Wanted to feel his naked body against hers. Wanted to feel the rain sluicing off of them. Wanted to feel everything all at once. She'd always been greedy that way. Hungry for experience, thirsting for excitement, desperately seeking to hide her pain through pleasurable sensations.

His hips kept moving against her. He was measured, slow, taking his time. He wasn't as desperate as she. Either that or he was much better at hiding his need. Maybe it was just that he liked to draw things out. Liked how he was torturing her.

He possessed a lot of control. Here was the kind of man you could spend a whole weekend in bed with and never grow tired of making love. Sore, yes, tired, no.

Shane kissed the length of her neck, nibbling and nipping as he went. She thrilled to the vibration of his lips on her throat.

"I want you naked," he said, although she could barely hear him above the noise of the rain and her steadily pounding pulse. "I need to touch you."

Yes! It was exactly what she wanted, too!

Sighing happily, she burrowed her face against his chest, shielded her eyes from the pelting storm. She slid two fingers down the column of his throat. He swallowed as she stroked his Adam's apple.

They nuzzled and kissed. Tasted and teased. He treated her with tender licks. His tongue was an instrument of delicious delight. Somewhere along the way, his hand had inched inside the collar of her dress, easing aside the soft material, skating in to unhook her bra.

The feel of his rough, masculine fingertips against the soft, gentle skin of her breasts was highly arousing. Her nipples hardened tight as diamonds.

Then he dipped his head and began unbuttoning the top of her dress with his teeth. One by one, they popped open.

Her knees weakened. If he hadn't been holding her pinned to the wall, she would have melted straight into the floor. They were going to get naked right here on the top level of the ferry. Right here in the rain, hidden from view by a support pillar, but standing underneath a full flowing sky.

She shoved her hands underneath his shirt, as eager to get at him as he was to get at her. Her hunger escalated his need. Frantically, he stripped off his own shirt and tossed it, sopping wet, to the ground.

Lightning flashed, illuminating him.

He was magnificent.

Her breath left her body at the sight of his muscular bare chest. He was exquisite. Not an ounce of flab on his hard-honed frame. This was indeed a man.

And she couldn't wait to get him out of his pants.

Thunder growled, low and sexy.

Her shirt hung open. Her bra was unhooked. He pulled both garments off her shoulders in two forceful moves and then he dropped to his knees in front of her. His eyes stared at her bare breasts with awe and reverence.

His caresses grew frenzied. She realized she was just as frantic as he was, maybe even more so.

Their breathing grew ragged, husky. It all seemed so urgent. She must have him or she felt as if she would literally die. Things were totally out of control and she loved it. This was the way she lived her life, acting on impulse, obeying her gut instincts.

She told herself he was nothing more than a way to take her mind off her problems. A diversion she would soon tire of. That was okay. She wasn't going to fall into the trap her mother had fallen into so many times. She was not going to lose herself in a man. Sex, yes, but with just one particular man, hell no.

But this man seemed to have other plans.

He twisted away from her and her body throbbed to have the contact back. In the darkness, his gaze collided with hers. The expression on his face was feral, primal.

She was vulnerable. Alone with a stranger. She acknowledged this. She shrank back into the shadows, suddenly realizing how vulnerable she truly was. This crazy foolishness was beyond comprehension.

Yet, in spite of the passion, in spite of her out-of-control urges, in spite of her raw vulnerability, something told her she could trust him. That he would keep her safe. And that scared her more than anything else. She had an urge to bolt over the side of the ferry, plunge straight down into the inky water and swim away.

"God, Tish," he said with a catch in his voice. "You are so beautiful."

She'd been told she was beautiful before, but never with such heartfelt rendering.

Tish found herself pressed hard against him. They were chest to breasts, skin against skin. He wrapped his arms around her, seized her mouth with his, tipped her backward until her hair trailed the ground.

She exhaled sharply and he swallowed up the sound.

He read her need and his hands explored unfamiliar territory, slipping up the skirt of her dress, gliding up her thighs and sliding around to grasp her rear end.

The next thing she knew his hand was inside her panties and she was on fire. Burning up inside, shoving her pelvis hard against his.

"Finger me," she demanded.

But he didn't have to be told. He was already doing it. He pushed his thick middle finger inside her, stroking her ache.

"Devil," she growled.

"Wench," he growled back.

She nipped his shoulder, sank her teeth into him.

He touched her in places that ignited thoughts of what it would feel like when he was between her thighs, pushing deep enough inside her to soothe that throbbing ache.

He lowered his head, made love to her breasts with his wily tongue. He zeroed in, plucking a straining nipple into his mouth.

Tish wobbled in his arms. He braced his hand against her spine.

"I'm going to make love to you now," he said.

"Yes."

It was that simple. Her acquiescence. He had her. She would do anything he wanted. God, she was lost. And it felt wonderful.

His mouth caught hers again in a possessive kiss that made her quiver. Caught her, arrested her. She wasn't going anywhere until he'd branded her as his own. They were in a whirlwind, swept up by a maelstrom of chemistry and passion and need. Shane unzipped his pants, wrestled himself out of them and his underwear.

She shimmied out of her skirt, shucking her panties, and then shifted her gaze back to the magnificent man in front of her.

They stood completely naked on the upper deck of the ferry, in the middle of the night, in the crescendo of a thunderstorm, completely vulnerable to each other.

It was, quite honestly, the most exciting moment of Tish's life. She let her eyes drop from his. Allowed her gaze to travel over the length of his bare chest, down his taut belly to his very impressive package.

She lifted her eyes to meet his again and saw he was assessing her as avidly as she'd been assessing him. The corner of his mouth quirked upward in approval. That lopsided grin shot an arrow straight to her heart.

The emotions playing across his face riveted her.

A strange feeling overcame her, a combination of fear and excitement and danger and trust. Yes, trust. In spite of their wild circumstances she trusted this man.

That she trusted him scared her. A lot.

The impulse to back out was suddenly overwhelming. But then he clamped a hand around her bottom and drew her up tight against his hardness and she just melted. Into him, into the rain, into the darkness of the steamy night.

He braced her back against the support column. He took her right leg and guided it around his waist. She understood what he wanted and pulled her left leg up as well, until she was pinned against the pillar, totally supported by the strength in his body.

And she trusted him to support her. That was the miracle.

He leveled into her, slipping in with surprisingly gentle movements considering how fired up they both were.

She hissed in a breath. The minute Shane was snugged inside, her muscles contracted around him.

"Oh, no ma'am, don't start that yet," he said, "or I won't last a minute."

But he felt so good. So big and thick inside her that she couldn't resist squeezing.

"Ah, Tish, I can see I'm going to have to distract you if I want to satisfy you."

His mouth sought hers, kissing her thoroughly, imprinting her with his taste. She could hear the rasp of his breathing through the sound of the slowing storm.

"That's it," he whispered. "Settle down. Enjoy the ride."

And then he began to move.

Their bodies fit. Hand in glove.

She felt every manly inch of him as he slid in and out of her warm moist folds, his movements languid and pointed, clearly designed to drive her quite mad. She could feel it coming.

The storm.

Not the one lashing them against the ferry. But the one gathering in her womb.

Legs braced wide, penis sliding in and out of her, Shane anchored her to the wall, his strong arms holding her in place. Like a dedicated explorer, he took his time, getting to know the feel of her.

She slid the fingers of one hand down his back, feeling the bumps in his spine, grateful for him, for this moment, for this delicious pleasure.

His thrusts quickened. She egged him on with hot little gasps and soft, hungry moans.

Tension mounted.

Shane drove into her. Forceful now, demanding. His early gentleness evaporated in the face of urgent need.

Fearing she was going to slip, she tightened her legs around his waist. He cupped her buttocks in his hand, spearing her hard, banging into her until she was shaking all over.

The inside of her thighs rode his hips. He was pounding her, driving as hard as the pelting rain, his penis a searing sword of pleasure so intense it almost hurt.

"That's right," she cried. "Make me come."

She could feel his legs quivering, knew he was on the verge of climax. Oh God, it was gonna be big.

They exploded.

Shattering into pieces. Blasting apart. The orgasm tore through them simultaneously. She felt it ripple through her womb. Felt the hot shot of his heat flood through her.

In that quivering second in time, everything changed forever.

Chapter 11

Tish. Tish?" Shane's voice tore her from the past. "Where did you go?"

"Huh?' She blinked and found herself back on the porch at the Benedict ranch, staring deeply into her ex-husband's eyes.

The sizzle was still there. Deadly as ever. Tish gulped. The chemistry might linger, but she'd accepted the fact that Shane no longer belonged to her. The expression in his eyes was just the caress of a memory and the passion that had once defined them. But they'd gone beyond that.

They had, she realized with a start, grown up.

They could feel this passion and not act on it. She could let the sensation of want and need wash over her and then move on. She liked the cleanness of what was left behind. She'd never thought she could find physical restraint appealing, but there it was.

"You zoned out on me."

"Did I? I'm sorry. What were you saying?" she asked in a rush, praying her heated memories didn't show on her face.

"I'm proud of you," Shane said.

"What?"

"You're one tough cookie."

"Since when did you admire toughness in a woman?"

He looked bewildered by the question. "I've always admired your toughness."

"Ya coulda fooled me. I thought my toughness was the thing that broke us."

He didn't say anything else, just pressed his lips together, reached over with his scarred hand, and flipped open the photo album. He was so close she could smell the scent of his soap, feel his body heat. The memory of their lovemaking on the Galveston ferry was burned into her brain for eternity.

Their gazes were welded. The sound of the autumn breeze sweeping through the oak trees filled the silence between them, the wind whispering as it rustled and danced around tree branches burdened with acorns.

They both knew what had really broken them. The tension rose, curling around him and around her, ensnaring them in the hurts of the past. She dropped her gaze, stared at his hand. Shane caught her staring. She longed to bring his damaged hand to her mouth, press her lips to his scars, healing him with her kisses. But of course she could not, did not.

Hurriedly, she shifted her gaze from his hand to the book between them. There was a picture of five-year-old Shane, cocking that lopsided grin that would later become a ladykiller. He had a bottom tooth missing and his eyes were sparkling mischief. He was sitting on a back porch stoop, a black and white spotted puppy in his arms, licking his chin.

"This is definitely going into the *Our Love Story* video." Tish peeled back the plastic covering and slipped the photograph from the album. "Along with a quote about what little boys are made of."

"I never really liked that picture," Shane muttered.

"Why not? It's adorable."

"My ears stick out like cup handles."

"All little boys' ears stick out like cup handles. Elysee is going to love it."

"Find another picture," he said gruffly.

Something Shane had once told her occurred to Tish out of the blue. "The cup-handle ears aren't the reason you don't like that picture, is it?"

"Huh?"

"That's your dog Bandit."

He nodded.

"You told me you saw Bandit get hit by a car and it hurt you so much you refused to get another dog. Remember when I wanted to get a collie?"

"Yeah."

"You lost Bandit not long after that picture was taken, am I right?"

Shane made a noise of surprise that she'd guessed. "It was the same day."

She studied him and the look in his eyes made her glance away before she started tearing up. She couldn't very well tarnish her reputation for toughness. Tish slipped the photograph of Shane and Bandit back between the plastic and quickly flipped the page.

Next was a snapshot of Shane and his sister with their parents on an amusement park ride. Shane looked to be eight or nine, his sister, Amy, about four or five. All of them were waving for the camera—a happy nuclear family on vacation. Tish felt jealous.

"How's Amy?" she asked, battling back her feelings.

"Finishing her graduate degree in journalism at Columbia this year. She's had a great job offer from the *New York Times,* although she's still weighing her options. She has a serious boyfriend. Everyone's expecting an engagement announcement from them soon."

"How are Charlotte and Ben?" Tish asked, referring to his parents.

"Dad retired this fall and they've taken off on that around-the-world cruise they've been dreaming of for years."

"That's wonderful," she said and meant it. She'd always adored Shane's mom, and while she'd been a little scared of his stern Vietnam veteran dad, she respected and admired Ben Tremont.

"How's Dixie Ann?" he asked.

"What can I say? She's Dixie Ann."

"Married? Dating?"

"In between men right now."

"Where's she living?" Shane propped his long, lean legs up on the porch railing.

"San Diego."

"Nice place. You visit her much?"

"Not much. You know my relationship with Dixie Ann. I bet your parents were thrilled when you told them you and Elysee were getting married. I know your dad shares Nathan Benedict's politics."

"I haven't told them yet."

Tish's eyes flew to his face and her heart gave a strange little bump. Why didn't they know about his engagement to Elysee? He and his parents had always been close. She figured they would be the first people he would tell. "Hmm."

"Hmm, what?"

"Hmm, nothing."

"Don't read anything into it."

"What? I didn't say anything."

"You said *hmm*."

"That's a sound, not a word."

"It's hard getting through on those ship-to-shore calls," he said defensively. "I phoned them after I got out of the hospital, to let them know I was doing okay and staying at the ranch to recuperate, but that was before—"

"You asked Elysee to marry you," she interrupted.

He ran his good hand through his hair, ruffling the damp locks, and angled her an exasperated look. "Yeah."

"Are you just going to let Charlotte and Ben read about your engagement in the papers?"

"No, no." He shook his head. "Of course not. I'll call them before the engagement party next weekend."

"So this photo is okay to use?" She tapped the picture of Shane and his family.

"Sure."

"Oh . . . I forgot all about this picture." She pointed to the photograph below it. "I absolutely love how adorable you look in it."

It was a snapshot she'd taken of Shane not long after they'd started dating. He was lounging in the middle of her bed in his underwear, his back propped against the headboard, hands cradling the back of his head, elbows jutting outward, looking like a thoroughly bad boy.

A trickle of sweat slid down the back of her neck in spite of the balmy temperature. Her pulse quickened, as it always had when she was near him. She felt a rush of sexual awareness so potent she had to bite down on her bottom lip. Thank God they weren't alone on this ranch. If they had been, Tish didn't know if she could have stopped herself from kissing him.

She heard his breathing speed up. Bravely, she tilted her head and peeked over at him. He was staring at her intently, at the bead of sweat that had tracked from her neck and was now sliding slowly toward her cleavage.

"Remember," he murmured, his breath fanning coolly against her skin, "what you were wearing when you took this picture?"

She caught the wicked gleam in his eyes.

His gaze held hers captive.

"What?" she breathed.

"Absolutely nothing."

She could not look away. Not that she wanted to. His finger crept up to touch a curl at her shoulder.

"You looked glorious, with all that red hair tumbling over your bare skin."

"That was a long time ago."

"Not that long ago."

"So much has happened since then." She inhaled. His hand was still at her shoulder. "Too much."

Quickly, Tish thumbed the next page, and what she saw made the breath catch in her lungs. She'd forgotten about this picture. Hadn't looked at the album in over two years.

It was a Polaroid of her and Shane on their honeymoon at Galveston Island. They were coming out of the Gulf of Mexico, soaking wet, Tish riding on Shane's shoulders. The afternoon sun was glinting off their sun-burnished skins; his hands were locked around her ankles to keep her from falling off. But there was no need, for she was perfectly balanced on the broad platform of his shoulders. They were laughing with their eyes shut and water rolling down their faces. They looked like they were in perfect harmony. Sharing one mind. One thought.

Yin and Yang.

Whole.

A beachgoer had snapped the photograph of that perfect moment in time. The man had told them he'd been so captivated by their unity, their pure joy, that he'd taken the picture because special moments like that didn't happen often. After they'd come ashore and dried off, he handed them the Polaroid and walked away. Leaving them with a visual of one precious second in time.

They did look happy. Poor lovestruck fools. They had no idea what they were in for.

A knot formed in Tish's throat. "We *were* happy once, weren't we?"

"Yeah," Shane said. "But that was before..."

His words trailed off, and the name neither one of them had the courage to say lay in the air between them.

As she stared at the photograph, the earth tilted and it felt as if she were being catapulted into outer space, flung far from sense and reason. Her loss was now a physical thing in her hands. Something she could touch and see. A thousand flashes of memory formed in her head. Formed and coalesced, melded and changed, jumbled and shifted. His kisses, their bodies, the taste of cake, the fizz of champagne.

Everything burned bright and clear and oh so painful—Tish's dreams, her hopes, her regrets.

Shane didn't move.

She could hear him breathing huskily beside her and she knew he felt it, too. This loss, this hurt she'd been trying so hard to bury for two long years. She started to flip the page, to run from those naïve newlyweds, but Shane's hand, raw and pink with scars, anchored the corner.

Tish couldn't turn the page. Not without his permission. Not without wrestling the book from him. How long was he going to make her sit here looking at her biggest failure, her greatest mistake?

No, no, not a mistake. Marrying Shane had never been the mistake.

"Tish." He spoke her name softly, but the sound was sharp, intense.

She couldn't look at him.

Instead, she turned her head, peered at a cow scratching her polled head against a fencepost. Brought her arms up, crossed them over her chest, futilely thinking the gesture would protect her. That it would hold in all these feelings she didn't want to feel.

What the hell am I doing here?

"I don't think Elysee would be too keen on having this picture in her video," she said. "In fact, I don't know why I'm hanging on to it. Why don't we destroy it together? A symbolic letting go so you can start your new life with Elysee fresh and free of me."

"No!"

They both heard the sudden heat of the word as it exploded from his lips. What did it mean? His abrupt rejection of her suggestion to destroy their honeymoon photo?

Don't read anything into this. Don't get your hopes up. You're only asking for more pain.

"Shane?"

Immediately, he backpedaled from the impact of that single reverberating "no." He pulled away from her, let go of the page. "What I mean is, there's already been enough destruction between us. There's not going to be any harm in you keeping the photograph."

"You know," she said, "I think this was what Elysee wanted from us. To take a look at the past and let go of it. To realize that while we've had some good times, we weren't necessarily good for each other."

"We were good for each other," he said gruffly.

She met his eyes. *So then why did you leave?* But she didn't ask the question that was in her head. She knew the answer, but didn't want to make him say it.

"Not good enough," she said instead. "But you and Elysee, you guys *are* good together. She needs you and you need to be needed. That was something I just couldn't give you."

"Wouldn't give me."

"Couldn't, wouldn't, the end results were the same."

"Tish." He gave her that "you've-disappointed-me" look that used to send her heart sinking to her shoes. Whether it was true or not, she'd often felt like she fell short in his eyes.

"It's okay, Shane, really. And I think Elysee Benedict is a very wise person. I like her. She's great. I don't know how she had the courage to hire me as her videographer, but this..." She toggled her index finger in the air between them. "She was right. This is clearing up a lot of old baggage between us."

"Is it?"

"I think so." She canted her head. "Don't you?"

He surprised her by giving her one of his signature lopsided grins. "Yeah."

"Everything's going to be okay, isn't it?"

He nodded.

"We can be friends." She touched his wounded hand.

"Friends." He repeated the word like he'd never heard it before, pushing it tentatively around on his tongue.

"Friends," she echoed.

Her hopes lifted. Could they really be friends? The

thought was enticing. To have him in her life in some small way would be a gift beyond measure.

Friends?

Shane watched her walk toward her car, the alien concept stomping around in his brain. His gaze landed on her swaying behind. Immediately guilt had him by the short hairs. Was it even possible that he and Tish could be friends, considering their sexual chemistry? And if they could, would it be fair to Elysee?

Anger fisted inside him. Anger at Elysee for bringing Tish here. Anger at Tish for trying to be his friend. Anger at himself for being so damned conflicted about what he wanted.

What was the matter with him? Ever since the accident he'd been acting like a pansy, letting circumstances push him around rather than taking action. The only purposeful thing he'd done since leaving the hospital was ask Elysee to marry him, and he'd been second-guessing that decision from the moment he'd made it. What had happened to the old Shane? The man who took a stand and never wavered from his course of action?

Shane stalked back inside the ranch house and headed for the gym. He knew of no other way to dissipate this mishmash of regret, anger, sadness, guilt, helplessness, and longing. He ground his teeth, marched down the hallway, and pushed through the doorway into the gym.

"When you want to hit something, son, take it out on a punching bag," his father had instructed him. "Whale away until your anger is gone."

He strode to the box where they stowed the gym gear, pried it open, and rummaged around for a pair of boxing gloves. He put one glove on his bad hand, but then fumbled with the other glove, failing repeatedly to get it on.

In frustration, he slung the glove to the ground, and muttering a dark curse laid into the punching bag with his bare-knuckled left hand and his ineffective right hand.

He slammed into the heavy punching bag. Jarring pain shot up through his arm.

Again and again he punched, harder and harder, punishing himself, accepting the physical pain, inviting it in to gratefully crowd out his emotional turmoil.

His muscles bunched. Sweat slicked his brow. He grunted in ragged breaths.

Throughout his entire life, Shane had been all about self-control. His father had drilled it into his head. He was from a military family. A Tremont. He had a reputation, a code of honor to measure up to.

Even as a kid, he'd tried to do the right thing, to uphold his legacy. He could hear his father's voice, the echo of platitudes in his head. "You make a decision, you stick with it. Doubt is weakness. Don't ever show weakness. No second-guessing. It's better to make a mistake and fail than to be a wishy-washy girl of a man."

Whenever he thought back on his childhood, all he could remember craving was his father's admiration and respect, two things not easily earned from Ben Tremont.

"Dad, watch me go off the diving board."

"Don't whine for my attention, boy, just jump."

He'd stood at the end of the diving board, six years old and staring down into the swimming pool, unable to jump now that his father was watching.

Ben stood on the sideline, hands on his hips, scowl on his face. "Don't be a pussy. Jump."

His toes had curled over the end of the board. Paralyzed by his father's expectations, he couldn't do it.

In disgust, Ben had climbed up the ladder, grabbed him

by the seat of his swim trunks, and threw him into the water. "Hesitate and you're dead."

Shane smacked the punching bag. The pain was strong, but his anger was stronger. Punch, punch, punch.

Why was he so mad?

Punch, punch, punch.

He pounded the bag, beating back not only his frustration but the sexual desire he still felt for Tish that he was so ashamed to acknowledge.

Shane recalled another childhood memory. He had been twelve years old this time and eager to go on his first hunting trip with Ben and his cronies. Crouching in the deer blind, shivering cold, rifle clutched in his hand, pulse pounding with fear and adrenaline.

The big antlered mule deer walked into the clearing nibbling corn from the deer feeder they'd set up to lure him in.

Ben's mouth was pressed against Shane's ear as he whispered, "Look down the sight. Take aim at his heart."

Shane raised the gun, peered down the barrel, the buck in his crosshairs.

"Commit," his father commanded.

Shane's finger curled around the trigger, his breath fogged frigid air. The deer turned, lifted his head, staring through the small rectangular window of the blind and straight into Shane's eyes.

"Fire!" Ben's demanding whisper sounded like a shout in Shane's ear.

He pulled the trigger just as impulse telegraphed this thought to his brain: *I don't want to kill the deer.*

His arm moved in response to his thoughts, throwing off his aim. The gun blasted, the noise reverberated in the small enclosure, inside his head. The air filled with the acrid smell of gunpowder. Shane flung the gun away from him, closed his eyes.

His father cursed, grabbed him by the scruff of his neck and shook him. "Come on, boy. You're going to finish what you started."

Ben dragged him through the underbrush, tracking the blood drops spattered over the fallen autumn leaves. They walked for half an hour before they found him, lying against a cedar tree.

The buck thrashed on the ground, eyes glassy, breath raspy—dying. Slowly, painfully.

Bile rose in his throat and he dropped to his knees to retch in the weeds. He'd caused this.

Ben laid a heavy hand on Shane's shoulder. "The animal is suffering, son. Suffering because you second-guessed yourself. Now get up and finish what you started. Put this animal out of his misery."

Shane had learned an ugly but important lesson that day. He'd made up his mind. No more second-guessing. From now on he would not hesitate. He would do his duty. He would finish what he started.

And except for his marriage to Tish, he'd lived by that vow.

Wham, wham, wham. He pummeled the punching bag. His right hand was past pain now. It was numb. Dulled by the repeated punches.

He'd failed with Tish. Failed his marriage. Failed himself. He hadn't stood by his commitment and they'd both suffered.

She pushed you away.

But that was no excuse. She'd needed him and he hadn't been there. Not sticking with Tish was the biggest mistake he'd ever made. But it was over and done with now. He had a new commitment. He was engaged to another woman. A good, kind, trusting woman. And not just any woman, but the daughter of the President of the United States.

Exhausted, he dropped his aching arms to his sides, stepped back from the punching bag, rested his back against the wall and slowly sank to the floor.

He'd made promises. To Elysee. To Nathan Benedict. To himself. Promises he intended to keep.

Elysee needed him in a way Tish never had. He was determined to take care of her, especially since he'd messed things up so spectacularly with Tish.

So what if the sexual chemistry between him and Tish still lingered? It didn't change the fact that he'd made a commitment to Elysee. She trusted him and he would not betray her.

No matter how much he might long to make love to his ex-wife, he'd do whatever it took to eliminate those desires. Slam a punching bag into oblivion, take cold showers and stay as far away from Tish as he could get.

It wasn't going to be easy to accomplish with her underfoot as their wedding videographer. But this time he was determined. He was not going back on his promise. There'd been too much hurt already.

Chapter 12

When Elysee had told Tish she was going to fly her to Washington DC to video the engagement party, she'd assumed they would give her a coach ticket on a commercial airline. What she hadn't counted on was traveling via *Air Force One.*

When the stretch limo pulled up to the private airfield in Houston with Tish sitting in the backseat, her mouth dropped open at the sight of the presidential airplane parked on the tarmac. Just looking at the 747 with the emblem of the United States flag painted on its tail made her want to put her hand over her heart and recite the Pledge of Allegiance. For the first time she fully understood the sense of pride Shane felt working for the Secret Service.

It *was* awe-inspiring.

As the limo driver held open the door and she alighted in blue jeans and a flowing, amber-colored tunic top, she felt even more out of place than she had in the limousine.

She'd ridden in limos before, at her senior prom and a couple of times when her mother was dating men with lavish expense accounts. In comparison to this sleek, polished piece of equipment, those limousines had seemed old and shabby.

A no-nonsense-looking woman dressed all in black and holding a clipboard asked for her name and identity before she got within ten feet of the plane. Tish fumbled for her wallet, overwhelmed by what was happening and pulled out her driver's license. She explained who she was and why she was there. The woman took Tish's suitcase and passed it to a cohort for inspection before they stowed it in the plane.

When the woman reached for her camera bag, Tish clamped a hand around the strap. "This stays with me."

"Fine." The woman nodded curtly. "But it must be examined first."

Tish nodded, pulled out her expensive digital camera and accessories. She cringed while the woman turned on the camera, flipped settings, played with the focus.

After she made it past that gatekeeper, a Secret Service agent frisked her. The frisking put Tish in mind of the favorite sex game she used to play with Shane. Where he was the Secret Service agent and she pretended to be a foreign spy out to seduce him for state secrets. Her face heated at the memory.

"You may proceed," the agent said, sounding stern and not smiling.

She remembered that, too. How Shane could look at her sometimes so coldly and unemotionally. She hadn't really realized until now it was something he'd learned in training.

The revelation startled her.

Maybe all those times he had seemed to be stonewalling, he was actually struggling hard not to show his feelings, thinking it would make him seem weak somehow.

She bit down on her bottom lip and followed the female staff member who ushered her inside the plane.

Ascending the retractable stairs at the rear of the plane was a mythic experience. She was being granted entry where few had ever gone.

Once inside *Air Force One*, the staffer led her immediately up another staircase to the middle level. It looked more like a hotel or an executive office than a jetliner, except for the seat belts on the chairs.

"The lower level on the plane serves as a cargo hold," the woman said, acting as tour guide. "Most of the passenger room is here on the middle level. The upper level is largely dedicated to communications equipment and the cockpit. The president has onboard living quarters, with his own bedroom, washroom, workout gym, and office space."

The woman paused, letting Tish catch up. She'd been lingering, looking around at the masterfully handcrafted furniture with a photographer's admiring eye.

"All in all," the woman continued, "*Air Force One* can comfortably carry seventy passengers and twenty-six crew members. Passengers are not allowed to move forward within the plane. If the President should wish to speak with you, he'll walk back here to see you."

Staff members were moving to and fro. Security, military men and women, and members of the press were all dressed in either uniforms or suits. Tish felt out of place and extremely underdressed.

Why hadn't she realized what a big deal this was? Feeling like the proverbial local yokel, she stood in the middle of the aisle, confused and fighting the urge to turn around and run right out the way she'd come. She even turned her head toward the exit, checking the escape route.

She spied Shane's physical therapist, Pete Larkin, coming up the ramp with Shane bringing up the rear. At the sight of her ex-husband, Tish's breath slipped from her lungs, falling like mercury through a thermometer during a Blue Norther. Even before their tête-à-tête on the porch at the Benedict ranch house, Tish had been battling old memories and feelings she thought she'd put to rest.

He looked like Sir Galahad with a beam of sunlight streaming in through the window from over his shoulders, as if he were a mythological god bringing illumination to those inside. He wore the ubiquitous Secret Service sunglasses, even though he was no longer Elysee's bodyguard.

Old habits died hard.

For some strange reason that thought lifted her spirits. Like what? Was she subconsciously thinking of herself as one of Shane's old habits?

Stop it. Stop it right now.

He spotted Elysee sitting in the corner, but apparently he hadn't seen Tish. His face softened into a gentle smile as he went toward the President's daughter.

Elysee smiled back and tilted her face up to him. He leaned down and pressed a kiss to her cheek. Elysee looked at him as if he'd singlehandedly created the world.

It was a sweet, romantic moment that knocked the breath from Tish's lungs. She felt mean and petty and hurt. Jealousy was an ugly thing.

Panic spread through her veins like a firestorm.

It's all a mistake. Coming here today. Going to Washington. Agreeing to be the videographer for their wedding.

Not fighting harder to keep Shane.

What made her so self-destructive? Why couldn't she latch on to what was wrong with her and fix it? Why wasn't she able to control her spending? How come she swept her finances under the rug? Why had she just given up on their marriage?

He gave up on me first!

Misery had her jonesing for Ben and Jerry's Cherry Garcia. Either that or a double shot of really strong tequila. Unexpected hysteria clamped down on her mind.

I can't do this. I can't stand by and watch while Shane marries another woman.

Her knees trembled and her heart was in free fall, tumbling out of her chest and into her feet.

Elysee noticed her, waved, and called out, "Tish, come sit with us."

I'd rather stick a hot poker in my eye, thank you very much. "Okay."

Pasting on a fake smile worthy of a politician, Tish ambled over to a quartet of plush leather chairs arranged so they faced each other. Elysee and her secretary, Lola, sat on the forward-facing chairs, while Shane and Tish sat side by side on the backward-facing chairs.

If she were to reach out her right hand she could trail her fingers along the left sleeve of Shane's dark jacket. Instead, she made sure that both hands were tightly clutching her camera bag.

"Something to drink?" asked an attendant.

"V-8 juice, please, if you have it."

"Certainly, miss." The flight attendant departed.

Silence descended. Tish was aware that Elysee was studying Shane, who was looking over at her, an enigmatic expression in his eyes. He'd taken off the sunglasses and tucked them in the front pocket of his jacket. Lola was discreetly staring out the window.

Tish inhaled sharply. Oh God, this trip was going to be horrible.

"So what do you think about *Air Force One*?" Elysee asked. Tish could tell she was struggling to make pleasant conversation.

"Impressive. Photographs don't do it justice."

"It is difficult, catching the atmosphere of something on camera." Elysee gave a forced laugh. "But of course you know that. You spend your life trying to breathe dimension into a one-dimensional medium."

It sounded like a criticism, even though Tish knew Elysee hadn't meant it that way.

"Oh," Elysee said and brought two fingers to her lips. "That sounded stupid, didn't it? It's just that Shane told me how hard you work to capture the core emotional content of a moment with your camera. He said you focus in on the small details. An untied shoelace on a two-year-old ring bearer, a single bead of perspiration on the upper lip of the father of the bride, a bridesmaid fondling her own bare ring finger."

"He said that?" Tish slid her gaze in Shane's direction.

"Don't sound so surprised," he said gruffly.

"I never realized you ever paid much attention to my work." She studied him with fresh eyes.

"I was proud of you; of course I paid attention."

"Really? When was that? Before or after you bitched at me for buying this camera?" She clutched her camera bag to her chest.

"Tish." He leveled a warning glance. "You're distorting things."

"You're right." She held up her palms. "Ancient history."

"I didn't mean to stir up controversy between you two," Elysee apologized.

"You didn't," Tish and Shane said in unison and glared

at each other. The undercurrent of tension was still there, strong as ever.

The flight attendant returned with the V-8 juice she'd ordered and Tish set it in the cup holder nestled in the arm of her chair and rested her camera bag at her feet.

A commotion at the door drew Tish's attention to the entrance. A knot of Secret Service surrounded the President as he entered the plane. Awestruck, she stared openmouthed as the Commander-in-Chief made his way over to Elysee.

Nathan Benedict's presence was palpable. Not only because of everyone's reaction to him, but from the aura emanating from him. He had steel gray hair and a no-nonsense stride. He slipped out of his suit jacket, handed it to an underling, and rolled up the sleeves of his starched white shirt. He hugged Elysee, shook Shane's hand, nodded hello to Lola, and then turned to her.

"You must be Tish," he said warmly. "My daughter speaks very highly of you and your work as a videographer."

"It's a great honor to meet you, sir."

"Likewise."

"Please, take my seat, Mr. President; sit with your daughter."

She was up and moving, desperate to get away from the sudden claustrophobia squeezing her lungs. This was too much. She was ill-prepared for such a momentous encounter. She couldn't look the President in the eye. Not when she was still aching for Shane, who was about to marry his daughter. She was terrified that this perceptive man would see her secret etched upon her face.

"No, young lady, sit, sit." The President gestured toward the chair she'd vacated.

"I'm more comfortable standing."

"We're about to take off," he said, a bemused smile playing across his lips. "You have to sit down."

Tish pointed over her shoulder at vacant seating in the rear corner. "I'll be more comfortable over there."

He studied her a moment, obviously reading her nervousness.

"As you wish."

She snatched up her camera bag and grabbed her V-8 juice from the cup holder on the chair. She moved to the right. The President went in the same direction.

"Oh, sorry," she mumbled and stepped left at the very instant he did the same.

"Hold still, young lady, and let me get around you." Nathan Benedict chuckled and reached out with both hands to grab her shoulders.

Call it a subconscious response. Call it extreme nervousness. Or call it what it really was—her self-destructive mode kicking into high gear. Either way, it was a major snafu.

The second he reached for her, Tish raised her arm in a protective gesture, forgetting she was clutching a glass of viscous V-8 juice.

Her hand went up.

The glass came down.

Thick red juice splashed, blooming like blood in the center of Nathan Benedict's pristine white shirt.

The President made a startled sound.

Tish gasped.

"She stabbed the President!" someone shouted.

The Secret Service converged in a swarm.

The next thing Tish knew she was pinned to the floor by six burly bodyguards.

People were shouting. Hard knees jammed into her back, pressing down on her lungs, making it hard for her to breathe. Someone sat on her legs. Her knees dug into the carpeting. Both of her hands were staked to the ground by thick wrists heavier than iron shackles and her camera bag had disappeared.

Panic seized her. Her camera was her most valuable possession. It had cost her fifteen thousand dollars and her marriage.

"My camera!" she cried. "Where's my camera?"

Above all the hubbub she heard Shane calmly explaining that they could let her go, because while his ex-wife was a monumental klutz, she'd hardly intended to assassinate the leader of the free world with a glass of V-8 juice.

"Get off my wife." The words were on the tip of his tongue. Shane almost spoke them, but just in the nick of time, he managed to bite them back. Instead he said, "All clear, suspect no threat to the eagle."

"I'm fine," Nathan Benedict reiterated as another agent whisked him away. "It's nothing more than spilled tomato juice."

"I can't breathe," Tish mumbled, her face pressed against the floor.

A shock of concern passed through him. "Get off," he snapped at the bodyguards. "You're hurting her."

Slowly, the Secret Service agents let her up and backed away, holstering their drawn weapons as they went. Shane understood why they'd done what they'd done, but he couldn't help feeling as if they'd acted overzealously.

He reached down to take Tish's arm. "You okay?"

She raised her head, pushed up on her knees, and threw him a scathing glance. Reluctantly she took his proffered hand, but once on her feet she immediately twisted from his grasp and glowered at him darkly.

"Are you pissed off at me?"

"Why on earth would I be pissed off at you?" Her voice was laden with sarcasm.

"I don't know. That's why I'm asking."

She just glared and leaned over to dust off the knees of her jeans. When she did the gauzy top she was wearing fell forward, giving him a clear view of her cleavage.

Tish's skin was so creamy and soft. He remembered exactly what it felt like to press his face into the delicious scoop of her cleavage. He could smell her scent—an intoxicating cinnamon, ginger, and licorice mix. His heart did a weird somersault.

It had been a very long time since he'd been privy to that amazing view and he hadn't realized exactly how much he missed it. Shane blinked and just stood there for the few seconds it took to remember where he was and what he was supposed to be doing.

You're an adult, he scolded himself. *Not a randy teenager. Knock it off. Remember what you promised yourself. Remember, you're engaged to Elysee.*

Tish raised her head and her eyes met his. For that split second in time it was just him and Tish and the way things used to be.

Once upon a time, when it came to sex, they'd been insatiable for each other. Even in the rockiest moments of their marriage, their lovemaking had been monumental. She could turn him on with just one sultry, well-placed glance. Fortunately for Shane, she was scowling at him as if he had leprosy.

"Where's my camera?" she demanded.

"Hang on."

"I want my camera."

Shane glanced around and saw that Cal had it slung over his shoulder. He also saw his old partner had noticed Tish's cleavage. Shane had the sudden urge to smack him right in the kisser.

"Cal?" He stepped closer and held out his hand. "May I have the camera?"

"You sure that's a good idea?"

"She's not a security threat," Shane growled. *And stop looking at her like that.*

"Maybe not intentionally," Cal muttered low enough where only Shane could hear. "But she's got 'walking disaster' written all over her. Remember the first time you met her?"

"Give me that." He snatched the camera from him. "And mind your own damned business."

Cal arched an eyebrow. "Guarding the first daughter is my business. What's yours, Tremont?"

Shane glared. He knew where Cal was coming from, but he also knew Tish was mentally browbeating herself for having caused such a scene. She took things so personally.

"I feel so humiliated," Tish moaned softly when Shane brought the camera back to her.

"Don't be. It happens."

"What about the President?" She worried her bottom lip with her teeth. "Is he okay?"

"He's gone to change his clothes. Don't worry about it. No damage done. President Benedict knows you were just nervous."

"I don't get how you do it." Tish shook her head.

"Do what?"

"Move in these circles and act so cool."

"Practice," he said. "FYI, whenever you bend forward, that blouse shows off a lot more than it should."

Tish splayed a hand to her cleavage. "Really?"

"Really. Why do you think Cal was staring?"

"Oh, no, and I leaned over the President to pick up my camera. Do you suppose he—"

"Saw your ta-tas? Probably."

"I flashed the President?" Tish groaned and covered her face with a hand. "God, kill me now. Thanks for telling me. I'll be extra careful until I get a chance to pin it up."

Sympathy stirred inside him. Shane reached out to touch her, wanting to reassure her that everything was going to be all right. The minute his fingers brushed her skin, he knew it was a grave mistake. Immediately, he drew back his hand.

Madness.

The heat was back again, hotter than ever. A maze of emotions rushed through his blood. Shane steeled himself. He had no right to feel this way. He was grateful that his back was to Elysee. He'd hate for her to read in his eyes what he struggled so hard to hide.

The pilot's voice came over the loudspeaker. "If everyone could take their seats, we'll be on our way."

Everyone was already sitting down except for Tish and Shane. And everyone was staring at them.

"Shane?"

He turned to take his seat beside Elysee. She crooked her finger at him. He leaned in.

"Why don't you take Tish to the back and get her settled in? I think she'll feel more comfortable back there. Go ahead and sit with her until we're airborne. She's probably feeling very embarrassed and could use some moral support from a familiar face."

Elysee's thoughtfulness was the thing he admired most about her. Honestly, he didn't deserve her. Not with the way these contradictory emotions were running through him.

"You're one hell of an understanding woman, Elysee Benedict," he said and gently chucked her under the chin. "You know that?"

She smiled sweetly. "I try. Now, shoo. Go on, so we can take off."

He escorted Tish to the back of *Air Force One*, found two empty seats side by side, stowed her camera in an overhead bin and then plunked down beside her.

Tish raised an eyebrow. "You're staying back here with me?"

"Elysee thought you could use the company."

"Hey," she said, "don't do me any favors. I don't need you. Go sit with your bride-to-be."

"You *are* pissed off at me."

"Oh please, stow your ego. I have better things to think about than you."

"Look, you've got a right to be upset. I know it's disconcerting to be tackled by six Secret Service agents."

"It was V-8 juice, for God's sake. What's the potential crime? Assault with a deadly beverage?"

"You've got to understand the Secret Service's position."

"If I could do that, we'd still be married."

She had a point. "You've got to understand. We're always waiting for an attack. On constant alert. Our adrenaline switch is always ramped to high. We're trained to react to danger with a hair-trigger response. They overreacted, sure. But they live and breathe for the President."

"And while you were guarding Elysee, you did all that for her?"

"Yes."

"I'm glad you weren't on protective detail when we were married."

"How come?"

"Heady stuff. I would have been fiercely jealous. No wonder Elysee is head over heels for you. All the macho, save-the-day stuff makes a girl feel tingly."

"I never made you feel tingly?"

Her eyes met his. "You seriously underestimate yourself, Tremont."

"So I do make you tingly?"

"Stop fishing for a compliment."

He grinned.

The plane taxied down the runway.

"Besides," she muttered under her breath, "it doesn't matter whether you make me feel tingly or not. You're with Elysee. There's no more tingly feelings allowed between you and me."

Now *he* was feeling tingly.

Think about something else.

But that was hard to do considering how good she smelled and how her quick-witted teasing was bringing back fond memories.

Take a deep breath. The feeling will pass.

"How's your friend Delaney?" he asked, desperate for something neutral to talk about, something that wouldn't stir unwanted feelings.

"She's fine. Got married."

"She and Evan?"

"Actually no, she married a cop."

"No kidding."

"He's very sexy."

"Sexier than me?"

"There you go again, fishing for a compliment. You'd think we were still married or something."

"We're not," he said hurriedly.

"No."

The plane thrust forward, leaving the runway. Glancing down, Shane noticed Tish was gripping the armrests with white-knuckled intensity as they became airborne. He remembered she hated flying.

"Do something to distract me from takeoff, will you?" She had her eyes squeezed shut.

He put a hand on her forearm and she let out a tight sigh. "We were such total opposites. It's little wonder our marriage didn't work."

"But the sex was good." She opened one eye to peer at him and looked so damned adorable his pulse skipped a beat. "Right?"

"It was great." God, why was he doing this to himself?

"Best you ever had?" Tish smirked.

"Now who's fishing for compliments?"

"I just want a ballpark figure. On a scale from one to ten, ten being the best you ever had. Where did I fall?"

"Eleven," he said without hesitation.

Tish lowered her voice. "Where does Elysee fall?"

Shane shot a guilty glance toward the front of the plane. Elysee was dictating something to Lola, who was taking notes on her BlackBerry. The airplane noises drowned out the sound of their conversation. "We haven't—"

"Done the deed?" Tish's grin turned impish.

"We're waiting. You know. To consummate."

"I find that hard to believe."

"Why's that?"

"I'm just saying celibate Shane doesn't sound like the Shane I knew."

"Things change. She's the President's daughter."

"And I was raised by Dixie Ann."

"That's not what I meant."

"I was really an eleven?" Her voice turned husky.

"No," he said. "I lied."

"Huh?"

"You were at least a twelve." He was getting in deep here. He should stop this and he knew it, but the smile on her face lit him up like hot chocolate on a cold winter day.

"Twelve is not on the scale."

"My point exactly. When it comes to sex, you're off the charts. No one can hold a candle to you."

"But when it comes to my money management skills, I've got a feeling I'm off the charts in the opposite direction. Say negative fifteen?"

"Let's not get into it. We've been down that road before with no resolution."

"Come on, admit it," she said. "Sex is the only reason we hooked up in the first place."

"You don't really believe that."

She cocked her head. "No? Then why were we together? If it was more than just sex, why didn't we fight harder for each other?"

Shane shifted in his seat and met her gaze. He felt a heavy, hollow feeling deep inside him. "What do you want me to say? Just tell me and I'll say it."

"I don't want you to say what I tell you to say. I want you to say what you really feel."

"I'm way past the point of understanding anything about what I feel where you're concerned," he admitted.

"At last, honesty. This is nice," she said. "That we can still tease each other, but it doesn't have to mean anything."

Her quick wit had always made him feel inadequate. She could out-quip him every time.

"Shane?" she said.

"Uh-huh?"

"You can let go of my hand now. We're at cruising altitude. That scared feeling I get on takeoff has passed."

He moved his hand away. His palm was hot and damp from holding hers.

"In fact," she murmured, "why don't you go back to Elysee? I'm sure she's wondering what's keeping you. What is keeping you?"

Her eyes met his and made him long for all the things he'd forgotten. How it felt to soap up her body when they showered together. How she could almost keep up with him when they ran in the park. How she was a terrible cook and how all her recipes had something to do with Ramen noodles.

There was so much he wanted to tell her. Express his regret over the way things ended. Apologize, maybe, somehow. But how could he do that? They were surrounded by Secret Service and generals and a senator.

And there were just no words. If words could fix what had gone wrong, he would have spoken them two years ago.

He would have saved his marriage.

Elysee Benedict felt sorry for Tish. She was such a nice person, but she seemed to make a habit out of doing the wrong thing. For instance, beyond the V-8 juice incident with her father, she had let a wonderful man like Shane slip through her fingers.

Not the ploy of a brilliant woman.

Elysee glanced over her shoulder at Shane and her

heart swelled with pride. He was so handsome and strong and brave. He'd laid his life on the line for her, taken a tremendous hit and she would be forever grateful.

Poor Tish.

Her gaze shifted to the other woman. Her color was pale and she looked to be on the verge of airsickness.

Poor, poor Tish.

She was proud of herself for sending Shane back to sit with her. She could afford to be generous. Shane belonged to her now. She felt a sense of pride and gave herself a mental pat on the back. It was the same way she felt after hosting a charity event or visiting sick children in the hospital. Or deciding to get involved with WorldFem and helping Rana get Alma Reddy out of India.

Poor, poor, poor Tish.

It had to be tough. Watching while her ex-husband married the President's daughter.

Had hiring Tish for the job actually been a cruel thing to do? She hadn't intended it that way. She'd just thought it was time she found out about Tish, time to force Shane to deal with any leftover baggage from his first marriage before he took fresh vows with her. Her plan had seemed simple enough at the time, but now she found herself questioning her wisdom.

Too late now. Tish is already here.

Doubt nibbled at her. She looked over her shoulder again—searching for reassurance that Tish was okay. Elysee hated seeing anyone in pain. But she didn't have to worry. Tish was leaning back in the seat with her eyes closed and Shane was making his way back toward her, a big, strapping smile on his face. He settled into his seat across from her, taking his rightful place, and all her fears vanished.

Everything was right in Elysee Benedict's world.

Chapter 13

Why don't you take Tish sightseeing around DC?" Elysee suggested to Shane after they'd arrived at the White House. She'd come into Shane's bedroom on the pretext of helping him unpack. She hung up the suits from his garment bag and turned back to look at him.

The truth was she was anxious to get to the bank, take the antique coins out of her safety-deposit box, and liquidate them without anyone finding out what she was doing. If Shane knew what she was up to Elysee feared he might try to talk her out of it.

Or worse, tell her father she'd gotten deeply involved in WorldFem.

Rana had called her before she left Texas and begged her to keep their endeavor as quiet as possible for Alma Reddy's safety. She would have to take Agent Ackerman to the bank with her of course, but she hoped she could convince him they didn't need a full entourage. Plus, she didn't have to let him know exactly why she was going to the bank.

"Is there a particular reason you keep throwing me together with my ex-wife?" Shane asked.

"Come on, being with her isn't that bad, is it?"

Shane swallowed. "No."

She could tell this was hard on him. Elysee crossed the room to slip both arms around his waist and looked up into his dark brown eyes. "I feel sorry for Tish. She's alone here, except for us, and far out of her element."

"Why don't we all three go sightseeing?" He smiled down at her, ran his finger over her forehead to push away an errant strand of hair.

"You know what a production that would be if I came along," Elysee said, worrying she might not be able to talk him into this.

"I'd rather just stay here with you."

"Come on, please? Do it for me."

"What are you going to do while we're gone?"

"You forget my aunt Jackie and uncle Felix are arriving soon. We're having dinner with them tonight. You want to be stuck with them all day, too?"

"Aunt Jackie with the purse dogs?"

"And Uncle Felix the draft-dodging hypochondriac."

"Gotcha. Sightseeing with Tish it is, then."

"You'll thank me later," she teased, glad she'd found an angle.

"We'll see about that."

"It's a kind thing you're doing. Good karma and all that. I know Tish will appreciate the company." Elysee went up on tiptoes to brush her lips against his. "Dinner's at seven; see you guys then."

She hurried out of the room, glad she'd gotten Shane squared away. Now to find Agent Ackerman and get on over to the bank before her relatives showed up.

Her pulse rate quickened and her palms grew slick with anticipation as she thought about helping Alma Reddy escape her assassins. She felt like a spy.

And for a quiet woman who never rocked the boat, it was an exhilarating sensation indeed.

The last thing Shane wanted was to take Tish sightseeing. Not because he didn't enjoy her company, but precisely because he did. He knocked at the door of the Lincoln bedroom where Tish was staying at Elysee's urging.

Tish flung the door open. She grabbed him by the lapel and tugged him over the threshold. "Look at this room. Look at this furniture. Presidents have touched it. Celebrities have slept in this bed. How can I sleep in this bed with so much history surrounding me?"

"You probably won't."

She took his hand and pulled him over to the stately desk. "Look, look, a copy of the Emancipation Proclamation under glass. It makes me feel so American!"

He chuckled at her wide-eyed enthusiasm, but he fully understood. He remembered the first day he'd come to the White House, wide-eyed, overwhelmed, and trying his damnedest to look cool.

"Omigosh, Shane, can you believe it? We're here! In the White House. In the infamous Lincoln bedroom. Pinch me. I must be dreaming."

"You're not dreaming, sweetheart. You're here. You held on to what you wanted, never giving up, even when I wasn't very supportive of your dreams, and now you've made it."

She looked at him with sudden sadness in her eyes. "You've made it, too."

"Yeah."

"Too bad we couldn't have made it together," she said.

"Too bad," he echoed. They looked at each other and his heart lurched sideways.

"Do you ever get used to it?" she asked.

"Get used to what?"

She waved her hands. "Being under the microscope. Being watched."

"I'm one of the ones doing the watching," he said. "Or at least I used to be."

"How's the role reversal working for you?"

"It's an adjustment," he admitted. "You get used to the feeling of being watched, but you never forget you're under scrutiny."

"It restricts you," she said. "Limits your freedom, your choices."

"Yes."

"Kind of ironic, huh?"

"Kind of," he agreed.

"We're being watched right now, aren't we?"

"Uh-huh."

She rubbed her upper arms with her hands as if she'd gotten a chill. He realized to his dismay she was still wearing that peepshow blouse of hers.

He tried not to look, but he couldn't help himself. His gaze tracked down the length of her long neck to lodge firmly in her cleavage.

God, she was stunning. Hot, sensuous, and curvy.

Stop thinking like this.

He cleared his throat. "I came to see if you'd like to go sightseeing."

"With you?" She arched an eyebrow.

"Yes. It's Elysee's idea. You've never been to DC and she's entertaining relatives from out of town. She thought you might be feeling out of place."

"Sure," she said. "I'd love to take a breather from the fishbowl. Just let me get my coat."

* * *

Shane had called her sweetheart.

Tish could think of little else, which was a bit surprising considering they were at the Smithsonian. It was probably just a slip of the tongue, she told herself. He didn't mean anything by it. She knew that, but it didn't matter. *Shane had called her "sweetheart."*

The museum was crowded and they found themselves jostled together. Shane's arm would brush against her shoulder or her hip would collide with his. It shouldn't have been any big deal, but she was acutely aware of every tiny bump and touch.

She kept sneaking glances over at him, trying to gauge whether their contact was having any effect on him, but the guy was a regular Mount Rushmore. Stoic self-control. At least when it came to his emotions.

Nothing rattled him.

In profile, in the museum lighting, he was as ruggedly handsome as ever. Maybe even more so. His craggy features had always appealed to her more than classic good looks. His chin jutted out in determination, his cheeks were high slabs of masculine dominance.

Delight shivered over her spine. *Stop it.*

"I would so have loved to come here with you when we were married. Think of all the dark alcoves we could have explored." She wriggled her eyebrows suggestively.

"There's security cameras everywhere."

"Oh yeah, like you're not a bit of an exhibitionist, Mr. Get-Naked-on-the-Galveston-Island-Ferry-in-a-Rainstorm."

He grinned. "That was a helluva night."

"Incredible," she agreed.

Then they both fell silent. She could tell that he was

thinking about the consequences of that night, just as she was.

She had to distract herself. “Let’s check out the photography exhibits.”

“It’s where I was headed all along.” He held up a map of the floor plans. “We’re almost there.”

A warm, sappy sensation settled in her bones. He’d been thinking of what she’d like to see. *Stop it, stop it.*

“Oops, watch out.” He reached out, grabbed her elbow, and tucked her against his side, pulling her clear of a pack of unruly preteens in school uniforms.

This close she could smell him. She halfway expected for his scent to have changed—gone all highbrow like his new lifestyle. But he smelled like he did when she was married to him. Soapy clean and serious.

The kids passed by.

Head reeling, Tish stepped away from him and darted toward a display of architectural photographs. “Look, pictures.”

Shane came to stand behind her. She was acutely aware of the heat of his presence.

“I love this one.” She cocked her head to study the black-and-white photo of an old village church resting pastorally on a bluff overlooking a turbulent sea.

“Explain to me why it’s so special,” he said.

“The composition is magnificent.”

“I just see an old church.”

Tish clicked her tongue and shook her head. “Look closer. The photographer has perfectly captured the peace of the church and contrasted it with the churning waters below, suggesting underlying turmoil.”

“Hmm.”

“You still don’t get it.”

"The church represents faith?"

"And the sea?"

"Rebirth?" he guessed.

She shook her head.

"What then?"

"Temptation."

He inhaled sharply. "If you say so."

"Here, look at the clouds." She pointed. "See, in this part of the sky they're white, fluffy, safe."

"Safe," he echoed.

"Exactly. While over here in this corner we have the dark, brooding clouds, gathering quickly, promising trouble."

"So what does it mean?"

"I'm not going to spoon-feed you. Come on, you can think this through."

"I had no idea pictures were so complicated," Shane groaned.

"Regular pictures aren't, but photographs good enough to hang on the wall of the Smithsonian? You betcha they're complicated."

"I'm beginning to understand you now."

"Me?" She swiveled to look at him. "What do you mean?"

"Why you're attracted to photography. What it is that you see when you look through the viewfinder of your camera." He placed a palm against the back of his neck.

"You're saying I'm complicated?"

"Understatement of the century."

She felt a pleased little flush run up her neck, but swiftly turned back to the picture so Shane couldn't read the telltale signs in her face. "Examine the colors."

"What colors? It's in black and white."

“I know, but pay attention to the grays. The gradations between light and dark.”

“Uh-huh.”

“Can you see the complementary play of brightness against shadows?”

He squinted, his gaze following her fingers as she traced the air in front of the framed photograph. “I think so.”

“Is it making more sense to you now?”

“Not really,” he confessed. “Over my head. I’m too literal.”

She sighed. What could she do to get through to him, to make him see? “Let’s try a different approach. What do you feel when you look at the picture?”

He stared for a moment, and then straightened. “This is too much pressure. Feels like the art appreciation class I took as a gimme credit in college and almost failed.”

“It’s not rocket science. Look at the picture and tell me what you feel.”

“I feel stuck.”

“Interesting. So what is it in this picture that makes you feel stuck?”

He chuffed in exasperation. “I dunno. Let’s see. No roads, no cars, no people. There’s nothing going on. Stuck.”

“Oh no, no, no. That’s where you’re dead wrong. There’s something very important going on.”

“What’s that?” He cocked his head, trying to look at it from a different angle.

“In this serene, bucolic scene, a fierce battle is being waged.”

“Between good and evil?” he ventured. “That light and the dark, faith and temptation stuff?”

“Nope.”

He threw his hands into the air. “I give up.”

"Between balance and chaos."

"Ookay, if you say so."

She laughed. "Maybe you are too literal."

He stepped closer to the photograph. "The sea is wild, untamable, shrouded in mystery. The church is stable, grounded, rooted in tradition. Together they're balanced. But one without the other, apart, it's chaos."

Her pulse skipped for no discernible reason. "Yes."

"Why do I feel a sudden need to pray?"

"That's something for you to figure out." Her hands were quivering and she clasped them together to keep him from noticing. He was standing over her, his breath warm against the nape of her neck. He wasn't touching her, but she could feel him like a brand on her skin. She inhaled the honest, masculine scent of him and her heart pounded.

How easy it would be to turn around, frame his face in her palms, and kiss him. How easy to fall blindly into chaos.

Do it. Touch him. Kiss him. Hold on to him.

Tish clutched her hands into fists, fighting off her impulses. *No, you can't.*

Donning every ounce of emotional armor she could muster, Tish bit down on her lip, tossed her head, and gathered all her willpower to slip weak-kneed away from him. She wasn't going to trust what felt easy when it came to Shane.

Not ever again.

While Shane and Tish were wandering around the Smithsonian, Cal Ackerman and Elysee were in the safety-deposit vault at Citibank.

"You want to explain to me what we're doing here?" Cal asked.

"I do not." Elysee tossed her hair. She couldn't put her finger on what it was, but something about Ackerman rubbed her the wrong way. He made her bristle in a way no one else ever had.

"If it concerns your security," he said, "I have a right to know."

"It doesn't." Elysee sent him a scathing look. Agent Ackerman was going to take some getting used to. He wasn't at all like Shane. He was bigger for one thing and he made her feel unsettled instead of safe the way Shane did. "Now mind your own business."

He glowered. "FYI, your safety is my only business."

"Do you have a problem with me, Agent Ackerman?" she said in the most haughty first daughter tone she could muster. "I could have you reassigned."

"Who, me?" He held up his palms.

"That's what I thought," she muttered and turned to the safety-deposit box the bank officer had carried over to the table for her.

She turned the key in the lock and flipped open the lid, revealing the box full of valuable coins.

"Holy shit, what'd you do? Rob Captain Jack Sparrow?" Ackerman breathed.

Elysee narrowed her eyes at him. "Not a word of this to anyone."

"What's the big deal?" Ackerman shrugged. "It's your money."

"Exactly."

"How much is there?"

"Again, none of your business."

"How come you're sassier with me than you are with other people?" he asked.

"You have a way of bringing out the worst in me."

"Looks like the best to me."

Elysee felt her face flush.

Ackerman was standing over her, eyes assessing the coins. "That's some valuable change you've got stowed there. Collector's items."

"How would you know?"

"I collected coins as a kid."

"You?" She arched an eyebrow.

"That so hard to believe?"

"Yes. You look like the guy who beat up the kids who collected coins."

"I didn't get my growth spurt until my senior year. Before that I was president of the geek squad."

"Charming story, I'm sure." She dumped the coins into the black leather bag she'd brought with her.

"Whoa," Ackerman said. "You're not just going to waltz out of here with over a hundred grand worth of change in your carryall."

"Why not? I've got a badass Secret Service agent as a bodyguard. Who'd be dumb enough to try to snatch it?"

He looked pleased that she'd called him a badass. "Thank you."

"I didn't mean it as a compliment." She wrinkled her nose at him. "Come on."

"Where are we going?"

She shot him a look. "Where would you guess?"

"Coin dealer?"

"Bravo. He's got an I.Q. Who knew?"

"And who knew you had such a smart mouth?"

I don't, Elysee thought. *Not normally.* But this swaggering tough guy set her teeth on edge. She was definitely going to have to talk to her father about having him reassigned.

Elysee stood up with the carryall. It was so heavy she couldn't hold her shoulder straight.

"Here." Ackerman reached for the bag. "Give it to me."

"I can carry it," she protested.

"Not without signaling to everyone who sees you walking out of the bank toting a black bag you can barely carry that you're a target."

"Please, I spend my life as a target." She reached for the bag.

He held it over his head where she couldn't get to it. The thing had to weigh at least thirty pounds and he was holding it like it was a bag of popcorn.

"Give it up," he said and pushed the buzzer for the bank officer to let them out of the vault.

Elysee seethed at his high-handedness. "You're a very infuriating man, you know that?"

"So I've been told."

"And arrogant."

"Been told that, too. If you're planning on insulting me you're going to have to do better than that."

"Ass."

"Princess."

"Jerk."

"Sweetheart."

"If I wasn't a lady..." She broke off her threat.

"Ah, but you are." He winked, took her elbow, and escorted her out of the vault.

Chapter 14

The engagement party held at the Ritz-Carlton was unlike anything Tish had ever attended. Lavish far beyond normal standards. Elaborate ice sculptures. Exotic flowers in leaded crystal vases on every table. Extraordinary cakes constructed by world-renowned bakers. The opulence stole Tish's breath away. She felt as if she'd stepped into a fairy tale.

If this was just the engagement party, what in the world would the wedding be like? The notion spun her head.

Elysee's secretary, Lola, escorted Tish into the room just ahead of the guests so she could find a prime spot for filming. No other video cameras were allowed in. After the party, Nathan Benedict planned to hold a press conference, officially announcing his daughter's engagement to the world.

Tish had an exclusive.

You got the exclusive only because you used to be married to the groom.

It didn't matter, she told herself. However she got the gig, she had it and her career was going to be made because of it. She owed Elysee a debt of gratitude.

I'm living my dream.

This was more than she could ever hope for. Yet, in spite of her excitement, an exquisite sadness seeped into her limbs, weighing her down, making the camera feel impossibly heavy. Yes, she was on top of the world career-wise. It didn't get any higher than this. After the wedding was over she would be one of the most renowned wedding videographers in the world.

Why, then, did she feel so blue?

A string quartet played chamber music as the guests filtered in. She thought of her mother and wished Dixie Ann was here to see this. After settling her camera on its tripod, she dug out her cell phone, found an unobtrusive spot in the corner, and placed a call.

"Dixie Ann," she whispered as soon as her mother answered the phone. Her mother didn't like to be called Mom. She always said it made her feel old. "You'll never guess where I'm calling you from."

"Tish, honey, is that you? I can hardly hear. What's that noise?"

"I'm at Elysee Benedict's engagement party."

"Elysee who?"

"Elysee Benedict. You know, the daughter of the President of the United States."

"No!"

"Yes."

"You're pulling my leg. Stop teasing me right now, Patricia Rhianne Gallagher."

"Swear to God, I'm not."

"How?"

"Elysee hired me to videotape both her engagement party and the wedding."

Dixie Ann squealed. "I'm so proud of you! That's wonderful. You deserve something good in your life."

"Thanks, Dixie Ann."

"Have you seen the President? He's nice-looking for an older man. And he's single. You're a pretty girl, Tish. You've got just as good a chance to hook him as the next gal. Are you wearing something nice? 'Cause you know nothing attracts—"

"Affluence like affluence, yes," Tish interrupted. "I know. You've told me over and over."

Dixie Ann said longingly, "Oh, I wish I could be there with you."

"I know. That's why I called."

"So who's there? What are they wearing? What food's being served? What's the music? Are any movie stars there?"

"Oops, sorry, Dixie Ann, I've gotta go. Shane just came in. I'll fill you in on all the details later."

"Shane? He's there?" The excitement in her mother's voice hit top pitch.

"He's here." Tish looked across the room at him and her heart was in her throat. He wore a black tuxedo, and when he entered the room, he took stock of his surroundings, surveying the entrances and exits, eyeing the crowd. Secret Service to the bone. Even with his damaged right hand tucked in his pocket, he looked imposing and dangerous. James Bond had nothing on him.

Seriously, you gotta stop drooling over your ex.

"Tish, this is wonderful, wonderful news. You're videotaping Elysee Benedict's engagement party and you and Shane are getting back together and—" Her mother's excited voice jerked her back to the cell phone conversation.

"No, Dixie Ann, you've got it all wrong. Shane and I are not getting back together."

"Oh." The sound of Dixie Ann's disappointment grabbed hold of Tish's gut and twisted. "Then what's he doing there?"

"He's getting engaged to Elysee Benedict."

A long silence ensued. Tish could hear the sound of her own heart beating in her ears.

"What did you say? There must be something wrong with your cell phone reception because I thought you said your Shane was marrying the President's daughter."

"I did. He is."

"Oh."

"Don't sound so surprised. We've been divorced for two years."

"But the President's daughter? How did that happen?"

"Long story. I gotta let you go. I have to catch all this on camera."

"Call me back later. I want to hear everything."

Tish hung up, pocketed her cell phone, and then picked up her camera from the tripod and started moving around the room, filming as she went.

Shane sauntered across the ballroom to where Elysee stood chatting with the Prime Minister of Israel. The human sea of tuxedos, designer labels, and expensive haircuts parted before him.

Tish raised the camera and zoomed in on his face. Something deep inside the most feminine part of her tightened.

Lust.

Pure and raw and wild.

And from the looks in the eyes of half the women in the room as they tracked Shane's journey toward Elysee, Tish wasn't the only one having lusty thoughts.

They all wanted him.

This man who had once belonged to her.

Misery winnowed inside her. Her feelings jerked her in two directions at once. Ecstatic one minute, despair the next. She shuttled back and forth so quickly she feared emotional whiplash.

Just do your job. Focus on your work. It's the only thing that will save you.

She knew the truth of it. Tish took a deep breath, calmed her mind, and became one with the camera.

Elysee smiled at Shane. He took her hand.

Tish moved in closer.

By the time the President entered the room a few minutes later she was nothing more than a camera lens. Seeing without feeling, capturing what was before her. A fly-on-the-wall view. Detached and professional. Using her camera to tell the story, her aim to bewitch the viewers. But she would not fall under the spell. She'd learned the hard way you couldn't trust happily ever after.

Elysee's hair was piled atop her head in an elegant, old-fashioned style and she wore a floor-length dress of lemon chiffon. The color made her appear prettier than usual, less washed out. She was a plain girl but a sweet one, and Tish did the best she could to capture Elysee's better features—her smile, her graceful walk, her straight white teeth.

She changed lenses, looking for the best filter, the right focus for the President's daughter. How ironic was this, presenting the competition in her best light?

But there was no competition.

Elysee, with her chaste innocence, had won. She'd known how to play a man like Shane. A valiant knight. A staunch defender who proved his worth by slaying the mightiest of all dragons—his independence, sexual hunger, and pride.

Tish had lost because she'd held nothing in reserve. She

loved too messily, gave too much of herself too soon only to have it all end wrongly. Her stomach took a nosedive.

Back behind the camera. Close off your mind. Just capture the moment. Don't think.

She recorded everything—waiters moving through the crowd with champagne on silver serving trays. The press secretary calling for everyone's attention. Then Shane presenting Elysee with a beautiful marquis-cut three-carat diamond engagement ring.

The camera couldn't blunt Tish's jealousy, but she swallowed it back and kept filming.

She captured the President making the announcement to the room of friends and supporters. His beautiful daughter was marrying her stalwart bodyguard. Nathan Benedict welcomed Shane into the family with a warm embrace and a hearty pat on the back.

Everything was committed to the camera.

The crowd lifted their glasses in unison and toasted the happy couple. Everyone loved a good fairytale romance.

Shane and Elysee kissed. Sweetly, romantically. The crowd applauded politely. So civilized.

"When's the wedding?" someone asked.

"Christmas Eve," Elysee sang out.

"Who's designing your gown?" asked someone else.

"Top secret." Elysee blushed prettily.

"How did you two hook up?"

Elysee slipped her arm around Shane's waist and gazed up at him. "He was my bodyguard."

"Shane, is your family here tonight?"

From across the room, his gaze met Tish's. His dark, familiar eyes were all she could focus on. "Unfortunately my parents couldn't be here. They're on a worldwide cruise for their fortieth anniversary."

That answer drew a collective "ah" from the crowd.

"Where will you honeymoon?"

"Fiji." Elysee beamed.

Tish filmed without evaluating, without filtering content. *Get everything on camera. You can worry about the effects when you edit.*

She circled the couple. Shane watched her from his peripheral vision. She was glad her eye was pressed to the lens of the camera. She preferred that view to looking at the monitor. With the monitor, you couldn't hide behind the equipment. The last thing she wanted was for Shane to catch a glimpse of her eyes and read something in her face that she couldn't disguise.

Tish filmed him watching her. Zeroing in on his inscrutable brown eyes, his expression revealed nothing.

When he saw what she was doing, he winked boldly for the camera. She recalled that when they were married, she had loved to take his picture, how he would protest and then just finally give in because she wouldn't stop pestering him until he did.

He was even more attractive now than he'd been when she'd met him three years ago. And he'd been pretty darned cute then. But now, he was heartbreakingly, impossibly handsome as the corner of his lips tipped up in his lopsided smile.

Something low and hot fluttered inside her. Something dangerous and subversive. It felt as if she were climbing a rickety ladder in a hurricane, destined for a fall. Enough pictures of the happy couple for now, she decided. It was time to scope out the crowd for interesting reactions to the engagement announcement.

Tish honed in on the dignitaries. Capturing VIPs from various countries all over the world—fraternizing together at the bar. Whispering gossip in corners. Kowtowing to the President with compliments and flattery. It was the photo-op of a lifetime.

The string quartet was playing a waltz and people started dancing. The French Ambassador spun the Vice President's wife across the ballroom. A Democratic senator from California cozied up with an NRA gun lobbyist. The prince of a small European country dazzled an up-and-coming starlet. Tish wasn't very political herself, but she knew good content when she saw it.

Elysee danced with Shane. His arm was around her waist. Tish thought of the dance they'd shared at Louie's and her throat went dry.

Halfway through the waltz, Elysee saw Rana Singh walk into the ballroom, an anxious frown furrowing her brow. She was dressed in an exquisite ruby red sari, but she looked decidedly out of place and uncomfortable with her surroundings. Elysee's former nanny kept casting nervous glances over her shoulder at the male foreign dignitaries in the room.

Elysee's pulse skipped. Could one of these men be responsible for putting the price on Rana's head? She stopped dancing.

"Is something wrong?" Shane asked.

She looked up at her husband-to-be and briefly thought about telling him what was going on. But Rana had sworn her to secrecy and she wasn't about to do anything that could jeopardize Alma Reddy's life.

"These shoes are killing my feet," she said. That wasn't a lie. Her feet did hurt. "Do you mind if we sit this one out?"

"Not at all. Where would you like to sit?"

Elysee peeked around his elbow to see Rana edging toward the back corner of the room. Their gazes met. The expression in Rana's eyes was urgent.

Hurry.

"Um, I'll find a spot." She smiled at him. "Could you get me some water?"

"Certainly."

The second Shane turned away, Elysee hurried over to Rana. "This way."

She led Rana to a shadowy corner of the outside patio where earlier, she'd stashed the cash she'd gotten from liquidating her grandmother's antique coin collection inside a safe made to look like a rock. After lifting the safe from a flowerbed filled with chrysanthemums, she spun the tumblers on the combination.

Rana kept glancing over her shoulder. "I'm so worried. The last thing I want is to put your life in jeopardy."

"Please, don't worry about me. I have around-the-clock bodyguards. See, Cal is standing right over there watching me as we speak."

"Anyone can be bribed for the right amount of money."

Elysee's eyes met Rana's. "They're that desperate to kill you?"

"You don't understand how much I threaten those small-minded tyrants."

"What you're doing is very brave and dangerous," Elysee said.

"No more than you." Rana's smile was tight, slight.

The combination to the rock safe yielded and Elysee took out the money. Furtively, she slipped it to Rana. The woman quickly stowed the cash into the folds of her sari.

"Bless you," Rana said and kissed Elysee on the cheek.

"With this gift, you may very well have saved Alma Reddy's life."

Suddenly, Tish felt hot and dizzy, claustrophobic. The camera weighed heavy in her arms. She had to get out of this room. Without even thinking to turn off her camera, she hurried from the room. She passed a Secret Service agent posted at the doorway and went in search of the ladies' room.

She swung the camera up onto her shoulder and opened a door where she believed the bathroom was located, but ended up outside on a patio. A few guests were there, taking in the fresh air, enjoying a quiet moment away from the crowd.

Rounding a cluster of potted ficus trees, she spied Lola talking in hushed tones to a man Tish didn't recognize. The setting looked intimate. Glasses of champagne rested on the table in front of them and they were leaning in toward each other. Lola's shoulder touched the stranger's.

That's when Tish saw the red Record light and realized the camera was still on.

Lola looked up at her, saw the camera, and frowned darkly. "Is that thing on? Turn that camera off. Right now."

Jeez, what was she getting so fired up about? Was the guy beside her married or something?

"No, no," Tish said. "It's not on."

"Don't video me, Tish. I don't like to be filmed." Lola prickled.

"I'm not filming you. I was looking for the bathroom and got lost."

"Go back inside the ballroom and out the second exit. The ladies' room is the first door on your right."

"Thanks, thanks." Tish nodded at the man, but he had

his face turned away from her. Hmm, she was getting the feeling the guy was definitely married.

For shame, Lola.

As Tish turned and hurried away, she heard Lola mutter to her paramour, "What a pathetic woman."

Shane couldn't find Elysee. Perhaps she'd gone upstairs to change her shoes. He stood in the middle of the room, water glass clutched in his hand, trying to spot his fiancée. Instead he saw Tish rush into the ballroom from the adjoining garden courtyard. He noticed as the Secret Service agent positioned at the door touched his earpiece and mouthed a coded message into the microphone.

Tish was under surveillance.

Shane sighed. What had she done now?

He set the glass of water down on a table and went after Tish. He saw Cal cruise by a bowl filled with matches engraved with the date of Shane and Elysee's engagement and stuff them in his pocket.

Shane stepped through the doorway, peered down the empty hall, and then stepped back to speak to Cal.

"I thought you stopped smoking," Shane said.

Cal shrugged. "Hard habit to break."

"Did you see which way my wife went?"

Cal arched an eyebrow, but otherwise kept his face noncommittal as he'd been trained. Grace under pressure was part of the Secret Service agents' code. "Your *wife*?"

It was only then Shane realized his Freudian slip. "I meant my ex-wife. Which way did she go?"

"Ladies' room."

"Thanks." Shane went down the corridor to the ladies' room and knocked on the door.

The attendant who'd been hired for the evening's even
poked her head from the lounge. "Yes, sir?"

"There's a redhead in there with a camera." He hande
the woman a ten-dollar bill. "Will you tell her I want t
see her, please?"

"Just a minute, sir." She shut the door.

Feeling awkward, Shane waited in the hall. Cal stoo
at the other end of the hallway, watching him. Shan
stuffed his hands in his pockets, turned his back, and trie
to appear nonchalant.

What the hell was he doing out here anyway? So Tis
was upset about something. What did he care? It was n
longer his job to look out for her. This was Elysee's bi
night. He should be at her side.

But he couldn't shake Tish off his mind. She'd bee
upset about something. He'd seen it in her face. And n
matter how he might wish things were otherwise, he sti
cared about her. Probably more than he should.

The door to the ladies' lounge opened again and Shan
straightened.

It wasn't Tish, but the attendant. "She doesn't want t
talk to you."

"Tell her I'm not going away until she does."

The attendant sighed, rolled her eyes, and let the doo
close between them.

A couple of seconds passed. The attendant returned
"Actually, I'm cleaning this up a bit, but she said for you t
buzz off back to your fiancée."

That made him mad. He knew what word Tish ha
used in place of "buzz." Shane glanced down at the woman's nametag. "Stand aside, Mattie, I'm going in."

"You can't do that." Mattie moved to block the door
"It's the ladies' room."

"I'm aware of that, but I'm going in anyway," he growled and glowered, giving her his full burly tough guy routine. "I'm Secret Service. Now step aside."

The look on his face must have said it all, because Mattie hurriedly stepped aside.

Shane stalked past the mirrored sitting room where a handful of women were applying makeup, brushing their hair, and gossiping. They gaped when they saw him. He blew past them, his shoes trodding heavily on the tile as he walked down the row of stalls. He was pissed off. "Tish," he said sternly. "Where are you?"

"Go away!" she hollered from the last stall on the left. In spite of the command, her voice sounded shaky.

"Come out here," he said. "We need to talk."

"Go back to Elysee. It's her big day."

"Exactly. So get out here. Let's get this over with so I can get back to her."

"Just leave me alone."

What in the hell was wrong with the woman? He turned slightly, glanced back the way he'd come and spied a clutch of women standing in the doorway, craning their necks, looking for a show.

"That's it," he said and pointed for the door. "Out, out, everyone out." He marched toward them, scowling and shooing them out with extravagant hand gestures. "You, too, Mattie. Go on, everybody mind your own business."

"Ooh, he's so manly." One woman giggled. "He could boss me around anytime."

"But this is his engagement party to Elysee and he's come into the bathroom after another woman." One of the women glared at him. "What's that all about?"

"It's the wedding videographer," interjected a third woman.

"I heard she's his ex-wife."

"Out!" Shane rumbled, pointing at the door.

Tittering, they left.

Once he made sure the ladies' lounge was empty, Shane dragged one of the heavy sitting room chairs in front of the door to block further interruptions. Then he went back after Tish.

"Open the door," he demanded.

"No."

"Tish, don't make me bust the door down. I'm not in the best shape of my life here."

"Please, Shane, just go away." Her voice sounded so vulnerable, it sliced him like a blade. Emotion clotted inside him—a dark viscous knot of anger and regret, helplessness and concern.

"Tish, open the door."

"What is with you and following me into bathrooms? Can't a girl get a little privacy when she needs it?"

"If you don't come out here and talk to me, I swear I'm kicking down this damned door."

"You wouldn't."

"I sure as hell would." No one could irritate him as much as Tish when she was being stubborn.

"What would Elysee think? Directing so much passion toward me when you're marrying her?"

"It's not passion, dammit!" he yelled.

"You're yelling and threatening to break down doors. Sounds like passion to me."

"Okay, if that's the way you want to play it. Who cares what upset you? I'm leaving."

"Good."

"Fine."

"Good-bye."

"So long."

"I don't hear your feet carrying you off in the opposite direction," she said.

Shane fisted his good hand, shifted his weight. This was idiotic. He was arguing with a bathroom stall door.

"Patricia Rhianne"—he almost said *Tremont*, but managed to bite off the word before it came out of his mouth—"Gallagher, get out here this minute."

What was he going to do if she didn't come out? Shane had made such a big deal out of this he couldn't just walk away, although it was the sensible thing to do. Just walk away, go back to the party, back to his sweet-tempered Elysee, back to the new life he was forging for himself. But when it came to Tish, when had he ever taken the sensible route?

To his amazement, the stall door swung slowly inward and Tish peeked out at him, her eyes red-rimmed.

Tish? Crying?

Shane had only seen her cry once, and that was when... He bit down on the inside of his cheek at the rush of raw, hot emotion that suddenly filled the back of his throat.

"Have you been crying?"

"No," she denied viciously. "I had something in my eye. That's why I rushed into the bathroom. Happy now?"

"Sweetheart." Instinctively he reached for her, with his raw, scarred hand. "Tell me the truth. What's really wrong?"

Tish shrank back from him. "Don't you dare touch me, Shane Tremont. And don't you dare call me 'sweetheart.'"

He retracted his hand, understanding he'd started across a line that he couldn't cross. "I just want to help," he said, and helplessly let his arm drop to his side.

"Why?" She glared at him and her breasts rose sharply as she drew in a deep breath of air.

Tish had always asked hard questions of him. She made him think, often goading him into reconsidering his positions. She challenged him to examine his values and beliefs.

In the beginning of their relationship, he'd loved that about her. Toward the end, it had driven him crazy. She could never leave well enough alone. Always prodding, digging, wanting more answers than he had to give.

"Because I care."

"If you cared, why did you leave me?"

"You know why I left."

"I needed you and you abandoned me, you asshole."

Shane winced as her words struck him like a stunning blow. She was right and his failure ate at him. She didn't deserve this.

"What can I do to make it better, if you won't tell me why you were crying? Is it me? Is it Elysee? Is it the engagement? Is it too much for you to handle? Do you want out of the job?"

"I was *not* crying." She enunciated the words slowly, injecting her sarcasm. "I don't cry. It's not something I do. Got it?"

He watched the emotions play across her face. Anger sparked in her eyes, tightened her jaw. Frustration furrowed her brow, sadness dragged down the corners of her mouth.

She looked haunted.

"So what is it? Just tell me."

"Johnny," she said. "I was thinking about Johnny. Happy now?"

He couldn't believe she said it. He stared at her, his heart constricting in his chest, unable to believe she'd uttered their dead baby's name.

* * *

Until that very moment, Tish hadn't been thinking about Johnny. She'd spent the last two years learning how to bury that hurt so deep she couldn't find it. Hiding it under clothes she didn't need and shoes that were criminally expensive, disguising it with ice cream, locking it away in the attic of her mind along with those tiny little baby things.

But then Shane had insinuated she was pining over him, that she was jealous of Elysee, that she couldn't handle the stress of videotaping their precious wedding. And she'd just gotten mad. She was determined not to let him know she'd been tearing up over him and their shattered marriage. So she said what she knew would stop him in his tracks.

Once the name of their dead son had been uttered, the past jumped up and slapped hard against her.

Chapter 15

Tish was in labor, but it was too soon. Two and a half months early. Something was very wrong. She knew it deep inside her. Her baby was in serious trouble and there was nothing she could do about it.

And she was all alone. Shane, the bold, strong Secret Service agent who she'd thought would always protect her, no matter what, was out of town on an undercover assignment.

"Help me," she cried to the doctor. "You've got to help me. Help my baby. Something's wrong with my baby."

Please, God, don't let the baby die.

The doctor, with his green scrubs, chubby cheeks, and coffee-colored skin, stared at the monitor. Then he looked at her. He was a professional. He knew how to hide his feelings, but for one brief second, she saw both fear and pity in his eyes.

And in that awful moment, Tish knew the dream was over. Nothing would ever be the same again.

The wonderful, romantic fantasy that began that night in Louie's nightclub, the night Shane sauntered into her life and swept her off her feet, was shattered. The magic vanished. Shane couldn't protect her from this. She didn't believe in miracles anymore.

It was over.

"Is there someone I can call for you?" the doctor asked.

"My husband," she said. "Call Shane." When he got there everything would be all right. He would make it all right. Shane had that kind of power.

Dread, more powerful than anything she'd ever experienced before, took hold of her as a disabling contraction twisted through her body, mangling her womb.

"The baby," she gasped and grabbed the doctor's arm. "What's happening to my baby?"

The doctor didn't answer. He pulled away from her. Called to the nurses. The room filled with medical personnel. They were doing things to her, prepping her, hustling her down the hallway to the operating room.

C-section.

Before, she'd feared the word. Terrified at the thought of being cut open. Thinking she would be less of a woman if she couldn't give birth the "real" way. But now, all she could think was Yes, yes, yes. Cut me open, get him out. Save my son.

They placed a mask over her face. Told her to count backward from a hundred. The room was cold, sterile, lonely. She was scared. So scared.

Shane, where are you when I need you most? Shane. Shane!

"We've lost the fetal heartbeat," she heard a tense-voiced nurse call out.

Save my baby!

Where's Shane? She needed Shane. She could not do this alone.

"Shane!"

Then the world blurred, her eyelids sank closed, and she was gone.

Shane laid a hand on Tish's forearm. A gesture of sympathy. She stiffened beneath the weight of it. She didn't want his pity. Didn't want to see the regret in his eyes. He'd screwed up. She wasn't going to make it easy for him.

"I don't need you," she said. "Not anymore. You belong to Elysee. Leave me alone."

He looked hurt. Good. He'd hurt her plenty; now it was his turn.

Tish shrugged off his hand, turned and headed for the exit. Stepping carefully so that she didn't falter. Didn't stumble and give away what she was truly feeling.

But when she reached the door, she found a chair blocking her exit. She leaned over to push it aside, but Shane was already there. His hand brushed against hers as he shoved the chair away from the door.

Adrenaline rushed through her blood, strummed her nerve endings, shoved her senses into overdrive. The familiar feeling of heat and excitement she'd always associated with Shane filled her.

But there was more. She felt something different. Something starkly fresh and unexpected.

Danger.

The hairs on her arms lifted.

What was this? How could being with Shane suddenly feel dangerous and new?

She knew him so well. The texture of his hair. The sound of his throaty voice. The smell of his Shane-y scent. The way he phrased his sentences. How he preferred his eggs sunnyside up and liked the crust cut off his bread.

She knew what motivated him. What thrilled him. What turned him off. She knew how to push his buttons, how to provoke his anger. She also knew what words soothed him. How to appeal to his highly honed sense of honor and integrity.

So why this sense of danger?

Because it was taboo. Being alone in the ladies' room with a man who was engaged to someone else. And not just any someone else, but the President's daughter.

She wasn't the only one feeling this forbidden sensation.

Shane's Secret Service training might have taught him how to hide what he was thinking, but he couldn't fool her. His arousal strained at the zipper of his tuxedo pants.

For a breath-stealing second, she had an almost irresistible urge to reach out and touch him where it would affect him the most. She ached to feel the hard outlines of his male body pressed against hers just one more time.

Heat swamped her.

A purely physical response. She had an overwhelming urge to kiss him. Never mind that he was engaged to Elysee. *She* was the one who did this to his body.

Chemistry.

They still had it. Apparently, not even divorce could destroy it.

Tish raised her eyes to meet his.

They stared at each other.

From the chagrined expression on his face, she recognized that he knew she'd seen his acute reaction to the simple brushing of their hands.

"Don't worry," she whispered. "Your secret's safe with me."

Then without giving him an opportunity to respond,

she pushed through the door and rushed out into the corridor. Her heart pounded erratically, her palms sweaty.

Shane wanted her!

It doesn't mean anything. He's engaged to Elysee. He's not the kind of guy who cheats. His body just reacted. History, chemistry. It doesn't mean anything.

But she could still make him hard.

Tish suppressed a grin and forced herself to amble back into the ballroom, past the stern-faced Secret Service agents.

"Tish!" She glanced over to see Elysee waving at her from across the room.

Ho, boy. Feeling like a traitor, Tish hitched in her breath and went over.

"Have you seen Shane?" Elysee asked.

"He was in the hallway earlier."

Not a lie. Okay, so it wasn't the complete truth either, but there was no sense hurting Elysee with the details of what had transpired in the ladies' lounge.

"Where's your camera?"

Instinctively, Tish's hand went to her shoulder, but she'd already realized the familiar weight was missing. Oh gosh, she must have left it in the bathroom stall, forgotten because she was too preoccupied with Shane. Leaving her camera behind was equivalent to a first-time mother forgetting her newborn infant in the backseat of a car.

Panic smacked against her rib cage. She spun away, running back toward the bathroom.

Please let it still be there.

She crashed into Shane's chest just as he was coming into the ballroom.

His hands went up to grasp both her shoulders. "Whoa. Slow down."

"Let go." She tried to pull away from him but he held on.

Anxiety mingled with attraction. Fear dueled it out with chemistry. He was the reason she'd forgotten her camera in the first place. His fault.

"What is wrong with you, woman?" he growled.

"My camera."

"What about it?"

"I left it in the bathroom."

He let go of her then, followed her back into the hallway. Tish was barely aware that Elysee was behind them. There were several people in the corridor and they were all staring at her.

Tish clambered through into the bathroom, heels snapping against the tile as she hurried to the last stall on the left, shoved the door open and stuck her head inside. Her eyes went to the purse hook where she'd hung her camera bag.

When she saw the empty space, her heart dropped into her shoes.

While she'd been foolishly getting sexually charged up over her ex-husband, her camera—the most precious thing she owned—had been stolen.

The look on Tish's face was a knife to Shane's gut. He knew how important the camera was to her. Not only because it was the tool of her trade, but because behind it was the only place she felt truly safe in the world.

On the outside she presented a bubbly, optimistic, free-spirited front. She even had herself convinced she was an outgoing extravert who loved fast-paced activities.

But Shane knew better.

When things got too rough and the world got too fast,

she would retreat behind her camera. Even during their marriage, when he would try to pull her into his arms and give her the safety and security she'd never had growing up, she hadn't really been able to accept it. Oftentimes in the middle of cuddling, she would slide off the bed, pick up her camera, and start filming him. As if what she saw through the viewfinder was her only avenue to real intimacy.

It had irritated him to no end. During their marriage, what she hadn't seemed to understand was that for Shane, the camera was a barrier to their intimacy, not a conduit. She always had a camera with her, no matter where they went. She had never really let him into her life at all, he realized with a start. She always kept him a camera's width away.

"Oh, Tish," Elysee exclaimed. "This is awful."

It was only when she spoke that Shane even remembered his fiancée was standing behind him. He turned his head toward Elysee, saw four Secret Service agents clumped up in the ladies' lounge beside her. A group of curious onlookers craned their necks behind Elysee's wall of bodyguards.

Tish started humming.

Uh-oh.

Shane flashed a glance at his ex-wife and her pallor confirmed his fear. He understood her, and that understanding scared the hell out of him. Tish was teetering on the verge of cracking up. She'd been under tremendous stress and having her expensive camera stolen was the last straw.

And he was at fault.

He had followed her into the ladies' room earlier, pressured her into talking to him, stirred the old sexual chemistry between them, and caused her to forget her camera.

A memory flashed in Shane's mind.

He remembered coming home one day to find Tish in the nursery. Surrounded by sacks and packages and boxes of brand-new baby things—clothing and bassinets, diapers and bibs, stuffed animals and picture books. She was humming a lullaby and putting away the things she'd bought, a dreamy smile on her face as she swayed gracefully.

A mother getting ready for her new infant.

Just one problem. It was after they'd lost Johnny.

Whenever she hummed like that it scared the living shit out of Shane and he knew of only one way to stop it. He had to get that camera back.

Sir Galahad to the rescue again, eh? It didn't work before, what makes you think it'll work now?

He didn't have an answer. He just didn't know what else to do. It had only been a few minutes. Whoever had stolen the camera couldn't have gotten far.

"Get to the exits," he barked to the Secret Service agents. "Don't let anyone leave the floor until we've found that camera."

"Shane?" Elysee raised a hand to her throat. "We've got guests. VIPs. Dignitaries. We can't ruffle political feathers, but we can buy Tish a new camera."

Elysee didn't get it and he didn't have time to explain.

"Come with me," he said to Cal. "We're searching the rooms in this wing. Elysee, go back to the ballroom and make some politically correct excuse why the guests can't leave yet."

Everyone jumped to obey him.

Tish stopped humming. A good sign.

He and Cal tore down the corridor. Cal took the rooms on the left side of the hall, Shane the ones to the right. He wrenched open the door to a conference room, did a quick search. Nothing seemed disturbed.

He tried the next room, then the next.

In the fourth room, he found what he was looking for. The French doors leading out into the courtyard stood ajar.

Shane rushed into the courtyard just in time to see a shadowy figure sprint across the lawn. Instinctively, his wounded hand reached for the shoulder holster that wasn't there. God, he wished he had his gun. He felt naked without it. Just as Tish must feel without her camera.

"Stop!" he called out. The thief didn't know he didn't have a weapon. "Secret Service!"

The culprit kept running.

Shane swore under his breath and took off at a dead sprint. But the thief had too much of a head start and Shane just couldn't keep up. His lungs throbbed, sending sharp pulses of pain shooting through his chest. He'd become sadly out of shape since his accident.

The thief broke through the privacy hedges to the street beyond. By the time Shane got there, he was out of breath. He stood a moment in the darkness, heaving in air, body quivering, wondering how he was going to break the news to Tish that her camera was gone.

Then he spied the camera bag lying in the dirt underneath the Japanese boxwoods.

Feeling like a conquering hero, he shrugged off the pain and made his way back to the party with the bag. He slipped inside to find Elysee holding court, Tish sitting quietly beside her.

The minute Tish spotted him she was on her feet, her eyes wide, overjoyed to see her bag.

"You found it!" she breathed and reached out to take the camera bag like it was her long-lost baby. She clutched it to her chest for a moment, then unzipped it and took the camera out.

"Is it okay?" Shane asked.

Elysee came over and slipped an arm around his waist. "Are you all right, Tish?"

Tish shook her head. "I'm fine," she said. "But whoever stole the camera took the disk."

Thanks to Shane, Tish had her camera back. Everything was going to be okay.

"I don't understand. Why would the thief leave an expensive camera like this, but steal the disk?" Elysee asked.

"They weren't after the camera," Shane said.

"Who'd go to such lengths for a disk of our engagement party?" Elysee wrinkled her nose in confusion.

"Tabloids," Tish said. "They'll pay millions for exclusive shots of the first daughter's engagement party."

"Oh, no." Elysee groaned, crossed her palms and pressed them against her heart. "I hadn't thought about that."

Tish felt instantly protective of her. "It's okay."

"No it's not." Elysee shook her head. "It's going to be a nightmare for security and..."

"Fear not." Tish grinned and dipped her hand into the pocket of her dress, pulling out a compact camera disk.

"Is that what I think it is?" Elysee breathed.

"Yep. I'd just changed out the disk before the camera went missing. I've got your engagement party pictures right here. You're safe."

"I'm not sure I trust her," Lola Zachary said to Elysee after the engagement party, when they were alone in Elysee's bedroom at the White House.

Elysee wasn't really listening to Lola. She was thinking about Shane. She'd wanted to spend some quiet time with him after the party—maybe kissing in the garden under the full moon. They hadn't spent nearly enough time kissing, but protocol and circumstances had reared their heads. All she'd gotten from him that night was a chaste kiss.

While she liked the excitement of waiting until their wedding night to have sex, the lack of physical contact with him was starting to get to her. They were engaged, after all. Nothing wrong with letting him get to third base. She imagined Shane's hand sliding up her thigh, disappearing under the hem of her skirt, and her face heated.

"Did you hear me?" Lola asked.

"Huh?" Elysee blinked.

"You shouldn't trust her."

"Trust who?" Elysee unzipped her dress and stepped out of it.

"Tish Gallagher." Lola held out her hand for the garment. Elysee scooped it off the floor and passed it to her.

"What do you mean? Tish is great. She saved the engagement party. If she hadn't changed that disk when she did the photographs could be all over the Internet by now."

"Please, Elysee, you are so naïve." Shaking her head, Lola went to the closet, plucked a wooden hanger from the rack and hung up Elysee's dress. "Sometimes I can't believe you're really Nathan's daughter. Your father has been in politics all of your life. Hasn't that taught you anything about human nature?"

Lola was always so serious. Sometimes, Elysee wished she'd either lighten up or shut up.

"What are you saying?"

"Tish is Shane's ex-wife."

"And?"

"There's a possibility she could be trying to sabotage you. I mean, think about it: what professional photographer leaves her camera bag in the bathroom? Those cameras are heavy. Wouldn't you notice there's no big heavy camera bag hanging off your shoulder when you left the ladies' room?" Lola relished being the voice of doom and gloom. She was an excellent personal assistant, but sometimes her negativity grated on Elysee's nerves.

"Don't you think if Tish were trying to sabotage my engagement to Shane that she wouldn't have told me she'd changed the disk? That she would have sold them to the tabloids herself and probably made a lot more money than what she's getting paid to put together the wedding video?" Elysee asked.

"Not if she felt guilty and decided at the last minute not to go through with her scheme."

"You make her sound so Machiavellian."

Lola arched an eyebrow. "Maybe she is."

"You have a tendency to look on the dark side of life," Elysee chided, plunking down at the vanity and reaching for the cold cream to remove her makeup.

"Sometimes you're such a child."

Elysee bristled and sat up straight. It took a lot to ruffle her feathers, but calling her childish was one way to do it. She worked so hard to be grown-up, especially since she'd been thrust into the role of her father's companion on the political trail after her mother passed away. To be thought childish was her Achilles' heel and Lola knew it.

"I'll thank you to leave me for the night," she said coldly. "And I don't want to hear another word against Tish."

"But…"

"Not another word." Elysee raised a cold-cream slathered hand. "Understand?" Her assistant gritted her teeth so loudly she could hear her from across the room.

"As you wish." Lola hurried for the door, head down. As she passed by the vanity, Elysee heard her mutter, "It's your funeral."

Lola's words ended up poisoning Elysee's sleep.

Could her assistant be right? Was she being foolish by assuming that Tish cared only about producing a great video and launching her career? Did Shane's ex-wife still have romantic feelings for him?

More important, did Shane still have feelings for Tish?

The thought struck terror in her heart. Damn Lola anyway, for making her doubt the only man, other than her father, that Elysee had never doubted.

Disturbed by the direction of her thoughts, Elysee forced her mind onto other things. She thought about Rana Singh and what Rana had told her about Alma Reddy's journey to America. Alma would arrive in Houston via a cargo freighter through the gulf shipping channel. Elysee had promised to offer safe harbor at the ranch until Alma and her husband could be reunited.

Ah, romantic love.

She sighed, the thought bringing her restless mind back to Shane. She tossed the covers aside and crept out of bed. She knew of only one way to put a stop to these gnawing concerns. She needed to have a serious talk with him. He was her fiancé. They shouldn't keep secrets from each other.

After donning her bathrobe over her pajamas, Elysee stepped from the bedroom and padded past the sentinel posted at her door. Cal Ackerman was reading a J.D. Robb novel.

Elysee missed having Shane as her bodyguard. She recalled other nights when she'd had trouble falling asleep. How he would play chess or watch a silly movie with her until she got drowsy. She thought about how he'd listened while she chattered on and on about her trivial concerns. How he'd often gone down to the White House kitchen and brought back warm milk and chocolate chip cookies for her, just like her mother used to do when she was a little girl.

Sometimes, if she begged him long enough, he would show her things he'd learned in the military and Secret Service training. Self-defense techniques and methods of disabling opponents. She liked those lessons most of all, and yet those had been the ones he'd been most reluctant to teach her.

Affection for Shane rushed through her, filling her chest with a warm tightness of emotion. He was such a good man. A real hero. A great friend. Could anyone really blame Tish for still being in love with him?

The thought brought a stab of fear, draining the joy from her heart. Had she indeed made a grave mistake in hiring Tish? Was she, as Lola contended, ridiculously naïve?

"Need something?" Cal asked, resting his open paperback on his knee. His sharp eyes met hers.

Elysee shook her head. "Go back to your book."

"Where you headed?" He closed the novel, set it on the small hallway table beside him, and got to his feet.

She hated this part of being the President's daughter. Zero privacy. She jerked a thumb in the direction of the room where Shane was staying.

"Shane's not in his room," Cal said. She noticed then that his gaze had strayed to where her breasts curved beneath her pajama top. A strange thrill of excitement raced through her. Shane had never looked at her with such frank sexual interest.

Doubt squeezed her hard. Suddenly, her stomach rolled queasily. Elysee raised a hand to her mouth. Could he be with Tish? "He's not?"

"No."

"Do you know where he is?"

"I think he and your father are discussing security for your wedding." Cal's gaze locked on hers, he settled his hands on his hips. He was not a particularly handsome man, but he was potently male. He was taller even than Shane and a few pounds heavier. All muscle and edge.

Nervously, Elysee looked away and wet her lips with her tongue. "But he shouldn't be up this late. It's after midnight. He's still recovering from his injury."

"Once a bodyguard, always a bodyguard." Cal shrugged as if it explained everything.

That notion made her feel better. Of course Shane was talking to her father about security matters. Nothing meant more to him than her safety. He was her hero. She had absolutely nothing to worry about, unless she wanted to fret about the bizarre warmth that suddenly heated her stomach whenever she met Cal's eyes.

This was ridiculous. She was imagining things. She was engaged to Shane. She wouldn't attach a meaning to a momentary exchange of meaningful glances with her new bodyguard. She was engaged to Shane and he would take care of her, no matter what. He was the man her mother had promised would come into her life. Elysee was certain he was The One.

But how can you be absolutely sure?

Especially when Cal kept staring at her like she was a

birthday cake. *He's not. You're reading something into his look that isn't there. You're just getting cold feet, like you did with the other three guys. The problem isn't Shane, or the way Cal is looking at you, or even Tish. It's your own fear that you've made the wrong choice.*

Again.

"You want me to call Shane?" Cal reached for the two-way radio clipped to his belt. She noticed how his large fingers skimmed over the smooth, black leather. "Tell him you're looking for him?"

Elysee could go find Shane and ask him about his feelings for Tish. Or she could accept things at face value and go back to bed. Shane had asked her to marry him. They'd officially announced their engagement. She twirled his engagement ring on her finger. It was the prettiest engagement ring she'd ever gotten.

He loved her.

She loved him.

There was no need to talk about the past. It was over. The future lay ahead of them. What was the point of cornering him for an answer? Did she really want to know the truth? What would she do if Shane told her he still had feelings for Tish? Would she fire Tish? Would she let Shane out of the engagement? Elysee nibbled a fingernail.

And then there was the flip side. If Shane assured her that he felt nothing for his ex-wife, could she believe him?

There was a catch-22 between truth and ignorance.

Elysee shook her head at Cal. "No, no, don't call him."

Turning, she went back to bed, making the conscious decision to embrace ignorance.

And forget all about the sultry look she'd just seen in Cal Ackerman's eyes.

Chapter 16

The first thing Tish did when she got back to Houston on Sunday evening was make two copies of the engagement party disk. Tomorrow, she promised herself, she would give one to Elysee, keep one for herself, and lock the original up in her safety-deposit box.

After nearly losing her camera to a thief, she wasn't taking any chances. This job was the only thing she had left. She wasn't about to screw it up. She could only give thanks she'd changed the disk before the camera had been stolen.

The second thing she did was quickly review the engagement party video before breaking it down frame by frame. Sitting in her office, staring at the screen, watching Shane and Elysee announce their engagement, seeing Shane give her the ring, just broke Tish's heart.

When Shane touched the small of Elysee's back, Tish felt the warmth of his hand against her own back and recalled the way he'd held her when they'd danced at Louie's. Such a small thing. Why did it feel like such a big deal?

Because his hand—his poor damaged hand that had

once been whole, had once belonged to her—was now resting against another woman's back.

Betrayal, hot and salty, rose in her throat strong as brine. Why did she feel betrayed? They'd been divorced for two years. She had no right to feel this way.

Tish sat cross-legged on the floor, heart thumping, eyes filled with tears. She had to get these thoughts out of her head, couldn't stand the pain of them one second longer.

Forlornly, she drew her knees against her chest and fought back the tears that threatened to roll down her cheeks. She'd lost so much, but she refused to cry. She was tough. She was strong. Somehow, she would get through this.

In that moment, she turned where she'd always turned when she no longer had Shane to turn to. Hand trembling, she picked up the phone and dialed Delaney's number.

"I'm back from Washington," Tish said the minute her friend answered the phone. "It's official, Shane's engaged to the President's daughter. It'll be in all the newspapers and on the television news tomorrow."

"I'm coming over right now. What flavor of ice cream should I bring?"

In the background, she heard Delaney's husband, Nick, calling out to her, "Who's phoning this late? Tell them to get some sleep and call back in the morning. Come back to bed, Rosy." Rosy was Nick's pet name for Delaney because when they'd first met, she'd blushed so much.

Guilt took hold of her. She was being too needy and inconsiderate of her friend's new life. No matter how close they were, she couldn't expect Delaney to drop everything and come running whenever she slammed up against a painful memory. Delaney was married now, with a husband of her own to consider. Tish should be respectful of that.

"It's okay," she said, forcing false joviality into her voice, "I don't need any ice cream. But thanks."

"Are you sure?" Delaney sounded bewildered.

"Sure, I'm sure."

"Wow."

"Wow, what?"

"You really must be over Shane."

"Yeah," she murmured. "I guess I've finally come to grips with the fact he's moved on."

"That's terrific," Delaney said, sounding dubious.

"Seriously, I'm okay. You don't need to come over and hold my hand."

"Really?"

"Yeah."

The calmness inside her didn't feel faked. She was comfortable. Safe. Secure. She'd screwed up by leaving the camera bag in the bathroom at the Ritz-Carlton, but in the end, she'd triumphed. She'd saved the engagement party video.

That's all that mattered. She didn't want him thinking his impending marriage to Elysee would destroy her.

"I'm happy for you," Delaney said. "But are you absolutely certain you don't need me to come over?"

"Nope, I'm fine."

"Truly?"

"Delaney..."

"It's just that I know you. Even if you don't admit it to yourself, deep in your heart you always hoped that you and Shane would eventually get back together."

"I've come to terms with the fact that's not going to happen," she said, proud of herself that she was able to say it without falling apart.

"You've made amazing progress," Delaney praised. "I

must admit, I was really worried when I heard you were going to be filming Shane and Elysee Benedict's wedding, but I guess this will give you the closure you need to move on."

"Yep." She was feeling fine. Really she was. But maybe it would be a good idea to get off the phone before other emotions bubbled up. "Just wanted to let you know I'm back from DC and everything's fine."

"Thanks for calling. Sleep well."

"You, too." Tish hung up the phone feeling that her last lifeline had just been severed.

Shane lay in his bed at the Benedict ranch staring up at the ceiling, feeling as if he didn't belong. In this place, in the dead of night, he was lonelier than he'd ever been in his life.

As a bodyguard, insomnia came with the territory. It was difficult to sleep when your job required vigilance. But he wasn't a bodyguard anymore. He didn't know what he was. He was Tish's ex-husband, Elysee's fiancé. But who was he deep down inside?

Shane didn't know anymore.

Uncertainty had never been an issue for him until he'd been injured, but now it haunted his every waking hour. He thought of his father. He could hear Ben Tremont's voice in his head saying, *"Self-doubt is a weakness."*

But wasn't supreme self-confidence just as bad as self-doubt? If you didn't have some doubt when you were on the wrong path, weren't you cutting off that inner self who knew what was right? Arrogance was a weakness, too. And in the past, he'd been guilty of it.

Maybe that was what he was supposed to learn from the accident. That it was okay to be unsure. That uncertainty could bring you back into balance if you didn't fight it. He'd been out of balance for so long. Was he too far gone now to find his way back?

Anxiety pushed him to a sitting position. Shane switched on the lamp beside the bed, held up his hand in front of him, searching for answers in the ribbon of red scars crisscrossing his palm. He tried to mime pulling a trigger, but his fingers would barely move. Weeks of physical therapy and he hadn't progressed any further than this?

How long before he could fire a gun again? Would he ever be able to fire a gun again?

That was the million-dollar question. If he couldn't fire a gun, how could he be a bodyguard? And if he wasn't a bodyguard, who was he? His questions brought him full circle without any answers.

A sensation of claustrophobia gripped him the way it had the night he went to Louie's. He felt as if he couldn't breathe, as if the walls were closing in.

And on the heels of that feeling came another feeling. It started in the pit of his gut and dug in deep, spreading throughout his body. It was a feeling he'd honed and cultivated as a Secret Service agent. The instinct that told him something bad was about to happen.

No matter how he tossed and turned and tried to ignore it, he couldn't help thinking that something bad was going to happen to Tish.

In his head, he replayed what had gone down at the DC Ritz-Carlton. What if whoever had snatched Tish's camera hadn't been a tabloid journalist as they'd assumed? What if it had been someone with a far darker purpose?

But what purpose could that be?

Shane didn't know, but the worrisome feeling in his

gut wasn't dying down. He had to check this out. He flung back the covers, jumped out of bed. He dressed and then quietly, secretively, as only a good agent could do, he slipped from the ranch house without being detected. Leaving the property wasn't as easy. He had to start his SUV, head down the only access road, get security to open the gate and let him out.

Truth was Shane just had to get off the ranch. He had to check on Tish and make sure she was okay.

Why don't you just call her?

In the middle of the night? And say what? "Sorry to wake you, but I got a feeling?"

Okay, here's the deal—just drive by her place. If everything looks copacetic, then drive on by. She'll never have to know you were there.

He traveled toward Interstate 45. Forty minutes later, he was pulling up to the curb outside Tish's garage apartment in the old-money neighborhood of River Oaks. He'd gotten her address off the business card she'd given Elysee. He suspected she'd moved to this area to be closer to her friend Delaney.

When he saw that the light was on in her apartment, his heart rapped hard against his chest. He blew out his breath. She was awake. Now what?

Good God, Tremont, you're acting like a stalker.

He wasn't stalking her. He was worried about her. His gut was gnawing at him, telling him something was wrong.

What if Elysee finds out you slipped away in the middle of the night to come park outside your ex-wife's apartment simply because you had a feeling?

And what would keep Elysee from thinking, Yeah, right. Then why is her business card in your front shirt pocket?

He clenched his jaw, swallowed back the pain clogging his throat. He did that a lot. Swallowed back his pain; sucked up his sorrow. It was what a man was supposed to do. Shane hailed from a long line of heroes. Heroes didn't whine or complain. They didn't mourn for what they'd lost. They accepted circumstances as they were, buried their emotions, took stock of the facts, and moved on without regrets.

So why couldn't he do that?

Because you're not really a hero. Not like your grandfather, not like Dad. They were real heroes. Real wars. Real men. You're nothing but a glorified babysitter.

He looked down at his damaged hand that could barely hold the steering wheel, and his heart plummeted to his feet. Hell, he wasn't even a glorified babysitter anymore. He was useless. Washed up. Wiped out.

Pity over everything he'd lost grabbed him by the throat, but he refused to let it take hold. To hell with pity. He was going to get the use of his hand back. He would prevail. He was a Tremont and Tremonts were heroes. It was his legacy.

He looked up, realized where he was and cringed. How had he come to this? Sitting outside Tish's apartment, blaming his being here on a gut feeling. It was pathetic. What was he hoping to accomplish? He should either knock on her door or get the hell out of here.

Shane started the engine, but he couldn't seem to make himself put the Durango in gear. His gaze was locked on Tish's window.

There wasn't another woman like her on the face of the earth.

So why did you let her go?

It wasn't him. He'd tried his best. Ultimately, she was

the one who'd turned her back on him. Even if he was the one who finally pulled the plug by walking out the door.

The emptiness he'd been feeling at the Benedict ranch hadn't abated. In fact it was stronger now, as the old memories tumbled in on him. Memories that knotted his throat and misted his eyes.

You're still in love with Tish.

He couldn't still be in love with her. He was marrying Elysee Benedict on Christmas Eve.

Marrying Elysee while his heart still belonged to Tish.

His gut twisted. *Okay, fucking fine.* He would admit it. He was still in love with her. But so what? She didn't love him. If she still loved him she wouldn't have let him walk out that door. She would have told him the things he needed so desperately to hear.

Get the hell out of here. Go back to the ranch. Forget about what you lost. Forget about what your gut is telling you. Tish is building a new life. You're building a new life now with a good woman who truly needs you. You have everything you've ever wanted.

Except for Tish.

Determinedly, Shane fumbled for the gearshift with his bum hand and finally managed to slip it into drive. He stomped down on the accelerator, but as he pulled away, he tossed one last look over his shoulder at Tish's bedroom window.

And that's when he saw a dark figure creeping along her balcony.

After calling Delaney, Tish pushed aside all her sorrow and memories and got down to work. She was running the video disk from the engagement party through her state-of-the-art editing program on her computer.

She would watch a segment, freeze it, and make notes for special effects she wanted to add or cuts she wanted to make. She also jotted down a list of music selections to mix in, but she would need to run her ideas by Elysee before finalizing it.

There was the ballroom where the ceremony had been held. And here came Nathan Benedict and his entourage. She paused the scene and made notes before continuing on to the next segment.

The work held her mesmerized as she slipped into professional mode and stopped seeing Shane and Elysee on a personal level. They were just another high-profile couple getting engaged. She wasn't going to let viewing the video trigger any more emotions inside her. This was a job. That's all it was.

She'd managed to block her emotions so well in fact that she got lost in what she was doing. Time flew, and the first indication of trouble was the smell of gasoline filtering in through her bedroom window.

Where was that smell coming from?

Her nostrils twitched.

Had she left the gas burner on the stove turned on? No, she hadn't cooked since she'd been home.

Concerned, she pushed back her chair and thought she heard a noise from the balcony outside her window. She cocked her head, listening.

The noise repeated.

What was that sound? She furrowed her brow, and strained to identify it.

She heard sloshing. That was it. Like a liquid being tossed from a container.

Slosh, slosh, slosh.

A liquid like gasoline.

Fear lifted the hairs on the nape of her neck. She felt a stab in her gut, like a knife plunging in and twisting as the full impact of the sound registered deep within her psyche.

Someone was outside on her balcony dousing her apartment with gasoline!

Call 9-1-1.

The instinctive impulse hit at the same moment a match sparked outside her window.

Whoosh!

The gasoline burst into flames, lighting up the balcony behind the curtains on the French doors and she saw, barely visible beyond the fire, a hooded figure dressed in black.

Tish stood frozen, unable to believe what she was seeing. Someone was trying to burn her out!

Get out. Get out of the apartment. Get out now.

There was no time to call 9-1-1. She had to depend on her neighbors for that.

Briefly, she thought about trying to save things. Her clothes, her shoes, computer disks, but the room was already growing blistering hot as the heat blew the glass from the French doors.

Smoke billowed into her bedroom.

Hurry, hurry.

She wore only Lycra workout pants and an oversized T-shirt that served as her pajamas. Adrenaline pumping, heart thumping, she spun on her heels, ran from the room, racing for the only other exit out of the apartment.

The fire crackled behind her like an evil, cackling witch, destroying, eating up her life. Smoke, heavy and black, filled the hallway.

How was it burning so quickly?

Get out.

She paused at the door just long enough to slip her feet into her flip-flops and glanced around for the camera bag backpack she'd hooked over one of the kitchen chairs when she'd gotten home.

Where was the backpack? She had to have it. Her wallet was inside it, her identification, her laptop, the backup disk and the original she'd made of Shane and Elysee's engagement party, and of course her camera.

Smoke curled into her lungs, thick and acrid, and obscured her vision. Frantically, she ran her hands along the back of first one kitchen chair and then the other, desperate to find the backpack.

Had she left it in the living room?

She swung her head around, but the fire was already in the living room, too.

Forget the backpack. Get out or die!

Tish coughed against the billowing plume of smoke, barely able to breathe. Her head spun. Admitting defeat in finding her backpack, she staggered for the door but stumbled over something on her way out.

Her foot hung up on it and tripped her.

She fell to her knees, coughing, choking.

She'd stumbled on the strap of her backpack. It was on the floor underneath the chair.

Lungs aching, she hooked the heavy backpack over one shoulder, reached up to fumble for the lock on the door, determined to get outside to the sweet salvation of fresh, night air.

Her head was foggy, her chest constricting.

Get to your feet. Get out the door. You're almost there.

Her stupid feet wouldn't obey.

The sound of the fire was deafening now, coming

closer, swallowing everything in its path with a vicious heat.

Okay, fine. If her legs wouldn't work, then she would crawl out of here.

She grabbed for the doorknob, dragged herself to a sitting position, twisted the knob and tumbled out onto the front stoop. She sucked in a merciful breath of smoke-free air. In the distance, she heard sirens. Some sharp-eyed neighbor had called the fire department. Good thing.

Safe. She was safe.

But then a pair of strong masculine hands slipped around her neck.

Oh my God, it was the arsonist and he was going to finish off what he'd started.

Her eyes burned from the smoke and profuse tears streamed down her cheeks. She couldn't see her assailant's face, but she would fight him with every last breath in her body.

In a blind panic, she cocked her knee and kicked savagely at his crotch. She heard a sharp exhalation of air, knew she had made solid contact. And that she'd probably knocked the air out of his lungs and he couldn't speak.

Yes! her brain crowed in triumph.

Can't stop now. Must get away.

She curled her fingers like claws and went for his face, scratching, searching for his eyes.

He grunted as she dragged her fingernails over his skin, committed to doing as much damage as possible. *Take that, you bastard.*

He grappled with her. He was so heavy. How could she fight him?

The sirens were growing closer. If she could only hang on for a few more minutes, help was on the way.

She blinked hard, desperate to see. She was on her back on the front stoop, perilously near the edge of the eight-foot plunge off the stairway.

If she could just buck him off of her. But how? He was twice her size.

She arched her back, spit and scratched, kicked and clawed. She pulled her knee up, used it as a fulcrum, and levered his legs off of hers. She wriggled and kicked, shoving him closer to the edge.

"Tish!" he gasped, just as she was preparing to kick him over the side. "Stop it, stop fighting. It's me. It's Shane."

Chapter 17

So let me get this straight," said police sergeant Dick Tracy. The paunchy man narrowed his eyes at Shane. "You were standing outside your ex-wife's bedroom window in the middle of the night."

Shane and Tish were sitting in front of the Houston PD sergeant's desk, both bloodied and battle-weary. The fire department had shown up to put out the fire but her apartment had been utterly destroyed. Several patrol cars had arrived along with the fire trucks. One of the cruisers had brought them downtown to make their statements and fill out a full report.

Shane's face was raw from where she'd scratched him. Tish had skinned her chin in the scuffle and didn't even remember it. And every time she touched her face, soot came off on her hands.

Clutching a grimy tissue in her hand, Tish longed for a shower. They had Styrofoam cups of rotgut cop coffee in front of them. She'd taken one sip when Dick Tracy had given it to her but hadn't been desperate enough for a second swallow. Where was Starbucks when you needed them?

Tish kept looking from the balding, middle-aged cop to

the nameplate on his desk that confirmed he was indeed named Dick Tracy. "Honest to God, your name is really Dick Tracy?"

"Yes," he snapped.

"Dick, not Richard?"

"That's right." Dick Tracy glowered.

Shane kicked her lightly on the ankle, and telegraphed her a silent message with his eyes. *Shut up before you get us into more trouble.*

"Your mother must have had a fondness for comic book heroes," Tish said.

The cop scowled. "I don't know what you mean."

"Naming you after a comic book detective. I suppose you didn't have much choice except to become a cop. A name like that is destined to define your whole career path." Tish was blathering and she knew it, but she didn't want to talk about the fire. Focusing on Dick Tracy's curious name was a nice distraction. "Must be hard to live up to such a moniker, though. I mean here you are in your what...late forties and you still haven't made it to detective? That's gotta eat at you. Ouch!"

Shane's kick was more solid this time, his frown darker. *Are you nuts?*

Dick Tracy slid a glance over at Shane. "I can see why you're divorced. What I don't understand is why you were spying on her."

Yeah, Tish thought. *Good question. I can't wait to hear the answer to that one.* She folded her arms over her chest and waited expectantly.

"I wasn't spying," Shane denied.

"Were you stalking her?" Dick Tracy leaned forward, sizing Shane up with a critical eye.

"I am not a stalker." Boldly, Shane also leaned forward

until his nose was almost touching the police sergeant's. A shiver skated up Tish's spine. It thrilled her when Shane got all tough and manly.

"Did you start the fire?"

"I did not."

"So." The cop's voice dripped sarcasm. "You just happened to be in the right place at the right time."

"Basically."

"I gotta warn you, I don't believe in coincidences. If you weren't spying on her, stalking her, or looking to burn her house down, why were you there?"

Tish curled her hands into fists. She was anxious to know the answer to this one.

The question had been nagging at her from the start. She knew Shane hadn't started the fire, even though Dick Tracy seemed inclined to believe otherwise. Personally, she didn't have a single doubt on that score. When it came to her physical safety, there wasn't a person on the planet she trusted more than Shane.

Shane made a noise, half-snort, half-sigh. He wasn't looking at Dick Tracy. His gaze was hooked on Tish. "You wouldn't believe it if I told you."

"I might. Why don't you try me?" the cop said, expressing exactly what Tish had been thinking.

"I was there to watch over her," Shane answered, then immediately snapped his jaw shut.

A sudden, inexplicable thrill caused goose bumps to raise up on Tish's arms. Shane had been watching over her? Was this the first time? Or had there been others?

Her gaze searched his face, looking for answers in his eyes, but he wasn't looking at her. He was focused intently on Dick Tracy, never breaking eye contact, trying to prove he had nothing to hide.

"You were watching over her." A Skeptics-R-Us expression drew Dick Tracy's eyebrows down. He shuffled through the notes on his desk. "Does your fiancée, Elysee Benedict, the first daughter of the United States of America, know that you slipped out of bed in the middle of the night to come into Houston and stand outside your ex-wife's apartment to watch over her?"

Shane didn't answer him.

Dick Tracy swung his gaze to Tish. "You have any idea that your ex-husband likes to swing by in the middle of the night to 'watch over you'?"

She didn't know how to answer that. She looked from Shane to the police sergeant and back again.

"Just tell him the truth, Tish." Shane nodded.

Tish drew in a breath. "I had no idea."

"I don't swing by in the middle of the night. This is the only time I've ever done it."

"The only time?" Dick Tracy pointedly cleared his throat.

Shane shifted in his seat. Tish could tell that talking about this was making him uncomfortable. "Maybe there were a couple of other times, when we were first divorced and she was living in our old house all alone. I just wanted to make sure she was okay."

He'd come back to check on her after the divorce?

Tish's heart and stomach contracted in tandem waves and a pea-sized knot of pain embedded itself in the dead center of her sternum. He'd come back to check on her after the divorce.

"I don't get it," Dick Tracy said. "If you cared enough about this woman to check on her after your breakup, then why did you divorce her?"

Tish perched on the edge of her seat, muscles tensed, waiting for Shane's reply.

Shane took a sip of coffee, winced, and quickly set it back down on the desk. He was stalling, trying to decide what to say. Tish recognized the tactic. "It's complicated," he muttered at last.

"I'm all ears." Dick Tracy cupped both hands behind his ears.

Breath bated, Tish leaned forward and almost fell off the chair. Would he reveal his true emotions to Dick Tracy? Would she at long last find out what had really propelled him out the door that last morning they were together?

Would he tell the cop about Johnny? Briefly, she closed her eyes and bit down on her bottom lip to stay the tears that threatened to tumble.

"My being there has nothing to do with the fact that someone burned her apartment to the ground tonight."

"No?"

"No."

Shane and Dick Tracy continued their macho stare-down. One minute passed. Then two. The police sergeant finally caved. He dropped his gaze, plucked a pencil from the cup holder on his desk, and started doodling on a Post-it note.

Tish slumped back against her chair. She wasn't going to learn anything about Shane's true motives. Not tonight. Hell, if the police couldn't wring the truth out of him, she'd probably never know for sure.

"Let's take a different approach. Forget the past. Why were you at her place tonight? Why this night, out of all the other nights, did you decide she needed watching over?"

"I woke up with a bad feeling she was in danger."

Dick Tracy snorted and flipped his pencil back in the

cup holder. "Psychic, are ya? Wait, wait, don't tell me. You had a vision that someone was going to torch your ex-wife's apartment and try to kill her?"

"I didn't know what was going to happen. I just woke up with this feeling in my gut that she needed me."

Tish couldn't help herself. She gave a half-laugh. "Oh, that's rich. When we were together, when I really needed you, where were you? Off protecting someone else. But now you're engaged to Elysee frickin' Benedict and suddenly your gut's telling you to come look after me?"

"Well, yeah."

Tish rose to her feet, sank her hands on her hips. "Maybe you should discuss these tendencies with a shrink, if you want *this* marriage to last."

"Your wife's got a point," Dick Tracy said.

"We're not married!" Shane and Tish said in unison.

Dick Tracy raised his palms. "Okay, I get it. You're divorced and hate each other."

"We don't hate each other," Shane said.

The cop made a derisive noise. "Look here, I get off duty in an hour. I don't have time for this. Let's just make a statement and you'll be free to go, but I don't want either one of you leaving the area until this investigation is over. Got it?"

They nodded.

"Sit back down"—Dick Tracy pointed to the chair Tish had vacated—"and let's get this over with."

Tish plunked back in her seat and told her side of the story. Then Shane told his.

"Do you have a patrol officer who can take me back to my vehicle?" Shane asked the police sergeant when all the requisite paperwork had been completed.

"Nope. Shift change."

"How are we supposed to get out of here?"

"Oh, don't worry about that. You've got a ride coming." Dick Tracy's eyes gleamed.

"Yeah?"

"I had my assistant call the Benedict ranch. They're sending a car."

"You did that on purpose." Shane splayed his palms on the sergeant's desk.

Dick Tracy shrugged, grinned. "Just doing my job. After all, you can tell the most about a suspect when he's under pressure. If I'm not mistaken"—he nodded toward the entrance—"your ride has arrived."

Simultaneously, Shane and Tish turned, just as the doors of the precinct flew open and a clot of Secret Service agents, led by Cal Ackerman, marched into the station.

And there, in the center of the group, looking as innocent and sweet as Cameron Diaz in *My Best Friend's Wedding,* stood Elysee Benedict.

As the rising sun edged up into the morning sky, Shane found himself stuffed into the backseat of the limo with Elysee on his right side and Tish on his left. Cal Ackerman and another agent sat in the seat across from them. Once upon a time, he would have been sitting next to Cal. Now he was sandwiched between his ex-wife and his wife-to-be.

It was a surreal sensation.

"Here," Tish said, rummaging around in the backpack that served as her camera bag and coming up with a disk. She passed it to Elysee. "Hang on to this for me. The original burned up in the fire, but luckily I'd made two copies and stowed them in the camera bag."

Elysee slipped the disk into her pocket and looked over

at Shane. "Do you think the fire could be related to the disk?"

"I don't know," he said.

Elysee looked back at Tish. "You're coming to stay at the ranch where you'll be safe and that's all there is to it."

"No, no," Tish said. "I can get a hotel room."

"Don't be silly," Elysee said matter-of-factly. "It's the perfect solution. You need a place to stay."

Shane's gaze flashed to Tish's face. He shouldn't be looking at her. Not in front of his fiancée, but he couldn't seem to stop himself. Her hair was disheveled, her mass of corkscrew auburn curls cascading over her slender shoulders. Black soot smeared her cheeks and forehead. Her chin was skinned, marring her peaches-and-cream complexion. He'd always loved the sun-kissed hue of her skin.

Tish averted her eyes, stared down at her lap. Shane realized for the first time that she was wearing her version of pajamas—well-worn workout pants and an oversized T-shirt.

His old T-shirt.

When they'd been married, he'd bought her sexy lingerie. Teddies and baby doll pajamas and silky nightgowns. She'd worn them to seduce him, but once the garments had been discarded in favor of lovemaking, once they were spent and ready for snuggling, she would get up, dig out pants worn soft from wear and one of his T-shirts, and slide back into bed.

Elysee, on the other hand, was a total girly-girl about her bedclothes. She slept in satin and silk. He knew because he'd been her night shift bodyguard and she'd occasionally get up in the middle of the night, with a gauzy dressing gown over her delicate underthings, and challenge him to a game of chess.

Weird that in waking life Tish was overtly sexual, while Elysee was demure. Yet in their sleeping attire Tish preferred comfort and cotton, while Elysee went for high style and lace.

Women. Who could figure them? Certainly not him. If he could, he'd still be married to Tish.

"We need to swing by Tish's place so I can pick up my Durango," he said as the limo cruised through downtown Houston. To keep from staring at Tish, he studied the carpet, noticed there were little pieces of what looked to be red gravel underneath Cal's shoes.

"I've already dispatched someone to retrieve it, sweetheart," Elysee assured him, still smiling. Her congeniality was almost eerie, but there was something else in her eyes. An emotion he couldn't identify.

Here was another weird thing. Elysee hadn't asked what he'd been doing at Tish's place in the middle of the night. Wouldn't a normal woman be jealous, or at the very least, curious?

Elysee reached over his lap to touch Tish's hand. "I'm so sorry for what happened to your apartment. I'm just glad you managed to get a call off to Shane and he was able to race to your place in time to save you from the arsonist."

Shane tensed, fisted his hands against the tops of his thighs. What was Tish going to say?

"I didn't..." Tish flashed a quick glance at Shane's face.

Was she going to tell Elysee the truth? He tensed, bracing himself for what might come next.

Tish shifted her gaze to Elysee, who was looking over at her so wide-eyed and trusting. She cleared her throat. "Yes, yes, I was lucky."

Relief loosened Shane's limbs, but it was quickly

replaced by guilt. He shouldn't be getting off this easily. If the roles had been switched he could bet Tish would be grilling him like a steak.

"So it's settled. You'll stay at the ranch until you can get back on your feet," Elysee commented.

Tish sneaked another glance at Shane. He kept his face impassive, although he would have felt more comfortable if someone had detonated a grenade in the limo. He looked across at Cal Ackerman, who was smirking at him. He deserved it. He'd broken the bodyguard's code. Never get personally involved with the person you were hired to protect.

"All right, then."

"Isn't that wonderful, darling?" Elysee linked her arm through his and squeezed tight.

"Wonderful," Shane echoed and forced an optimistic smile. How in the hell had he gotten himself into this? Then he looked down at the hand Elysee was touching. His injury had made him vulnerable in more ways than one.

If not for a sleep-deprived backhoe driver, he would not be in this fix: about to marry one woman while he was still in love with the other. What was he supposed to do about that?

Nothing. You don't do anything.

Indecision held him tight in its grasp, which was bizarre because he'd always made decisions fast and followed through quickly. It was that ability that had driven him out of bed in the middle of the night. His instinct to act was the very same thing that had saved Tish's life, but it had landed him in this situation.

Indecision took hold. Made itself at home in his chest. Curled up tight against his spine.

Indecision.

The very thing Shane feared most.

"Don't marry him."

"What?"

Four hours after Elysee and her entourage had retrieved Shane and Tish from the police station, Elysee sat at her writing desk. Telephone in hand, she'd just ended a conversation with a department store retailer. Shane was at his morning physical therapy session. Tish had been ensconced in a guest bedroom to try to get some sleep after her ordeal. Elysee blinked at Cal Ackerman, who'd come into the room while she was on the phone.

"Shane." Cal strode across the room toward her. "Don't marry him."

His statement threw her off balance. She settled the cordless phone into its docking station, straightened in her chair and met his edgy gaze. Her pulse quickened. She lifted a hand to her throat. "Why not?"

"Because." Cal took a deep breath. "You deserve someone who loves you."

"Shane loves me," Elysee said, but even as she spoke the words she felt hollow deep inside.

Cal shook his head. "Not the way you should be loved."

He was standing mere inches away, and Elysee could feel the heat emanating off his big body.

She gulped. "What do you mean?"

"You know," he said in a tone that raised the hairs on her forearms.

"I don't." *What a fib.* "If you'll excuse me, Agent Ackerman, I've got a wedding to plan."

He laid a big palm smack-dab on top of the papers in front of her and leaned in close. "You're making a big mistake."

Elysee's knees felt weak. Good thing she was sitting down. She didn't know what to make of this, but suddenly, she flashed to a mental image of a buck-naked Cal climbing out of the shower. She closed her eyes, shook her head, but the image persisted.

"You've overstepped your bounds, Agent Ackerman," she said sharply, unnerved by what she was experiencing. She shouldn't be feeling what she was feeling. Not when she was engaged to another man. "I'll thank you to remember your place."

"Pulling rank?" His tone was amused.

"Yes." She lifted her chin. "I am. I'd appreciate it if you'd step back across the room."

"What's the matter, Elysee?" He dropped his voice. His head was so close that if she turned, his lips would be on hers. "Afraid of what you're feeling?"

She spun away from him, scrambled to her feet, so unnerved she could barely speak. She stood with her back to the wall, struggling to catch her breath. "I'm appalled at your effrontery, sir."

"Who're you trying to kid? Me or you?"

Her hands curled into fists. "Please, you're making me uncomfortable."

"No one's ever made you uncomfortable before?" He arched an eyebrow.

Not like this! She'd never been so upset with someone while at the same time desperately aching to kiss them. *What's the matter with me?*

"Do you value your job, Agent Ackerman?"

"Not as much as I value stopping you from making a major mistake."

The honesty in his words, the serious expression on his face, startled her. "Duly noted. Thank you for expressing your objections. Now, if you'll just mind your own business, we'll forget this entire conversation. Otherwise, I'll have to ask my father to have you replaced."

A knock on the bedroom door pulled Tish from a restless sleep, where she'd dreamed of a shadowy menace chasing her. In the grogginess of half-sleep she remembered the fire and a rush of sadness rolled over her.

Another knock sounded but before she could organize her thoughts for a response, the door opened and Elysee poked her head in. "You awake? "

"Just barely." Tish stifled a yawn.

"Get up, we're going shopping."

"Shopping? Like this?" Tish waved a hand at her rumpled clothes. "It's all I have to wear. I can't go to the mall looking like this." She cocked her head at petite, five-foot-two, size-four Elysee. She was five-nine and wore a size twelve. "It's not like you and I could share the same clothes."

"We're going shopping presidential style."

"How's that?"

Elysee crooked a finger. "Come with me."

Feeling grumpy, dowdy, and decidedly homeless, Tish begrudgingly got out of bed. She ran a hand through her tangle of curls, stuffed her feet into her flip-flops, and followed Elysee out of the room, her curiosity piqued.

Elysee led her through the house to the sitting room where she'd first interviewed Tish. Today, the room was filled with racks and racks of clothes, from Macy's, Nordstrom's, Ann Taylor, and Neiman Marcus. Salesclerks stood in a line, waiting at the ready for Elysee's beck and call.

And then Tish saw them.

Shoes. Boxes upon boxes of shoes. Jimmy Choos, Christian Louboutins, Manolo Blahniks, Dolce & Gabbanas.

Her heart pattered. "What's all this?"

"It's a little difficult for the President's daughter to pop down to the local mall, so the mall comes to me."

This was Tish's biggest fantasy come true. A shopaholic's erotic dream. It was the most amazing thing that had ever happened to a poor girl with a bad credit rating.

"It's awfully nice of you," Tish said, fingering a beautiful silk camisole. "But I can't afford this stuff. My pocketbook is geared more toward Target."

"Sweetie." Elysee patted her shoulder. "This shopping spree is a gift. From Shane and me."

Tish backed up, backed away from all the lovely, lovely clothes. She raised her palms in front of her, and shook her head. "No, no. I can't accept this."

Elysee blinked. "Why not?"

"It's too much. It's too extravagant." *It's from you and Shane. My ex-husband whom I still love.* The whole situation was just too damned weird.

"But you have to have clothes."

"If someone could just give me a ride to the nearest Wal-Mart I'll pick up a pair of jeans, a couple of blouses, a package of underwear, and I'll be good to go." She realized for the first time that she was truly stuck here. The car she'd borrowed from Delaney was parked under the carport near her burned-out apartment.

"Tish Gallagher, you're the first daughter's wedding videographer. You've got to look the part."

She gazed at the clothes again and sighed with longing. "Seriously, Elysee, I can't accept."

"Seriously, Tish, why won't you just let us help you?"

Because I don't deserve it. Because you're so nice and I'm lusting after Shane and you don't even know it.

"If it makes you feel any better, you can deduct the cost of the clothes from the final installment on our wedding video."

"Really?" Now that was an idea she could wrap her head around.

"Really."

"Okay."

"Now, let's shop."

Two hours later, Tish's wardrobe had been replenished. While the retailers were tallying totals and packing up their inventory, Elysee and Tish were served a late lunch of finger sandwiches and pasta salad on the veranda.

"So tell me, what's Shane like in bed?"

"Huh?" Tish choked on a mouthful of raspberry tea.

"Is he forceful?"

"Um, are you sure you really want to discuss this with me, again?" Tish asked.

Elysee lowered her voice. "I don't have anyone else to discuss this sort of thing with."

"What about your girlfriends?"

"Honestly, it's difficult keeping friendships when you're in the public eye." Elysee took a deep breath.

"I'm sure it is."

"So tell me what he's like in bed."

"Elysee, that's personal."

"Was the sex bad between you two? Was that why your marriage fell apart?"

She shouldn't have said what she said next, but she couldn't seem to stop herself from bragging. "If great sex could keep a marriage together, let's just say Shane and I would have been superglued for life."

"Really." Elysee struggled to keep the smile on her face.

Tish felt as if she'd just kicked a puppy. "I'm sorry, I shouldn't have said that."

"No, no, I'm glad you told me. I need to know these things." Elysee took a breath. "So why did you divorce him?"

"I didn't divorce him. Shane divorced me."

"I didn't know."

"Now you do."

A long silence ensued. Elysee toyed with a cucumber sandwich. "Why did he divorce you?"

"Because I didn't need him the way he thought I should and then the one time I really needed him, he wasn't there for me," she said, hearing the bitterness in her own voice.

"That doesn't make any sense." Even when Elysee frowned, she managed to look sweet and innocent. It grated on Tish's nerves.

"Don't let it worry you, Elysee. Your marriage will be fine. You're plenty needy enough for Shane."

It was an awful thing to say. Especially to Elysee, who'd been nothing but kind to her. Immediately, Tish felt like the crud in the bottom of a dirty refrigerator. No, wait, she was lower than that. She was ring-around-the-toilet crud.

Elysee burst into tears, pushed back her chair, and ran sobbing from the room.

Great going, Gallagher. You're turning out to be quite the puppy kicker.

Chapter 18

I don't want to interrupt your workout, but I have a favor to ask."

Shane glanced up to see Tish standing in the doorway of the elaborate gym. Embarrassed by the puny little one-pound weight cradled awkwardly in his right hand, he hid it behind his back.

She looked absolutely breathtaking in a green silk blouse that molded to her lush breasts and designer blue jeans that hugged her sexy ass. His body stirred, responding in a totally inappropriate way.

"Where's your physical therapist?" she asked, sauntering into the room.

"He got a phone call."

"So you're in here all alone?" She craned her neck, looked around the corner at the bank of treadmills. She moved with the grace of a dancer, lithe and totally at ease in her own skin. She ran her hand along the padded cushion on the nearby butterfly machine. She'd always been a very tactile person. Kinesthetic. Physical. Shane clamped his teeth shut, remembering how much she'd liked to touch and be touched.

"You needed to ask a favor?" he said gruffly, to hide what he was feeling.

"Will you give me a ride back to my place?"

"Your place burned down."

"I know, but my car's there. Or rather Delaney's car is there. She let me borrow it after mine got repossessed."

"Your car got repossessed?" The damned weight was getting so heavy, the weakened muscles in his wrist were yelping with pain. He clenched his jaw.

Her cheeks flushed red with embarrassment. She made a face, waved a hand. "I know, I know. I'm irresponsible, unreliable, immature."

"I didn't say that."

She was trying so hard to be tough and brave, enduring a burned-up apartment, a repossessed car. A sudden tenderness swept through him so raw and stark it had him shaking his head. He wanted to pull her into his arms, hold her close and tell her everything was going to be all right. But he had no right to comfort her. He'd given up his right when he'd filed for divorce.

"You were thinking it."

"I was thinking..." No he couldn't say what he was thinking. A spasm shot through his right hand. He dropped the weight. It fell to the floor with a loud thunk. He shook his hand trying to free it of the charley horse. "How heavy that weight was getting," he finished, wincing.

"Cramp?"

"Uh-huh."

"Here," she said, stepping across the room toward him, hips swaying in that sassy walk of hers. "Let me."

He started to say no, that it would be all right, but before he could pry the words from his mouth, she was there, reaching for his hand.

Touching him.

Tilting her head and studying him.

She placed the pad of her thumb in the center of his savaged palm, her fingers wrapping around the back of his hand. Her skin was so warm against his, but he was self-conscious about the scars.

Her thumb kneaded his palm in widening circles. She was so close. Too close.

He could feel the blood pumping through his veins as he stared at her moist, luscious lips. He remembered exactly how they tasted like summer raspberries. A taste he craved.

Swallowing past the lump of aching desire blocking his throat, Shane pulled his hand from hers. "The cramp's gone."

He lied. It wasn't gone. But for the sake of his sanity he had to distance himself from her. Before he ended up doing something that would ruin everything for both of them. He couldn't have her. He was engaged to Elysee and the river of ancient history was too wide to cross.

"Come on," he said gruffly. "I'll give you that ride."

"Yes," she agreed with a quick nod.

Forty minutes later they stood in her driveway, surveying the burned-out ruins of her apartment.

A gasp rose to Tish's lips the minute she grasped the extent of the damage. He watched the impact on her face, saw how her features sank and crumpled. He had an overwhelming urge to reach out and put an arm around her shoulders to steady her, but he did not.

The arson investigator and his team were there, sifting through the rubble.

"Who are you people?" the investigator asked.

"It's my apartment. Or it was," Tish said, eyeing his helpers as they relocated pieces of her charred life and sifted them into different piles.

"You can't be here. The investigation isn't complete."

"We just came for my car." She jerked her thumb over her shoulder in the direction of her landlady's garage.

"All right, but please back away from the perimeter."

"Is everything completely destroyed?"

"Pretty much."

"Do you have any idea who might have started the fire?" Shane asked. He stepped closer to the investigator, his shoes crunching loudly in the red lava landscape gravel that fronted the garage.

The investigator shook his head. "We can't release any information at this time. I'm going to have to ask you folks to get what you came for and be on your way."

"Hey," one of the team members called to another. "I found something intact. It was buried under a stack of burned-up books."

All eyes swung the man's way. He was holding up a bookend, a sculpted little girl with a pail of water in her hand carved from the burl of two banyan trees that had twined and grown together. Somehow it had come through the fire unscathed, probably because it had been buried under the books. Shane recognized it and felt an immediate sorrowful tug in his gut.

He'd bought the Jill half of the Jack and Jill bookends for Tish at a rummage sale while they were on their honeymoon in Galveston. She'd fallen in love with it the moment she'd seen it.

"Remember the day you bought that for me?" Tish whispered.

"I remember," he said gruffly.

"We never did find Jill's mate."

"No Jack."

"Can I have it?" she asked the arson investigator. "Please."

"I'm afraid it's evidence until the investigation is closed."

Evidence of what? Shane wondered. *A memory gone bad? A promise forgotten?*

"All right," she told the investigator, then to Shane she said, "I'm ready to leave now."

Shane walked her to the car and opened the door for her. She slid across the leather. He handed her his cell phone. "Here, take my cell."

"What for?"

"Your cell phone burned up in the fire. You're a woman driving alone in a big city and it's almost forty miles to the ranch. Take my phone."

"But aren't you following me back?"

"No, I've got a couple of things to do first."

They looked at each other. Was that longing in his eyes? Sadness?

She took the cell phone. "Thank you."

He moistened his lips and for one wonderful moment she thought he might kiss her good-bye. "That was weird about the Jill bookend. The only thing that survived the fire intact."

"Weird," she echoed, her eyes hooked on his mouth. The tension, the emotion, the sad yearning for days gone by vibrated the air between them.

"I never found the Jack bookend for you like I promised."

"No."

"I should have found it," he said. "I should have kept my promise."

"It doesn't matter."

"It does matter, Tish. I let you down."

"It's too late for that, Shane."

Was it her imagination or was his hand trembling ever so slightly? She saw the anguish in his eyes. What did he want from her? What did he expect?

"I could go on the Internet tonight, check out eBay, search for the bookend."

"You don't have time for that. You've got a hand to heal. You're getting married in a month. You've got preparations to make. Besides, what use do I have for bookends? My books are all gone."

"Tish," he murmured her name again.

"I release you, Shane, from any obligations you might still be feeling toward me. You don't owe me a thing."

"But I made a promise."

"Things happen. People aren't always able to keep the promises they made in good conscience. Let yourself off the hook, Shane. I'm not holding it against you that you never bought that other bookend for me."

"You've changed." He looked at her as if really seeing her for the first time.

"I have to go. Elysee is expecting me. We're going to work on the video." She had to get out of here before she did something completely stupid, like telling him she was still in love with him. She started the engine.

"Drive safely." He raised his hand.

She slammed the car into gear, backed out of the carport, and left him standing there, looking utterly confused.

Seeing the burned-out remains of Tish's apartment brought Shane face-to-face with the realization of how easily she could have died in that blaze. He could have lost her forever.

Until this minute he hadn't fully understood the depths of how much he missed her. Of how he would miss her if she was suddenly gone.

He couldn't let this lie. Last night, someone had tried to kill Tish and he was determined to find out why. Jaw clenched, he climbed into the Durango and drove to the police station.

Dick Tracy was reluctant to speak with him.

"The investigation is ongoing," he said in that noncommittal way cops have perfected, when Shane prodded for answers.

"In other words," Shane said, "you've got nothing."

"I didn't say that." Tracy leaned back in his chair, sizing him up with one long, cool, appraising glance.

"And?" The conversation made him feel like a dentist trying to extract impacted wisdom teeth.

"And what?"

Tracy was apparently in no frame of mind to surrender his secrets, but Shane was in no frame of mind to leave this police station without some answers. "Any new leads? Any clues?"

"I don't have to tell you anything."

As Nathan Benedict's future son-in-law and a former Secret Service agent, Shane could have thrown his weight around. He had connections. One well-placed phone call and he could force Dick Tracy to turn over the evidence. But that would take time. He wanted answers now.

"Sergeant Tracy." He leaned across the desk. "You seem like a reasonable man who's just doing his job. Don't make me pull strings."

"You threatening me, Tremont?"

Okay, wrong tactic.

"Not at all," Shane said smoothly when he was feeling

anything but smooth. Inside, he felt ragged and edgy. "I'm law enforcement, too. I was hoping you'd share what you've learned."

Tracy considered him a long moment. He opened up his desk drawer and drew out a plastic evidence bag. He tossed it in the middle of his desk. It was a matchbook with Shane's and Elysee's names on it, along with the date of their impending nuptials—Christmas Eve. "Evidence team found this on the ground outside your ex-wife's apartment, along with several cigarette butts. Someone's been watching her. You have any idea who?"

"Those matchbooks were given away at our engagement party. Anyone could have grabbed a handful."

"Not anyone. Only the people with access to you and your fiancée."

"What are you saying, Officer Tracy?"

"I'm saying the culprit is probably someone you know and trust."

Elysee lay on her bed, head buried under her pillow. Tish was one hundred percent correct. She *was* needy. Her neediness was the reason she'd thrown herself headlong into WorldFem and helping Rana. She'd thought that by empowering other women, she could empower herself. Her neediness was what had broken up her first three engagements. Was it also sabotaging her relationship with Shane?

If she were being honest with herself she would admit his need to be needed was the very thing that had attracted her to him. He was the strong shoulder she'd been looking for to cry on and he liked that role.

Was their relationship based on anything more than mutual co-dependency?

It was a troubling thought.

She rolled over, brought the pillow to her chest and stared up at the ceiling with a painful blend of hope and longing. Was there any possibility that she could hold on to Shane? Or was she doomed to make Tish's tragic mistake?

Elysee knew she could never compete with Tish. The woman was so sexy and smart and brave. Elysee had no illusions about herself on that score. She was flat-chested and narrow-hipped and gap-toothed. She had been a solid C student no matter how hard she studied—which was why she hadn't bothered with college. And she was such a coward that she had to call the Secret Service to swat spiders for her. She was a dowdy, dumb wimp.

Don't marry him. The words Cal had spoken to her that morning rang in her head.

But how could she back out now? The last thing on earth she wanted was to hurt Shane. He'd already suffered so much.

Marriage should be forever. If Shane's not The One, it's better to break an engagement than a wedding vow.

Elysee covered her face with her hands as she imagined the tabloid headlines. *Fickle First Daughter Flakes on Fiancé Number Four.* She thought of the engagement party and the money her father had already spent.

Shane was a good man, a kind and honest man. Their marriage would be filled with mutual respect and admiration. On that score, she had no doubts.

But what about love? quizzed a tiny voice deep inside her. Cal was right. She deserved someone who'd love her fully, completely, wholeheartedly, without any reservations, the way her father had loved her mother. The way Alma Reddy and her husband loved. Could she and Shane ever love each other like that?

She had to find out.

Elysee went to Tish's room, knocked tentatively on the door. When she didn't answer, Elysee tried the handle. It was unlocked. She knocked again, pushing the door open as she went. "Tish?"

The room was empty.

But Tish's camera sat on the dresser, input/output cords hooking it up to the television. Elysee slipped the disk of their engagement party that Tish had given her in the limo out of her pocket and inserted it into the camera. She turned on the television and perched on the foot of Tish's bed to watch.

The sound of her father's voice announcing her engagement to Shane drew her attention to the video. Her stomach wrenched with emotion—regret, sadness, guilt, and an inexplicable feeling of hope. The camera view panned the room, then came back to linger on Shane and circled the room again.

This time, when the camera caught Shane's face, he was looking right into the lens with such an expression of abject longing it took Elysee's breath.

How sad and lost he looked. Why would he look that way on the day of his engagement?

Puzzled, she tilted her head to study his features.

Why was he staring into the camera?

Why was the camera so focused on Shane's face?

Realization hit her like a landslide. It was obvious to anyone with two good eyes and half a brain.

Shane was looking at the person behind the camera and the person behind the camera was fixed on him.

Tish.

In an instant, Elysee's body went as cold as if she'd been doused with ice water.

Shane was still in love with Tish and she with him.

Her stomach churned. Her heart constricted. And here she'd been repeatedly throwing them in each other's path. Oh, Lola had been right. Hiring Tish to videotape the wedding had been a terrible idea.

It's not Tish's fault if he still loves her. You love who you love.

The question was, did she love Shane as much as Tish did?

Elysee realized she didn't know the answer to that question. What she felt for Shane was very calm and quiet and familiar. No Fourth of July fireworks. No angst. No intense yearning. Were her feelings for him predicated on nothing more than admiration, friendship, and gratitude that he'd saved her life?

She realized she did not know. Until now, her life had been dictated first by romantic notions engendered by her mother, and then by her father's expectations. She didn't blame her parents. They'd done what they'd thought best for her. She blamed herself for not questioning her values and beliefs before.

In that moment, Elysee knew what she must do.

Tish was roadkill.

Flattened.

Squashed.

Annihilated.

She drove blindly, not really knowing where she was going. Not caring. Desperate to blunt the devastation suffocating her heart.

Her apartment had burned to the ground. Her ex-husband, whom she still loved, was marrying Elysee and there was nothing she could do about it. Anxious for someone to talk to who wasn't involved with the sainted first daughter, Tish pulled into a shopping mall parking lot, cut the engine, and punched Delaney's number into the cell phone Shane had given her.

"Hello." Her voice came out dry and reedy.

"Tish?"

Relief washed over her. "Yeah."

"Are you all right?"

Tish couldn't speak. Emotion was a wad of tears jammed up tight against her throat. She wasn't going to cry.

"I read about the fire in this morning's paper. I've been calling and calling your cell phone, but kept getting your voice mail. I was so worried."

"I'm fine." Tish finally managed to choke out the words. "My cell phone burned up in the fire."

"I tried calling your mom, but when she hadn't heard from you either, I really started to panic. I had Nick check the local hospitals."

"I'm sorry I worried you."

"I'm just happy you're okay. It scared me when the paper said the fire was a suspected arson and that you were at home at the time of the blaze."

"Yeah."

"Were you hurt?"

"No."

"That's good. I'm so glad you're all right."

"Shane was there."

"Shane?"

"Yeah." She was having trouble putting more than three words together.

"What was he doing there?"

"I don't know." Truly she did not. She wasn't sure that

she believed his claim that he'd had a dream she was in trouble. Why hadn't he just picked up the phone and called her? The man was seriously messing with her head.

"Why would someone try to burn down your apartment?" Delaney asked.

"I don't know." She was starting to sound like a scratched CD, endlessly repeating.

"You're really not all right at all."

"No," she agreed. "I'm not."

"Where are you?"

"On my way back to the Benedict ranch. I'm staying there until the wedding." Her voice sounded stronger now. That was good. "But I'll be all right. I'm just shook up."

"Are you sure? You know you're more than welcome to stay with me and Nick."

"I know. Thank you. I might take you up on your offer." Her heart swelled with love for her friend. "But enough about me. How are you doing, Delaney? It seems forever since I've seen you."

"That's because you've been jetting off with the presidential set," Delaney joked. "You're going to get so big you'll forget all about your friends."

"That'll never happen," Tish said fiercely.

"You say that now . . . ," she teased.

"And I mean it."

"I do have a bit of news."

"Oh?"

"I wanted to tell you in person, but Tish, I'm so excited. I don't think I can wait."

"What is it?"

Delaney inhaled a sharp sigh of joy. "Nick and I . . ." She paused.

"Uh-huh?"

"We're pregnant!"

Tish's body went limp and she almost dropped the phone. She sat there gulping in breaths of air.

Delaney was having a baby. Nothing was ever going to be the same between them again. She felt joy for her friend, but at the same time she feared for the tiny life growing inside of Delaney. She knew how precarious that precious life was. How it could all turn on a whisper of a second. Hopes could be dashed. Dreams eradicated.

"Tish? You still there?"

"Uh-huh."

"Did you hear me?"

"I heard you. I'm just stunned. I didn't know you and Nick were trying to have a baby."

"We weren't." Delaney giggled. "We just got a little careless. But Tish, Nick's so happy. You should see him. He already went out and bought a little baseball glove. It's adorable."

"How far along are you?"

"Just eight weeks."

"Are you hoping for a boy or a girl?"

"We don't really care as long as it's healthy. I sort of want a boy, but I think Nick prefers a girl."

"I'm so happy for you two."

And she was. She was! Tish wasn't jealous of Delaney, just deeply sorry for herself. For all the things she'd lost. From her baby to her husband to her home to her clothes. Photographs and keepsakes. Memories of her life up in smoke.

Tish bit down on her bottom lip. She would not give in to self-pity. She was made of sterner stuff. She'd survived losing a baby in the early third trimester of her pregnancy and the dissolution of her marriage. She would survive this, too.

"Why don't you come here? It would be a joy to have you," Delaney said. "It would be like college. Except with Nick hanging around."

She thought of living with Delaney. The eager smiles on her friend's face as she decorated the nursery. The knowing glances she'd exchange with her husband when she thought Tish wasn't looking. She simply couldn't bear it.

"You and Nick need your alone time right now. I'll be fine at the ranch."

"You're sure?"

"Positive."

"If you change your mind, you know where to reach me."

"Thank you."

Silence hung between them. The gulf had already begun.

"I was worried about telling you," Delaney said. "I kept thinking about Johnny. I don't want you to feel..."

"Honey, don't you dare worry about that," Tish said, forcing her voice to sound lighthearted and carefree. "I'm fine."

Fine as ground glass.

"I just..."

"Listen, I've gotta go. Elysee wants me to go over the engagement party video with her. I'll call you later. In the meantime kiss Nick for me and congratulations to you both."

"Tish..."

"Love you. Bye," Tish said and hung up.

For the longest time, she stared down at the cell phone. Briefly, she thought of calling Jillian to see if she could stay with her, but then she remembered Jillian was in San

Francisco for six months and she'd sublet her downtown condo. Rachael lived with her roommates, so that was out. And Dixie Ann was in San Diego.

Her house was burned to the ground. She had to be careful with her money. Her best friend was pregnant. She couldn't stay with either of her other two friends. And there was the possibility that whoever burned her apartment wanted her dead. She was stuck on the ranch with her ex-husband and his fiancée.

Things couldn't possibly get worse.

The laughter started deep inside her and built. Shaking her body, rumbling up through her diaphragm, into her lungs, and finally out through her lips until she was laughing hysterically, uncontrollably. Until she couldn't breathe.

Hell, she thought, it was a lot better than crying. At least when you laughed at rock bottom, your eyes didn't get all red and puffy.

Chapter 19

After his return from taking Tish to get her car, Shane went in search of Elysee. He traveled the path from the garage through the gardens, past the place where he'd first kissed Elysee—that sweet, chaste kiss that had caused him to put her up on a pedestal.

He stared down at his mangled hand. He tried to make a fist but could not contract his fingers inward any more than an inch. All this time in physical therapy and this was the best he could do?

Disgusting.

Worthless. He felt absolutely worthless. Last night, he hadn't been able to stop an arsonist from burning down Tish's apartment. Nor had he been able to save her from the fire. She'd saved herself. Not only saved herself but then nearly booted his sorry ass off the stairs.

What kind of man was he now? Broken. Useless. Unable to protect the people he loved. Viciously, Shane kicked at the loose pebbles on the garden path. His heel skidded in the gravel. He lost his balance and fell smack on his ass.

Chagrined, he stared up at the main house and saw Pete

Larkin standing on the back porch sneaking a smoke. A fitness trainer who smoked? Just his luck. Shane's humiliation was complete. Someone had seen him.

Scrambling to his feet, he tried to look cool and failed miserably. He limped. His hand hurt. His face was covered in scratches. He was a mess.

Suck it up. Your grandfather stormed the beach at Normandy. Your father made it back from Vietnam in one piece. This is nothing.

He could take the humiliation. He could handle the pain and his physical limitation. What he couldn't handle was having Tish so close, unable to touch her, fighting his desires, all the while remembering he was engaged to the President's daughter.

How had things gotten so damned fucked up?

The temptation to get into his Durango and just drive and drive and drive until he hit water was overwhelming. Too bad he wasn't the kind of guy who ran away when things got tough.

Oh, no? Who the hell bailed out of his marriage? That doesn't sound like the actions of a stick-to-it guy.

The thought clipped him low in the gut. All his life he had believed he was the kind of man who accepted responsibility willingly. He hadn't been a foolish teen. No drunken escapades, no irresponsible sex.

Well, except for that time on the ferry with Tish, when protection and condoms hadn't even entered his lust-soaked mind.

Twice in his life, he hadn't lived up to his image of himself. Once when he'd been so caught up in passion he'd gotten Tish pregnant, and then a year later when he'd walked out on her.

Guilt knifed him. Sliced open his gut, eviscerating him

and letting every emotion he'd been trying to hold inside come tumbling out in a rush of messy heat.

There was one big divider between the way he tried to live his life and Shane's actual behavior. One thing and one thing only had led him from the straight and narrow path he'd always walked.

And her name was Tish Gallagher.

But Tish had changed.

Shane had never seen her so calm, so accepting, as he had seen her this afternoon. He didn't know what to make of her transformation. He was gobsmacked.

Face it, Tremont. It's finally over. You should be relieved. Now you can get on with your life.

But he wasn't. He couldn't.

He scratched his head. His hair had grown out. He would need to get it trimmed before the wedding. When he'd first seen Tish again his hair had been nothing but little spikes of stubble all over his head. Now, so many things had changed, yet the most important one was still the same.

He was engaged to marry Elysee Benedict.

And he had Tish's blessings.

Fury grabbed him then. Fisted his gut. Burned his throat. He had no idea why he was so angry, but it felt damn good. Ever since the accident, he'd been walking around in a muddle. He hadn't stopped to ask himself what it was that he really wanted.

What did he want?

Tish. He wanted Tish.

You can't have her.

The strength of his desire knocked him on his ass. For two years he'd fought his desires, hidden his feelings, tamped down his emotions. He'd been a good Secret Service agent. No, he'd been a great Secret Service agent.

But what was he now?

Maimed. Muddled. Lost.

Shane refused to put up with this helpless feeling. He had to do something. Had to prove he was still a man. He had to get his courage back.

By the time he reached the back porch, Larkin had ducked back inside but the air was still redolent with the smell of his cigarette. Shane went in through the rear entrance, past the kitchen where preparations for the evening meal had already started. Elysee was throwing a small dinner party for her charity.

Lola was in the kitchen, confabbing with the executive chef about special dietary restrictions for one of the houseguests they were expecting for the President's visit. She spied Shane and graced him with her usual glare. For some reason, the woman hated him.

"Have you seen Elysee?" he asked Lola.

"I believe she's upstairs in her room."

"Not upstairs, Lola. Here I am."

Shane turned to see Elysee coming into the kitchen.

Their eyes met.

Her automatic smile was the painted-on version she doled out to the media. "Shane," she said. "We need to talk."

His breathing stilled and he felt a supreme sense of calm. "I know."

"Let's go somewhere more private for this conversation."

He realized all the ears in the room were attuned to them. He held a hand out to Elysee. She took it. They turned toward the back door. Shane saw Cal in a corner of the room glaring at him, arms crossed over his chest. When they started out the exit, Cal followed.

"I can handle her security from here." Shane stopped in front of his old partner.

"Can you?" Cal bristled.

Shane narrowed his eyes. "What's that supposed to mean?"

"You can't even hold a gun. How are you going to protect her?" Cal chuffed.

Elysee splayed a hand against Cal's chest. "It's okay. I'll be all right with Shane. We're just going for a stroll around the lake."

The look Cal gave her betrayed the same feelings that stirred inside Shane whenever he looked at Tish. The realization that came to him was sudden but certain. Cal Ackerman was in love with Elysee Benedict. The question was, did Elysee know?

"You've got nothing to fear," he said, reassuring his old partner. "I'll bring her back to you safe and sound."

Cal nodded curtly. "Fifteen minutes. After that, I'm coming after you."

It sounded like a threat. Shane didn't know what to make of this new development. Elysee slipped her arm through Shane's. Cal audibly ground his teeth. He had the feeling Cal would've gladly ripped his throat out.

Neither one of them spoke until they were treading the path leading away from the ranch house and toward the lake—the very place where Shane had proposed.

Elysee took a deep breath and stopped underneath an oak tree overlooking the water. "I don't really know how to say this," she began, but then didn't go on.

He cupped her cheek with his palm. "Whatever you have to say, it's going to be okay."

Her blue eyes, clear and soft, focused on his. "Is it?"

"I promise."

"You're such a good friend; that's why this is so hard for me." She was breaking up with him. He didn't know whether to jump in and help her out, or let her be the one in control.

In the end, he decided she needed to be empowered more than she needed the easy way out. He smiled at her. "No matter what you say next, Elysee, I just want you to know that you'll always be my friend."

"Really?" Her expression was somber.

He leaned down to touch his forehead against hers. "Really."

She exhaled sharply and sank against his chest. "Oh, thank heavens. The last thing I want is to lose your friendship."

"You won't."

She stepped back from the circle of his arms. "You already know what I'm going to say."

He nodded.

"You're still in love with Tish." Elysee's voice caught and her eyes misted with tears.

"Yeah." Darn if he wasn't feeling a little misty himself. "But she doesn't love me anymore."

Elysee laughed.

Confused, Shane tilted his head. "What?"

"You great big fool. She's truly, madly, deeply in love with you."

His heart thumped. "Are you sure?"

"You're not?"

"But I hurt her something terrible."

"She's a forgiving person."

"You really think I have a chance of winning her back?"

"Not as long as I have this on my finger." Elysee twisted off her diamond engagement band. She took his hand, placed the ring in his palm, and closed his fist around it. "Although Daddy's going to be disappointed. He really likes you."

"This isn't about your father."

"I know."

His gaze searched her face. "Elysee," he said and slipped the ring into his pocket. "I'm sorry if I hurt you in any way."

"You didn't hurt me." She smiled warmly. "You gave me a precious gift."

"What's that?" he asked gruffly.

"Unconditional friendship. Unfortunately, we both mistook what we were feeling for love. True love is something deeper," she said softly. "It's what you have with Tish. It's the thing I've been searching for my entire life, but I just haven't been able to find."

"It might be right under your nose," he said.

"What do you mean?" She canted her head.

"Cal Ackerman's in love with you."

Audibly, she sucked in her breath and her eyes brightened. The wind gusted, blew tendrils of brown hair about her face. "Did he say something to you?"

"No."

"Then how do you know there's something there?"

"The look in his eyes, the possessive way he glares at me whenever I touch you. Dead giveaway."

"I'm not sure that's enough to go on."

"It's up to you to find out."

Elysee tapped her foot in frustration. "Why can't men just say what they're feeling?"

"Something in the masculine gene prevents it, I guess," he said, thinking about Tish, about all the things they'd been through, about all the things he'd never been able to say to her but should have.

She snorted. "More like pure hardheaded stubbornness if you ask me."

"How do you feel about Cal?"

"I don't know how I feel about anything right now."

"That's understandable."

"Three days after our official engagement and it's all over." She ruefully shook her head. "My shortest engagement yet."

"Maybe next time, you should just elope." He grinned.

"Maybe I will." She grinned back.

"You're going to find him, Elysee," he reassured her. "The man you're supposed to be with. And when you do, you're going to know with absolute certainty."

"The way you knew about Tish?"

"Yeah." His voice cracked oddly.

"What happened between you two? What was it that broke apart a love that seemed so strong?"

Shane couldn't answer that. He couldn't tell her about Johnny. It was too painful. Instead, he shook his head. "I lost my faith in love."

She touched his shoulder. "We all have crises of faith."

"Not you. Not about love. That's one of the things that I admire most about you. Your resilience, your unwavering belief in happily ever after."

"Some people call it romantic foolishness."

"They're wrong. You gave me hope. You gave me back my faith. And that's a gift I'll never forget." He leaned down and kissed her cheek. "Thank you."

He straightened and she beamed up at him, her warm smile filling his heart with their special friendship.

"We better get back," she said. "You've got something very important you have to do."

"What's that?" he asked.

"Go find Tish and tell her everything she needs to hear."

While Shane and Elysee were walking around the lake, Tish had returned to the ranch to retrieve her camera equipment and her clothes and get the hell out of there before she ran across her ex-husband and his bride-to-be. She hurried past the Secret Service agent positioned in the hallway near her bedroom. She found the montage of photos of Shane and Elysee spread out on the desk the way she'd left them that morning.

Seeing their happy faces was a knife to her gut. How was she ever going to put this video together? Looking at the pictures over and over, feeling that constant weight on her heartstrings would be torture.

The sudden urge to go shopping was overwhelming.

No, no. That was a cop-out. She knew it now. Shopping was the way she'd smothered her feelings. No more smothering. No more denial. She would embrace the pain. It was the only way through it.

You can do this. You're not a coward. See this thing through.

Once and for all, she would prove she was a consummate professional. Nothing was going to stop her.

Haphazardly, she tucked the pictures back into the photo albums. She grabbed the stack and stood up. A clipping floated out, drifted to the floor.

Tish leaned over to pick up the piece of paper.

It was an article from *People* magazine about the backhoe accident on the UT campus. The headline read SECRET SERVICE AGENT SAVES FIRST DAUGHTER'S LIFE.

There was a photograph of Shane lying in a hospital bed looking frail and pale. His head was shaved, his scars fresh. The picture hit her with a visceral punch. Bile rose in her throat and her body went cold all over. For the first time she recognized how close Shane had truly come to dying.

Tish couldn't bear looking at the photograph, seeing him so helpless. That wasn't her husband. That wasn't her Shane. Breathing heavily, she flipped the clipping over, pressed the article facedown on the desk.

Resolutely, she again hoisted the photo albums in her arms. As she did, her gaze slid over the flip side of the *People* article.

It was a piece about an Indian woman working with the WorldFem organization to put a stop to the horrific practice of honor killings. Because of her work, she'd been placed on a death list, targeted by an assassin. Tish's eyes drifted to the photograph. She'd seen this woman before.

At Shane and Elysee's engagement party.

A thought stirred at the back of her mind, not yet fully formed. Yes, this was definitely the woman she'd seen. Could this woman be the key to why someone had tried to steal her disk?

Pondering that question, Tish took the third copy of the disk from her purse and slipped it into the camera, which was hooked to the DVD player. Seconds later, she was reliving the engagement party.

Fast-forward through the pomp and circumstance. Fast-forward through Shane giving Elysee the ring and kissing her. Fast-forward through Nathan Benedict announcing their engagement. Fast-forward past the congratulatory toasts.

To the part Tish was searching for.

Elysee was surrounded by well-wishers, blushing prettily, innocently. Then the camera caught a furtive woman wearing a scarf over her head hovering in the shadows. Tish watched as Elysee made her excuses, slipped through the crowd, headed toward the woman. They shook hands and Elysee led her through the French doors and out onto the patio.

Her pulse quickened. She didn't even remember filming this. Her mind must have been too befuddled by the engagement.

The camera angle swung away from Elysee to put Shane in the foreground. He was talking to Cal Ackerman. The camera lingered longingly on his face, spelling out for anyone who wasn't too blind to see that the person behind the camera was hung up on her subject.

Tish yanked her eyes off Shane and searched the background. Dammit. There wasn't any more footage of Elysee.

Wait, wait. There it was. Out on the patio when she'd accidentally left the camera on without knowing it.

It was the mystery woman and Elysee was handing her something. Was the footage of this woman the real reason someone had wanted her disk in the first place?

Tish had no answers. None of it seemed to have anything to do with someone burning down her apartment. Were the two incidents even connected? She rewound the tape.

The camera moved again, back to focus on Shane. Was she besotted with the man or what? There were other people in the frame behind Shane. The Ambassador from India was speaking in a language she vaguely recognized as Hindi, to a man who had his back to the camera. They were both eyeing Rana Singh.

She still didn't get it. Something was going on, but it was over her head. Whatever was on this disk held no meaning for her, but it definitely meant something to the person who was on it.

"Turn off the video and eject the disk," a voice from the doorway commanded. Too late, she realized she'd left the door to her bedroom ajar.

Startled, Tish turned and immediately let out a gasp of shocked surprise.

For there, pointed at her face, was the business end of a very large handgun with a silencer attached to it.

Chapter 20

Pete Larkin motioned toward Tish. "Hand me the disk."

"What?"

"Don't make me shoot you."

"Who are you? What do you want?" she asked.

"Just the disk."

"Why would you want the disk of the engagement party unless—"

"I'm on it and it's not a flattering camera angle," he growled. "Give me the disk."

"You speak Hindi," she said, as a terrible thought took root in the back of her mind. Larkin was the man talking to the Indian Ambassador on the tape.

"Fluently."

"You've been to India."

"Many times.

"Oh my God," Tish gasped as her suspicions crystallized. "You're the death squad assassin I read about in *People* magazine hired to kill Rana Singh. That's why you want the disk. It can incriminate you."

"Ding, ding, she's smarter than she looks, folks." Larkin ripped the disk from her hand and stuffed it in his front pocket then lowered his gun, pressing it firmly against her rib cage.

"Pick up your car keys," he commanded, nodding to where they rested on the desk.

Once she had the keys in her hand, he took the gym towel that was slung around his neck and used it to cover the gun in his hand. He wrapped his arm around Tish's shoulder.

"Here's what's going to happen," he said. "We're going out the side exit. If we meet someone on the way out and you give any indication of what's going on, I'll kill them. Got it?"

Tish nodded. She had no reason to doubt his sincerity. The cold, calculating look in his eyes told her he was very capable of carrying out his threat.

"Walk at a steady pace, neither too fast nor too slow," he instructed. "When we get outside, walk to your car, get in on the passenger side, and scoot over behind the wheel. Now let's go."

He muscled her out of the room and forced her to walk down the corridor beside him. Larkin had slung his arm around her waist, his gun pressed icily into her side.

Tish had fleeting thoughts of escape, but before she could even form a plan, Larkin whispered, "Forget about trying to make a run for it. I have no compunction about shooting you here if I must."

The flagstone walkway was wet from water sprinkler overspray. Now Larkin's other hand was at the back of her neck and he was pushing on her spine with his thumb, keeping her in line by putting pressure on her nerve endings. He guided her around to the back of the house where visitors parked in a covered lot.

"You're doing fine. Just keep it up."

When they reached the Acura she did as he'd instructed, getting in on the passenger side, sliding over to the driver's seat. He slid in after her, never taking the gun from her side.

"When we get to the security checkpoint, give a friendly little wave and keep driving. The guards don't pay as much attention to who's leaving as to who's coming in. If you so much as raise an eyebrow I'll kill you both. Do I make myself clear?"

"Yes."

"Good. Now drive."

"You're not going to get away with this, you know. There are cameras hidden all over the place. When I don't come back, the Secret Service will review the security tapes and hunt you down."

"Wrong. I'm CIA. I know exactly where the security cameras are and how to disable them," he bragged.

"If you're CIA, how come you're working as a physical therapist at the President's ranch house? Not much foreign intelligence going on in Katy, Texas. Doesn't seem like a job they'd give to their best agent."

His scowl deepened. "I got sent here when Elysee was engaged to her previous fiancé, Yuri Borshevsky. He had KGB ties. Someone had to keep an eye on him—since I speak twelve languages including Russian and Hindi, guess who got picked?"

"Still, it seems like a menial assignment. Babysitting, almost."

"It is." Larkin gritted his teeth. Clearly this was a touchy subject. "Now shut your mouth and drive."

Her life was in her own hands. She had to do something to get away from him or he was going to kill her. Of that she had absolutely no doubt.

Drive off the road.

"If you try to drive off the road," he said, reading her mind, "you'll be dead before your head hits the steering wheel."

"Lovely imagery. Thanks for that."

"Just wanted to let you know I'm not screwing around."

"There's one problem with your threat."

"And what's that?"

"If you kill me now you'll never know who all I gave copies of the disks to."

"You made copies?" His voice hardened.

"Lots of them."

"You're lying."

"Are you willing to take that gamble?" She snuck a glance at him. His eyes narrowed, glaring, and his jaw tightened. She could see his mental cogs turning.

He swore violently and pressed the gun against her temple. "Who else has copies?"

The feel of the end of the gun against her head was more chilling than finding a rattlesnake in her bed. Her body went cold with fear; her fingers blanched white on the steering wheel. Her mind raced desperately around the possible avenues of escape.

Stay calm. You've got to stay calm or you're lost.

"We're in traffic. Someone could see you with that gun pressed to my head and call 9-1-1," she said quietly. "Why don't you put it out of sight?"

She could tell it irritated him to have to do what she said, but she also knew she'd made an excellent point. He slid the gun down the side of her head, past her neck, and repositioned it against her rib cage. It was only slightly less terrifying there than having it pointed at her skull.

"Hang a left at this next traffic light and remember my finger is on the trigger. You make a wrong move and the gun goes off."

"And you've got one hell of a mess to deal with."

"I've dealt with worse."

"Still," she said, struggling to keep hysteria at bay by sounding flippant and carefree. "You'll never know how many copies of the disk I made."

"It's a risk I'm willing to take. In fact, I think you're lying. I don't think you made any copies at all."

"But you'll never know for sure."

"Oh, I'm sure I know a way to persuade you to talk." His voice sounded so sinister, she dared a quick glimpse at him. His features were maniacal, and she knew this was no mission sanctioned by the CIA. He had to be a rogue agent who'd lost all sense of boundaries. One look at his ominous face and she knew he was talking about torture. Horror sickened her stomach. She had no doubt he was completely capable of carrying out such an awful deed.

Please don't let me throw up, she prayed.

She had mistakenly thought that by telling him she'd made copies of the disk he would spare her life, because there was no way of knowing whether she was telling the truth or not. She'd never counted on torture. If this deranged lunatic tortured her, she knew she would end up telling him anything he wanted to hear. Including the fact that she'd given a disk to Elysee.

Dear Lord, she'd placed the President's daughter squarely in the line of fire.

You have to get away from him. It's the only chance you have. It's the only chance Elysee has.

"Take the overpass," he instructed. "Drive at the speed limit. Not one mile above or below."

"Where are we going?" she asked, really not wanting to hear the answer but frantic for some kind of information that would help her form a plan.

"To the shipping channel. To the docks."

"Why are we going there?"

"Not that it's any of your business, but I've already made arrangements for the disposal of two bodies. A third corpse shouldn't pose much in the way of an added inconvenience." His grin was pure evil. "There's a lot of places to torture someone down along the waterfront where screams go unheard."

After his talk with Elysee, Shane hurried to Tish's bedroom to tell her that they'd broken the engagement, but she wasn't there. He went in search of anyone who might know where Tish had gone. The place was in a bustle because the President was coming in. He couldn't find any staff members who'd seen her.

Until he spoke to one of the valets, who told Shane he'd seen Tish get into her car with a man just a few minutes earlier. Shane pressed for a description but the valet said he hadn't been close enough to get a good look at the guy.

Shane thought about phoning Cal, but hesitated. He no longer had any idea who he could trust. For all he knew, Cal could be behind the arson fire. He hated to believe it of his former partner, but at this point, everyone who'd been staying at the ranch that had been at the engagement party was suspect. Especially Cal, since he smoked and had access to those matches. Especially since Shane had seen bits of red lava rocks—the very same red lava gravel that was in the garden outside Tish's apartment—underneath Cal's shoes in the limo the night of the fire.

Call Tish.

But, of course. He was so frantic with worry, he hadn't thought of the simplest solution first. He went into Tish's bedroom, picked up the cordless phone, and called his cell.

It rang six times, then switched to voice mail. He left a message asking her to call him immediately and hung up. That's when he realized Tish's camera was hooked up to the computer monitor and photos were scattered across the desk.

Tish might be a little flighty at times, but when it came to her work, she was a dedicated professional. She would never have gone off and left her camera on or her editing equipment strewn around. He examined the camera and saw the disk was missing.

Alarm jolted through him.

He stabbed his fingers through his hair, blew out his breath and let out a short but emphatic curse. Something had happened to interrupt Tish from her work. Where had she gone?

And with whom?

He pivoted. On his way back out the door he saw a decorative glass bowl filled with the same matchbooks Dick Tracy had found at the scene of the fire. He scooped up a handful as he went past and stuffed them into his pocket, convinced they held the key to the person with whom Tish had gone.

His training told him not to jump to conclusions, but his gut told him his fears were valid. Someone had taken Tish and her camera disk from the engagement party, he guessed. And he feared it was someone who meant her serious harm.

Shane's father had taught him that in times of crisis he should always listen to his gut and not to his head.

Listening to his head had sent him walking out on his marriage when he should have paid attention to what his gut had told him.

Instinctively convinced Tish was no longer on the ranch, he raced back to his Durango, got in and zoomed to the security checkpoint at the front gate. The guards had changed shifts, so the officer in the guard shack hadn't seen Tish leave, but it had been logged in that Tish and a passenger had left the grounds seventy minutes earlier.

"Passenger?" Shane asked of the guard. "Who was the passenger?"

"It doesn't say here, sir."

"Male? Female?"

The guard lifted his shoulders in a helpless gesture. "No notation was made regarding the sex of the passenger in the car with Ms. Gallagher. Would you like me to call the other guards at home?"

"No." Shane didn't have time for that. Besides, he had another plan. He would track her via the GPS device in his cell phone. Wherever she was, he could target her location.

Once he had a plan of action, Shane calmed. He would find her and when he got hold of the sonofabitch who'd taken her, his retribution would be both swift and relentless.

He felt a surge of protectiveness for Tish unlike anything he'd ever felt before. It was far stronger than his sense of duty, far deeper than his patriotism and his honor code. It wasn't about revenge. This wasn't about his ego. This was about Tish's safety. She needed him—this time, he was determined to be there for her.

The sun was slipping down to the horizon as Larkin shoved Tish ahead of him through the maze of shipping pods lining the docks. Huge freighters lay tied up at their berths.

There was a lot of activity around the new arrivals, but Larkin stayed clear of those areas, guiding her farther and farther away from any dockworkers and her possible salvation.

Larkin shunted her down dark and musty rows of heavy metal containers, and the smell of fish and brackish water was thick in her nose. With all the noise and hustle, it was doubtful anyone would have heard her cry for help. The gun poking hard into her back deterred Tish from even trying to call out.

Finally, he told her to stop beside one of the pods positioned right at the edge of the water. "Open it up," he said.

Oh God, was this where he was going to torture her and kill her? Was this pod to be her coffin?

She hesitated, unable to make herself open the door.

He jabbed her in the spine with his gun. "Do it."

She obeyed his demand, struggling to unlatch the heavy metal door. As she worked on it, his pager went off. Cursing, he tugged it off his waistband and squinted at the display. For a brief second his concentration left her and went to the pager. Her eyes went to the water: If she jumped off the pier could she swim away from him? Or would she simply be a sitting duck in the water, a perfect target for his bullets?

"Sonofabitch."

"What is it?"

"The President is arriving at the ranch in an hour and he wants a training session and a massage when he gets there," Larkin fumed. "He treats me like I'm his frickin' servant."

"Well, he is the President of the United States."

"Like I have time for this crap."

"You better show up. If you don't, someone might get suspicious of your whereabouts," Tish said.

He cursed again. "Okay, in you go."

"What?"

"The pod." He waved his gun. "Get in there."

"But it's dark inside." She peered nervously into the black depths. "It smells like mice."

"You'd rather I just shoot you now?"

"I'm in." Tish hopped into the pod.

Larkin slammed the door on her and turned the lock. She pressed her ear against the door, straining for the sound of his footfalls walking away.

He was gone.

Relief weakened her limbs and she sank to the floor of the pod, wrapping her arms around herself to stem the uncontrollable shaking that suddenly gripped her body.

Inside the shipping container was airless and empty. Tish had never known darkness could be so deep and black, except for in her own mind, in her soul, after she'd lost the baby.

And then she'd lost Shane.

Mentally, she had whirled out of control, spinning wildly, madly—a dizzying dance of consumer excess. Buying, shopping, throwing away money. Until she'd lost momentum and like a wobbly dreidel, fallen over, top-heavy, spent and out of balance.

Time passed.

She didn't have any idea how long it was. It could have been mere seconds. It could have been a dozen hours. She might have dozed. She might have only hallucinated that she dozed. She might have dreamed that she hallucinated about dozing. The isolation and visual deprivation were disorienting.

I'm going to die. I'm going to die in here alone without ever telling Shane that I still love him.

* * *

Shane arrived at the docks just after dusk. The location scared the hell out of him. He knew someone could easily go missing down here. He found the Acura parked behind an abandoned warehouse on the far side of the shipping channel.

That's where his search ended, when he peered in the window and spied the cell phone he'd given Tish lying on the console. Shane's gut spoke to him, and it was yelling some pretty ugly things.

You weren't there for her when she needed you most, Tremont. Face it, you failed her. If she dies, it's all your fault.

He gulped. Guilt and fear hitched a ride from his throat to his stomach and settled in like bad indigestion. He stepped away from the car, eyes scanning the night, senses attuned for danger. His Sig Sauer was nestled in its shoulder holster, but it gave him little comfort. Fear badgered him, too. *What are you going to do? Shoot with your left hand?*

Yes.

Your target better be as wide as a Wal-Mart.

He heard a sound in the darkness behind him. He whirled, simultaneously reaching for his gun, but his reaction time was too slow.

"Got the draw on you, Tremont," said a voice from the darkness. "Throw down your weapon."

"What the hell is going on here? Who are you? Where's my wife?" Shane demanded, searching the shadows for a face.

Surprise tripped down his spine when he saw Pete Larkin emerge with his own Sig Sauer pointed at Shane's head.

"Throw it down," Larkin repeated. "You're worthless with the thing anyway. I know what kind of shape your hand is in."

"What are you doing, Larkin?"

"Stop yapping and do it." Shane tossed his weapon on the ground. Larkin retrieved it and tucked it in his waistband.

Rage engulfed Shane, red-hot and blind. It wasn't long ago that he could have as easily killed Larkin as look at him. "What the hell is wrong with you? Where's Tish? Is she alive? If you've done anything to her, I swear I'll kill you."

"Don't sweat it. I'll take you to her. Reunite the love-birds. Put your palms on the back of your head, turn around, and start walking toward the water."

Calm down. You're no good to Tish in an irrational state. Remember your training. Detach from your emotions.

"What's this about?" he asked, struggling to keep his voice calm when he wanted nothing more than to launch himself at Larkin and rip his throat out.

"Something you shouldn't have gotten involved in. It was none of your damn business. Nothing to do with you. Either one of you."

"Clearly." Shane's mind was racing as he tried to formulate a plan. He didn't want to act too prematurely, didn't want to disable Larkin before the man led him to Tish. "Who are you working for?"

"CIA."

"Fucking spook."

"You think that's an insult?" Larkin laughed. "Take a left at the next shipping container and don't try anything or I'll blow your kneecaps off."

"You don't scare me."

"Then you're very stupid. I have no problem with killing anyone who gets in my way."

"I'm guessing your superior officers have no idea what you're up to. Since when is a wedding videographer a threat to national security?"

"Those spineless pencil pushers. Please. They don't have a clue what it's really like out here in the field."

"What did Tish do to deserve this?"

"She took my fucking picture."

"And?"

"She got my voice on tape."

"Sounds like your fault for doing business in a public place."

"It was Sumat Kumar's idea," he grumbled.

"The Indian Ambassador?"

"He wanted the meeting at the engagement party so I could see Rana Singh."

"He hired you to assassinate Elysee's former nanny?"

"And some rebellious Indian chick whose father is some kind of cabinet minister in India. He wanted her dead for marrying a guy he didn't approve of." He smirked. "Imagine if we had honor killings in the States. All the teenage girls would be dead."

"So what were you getting out of the deal?" Shane asked, as his mind frantically tried to come up with a plan. The only reason Larkin would be telling him all this was if he intended to kill him.

"Besides a shitload of money, you mean?"

"Besides that."

Larkin smirked again. "Kumar's promised to give me detailed info on their nuke capacity. The CIA won't give me another shit babysitting assignment like Yuri

Borshevsky after I drop that little Turkish delight in their lap."

"All this for two honor killings?"

"These dudes are rabid about keeping the practice alive. They don't want their women getting uppity."

"So you're just going to kill these women in cold blood for your personal gain?"

"Shut up, Eagle Scout, and take a right."

Shane did as Larkin said, his mind in high gear as he mentally tried out several possible ways to overpower the other agent. But every idea he formulated would have to wait until he found out what Larkin had done with Tish.

They stopped next to a padlocked shipping pod sitting near the edge of the dock. Larkin pulled a set of keys from his pocket, tossed them to Shane. He reached for them with his bad hand and missed. They fell to the dock.

"Pick them up."

He did.

"Third key on the ring."

He found the key.

"Open the pod."

He did.

"Get inside." Larkin snatched back the keys.

Shane walked in, fully expecting to be shot in the back of the head. But to his surprised relief, Larkin slammed the door and locked him up inside.

Chapter 21

Tish woke with a start when the door opened. She was curled into a ball on the floor and by the time she jerked her head around, the door had closed again.

But someone was in here with her. She could hear them breathing.

"Hello," she whispered. "Is someone there?"

"Tish?"

The sound of her ex-husband's voice sent joyous rapture reeling through her heart. "Shane!"

They found each other in the dark, mouths melding, arms embracing.

"Tish, Tish, you're alive. You're okay." He rained kisses on her face.

"How did you find me?"

"Through the GPS tracking in my cell phone."

"Larkin got you, too?"

"Yeah, I didn't see it coming. I had feared it was Cal Ackerman who'd torched your house—he had red lava rocks in the tread of his shoes and he smokes. I never suspected Larkin."

"I don't understand what's going on."

He told her then about his talk with Dick Tracy; the matches, the lava gravel; how Larkin revealed he had agreed to assassinate Rana Singh and Alma Reddy for Sumat Kumar in exchange for cash and detailed information about India's nuclear weapon capacities.

"Larkin got a beeper message that the President wanted a workout session and a massage at the ranch. That's probably where he was headed when he left here. If he didn't go, he'd blow his cover. I suppose you ran into him on his way out."

"Yeah."

"I told him I made copies of the disk."

Shane made a disturbing noise. "Did you?"

"Yeah."

"How many?"

"Two. One burned in the fire and Larkin took my copy."

"Who has the other one?"

"Elysee."

He made that noise again, clearly frustrated.

"I know."

"Larkin will be back as soon as he completes his obligation to the President. It's an hour to the ranch and an hour back. A workout session and massage will last a couple of hours. We have about four hours to come up with a plan to defeat him or we're dead," Shane said.

They fell silent.

"We're stuck here," she said after a long while.

"We'll probably die here."

"At least I'm with you," she whispered.

He held her close and she listened to the steady strum of his heartbeat. In spite of her fear she was overjoyed to be held in his arms once again, if only for a little while.

"We might as well sit down," he said. "I have a feeling we're going to be here for a while."

They settled in on the hard, cold metal floor and he tucked her into the crook of his arm.

Emotion knotted up tight inside her. There was so much she wanted to say to him, but she had no idea where to start. She lay with her head pressed against his chest, feeling his warmth, listening to the beat of his heart.

"Shane," she whispered.

"Yes."

"I need to talk."

"What about?"

"You, me, the divorce... Johnny."

He didn't say anything.

"You still can't talk about your feelings? Even with two years' distance?" She heard his ragged intake of breath. She waited. Finally, finally, when she'd just about given up, he spoke.

"It hurt me deep, Tish, that you wouldn't talk to me about the credit card trouble you were in. Why did you hide it? I was your husband. It was my job to help."

"I didn't talk to you because you shut me out!"

"How did I do that?"

"With impossibly high standards. Perfect credit scores and checkbook balanced to the penny. It was overwhelming. You were overwhelming."

"You honestly believed I would put money above your feelings?" He sounded stunned.

"I was afraid you would judge me harshly and I didn't want to disappoint you, Shane. What can I say? I hid the debt from you because I was ashamed." She paused, struggling hard not to cry.

"Tish." The whisper of her name twisted from his throat. She heard the anguish in it and a corresponding pain settled over her heart. "I really let you down."

"No more than I did you."

"Explain it to me now. Why did you buy all those things? Why did you rack up credit card charges we couldn't afford? Help me to understand."

"If I knew the answer to that then I wouldn't have done it, or I could have stopped."

"Was it to fill some kind of emotional void? Did it have something to do with your childhood? Was it about your mother emphasizing the importance of latching on to a man with money?"

"Partially, I'm sure."

"What else?"

"What do you mean?"

"Was I the cause in some way?"

"I don't know."

She wished she could see his face. His voice hitched. "I felt so betrayed when the creditors started calling and I found out exactly how much in debt you'd sunk us. Those cards were in my name, Tish. It was my account. I was responsible. You went behind my back and sullied my name."

"Well, you like being responsible," she snapped. "Why was it such a problem?"

"Was that the way you wanted me to feel? Like you'd cheated on me? Were you trying to get back at me for not being there when you went into labor with Johnny?"

"I don't know," she repeated.

"I think you do know. Maybe not on a conscious level, but maybe subconsciously you were trying to get back at me for not being there when you needed me most."

"No, subconsciously you're feeling guilty for not being there when I needed you most. Don't project your guilt onto me."

"If that's not it, then what were you getting back at me for?"

"I wasn't getting back at you. I was just trying to relieve my own pain." Her voice cracked loud and echoed off the metal walls of the pitch-black shipping container. "You didn't even seem to notice how I was suffering. You forgot about Johnny so easily."

"You're wrong. I didn't forget." His tone was brittle.

"You made me take apart the nursery before I was ready to let go. You never talked about him. You cut me off whenever I tried to talk about him."

"Tish, I couldn't talk about him. I'm the strong one. I'm the protector. Don't you get it? If I talked about him, I couldn't have stayed strong for you."

"Dammit, Shane, that's the problem. You want to take care of everyone. Like you're ten feet tall and bulletproof. But if you're always the strong one, your loved ones never get the chance to prove their strength, or to help you. It's lopsided and unfair."

Silence stretched in the void of darkness.

"I never thought of it that way."

"Well, think about it. You grew up with all that flag waving, gotta-live-up-to-the-family-legends-and-be-a-hero stuff. Not that you shouldn't be proud of your family history, but come on, nobody can live up to all that hype. By always striving to be this great heroic figure, you never let yourself be a real human being with less than honorable impulses."

"I struggle plenty with my less than honorable impulses," he said. "I just try not to show it."

"But that's what you've got to do! Let me see that my big hero is reluctant once in a while. That he's conflicted over his decisions. That he's not some frickin' perfect Dudley

Do-Right who makes everyone else feel like dirty rotten scoundrels because they can't live up to his standards."

"You mean like this?" Even in the complete blackness, his mouth found hers with unerring accuracy.

The minute their lips touched, Tish was electrified. She felt like a desert flower joyfully blooming after a rare soaking rain. God, how she'd missed him!

Their tongues met, starving, two years without this delicious meal. They kissed and kissed and kissed. The joining of their mouths was more intense than that night on the ferry. This was a kiss of reunion.

Of forgiveness.

Of coming home.

They melted into each other, eyesight cloaked by the blanket of blackness. But they didn't need to see. They knew each other so well: by touch and taste, smell and sound.

She uttered a low sound and slipped her arms around his neck. His fingers knotted in her hair, his energy blazed as hot as her own. They were tuned to the same frequency, both vibrating with heightened awareness of each other.

The ridges and swirls in her fingertips traced the landscape of his face as they kissed; absorbing the subtle yet distinct changes in terrain from the apples of his cheeks to the hollows below. She moved, feeling the shape of his head like a sculptor. Her fingers traveled over him with complex precision, felt with delicate, indefinable intuition. She ran her hand through his hair and traced the ridge of the scar at his temple.

Wounds.

They both had so many wounds.

How different things might have been if they could have had this conversation two years ago. If they'd both been able to find balance in their lives.

Transcended. She was transcended and emotionally reborn.

Balance.

It was what she'd been after all along. With balance came closure.

Closure. It was where Elysee had been trying to lead her. She'd found it now, in this dark container, with her ex-husband, whom she still loved with all her heart but was finally able to let go on to his new beginning.

He kissed her harder, as if sensing her changing mood, pulling her back with him to the passion, to the flame. His tongue swept her up in a divine pleasure that she'd thought lost to her forever.

It was as thrilling now as it had been before. Maybe even sweeter now, because of what they'd been through, of all that they'd suffered.

His hand snaked up underneath her shirt and he ran his hot palm up her belly. She moaned softly, encouraging him, shooting the rapids of desire, riding the river of reward. She didn't care if this was right or wrong. She wanted him.

Tingles of anticipation started at the base of her neck, crept across her face, over her scalp, darted along her shoulders, trickled down her arms and finally shuddered softly down her spine.

She sat in his lap, between his spread thighs: such big, muscular thighs, full of power and promise.

He tried to pull her shirt over her head with his injured hand, but he kept dropping the hem. "Dammit," he swore.

"Shh," she said. "Let me."

Stripping off her shirt and then unhooking her bra, she flung her garments away.

"Ah," he said. In the darkness, his mouth found the

hardening tip of her nipple. Tish sucked in her breath at the delicious shock of his warm moistness suckling her tender breast.

He curved one arm around her waist, pulling her closer against him. She sighed as a strange blend of electricity and chemistry fused with her emotions and sent a surge of bittersweet pleasure flashing through her.

The blackness surrounded them, encompassed them, defined them. She could feel his erection through the material of his pants, prodding against her pelvis. He rubbed his beard-stubbled jaw along her sternum, his mouth seeking her other nipple. The sensation sent a fresh set of chills tripping over her spine.

He pulled lightly on her nipple and she sank closer to him, pressing her pelvis into the seam of his jeans. She pressed her head alongside his, nuzzling him like a colt. He laughed and the sound was of delight.

He went for her lips again, but in this sightless chamber ended up kissing the tip of her nose.

She had been so foolish. So blind. To her faults and motivations, to his needs and expectations.

All this time, she'd fled from him. She'd hidden from him in shopping malls and behind cash registers. She'd run away down the long corridor of the past two years, through the labyrinth of her own distrustful mind.

Run away, not just from him, but from her betrayal of him. Of what she had done to their marriage. Run from the searing pain of loss. All this time wasted. All this extra heartache because she hadn't had the courage to face her emotional pain, accept it and move through it.

By diverting her mind from the truth with shopping sprees and spending binges, she'd never given herself permission to heal. She'd frittered away money to lift her spirits, to stuff up the holes in her heart. But there was no stuffing up the holes with pretty clothes and designer shoes. No easing of her sorrow, just a numbing of her soul.

"Tish," he whispered and she felt his body tense. "What is it? What's wrong?"

"Johnny," she whispered. "All these mistakes were from losing Johnny."

She cried then, fully, completely grieving for the lost child who'd vanished before he'd ever really been theirs.

Shane held Tish tight and just let her cry, being strong for her now in a way he hadn't been before. Not trying to soothe her, just letting her go with it. Letting her feel the grief.

The next thing he knew, he was crying, too. His body shook with great, silent sobs.

They held on to each other in exquisite agony. In their pain, they came together.

United.

"I'm sorry, I'm so, so sorry, sweetheart. I'm so sorry I failed you."

She clung to him and he to her. He rocked her in his lap, her bare breasts against his chest.

Through the glaze of his sorrow-soaked heart, Shane began to feel something more. Something beyond the anguish stirred. Something primal and rich, life at its most organic.

Their chances of getting out of this alive were slim. Death lay so very close by. But if he had to die, at least he was with Tish.

Paradoxically, in these last moments of impending annihilation, Shane had never felt more alive. He realized that before now the very thing that had most appealed to him about Tish was also the thing he had feared most. Her passion.

If he succumbed to passionate love, along with its acceptance he must give up the notion of free will and self-control.

He'd tried to avoid losing control when they were married. Encouraging her to clamp down on her feelings, to sweep under the rug any emotions he found too disturbing. He'd been wrong about that.

Shane found her lips by sliding his mouth from the top of her head downward, kissing everything he found along the way. Her forehead, an eyebrow, the bridge of her nose.

Intensity rose off her like heat from a radiator. Her skin quivered beneath his fingertips. He fumbled out of his clothes and she shimmied from hers—both panting, both aware of every nuance, every sound, every scent in the darkness.

Once they were totally, gloriously naked and lying side by side on a bed of their piled clothing, he draped his wounded hand across the dip of her waist and tugged her against him.

"We shouldn't be doing this, Shane. It would kill Elysee if she knew."

"Didn't I mention Elysee and I broke up?"

"You did not."

"I meant to the minute I found you. I guess I got distracted."

"Who broke it off? You or Elysee?"

"We both did. We realized what we had was nothing more than a strong friendship. And I realized something else."

"What was that?"

"I never stopped loving you."

"I never stopped loving you."

Joy saturated his bones, pumped through his heart, hummed in his veins. He had her back!

She kissed his chin. He relished the sweet caress of her tongue. Her touch went straight to his brain, spun magic.

"I haven't made love to another woman since the last time I made love to you," he whispered, breathing in the scent of her silky hair.

"Not with Elysee?"

"We haven't shared anything more than kisses. It's like being in some damned Regency romance novel," he said.

"Good, because I haven't been with anyone else either," she confessed. "No one else could measure up to you."

"Oh, Tish." He squeezed her tight, buried his face in her hair.

He kissed her again because he couldn't help himself. He didn't want to help himself. She was all around him. His nose filled with her spicy scent. The sound of her quickened breathing was in his ears. The feel of her smooth, high breasts pressed against his. He had to have her or die.

Desire ignited, surged through his blood, snatching him up on a swell of love.

This felt too right. Too good. Too damn vital to be the wrong thing.

She kept kissing him, doing incredible things with her devilish tongue. God, how he'd missed kissing her. He groaned loudly and plunged his fingers through her hair.

His penis ached, hard and taut, surging in anticipation. Hungry for the caress of her fingertips. If they were going to die, he wanted to die with Tish embedded in his brain while he was embedded inside of her.

She licked a heated trail down his throat to his chest

and playfully nibbled at a nipple. Shane sucked in a deep breath and forgot all about dying. Every cell, every nerve fiber in his body was attuned to what was happening between them.

His balls pulled up hard against his shaft, crying out for her attention. His breathing shortened, quickened. As if reading his mind, she reached down to gently stroke the head of him, her whisper-soft fingertips gliding over his skin.

Helplessly, he thrust his pelvis forward, pushing his penis against her palm.

Tish murmured a sound of feminine power. It was hard for him to let her take the lead, but he knew they both needed it this way. Her, so she could feel strong again. Him, so he could let his needs be met rather than having to be the one to always meet her needs. She needed to be needed. It was finally dawning on him how much power he'd denied her by insisting on taking care of her. He was just now learning that it was okay to be helpless once in a while. To let someone else take the wheel.

Her lips engulfed his erection, her tongue performing magic against his aroused flesh. He groaned aloud. All this time without her. God, he'd been such a damnable, proud fool.

His heart pounded, his excitement intensified. He suddenly felt shy and unsure. What was the protocol here? There were no rules for this. No code of behavior to follow.

"Shh," she murmured, briefly breaking contact. "Let go, relax. For once just let me take care of you."

Reeling from the rush of it all, Shane surrendered his need for control and let Tish have her way.

Soon, he felt his climax rising, pushing up through him.

Tish must have sensed it, too, because she broke contact, dragging her moist warm lips from his engorged penis.

She straddled him, her soft inner thighs rubbing against his hips. He gasped, but she dropped her mouth on his, silencing him in a rush of red-hot kisses.

His Tish, just as daring and passionate as always. Damn, he wished he could see her.

Chuckling deep in her throat, she rocked back on her knees, took him in the palm of her hand, guiding his throbbing head into her slippery crease. His hands went to her waist. His right hand couldn't grip her tightly, but he was holding her nonetheless. That little miracle was all he'd really needed.

He raised his trembling hand and curved it around her breast. The weight of it felt glorious against his savaged palm. "Such breasts," he murmured. "Such beautiful, beautiful breasts."

Tish cupped her hand around his hand cradling her breast and slowly, she began to move. "My wounded warrior," she whispered. "My big, strong, wounded man."

She moved up and down in a languid rhythm, halting her upward momentum only when it seemed he would fall from her velvet clutches. Down and up. Down and up again.

Her tempo increased. Shane stiffened. He was close. On the edge of explosion. He felt the current of it start deep inside him, rising up on a torrent of release.

He felt her tense as her internal muscles began their rhythmic squeeze. She hugged him inside her, held him close as the clutching spasms of her orgasm gripped him, too.

And in one hot, spectacular gush they came together. The simultaneous release rippled through them like ocean waves against rocky shores.

Tish collapsed against his chest, their bodies slick with the aftersheen of great lovemaking. He wrapped his arms around her as their hearts slammed against their chests and their breathing came in hungry gasps.

He buried his face in her hair, inhaled the sweet, honest scent of her. He'd never felt as vulnerable as he did in this moment of reunion, and yet he'd never felt more invincible.

This wasn't mere lust he felt. It wasn't just love. They were bonded for life. Even if stupidity and blind grief over losing their son had separated them for two long years, they'd never really been apart. He knew it now. They were connected on an eternal level that mistakes and heartaches could not destroy. They were two parts of a single beating heart.

Now and forever.

Then he realized something profound. Their separation had been necessary for them both to grow to this point. They'd had to be apart in order to learn the lessons they were supposed to learn. They'd rushed their relationship before, letting chemistry and passion sweep them past the getting to know you stage.

If Tish hadn't become pregnant, they wouldn't have married as quickly as they had. Shane had never regretted marrying her, not even in those bleak days after the baby's death. What he did regret was letting his pride and guilt get in the way of what had been truly important. He'd been so ashamed that he hadn't been there for her when she'd needed him most, that he'd let her down in the most fundamental way; he'd turned away from her emotionally. In doing so, he'd pushed her to desperate measures.

It was difficult for him to admit his weakness, but he needed Tish. Without her, he was out of balance, as she was without him. He felt the message sear into his soul.

In that moment, he realized something else. He'd become involved with Elysée because of that deep longing to be connected again. But he'd never been connected with her. He'd picked Elysee because she was safe. With her he would never have to feel the kind of pain he'd felt with Tish. But the absence of pain also meant the absence of pure joy. Caring passionately about someone meant you might get singed a little. Nor could you get hurt without caring passionately.

But they were together again. Newly minted and starting over. The joy of it was almost more than he could believe.

And then he remembered Larkin.

Chapter 22

Elysee sat in her bedroom, replaying the engagement party video, knowing she'd done the right thing by ending her engagement to Shane, but feeling embarrassed that she'd now gone through four fiancés. What was the matter with her? Why did she keep picking the wrong men? She stared at the video as if it held the answer to her questions. Why couldn't she find the kind of love that had bonded Shane and Tish together so tightly in spite of all their troubles?

What did she want out of life?

What was her heart's deepest desire?

Elysee realized she did not know. Until now, her life had been dictated, first by romantic notions engendered by her mother, then by her father's expectations. She didn't blame her parents. They'd done what they thought best. She blamed herself, for not questioning her values and beliefs before now.

She'd just let everyone tell her what she was supposed to believe, whether it was her parents or her friends, or the men she took up with or even America's perception of her.

The engagement party played on—the participants

laughing, talking, and celebrating. She was so caught up in her own identity crisis she barely noticed that she was caught on screen passing Rana the money meant to ensure Alma Reddy's safe passage into the United States.

This was pointless. Reviewing the evidence of yet another failed engagement was not going to solve anything. Elysee sighed and got to her feet.

Hindi. Beneath the noise of the party, Tish's tape had caught someone speaking in the language taught to Elysee as a child by her nanny. Someone was speaking words she could not believe she was hearing.

Ambassador Kumar was ordering someone to take out a hit on Alma Reddy. Her murder was to take place the minute she set foot on American soil.

With dawning horror, Elysee realized Alma was arriving tonight.

Shane and Tish dozed in each other's arms and woke sometime later to the sound of a freighter ship docking nearby. In the darkness, they scrambled to their feet, fumbled for their clothes, and got dressed.

Several minutes later, the door to the pod opened with a metallic groan. The beam from an ultra-bright flashlight blinded them.

"Change of plans," Larkin called out. "Alma Reddy isn't on this ship the way she was supposed to be. So I'm killing you two first, but before we get to that, I need to know how many copies you made of the disk and exactly where they are. And in case you need a little incentive, sister," he said to Tish, "I'm going to smash every bone in your hubby's fucked-up hand with this nifty little silver hammer I brought along with me until you tell me everything you know."

* * *

It had taken some doing, but in the hubbub of her fathe
arriving at the ranch and with Lola's help, she'd manage
to give her Secret Service detail the slip. Elysee had neve
been to the docks before. She'd tried frantically to reach
Rana on her cell phone, but had had no luck.

She'd lied to Lola and told the secretary she was
sneaking off for a rendezvous with Shane. Lola let Ely
see use her car and provided a distraction for the check
point security. Elysee had no idea who she could trus
besides Shane, and she hadn't been able to find him. She
didn't want to take the chance of leading a killer to Alma
Reddy.

Alma was due to arrive on a freighter at midnight and
Elysee had to be there to warn her. Once she knew both
Alma and Rana were secreted away someplace safe, she'd
call Cal Ackerman to come pick her up.

She arrived at the docks just in time to see the freighte
come pulling into the shipping channel. It was awfully
dark down there and pretty scary with all those big con
tainers stacked everywhere. Plenty of places for a hired
assassin to hide.

Up ahead, along the waterfront, she saw a flashligh
beam bobbing, a beacon in the darkness.

"Rana," she whispered. She had to get to Rana and
warn her. She rushed ahead into a little clearing amid the
containers, but stopped short in the shadows when she
saw Shane and Tish, their hands bound in front of them
with duct tape, being held at gunpoint by Pete Larkin only
a few feet away from where she stood.

Her heart slammed into her chest. What to do? Wha
to do?

Call 9-1-1.

She reached into her pocket for her cell phone, flipped it open, and pressed the 9.

In the quiet darkness that single soft beep was deafening.

Larkin's head came up.

Their eyes met.

Elysee whirled.

Larkin dove.

She dropped the phone.

He grabbed her ankle, pulled her down on the dock.

She shrieked.

He yanked her by the front of her shirt with one hand and pulled her to her feet, while simultaneously spinning toward Shane, his gun outstretched. He caught Elysee's neck in the crook of his arm, then pressed the gun against her temple.

"Don't move, hero," Larkin threatened.

Elysee held her breath.

Shane's eyes met hers.

Larkin began backing up, dragging Elysee with him.

Shane launched himself at Larkin.

Instinctively, instantaneously, Larkin swung the gun around and fired without aiming in Shane's direction.

Elysee heard a gasp of pain. "Shane?"

Her eyes widened. Shane hadn't been hit. Tish had been standing right behind him.

With a soft "Oh," Tish crumpled to the dock.

Shane whirled around just in time to see her collapse. He made a guttural sound of despair and dropped to his knees beside his ex-wife.

"You bastard!" Elysee cried.

Using a self-defense technique Shane had taught her, she reached up and pressed in just the right spot on

Larkin's carotid artery. Two seconds later he lay incapacitated on the ground.

"Secret Service," Cal Ackerman's voice rang out from behind them all. "Don't anybody move."

•

The pain in her shoulder burned like liquid fire. Tish opened her eyes to find herself in a hospital bed.

Where was she? How had she gotten here?

She blinked and glanced around. Shane was perched in a chair at her bedside looking weary and sad, gazing down at his wounded hand. Elysee stood at the window, arms crossed over her chest, staring at something on the street below. Lola was kicked back in a recliner across the room, tapping something into her laptop. And Cal Ackerman was leaning his shoulder against the doorjamb.

She reached over and touched the thick bandage at her collarbone. Ouch!

Her head felt muzzy, her memory vague. The last thing she remembered was making love with Shane in the shipping pod. She smiled. They were a couple again.

"Hey, you guys?" she croaked, pushing the words past her dry lips.

"Tish!" everyone said in unison.

Lola closed her laptop. Elysee moved away from the window. Cal stood up straight. And Shane, an exhilarated smile on his face, took her hand.

"How are you feeling?" Shane asked. "You okay?"

"Fine, fine, just confused. How'd I get here? How long have I been here? I'm starving."

"You've been unconscious for two days," Lola said.

"Two days!" Her gaze flew to Shane's. He nodded, confirming what Lola had said. "What happened to my shoulder?"

"Larkin shot you," Shane said through gritted teeth, "but the bullet was a clean through-and-through. When you fell you hit your head, and that's why you've been out. If it hadn't been for Elysee's quick thinking, Larkin would have killed all three of us."

"Only because none of you trusted me enough to let me know what was going on." Cal glowered. "If Elysee hadn't been wearing her tracking device..."

"Elysee saved us?" Tish laughed, feeling giddy and happy to be alive.

"What's so funny?" Elysee asked. "You don't think I'm capable of saving someone?"

"No, no, not at all."

"I'm tougher than I look." She blew on her fingernails and rubbed them against her shirt in a comical gesture that said, "Yeah, I bested a badass rogue CIA agent and it was easy."

Everyone laughed then.

"So what became of Larkin?"

"He's in big-time trouble. Thanks to your videotape, he'll be going to prison. Ambassador Kumar is in some pretty hot water himself."

Tish shifted her gaze to Elysee. "What about Rana and Alma? Are they okay? Did Larkin get to them?"

"They're both fine," Elysee said. "Rana had never really intended to ship Alma via freighter. It was just a story she concocted because she knew how ruthless the men coming after Alma could be. She had to stay two steps ahead of them. Rana didn't clue me in, thinking it would be safer for me if I didn't know Alma's real travel route. She never dreamed I would end up going to the docks."

"It would have been smarter," Cal chided, "if you hadn't ditched your bodyguard."

"Good thing you showed up," Shane said. "I hate to think what would have happened if you hadn't been there."

"But how did you know Larkin would be there?"

"I didn't know for sure it was Larkin, but your videotape led me to the docks."

"My videotape?"

"You caught Ambassador Kumar on tape hiring Larkin to murder Alma. They were speaking in Hindi and I understood it. So ultimately, Tish, you were the one who broke the case," Elysee explained.

"There was so much left to chance." Tish shook her head. "If Shane hadn't given me his phone with the GPS tracking, if you hadn't watched the video, I'd be dead. Thank you, Elysee, for saving my life."

Elysee smiled. "I think everything happened the way it did for a reason. We're connected. All of us."

Tish smiled back, recognizing the truth of it. They were all connected in some way.

"Your mother's been here," Shane said, "and your friends Delaney and Rachael. Jillian called from San Francisco. Everyone's been pretty worried about you."

"My head's so fuzzy. I really don't remember much of what happened."

Lola said. "Cal confessed that the reason he had red lava gravel on his shoes from the garden outside your apartment was because he'd gone there to tell you that Shane was still in love with you."

"You knew?"

"Please," Cal said gruffly. "I knew you two were meant to be together the night you took him home from Louie's."

Tish glanced over at Shane. Their eyes met and his smile tipped up at the corners. She was barely aware that Elysee, Cal, and Lola had tiptoed out of the room.

"I think we're alone now," he whispered.

"I thought they'd never leave." Her gaze took him in. He was dressed in faded blue jeans and a white button-down shirt with the sleeves rolled up. He managed to look both crisp and relaxed.

His face was full of tenderness. "I got something for you."

"Oh?"

He reached behind him for something on the floor and pulled up a package wrapped in a turquoise bow.

"You got me a present?" Her grin widened.

"Open it."

Eagerly, she pulled off the ribbon and lifted the lid. The minute she saw it her heart stilled and her bottom lip started to quiver. "Shane, it's magnificent."

From the box she lifted the Jack bookend, a perfect match to her Jill. "Where did you find him?"

"E-bay, and I paid a pretty penny for express-mail shipping. Jill's in the box, too. Dick Tracy brought her by yesterday. The investigation's closed since Larkin confessed to starting the fire."

Tish took Jill from the box, sat her next to Jack in her lap. They were together again, balancing each other.

"Thank you," she whispered. "Thank you."

"No," he said. "Thank you for loving me and never stopping."

She slipped out of bed and settled into his lap. Kissing him lightly on the lips, she slid her arms around his neck. He held her close. She could hear the steady lub-dub of his heart.

They sat there in the hospital room, gazing into each other's eyes, drinking each other in. All this time, never knowing, they'd been on a journey back to each other.

She stared into the depths of his breathtaking brown eyes and her heart filled with contentment. They were better now than they'd been. Stronger, wiser, braver.

"My love, my life, my wife," he whispered. "For now, forever, for always. Marry me again, Tish. This time we'll do it right."

There was only one thing to say. With a sweet sigh of pleasure, Tish said, "Yes."

Epilogue

Adjusting his boutonniere in his parents' backyard, the ex–Secret Service agent, turned business manager to his high-profile videographer wife, scanned the crowd.

All the usual suspects were there. Tish's friends—Delaney with her rounded belly and her husband, Nick; Jillian, who'd just made Assistant DA in Harris County; Rachael, who was still single and searching; Shane's parents and his sister, Amy; Tish's mom, Dixie Ann.

The special guest of honor, one class act, Elysee Benedict, was present. Cal was there, too, keeping an eye on Elysee.

They had so many friends, such a loving family. They were so blessed it was hard to believe that they had once gotten so off track. But that detour had taught them a very valuable lesson neither one of them would ever forget.

Balance. That was key. Shane had learned to stop identifying with an impossible image of heroism that he could never achieve and accept himself, flaws and all. Tish had learned to ask for what she needed rather than burying her emotions under excess spending.

Some big changes had been made, and they were all for the better.

Once the vows had been taken and the ceremony completed, his beautiful wife tugged off her wedding veil and handed it to her friend Rachael with a bold wink. Then she pulled him off to the side for a big kiss.

"I love you, Shane Tremont. I have from the moment you punched that bald guy on my behalf at Louie's."

"And I love you, Tish Gallagher Tremont. From the first night you took me to bed and wouldn't let me touch you."

He wrapped his right arm around her waist with the hand that was now almost healed. "I never stopped loving you, not one time during all the sadness and confusion over losing Johnny."

"Shh," she said. "It's okay. Everything is as it should be."

"I have a very smart wife."

And that's how Shane Tremont, middle-class boy from small-town America, found himself remarried to the love of his life.

After having not one but *two* grooms ditch her at the altar,

Rachael Henderson commits an uncharacteristic act of rebellion and feels liberated—until she's arrested by sexy Sheriff Brody Carlton . . .

Addicted to Love

Please turn this page for an excerpt.

The last thing Sheriff Brody Carlton expected to find when he wheeled his state-issued white-and-black Crown Victoria patrol cruiser past the WELCOME TO VALENTINE, TEXAS, ROMANCE CAPITAL OF THE USA billboard was a woman in a sequined wedding dress dangling from the town's mascot—a pair of the most garish, oversized, scarlet puckered-up-for-a-kiss lips ever poured in fiberglass.

She swayed forty feet off the ground in the early Sunday morning summer breeze, one arm wrapped around the sensuous curve of the full bottom lip, her other arm wielding a paintbrush dipped in black paint, her white satin ballet-slippered toes skimming the billboard's weathered wooden platform.

The billboard had been vandalized before, but never, to Brody's knowledge, by a disgruntled bride. He contemplated hitting the siren to warn her off, but feared she'd startle and end up breaking her silly neck. Instead, he whipped over onto the shoulder of the road, rolled down the passenger-side window, slid his Maui Jim sunglasses to the end of his nose, and craned his neck for a better look.

The delinquent bride had her bottom lip tucked up between her teeth. She was concentrating on desecrating the billboard. It had been a staple in Valentine's history for as long as Brody could remember. Her blonde hair, done up in one of those twisty braided hairdos, was partially obscured by the intricate lace of a floor-length wedding veil. When the sunlight hit the veil's lace just right it shimmered a phosphorescent pattern of white butterflies that looked as if they were about to rise up and flutter away.

She was oblivious to anything except splashing angry black brushstrokes across the hot, sexy mouth.

Brody exhaled an irritated snort, threw the Crown Vic into park, stuck the Maui Jims in his front shirt pocket, and climbed out. Warily, he eyed the gravel. Loose rocks. His sworn enemy. Then he remembered his new bionic Power Knee and relaxed. He'd worn the innovative prosthetic for only six weeks, but it had already changed his life. Because of the greater ease of movement and balance the computerized leg afforded, it was almost impossible for the casual observer to guess he was an amputee.

He walked directly underneath the sign, cocked his tan Stetson back on his head, and looked up.

As far as he knew—and he knew most everything that went on in Valentine, population 1,987—there'd been no weddings scheduled in town that weekend. So where had the bride come from?

Brody cleared his throat.

She went right on painting.

He cleared his throat again, louder this time.

Nothing.

"Ma'am," he called up to her.

"Go away. Can't you see I'm busy?"

Dots of black paint spattered the sand around him.

She'd almost obliterated the left-hand corner of the upper lip, transforming the Marilyn Monroe sexpot pout into Marilyn Manson gothic rot.

The cynic inside him grinned. Brody had always hated those tacky red lips. Still, it was a Valentine icon and he was sworn to uphold the law.

He glanced around and spied the lollipop pink VW Bug parked between two old abandoned railway cars rusting alongside the train tracks that ran parallel to the highway. He could see a red-and-pink beaded heart necklace dangling from the rearview mirror, and a sticker on the chrome bumper proclaimed I HEART ROMANCE.

All rightee then.

"If you don't cease and desist, I'll have to arrest you," he explained.

She stopped long enough to balance the brush on the paint can and glower down at him. "On what charges?"

"Destruction of private property. The billboard is on Kelvin Wentworth's land."

"I'm doing this town a much-needed community service," she growled.

"Oh, yeah?"

"This," she said, sweeping a hand at the billboard, "is false advertising. It perpetuates a dangerous myth. I'm getting rid of it before it can suck in more impressionable young girls."

"What myth is that?"

"That there's such things as true love and romance, magic and soul mates. Rubbish. All those fairy tales are complete and utter rubbish and I fell for it, hook, line, and sinker."

"Truth in advertising *is* an oxymoron."

"Exactly. And I'm pulling the plug."

You'll get no argument from me, he thought, but vandalism was vandalism and he was the sheriff, even if he agreed with her in theory. In practice, he was the law. "Wanna talk about it?"

She glared. "To a man? You've gotta be kidding me."

"Judging from your unorthodox attire and your displeasure with the billboard in particular and men in general, I'm gonna go out on a limb here and guess that you were jilted at the altar."

"Perceptive," she said sarcastically.

"Another woman?"

She didn't respond immediately and he was about to repeat the question when she muttered, "The Chicago Bears."

"The Bears?"

"Football."

Brody sank his hands onto his hips. "The guy jilted you over football?"

"Bastard." She was back at it again, slinging paint.

"He sounds like a dumbass."

"He's Trace Hoolihan."

Brody shrugged. "Is that supposed to mean something?"

"You don't know who he is?"

"Nope."

"Hallelujah," the bride-that-wasn't said. "I've found the one man in Texas who's not ate up with football."

It wasn't that he didn't like football, but the last couple of years his life had been preoccupied with adjusting to losing his leg in Iraq, getting over a wife who'd left him for another man, helping his wayward sister raise her young daughter, and settling into his job as sheriff. He hadn't had much time for leisurely pursuits.

"How'd you get up there?" Brody asked.

"With my white sequined magical jet pack."

"You've got a lot of anger built up inside."

"You think?"

"I know you're heartbroken and all," he drawled, "but I'm gonna have to ask you to stop painting the Valentine kisser."

"This isn't the first time, you know," she said without breaking stride. *Swish, swish, swish* went the paintbrush.

"You've vandalized a sign before?"

"I've been stood up at the altar before."

"No kidding?"

"Last year. The ratfink never showed up. Left me standing in the church for over an hour while my wilting orchid bouquet attracted bees."

"And still, you were willing to try again."

"I know. I'm an idiot. Or at least I was. But I'm turning over a new leaf. Joining the skeptics."

"Well, if you don't stop painting the sign, you're going to be joining the ranks of the inmates at the Jeff Davis County Jail."

"You've got prisoners?"

"Figure of speech." How did she know the jail was empty fifty percent of the time? Brody squinted suspiciously. He didn't recognize her, at least not from this distance. "You from Valentine?"

"I live in Houston now."

That was as far as the conversation got because the mayor's fat, honking Cadillac bumped to a stop behind Brody's cruiser.

Kelvin P. Wentworth IV flung the car door open and wrestled his hefty frame from behind the wheel. Merle Haggard belted from the radio, wailing a thirty-year-old country-and-western song about boozing and chasing women.

"What the hell's going on here," Kelvin boomed and lumbered toward Brody.

The mayor tilted his head up, scowling darkly at the billboard bride. Kelvin prided himself on shopping only in Valentine. He refused to even order off the Internet. He was big and bald and on the back side of his forties. His seersucker suit clung to him like leeches on a water buffalo. Kelvin was under the mistaken impression he was still as good-looking as the day he'd scored the winning touchdown that took Valentine to state in 1977, the year Brody was born. It was the first and last time the town had been in the playoffs.

Brody suppressed the urge to roll his eyes. He knew what was coming. Kelvin was a true believer in the Church of Valentine and the jilted bride had just committed the highest form of blasphemy. "I've got it under control, Mayor."

"My ass." Kelvin waved an angry hand. "She's up there defacin' and disgracin' our hometown heritage and you're standing here with your thumb up your butt, Carlton."

"She's distraught. Her fiancé dumped her at the altar."

"Rachael Renee Henderson," Kelvin thundered up at her. "Is that you?"

"Go away, Mayor. This is something that's gotta be done," she called back.

"You get yourself down off that billboard right now, or I'm gonna call your daddy."

Rachael Henderson.

The name brought an instant association into Brody's mind. He saw an image of long blonde pigtails, gap-toothed grin, and freckles across the bridge of an upturned pixie nose. Rachael Henderson, the next-door neighbor who'd followed him around like a puppy dog until he'd moved to Midland with his mother and his sister after their father went to Kuwait when Brody was twelve. From what he recalled, Rachael was sweet as honeysuckle, certainly not the type to graffiti a beloved town landmark.

People change.

He thought of Belinda and shook his head to clear away thoughts of his ex-wife.

"My daddy is partly to blame for this," she said. "Last time I saw him he was in Houston breaking my mother's heart. Go ahead and call him. Would you like his cell phone number?"

"What's she talking about?" Kelvin swung his gaze to Brody.

Brody shrugged. "Apparently she's got some personal issues to work out."

"Well, she can't work them out on my billboard."

"I'm getting the impression the billboard is a symbol of her personal issues."

"I don't give a damn. Get 'er down."

"How do you propose I do that?"

Kelvin squinted at the billboard. "How'd she get up there?"

"Big mystery. But why don't we just let her have at it? She's bound to run out of steam soon enough in this heat."

"Are you nuts? Hell, man, she's already blacked out the top lip." Kelvin anxiously shifted his weight, bunched his hands into fists. "I won't stand for this. Find a way to get her down. Now!"

"What do you want me to do? Shoot her?"

"It's a thought," Kelvin muttered.

"Commanding the sheriff to shoot a jilted bride won't help you get reelected."

"It ain't gonna help my reelection bid if she falls off that billboard and breaks her fool neck because I didn't stop her."

"Granted."

Kelvin cursed up a blue streak and swiped a meaty hand across his sweaty forehead. "I was supposed to be getting doughnuts so me and Marianne could have a nice, quiet breakfast before church, but hell no, I gotta deal with this stupid crap." Kelvin, a self-proclaimed playboy, had never married. Marianne was his one hundred and twenty pound bullmastiff.

"Go get your doughnuts, Mayor," Brody said. "I've got this under control."

Kelvin shot him a withering look and pulled his cell phone from his pocket. Brody listened to the one-sided conversation, his eyes on Rachael, who showed no signs of slowing her assault on the vampish pout.

"Rex," Kelvin barked to his personal assistant. "Go over to Audie's, have him open the hardware store up for you, get a twenty-five-foot ladder, and bring it out to the Valentine billboard."

There was a pause from Kelvin as Rex responded.

"I don't care if you stayed up 'til three a.m. playing video games with your geeky online buddies. Just do it."

With a savage slash of his thumb on the keypad, Kelvin hung up and muttered under his breath, "I'm surrounded by morons."

Brody tried not to take offense at the comment. Kelvin liked his drama as much as he liked ordering people around.

Fifteen minutes later, Rex showed up with a collapsible

yellow ladder roped to his pickup truck. He was barely twenty-five, redheaded as rhubarb, and had a voice deep as Barry White's, with an Adam's apple that protruded like a submarine ready to break the surface. Brody often wondered if the prominent Adam's apple had anything to do with the kid's smooth, dark, ebony voice.

Up on the billboard, Rachael was almost finished with the mouth. She had slashes of angry black paint smeared across the front of her wedding gown. While waiting on Rex to show up with the ladder, Kelvin had spent the time trying to convince her to come down, but she was a zealot on a mission and she wouldn't even talk to him.

"I want her arrested," Kelvin snapped. "I'm pressing charges."

"You might want to reconsider that," Brody advised. "Since the election is just a little more than three months away and Giada Vito is gaining favor in the polls."

The polls being the gossip at Higgy's Diner. He knew the mayor was grandstanding. For the first time in Kelvin's three-term stint, he was running opposed. Giada Vito had moved to Valentine from Italy and she'd gotten her American citizenship as soon as the law allowed. She was a dyed-in-the-wool Democrat, the principal of Valentine High, drove a vintage Fiat, and didn't mince her words. Especially when it came to the topic of Valentine's favored son, Kelvin P. Wentworth IV.

"Hey, you leave the legal and political machinations to me. You just do your job," said Kelvin.

Brody blew out his breath and went to help Rex untie the ladder. What he wanted to do was tell Kelvin to shove it. But the truth was the woman needed to come down before she got hurt. More than likely, the wooden billboard decking was riddled with termites.

He and Rex got the ladder loose and carried it over to prop it against the back of the billboard. It extended just long enough to reach the ladder rungs that were attached to the billboard itself.

Kelvin gave Brody a pointed look. "Up you go."

Brody ignored him. "Rachael, we've got a ladder in place. You need to come down now."

"Don't ask her, tell her," Kelvin hissed to Brody, then said to Rachael, "Missy, get your ass down here this instant."

"Get bent," Rachael sang out.

"That was effective," Brody muttered.

Rex snorted back a laugh. Kelvin shot him a withering glance and then raised his eyebrows at Brody and jerked his head toward the billboard. "You're the sheriff. Do your job."

Brody looked up at the ladder and then tried his best not to glance down at his leg. He didn't want to show the slightest sign of weakness, especially in front of Kelvin. But while his Power Knee was pretty well the most awesome thing that had happened to him since his rehabilitation, he'd never tested it by climbing a ladder, particularly a thin, wobbly, collapsible one.

Shit. If he fell off, it was going to hurt. He might even break something.

Kelvin was staring expectantly, arms crossed over his bearish chest, the sleeves of his seersucker suit straining against his bulky forearms. The door to the Cadillac was still hanging open and from the radio Merle Haggard had given it up to Tammy Wynette, who was beseeching women to stand by their man.

Brody was the sheriff. This was his job. And he never shirked his duty, even when it was the last thing on earth he wanted to do. Gritting his teeth, he gathered his courage, wrapped both hands around the ladder just above his head, and planted his prosthetic leg on the bottom rung.

His gut squeezed.

Come on, you can do this.

He attacked the project the same way he'd attacked physical therapy, going at it with dogged determination to walk again, to come home, if not whole, at least proud to be a man. Of course Belinda had shattered all that.

Don't think about Belinda. Get up the ladder. Get the girl down.

He placed his good leg on the second rung.

The ladder trembled under his weight.

Brody swallowed back the fear and pulled his prosthesis up the next step. Hands clinging tightly to the ladder above him, he raised his head and counted the steps.

Twenty-five of them on the ladder and seventeen on the back of the billboard.

Three down, thirty-nine left to go.

He remembered an old movie called *The Thirty-Nine Steps*. Suddenly, those three words held a weighted significance. It wasn't just thirty-nine more steps. It was also forty-two more back down with Rachael Henderson in tow.

Better get climbing.

Thirty-eight steps.

Thirty-seven.

Thirty-six.

The higher he went, the more the ladder quivered.

Halfway up vertigo took solid hold of him. He'd never had a fear of heights before, but now, staring down at Kelvin and Rex, who were staring up at him, Brody's head swam and his stomach pitched. He bit his bottom lip, closed his eyes, and took another step up.

In the quiet of the higher air, he could hear the soft whispery sound of his computerized leg working as he took another step. Kelvin's country music sounded tinny and far away. With his eyes closed and his hands skimming over the cool aluminum ladder, he could also hear the sound of brushstrokes growing faster and more frantic the closer he came to the bottom of the billboard.

Rachael was still furiously painting, trying to get in as many licks as she could.

When Brody finally reached the top of the first ladder, he opened his eyes.

"You're doing great," Kelvin called up to him. "Keep going. You're almost there."

Yeah, almost there. This was the hardest part of all, covering the gap between the ladder from Audie's Hardware and the thin metal footholds welded to the back of the billboard.

He took a deep breath. He had to stretch to reach the bottom step. He grabbed hold of it with both hands, and took his Power Knee off the aluminum ladder.

For a moment, he hung there, twenty-five feet off the ground, fighting gravity and the bile rising in his throat, wondering why he hadn't told Kelvin to go straight to hell. Wondering why he hadn't just called the volunteer fire department to come and get Rachael down.

It was a matter of pride and he knew it. Stupid, egotistical pride. He'd wanted to prove he could handle anything that came with the job. Wanted to show the town he'd earned their vote. That he hadn't just stumbled into the office because he was an injured war hero.

Pride goes before a fall, his Gramma Carlton used to say. Now, for the first time, he fully understood what she meant.

Arms trembling with the effort, he dragged himself up with his biceps, his real leg tiptoed on the collapsible ladder, his bionic leg searching blindly for the rung.

Just when he thought he wouldn't be able to hold on a second longer, he found the toehold and then brought his good leg up against the billboard ladder to join the bionic one.

He'd made it.

Brody clung there, breathing hard, thanking God for letting him get this far and wondering just how in the hell he was going to get back down without killing them both, when he heard the soft sounds of muffled female sobs.

Rachael was crying.

The hero in him forgot that his limbs were quivering, forgot that he was forty feet in the air, forgot that somehow he was going to have to get back down. The only thing in his mind was the woman.

Was she all right?

As quickly as he could, Brody scaled the remaining rungs and then gingerly settled his legs on the billboard decking. He ducked under the bottom of the sign and peered around it.

She sat, knees drawn to her chest, head down, looking completely incongruous in that wedding dress smeared with black paint and the butterfly wedding veil floating around her head. Miraculously, the veil seemed to have escaped the paint.

"You okay?"

She raised her head. "Of course I'm not okay."

Up close, he saw tear tracks had run a gully through the makeup on her cheeks and mascara had pooled underneath her eyes. She looked like a quarrelsome raccoon caught in a coyote trap, all piss and vinegar, but visibly hurting.

He had the strangest, and most uncharacteristic, urge to pull her into his arms, hold her to his chest, kiss the top of her head the way he did his six-year-old niece, Maisy, and tell her everything was going to be all right.

Mentally, he stomped the impulse. He didn't need any damsel-in-distress hassle.

The expression in her eyes told him anger had propelled her up here, but now, her rage spent, she was afraid to come back down. That fear he understood loud and clear.

Calmly, he held out a hand to her. "Rachael, it's time to go."

"I thought I'd feel better," she said in a despondent little voice as she stared at his outstretched hand. "I don't feel better. I was supposed to feel better. That was the plan. Why don't I feel better?"

"Destruction rarely makes you feel good." His missing leg gave a twinge. "Come on, give me your hand and let's get back on the ground."

"You look familiar. Are you married?" she asked.

He opened his mouth to answer, but she didn't give him a chance before launching into a fast-paced monologue. "I hope you're married, because if you're not married, you need to get someone else to help me down from here."

"Huh?" Had the sun baked her brain or had getting stood up at the altar made her crazy?

"If you're not married, then this is a cute meet. I'm a sucker for meeting cute."

"Huh?" he said again.

"My first fiancé?" she chattered, her glossolalia revealing her emotional distress. "I met Robert in a hot-air balloon. He was the pilot. I wanted a romantic adventure. The balloon hung up in a pecan tree and the fire department had to rescue us. It was terribly cute."

"Sounds like it," he said, simply to appease her. Mentally, he was planning their trip off the billboard.

"And Trace? I met him when he came to the kindergarten class where I taught. On career day. He was tossing a football around as he gave his speech. He lost control of it and accidentally beaned me in the head. He literally knocked me off my feet. He caught me just before I hit the ground and there I was, trapped in his big strong arms, staring up into his big blue eyes. I just melted. So you see I succumb to the cute meet. I've got to break the cycle and these romantic notions I have about love and marriage and dating and men. But I can't do it if I go around meeting cute. There's no way I can let you rescue me if you're not married."

The woman, Brody decided, was officially bonkers.

"Sorry." He shrugged. "I'm divorced."

She grimaced. "Oh, no."

"But this isn't a cute meet."

She glanced over at the fiberglass billboard lips, then peered down at her paint-spotted wedding dress and finally drilled him with almond-shaped green eyes, the only exotic thing about her.

The rest of her was round and smooth and welcoming, from her cherubic cheeks to her petite curves to the full bow of her supple pink mouth. She was as soft-focus as a Monet. Just looking at her made him think of springtime and flowers and fuzzy baby chicks.

Except for those disconcerting bedroom eyes. They called up unwanted X-rated images in his mind.

"I dunno," she said, "this seems dangerously cute to me."

"It can't be a cute meet," he explained, struggling to follow her disjointed train of thought, "because we've already met."

She tilted her head. "We have?"

"Yep."

"I thought you looked familiar."

"So no cute meet. Now give me your hand."

Reluctantly, she placed her hand in his. "Where did we meet?"

"Right here in Valentine." He spoke with a soothing voice. Her hand was warm and damp with perspiration. He drew her toward him.

She didn't resist. She was tired and emotionally exhausted.

"That's it," he coaxed.

"You do look familiar."

"Watch your head," he said as he led her underneath the billboard, toward the ladder.

She paused at the ladder and stared at the ground. "It's a long way down."

Tell me about it.

"I'm here, I'll go first. I'll be there to catch you if you lose your balance."

"Will you keep your hand on my waist? To steady me?"

"Sure," he promised recklessly, placing chivalry over common sense.

He started down the ladder ahead of her, found secure footing, wrapped his left hand around the rung, and reached up to hold on to her waist with his right hand as she started down.

Touching her brought an unexpected knot of emotion to his chest. Half desire, half tenderness, he didn't know what to call it, but he knew one thing. The feeling was damned dangerous.

"I'm scared," she whimpered.

"You're doing great." He guided her down until her

sweet little rump was directly in his face. Any other time he would have enjoyed this position, but not under these circumstances.

"I'm going down another couple of steps," he explained. "I'm going to have to let go of you for a minute, so hold on tight."

The long train of her wedding veil floated in the air between them, a gauzy pain in the ass. In order to see where he was going, he had to keep batting it back. He took up his position several rungs below her and called to her to come down. As he'd promised, he put a hand at her waist to guide her.

They went on like that, painstaking step by painstaking step, until they were past the gap, off the billboard, and onto the collapsible aluminum ladder. In that regard, coming down was much easier than going up.

"You're certain I already know you?" she asked. "Because seriously, this has all the makings of a meet cute."

"You know me."

"How?"

"I'm from Valentine, just like you. Moved away, came back," he said.

Only four feet off the ground now. His legs felt flimsy as spindly garden sprouts.

"Oh my gosh," she gasped and whipped her head around quickly.

Too quickly.

Somehow, in the breeze and the movement, the infernal wedding veil wrapped around his prosthetic leg. He tried to kick it off but the material clung stubbornly.

"I know who you are," she said and then right there on the ladder, she turned around to glare at him. "You're Brody Carlton."

He didn't have a chance to answer. The ladder swayed and the veil snatched his leg out from under him.

He lost his balance.

The next thing he knew, he was lying on his back on the ground, and Rachael Henderson, his one-time next-door-neighbor-turned-jilted-psycho-bride, was on top of him. They were both breathing hard and trembling.

Her eyes locked on his.

His eyes locked on her lips.

Brody should have been thinking about his leg. He was surprised he wasn't thinking about his leg. What he was thinking about was the fact that he was being straddled by a woman in a wedding dress and it was the closest he'd come to having sex in over two years.

"You! You're the one."

"The one?" he asked.

"You're the root cause of all my problems," she exclaimed, fire in her eyes, at the same time Brody found himself thinking, *Where have you been all my life?*

But that was not what he said.

What he said was, "Rachael Renee Henderson, you have the right to remain silent..."

THE DISH

Where authors give you the inside scoop!

♥ ♥ ♥ ♥ ♥ ♥ ♥ ♥ ♥ ♥ ♥ ♥ ♥ ♥ ♥

From the desk of Paula Quinn

Dear Reader,

I'm so excited to tell you about my latest in the Children of the Mist series, CONQUERED BY A HIGHLANDER. I loved introducing you to Colin MacGregor in *Ravished by a Highlander* and then meeting up with him again in *Tamed by a Highlander*, but finally the youngest, battle-hungry MacGregor gets his own story. And let me tell you all, I enjoyed every page, every word.

Colin wasn't a difficult hero to write. There were no mysteries complicating his character, no ghosts or regrets haunting him from his past. He was born with a passion to fight and to conquer. Nothing more. Nothing less. He was easy to write. He was a badass in *Ravished* and he's a hardass now. My dilemma was what kind of woman would it take to win him? The painted birds fluttering about the many courts he's visited barely held his attention. A warrior wouldn't suit him any better than a wallflower would. I knew early on that the Lady who tried to take hold of this soldier's heart had to possess the innate strength to face her fiercest foe...and the tenderness to recognize something more than a fighter in Colin's confident gaze.

I found Gillian Dearly hidden away in the turrets of a castle overlooking the sea, her fingers busy strumming melodies on her beloved lute while her thoughts carried her to places far beyond her prison walls. She wasn't waiting for a hero, deciding years ago that she would rescue herself. She was perfect for Colin. She also possessed one other thing, a weapon so powerful, even Colin found himself at the mercy of it.

A three-year-old little boy named Edmund.

Like Colin, I didn't intend for Edmund Dearly or his mother to change the path of my story, but they brought out something in the warrior—whom I thought I knew so well—something warm and wonderful and infinitely sexier than any swagger. They brought out the man.

For me, nothing I've written before this book exemplifies the essence of a true hero more than watching Colin fall in love with Gillian *and* with her child. Not many things are more valiant than a battle-hardened warrior who puts down his practice sword so he can take a kid fishing or save him from bedtime monsters... except maybe a mother who defiantly goes into battle each day in order to give her child a better life. Gillian Dearly was Edmund's hero and she quickly became mine. How could a man like Colin *not* fall in love with her?

Having to end the Children of the Mist series was bittersweet, but I'm thrilled to say there will be more MacGregors of Skye visiting the pages of future books. Camlochlin will live on for another generation at least. And not just in words but in art. Master painter James Lyman has immortalized the home of our beloved MacGregors in beautiful color and with an innate understanding of how the fortress should be represented. Visit PaulaQuinn.com to order a print of your own, signed and numbered by the artist.

Until we meet again, to you mothers and fathers, husbands and wives, sons and daughters, sisters and brothers, and friends, who put yourselves aside for someone you love, I shout Huzzah! Camlochlin was built for people like you.

Paula Quinn

Find her at Facebook

Twitter @Paula_Quinn

♥ ♥ ♥ ♥ ♥ ♥ ♥ ♥ ♥ ♥ ♥ ♥ ♥ ♥ ♥

From the desk of Jill Shalvis

Dear Reader,

From the very first moment I put Mysterious Cute Guy on the page, I fell in love. There's just something about a big, bad, sexy guy whom you know nothing about that fires the imagination. But I have to be honest: When he made a cameo in *Head Over Heels* (literally a walk-on role only; in fact I believe he only gets a mention or two), I knew nothing about him. Nothing. I never intended to, either. He was just one of life's little (okay, big, bad, and sexy) mysteries.

Then my editor called me. Said the first three Lucky Harbor books had done so well that they'd like three more, please. And maybe one of the heroes could be Mysterious Cute Guy.

It was fun coming up with a story to go with this enigmatic figure, not to mention a name: Ty Garrison. More fun still to give this ex-Navy SEAL a rough, tortured, bad-boy past and a sweet, giving, good-girl heroine

(Mallory Quinn, ER nurse). Oh, the fun I had with these two: a bad boy trying to go good, and a good girl looking for a walk on the wild side. Hope you have as much fun reading their story, LUCKY IN LOVE.

And then, stick around. Because Mallory's two Chocoholics-in-crime partners, Amy and Grace, get their own love stories in July and August with *At Last* and then *Forever and a Day*.

Happy Reading!

Jill Shalvis

http://www.jillshalvis.com

http://www.facebook.com/jillshalvis

♥ ♥ ♥ ♥ ♥ ♥ ♥ ♥ ♥ ♥ ♥ ♥ ♥ ♥ ♥

From the desk of Lori Wilde

Dear Reader,

Ah ,June! Love is in the air, and it's the time for weddings and romance. With KISS THE BRIDE, you get two romantic books in one, *There Goes the Bride* and *Once Smitten, Twice Shy*. Both stories are filled with brides, bouquets, and those devastatingly handsome grooms. But best friends Delaney and Tish go through a lot of ups and downs on their path to happily ever after.

For those of you hoping for a June wedding of your

own, how do you tell if your guy is ready for commitment? He might be ready to pop the question if…

- Instead of saying "I" when making future plans, he starts saying "we."
- He gives you his ATM pass code.
- He takes you on vacation with his family.
- Out of the blue, your best friend asks your ring size.
- He sells his sports car/motorcycle and says he's outgrown that juvenile phase of his life.
- He opens a gold card to get a higher spending limit—say, to pay for a honeymoon.
- When you get a wedding invitation in the mail, he doesn't groan but instead asks where the bride and groom got the invitations printed.
- He starts remembering to leave the toilet seat down.
- When poker night with the guys rolls around, he says he'd rather stay home and watch *The Wedding Planner* with you.
- He becomes your dad's best golfing buddy

I hope you enjoy KISS THE BRIDE.

Happy reading,

Lori Wilde

loriwilde.com

Facebook http://facebook.com/lori.wilde

Twitter @LoriWilde

♥ ♥ ♥ ♥ ♥ ♥ ♥ ♥ ♥ ♥ ♥ ♥ ♥ ♥ ♥

From the desk of Laurel McKee

Dear Reader,

When I was about eight years old, someone gave me a picture book called *Life in Victorian England*. I lost the book in a move years ago, but I still remember the gorgeous watercolor illustrations. Ladies in brightly colored hoopskirts and men in frock coats and top hats doing things like walking in the park, ice-skating at Christmas, and dancing in ballrooms. I was completely hooked on this magical world called "the Victorian Age" and couldn't get enough of it! I read stuff like *Jane Eyre*, *Little Women*, and *Bleak House*, watched every movie where there was the potential for bonnets, and drove my parents crazy by saying all the time, "Well, in the Victorian age it was like this..."

As I got older and started to study history in a more serious way, I found that beneath this pretty and proper facade was something far darker. Darker—and a lot more interesting. There was a flourishing underworld in Victorian England, all the more intense for being well hidden and suppressed. Prostitution, theft, and the drug trade expanded, and London was bursting at the seams thanks to changes brought about by the Industrial Revolution. The theater and the visual arts were taking on a new life. Even Queen Victoria was not exactly the prissy sourpuss everyone thinks she was. (She and Albert had nine children, after all—and enjoyed making them!)

I've always wanted to set a story in these Victorian

years, with the juxtaposition of what's seen on the surface and what is really going on underneath. But I never came up with just the right characters for this complex setting. The inspiration came (as it so often does for me, don't laugh) from clothes. I was watching my DVD of *Young Victoria* for about the fifth time, and when the coronation ball scene came on, I thought, "I really want a heroine who could wear a gown just like that..."

And Lily St. Claire popped into my head and brought along her whole family of Victorian underworld rakes. I had to run and get out my notebook to write down everything Lily had to tell me. I loved her from that first minute—a woman who created a glamorous life for herself from a childhood on the streets of the London slums. A tough, independent woman (with gorgeous clothes, of course) who thinks she doesn't need anyone—until she meets this absolutely yummy son a duke. Too bad his family is the St. Claire family's old enemy...

I hope you enjoy the adventures of Lily and Aidan as much as I have. It was so much fun to spend some time in Victorian London. Look for more St. Claire trouble to come.

In the meantime, visit my website at http://laurelmckee.net for more info on the characters and the history behind the book.

Laurel McKee

Find out more about Forever Romance!

Visit us at
www.hachettebookgroup.com/publishing_forever.aspx

Find us on Facebook
http://www.facebook.com/ForeverRomance

Follow us on Twitter
http://twitter.com/ForeverRomance

NEW AND UPCOMING TITLES

Each month we feature our new titles
and reader favorites.

CONTESTS AND GIVEAWAYS

We give away galleys, autographed copies,
and all kinds of exclusive items.

AUTHOR INFO

You'll find bios, articles, and links to personal websites
for all your favorite authors—and so much more.

GET SOCIAL

Connect with your favorite authors, editors, and
other Forever fans, and share what's important to you.

THE BUZZ

Sign up for our monthly romance newsletter,
and be the first to read all about it.